W9-BKL-332

Autumn: Disintegration

David Moody

THOMAS DUNNE BOOKS

ST. MARTIN'S GRIFFIN ✹ NEW YORK

To the original readers of my "Infected Books."
Thanks for waiting.

This is a work of fiction. All of the characters, organizations, and events portrayed in this novel are either products of the author's imagination or are used fictitiously.

THOMAS DUNNE BOOKS.
An imprint of St. Martin's Press.

AUTUMN: DISINTEGRATION. Copyright © 2011 by David Moody. All rights reserved. Printed in the United States of America. For information, address St. Martin's Press, 175 Fifth Avenue, New York, N.Y. 10010.

www.thomasdunnebooks.com
www.stmartins.com

Library of Congress Cataloging-in-Publication Data

Moody, David, 1970–
    Autumn : disintegration / David Moody.
      p. cm.
    ISBN 978-0-312-57001-9 (pbk.)
    1. Zombies—Fiction.   2. Survival—Fiction.
3. Regression (Civilization)—Fiction.   I. Title.
    PR6113.O5447A9525 2011
    823'.92—dc22

                                        2011027110

      First Edition: December 2011

    10 9 8 7 6 5 4 3 2 1

Autumn: Disintegration

Also by David Moody

Hater

Dog Blood

Them or Us

Autumn

Autumn: The City

Autumn: Purification

Acknowledgments

This book was originally announced back in 2006, and written shortly thereafter. At the time, the previously released Autumn books—some published independently, others given away for free—were doing well, a low-budget film adaptation of the first novel had been announced, and everything was moving along nicely. Then things went a little crazy . . . My novel *Hater* was released, Guillermo del Toro became attached to a movie version, and the Autumn and Hater books were subsequently acquired by Thomas Dunne Books in the United States and Gollancz in the UK.

Sounds like a dream come true, doesn't it? It was. It still is.

The only downside was that there were a lot of people waiting expectantly to read this book five years ago, only to have it snatched from them before they'd even seen the cover. So I'd like to publicly apologize and thank them all for waiting. Sorry for the unintentional but unavoidable delay. I hope you (finally) enjoy *Disintegration*.

I also want to thank my family and friends for their continued love and support. Thanks also to Brendan Deneen and all at Thomas Dunne Books, Jo Fletcher and all at Gollancz, John Schoenfelder, and Scott Miller.

Finally, thanks to the close-knit community of zombie authors of which I'm proud to be a part, particularly Wayne Simmons and Iain McKinnon, and also to Richard Grundy, Craig Paton, Antony White, Michael Dick, Jack O'Hare, David Naughton-Shires, David Joseph, Daniel Boucher, and all the other artists and designers who've contributed to the ongoing www.lastoftheliving.net project.

Autumn: Disintegration

Prologue

They said I should have burned her with the rest of them. When everyone died I cleared this place out room by room, not stopping till I'd got rid of every last one of them. I worked for hours until every trace of dead flesh had been removed from the building. Except for her. Except for the Swimmer.

I found her a couple of days later when she'd just started to move. Don't know how I missed her before, lying there dressed in her bathing costume. Poor bitch had been about to take a dip in the pool when it caught her. The doors had swung shut, trapping her inside. When I first found her she was shuffling about in the shadows like those on the other side of the boundary fence, constantly dragging herself from one end of the room to the other, backward and forward, walking into walls and lockers, tripping over upturned benches and other obstructions. She looked pretty comical crashing around, stupid almost, but I wasn't laughing. I was too scared. I still am.

When the others got here we talked for hours about getting rid of her. Ginnie and Sean were dead set against the idea of keeping her inside the building with us, even though there was no way she could get

1

out into any other part of the hotel. Howard and Amir came around to my way of thinking pretty quickly. It made sense to keep hold of her and watch her. Christ, those bloody bodies dragged themselves up onto their feet after they'd been lying dead for days and none of us knew what they might do next. I knew that the Swimmer would show us. In a perverse way she's helped us to stay alive. Shut away in the changing room, she's sheltered from the rest of the dead world outside, and over the weeks we've watched her change. We've watched her decay. She's shown us how the dead have evolved. She's shown us what they've become.

The changes have been gradual. Sometimes nothing seems to happen for days, but then she'll react differently to one of us and we'll know that the hundreds of thousands of bodies on the other side of the fence will soon be doing the same. None of what's happened to the world makes any sense, but what's happening to them makes the least sense of all: as they continue to rot, their control and coordination has somehow returned. It's like they're starting to think again and make decisions. Sometime soon, I'm sure, they'll reach the point where they've decayed to such an extent they can no longer keep moving— but when will that be? And what will they be capable of by then?

It was less than a week after the day the world died when I first realized she was watching me. A week of dumb, uncoordinated, and random movements, and then suddenly she could see and hear again. Her dark eyes stared back at me whenever I approached. And when Howard's dog barked she reacted too. She lurched toward the window and hammered her hands against the glass as if she was trying to escape. As the days passed her reactions slowed down, became more deliberate and less instinctive. I realized she was regaining control.

I've spent hours watching her since then. Sometimes I can't take my eyes off her, even though she disgusts me. I'm sure I saw her here before she died. I remember her once-pretty round face, heart-shaped lips, slightly upturned nose and short, dark brown hair, flecked with highlights. Her subsequent deterioration has been remarkable. Even in here, where she's isolated and protected from the weather and the worst of the insects, she has been reduced to little more than a grotesque shadow of the person she once was. The color of her flesh has changed from the white-pink of life to a cold blue-gray. Her skin has shrivelled in places and slipped in others. There are bags under her bulging eyes where her mottled flesh has sagged. Her body seems almost to be turning itself inside out. Gravity has dragged her rotting guts down and now they're dripping out between her unsteady legs. Even from the other side of the door I can smell the stench of her decay.

It's almost two months since this nightmare began. Recently the Swimmer's behavior has changed again. Perhaps it's my imagination, but she seems more aware than ever now—more aware of me and the others, and more self-aware too. I don't know if she has any memory of who she used to be or if she understands what she has become. Whatever she does or doesn't know, a couple of days ago I swear I caught her trying to open the door. I found her leaning up against it, banging her right hand down on the handle repeatedly. She eventually noticed me standing at the window and stopped. She looked at me for a few seconds, then stumbled back into the shadows. If she'd run at the glass I'd have been less concerned, but she didn't. She actually moved away. She saw that I was watching her and tried to hide.

Yesterday afternoon, for a short time, she seemed to forget herself. She stood in the middle of the room looking directly at me through the window. I couldn't take my eyes off her grotesque face and I found myself wondering again who she might have been before she died. Does she see me and remember what she once was, or does she see me as a threat? Am I her enemy?

I hate her. She's one corpse alone in a world filled with millions but, because she's in here with us, I've begun to aim all my pain and

3

frustration directly at her. Sometimes I feel like she's taunting me and it's all I can do not to destroy her. Yesterday, when she was watching me, I stood on the other side of the door with an ax in my hands for what felt like forever. I wanted so badly to cut her down to nothing and batter her into memory.

I know I can't harm her. We still need her.

1

Webb kicked his way through the litter behind the counter of the petrol station kiosk. They'd been here several times before and had cleared the place out, but maybe today he'd find one last packet of cigarettes that he'd missed last time, or a previously overlooked bottle of drink. It was always worth a look. Christ, what he'd give for a can of lager right now.

Wait . . . he could hear an engine. More than that, he could hear three engines—the bike and both the vans. Bloody hell, they were going without him! The fucking idiots were leaving him behind! No time to think. He scrambled back over the counter, stepped through the mess of twisted metal and broken glass where the entrance door used to be, then ran out into the middle of the forecourt.

"Wait!" he screamed, his voice quickly deteriorating from a strong yell to a strained smoker's rasp. Bent over double coughing, he glanced up and caught a glimpse of the roof of one of the vans as it raced back toward the flats. It was just a momentary flash of sunlight on metal, gone in a second but visible long enough to leave him in no doubt that he was now completely alone. Alone, that was, apart from a fractious mob of more than two hundred dead bodies closing in on him. The whine of the engines faded away into echoes. Still coughing, Webb covered his mouth, desperate to stifle the noise but knowing it was already too late.

What are my options? Can't go back into the store, the back door's blocked. They'll follow me in and I'll be trapped.

He glanced across the forecourt at the green and yellow liveried tanker they'd been siphoning fuel from. Could he climb on top of it and sit and wait until something else distracted them? It might well have worked, but it would have taken time. Although clear and blue immediately above him, the skies all around had been filling with threatening gray rain clouds all afternoon. It would be dark soon. He didn't relish the prospect of being stranded on top of the tanker all night, soaked through and surrounded by rotting flesh.

Only one option left. Run.

Webb surveyed the opposition and gripped his weapon tight. A baseball bat with four six-inch nails hammered through its end, it was a rudimentary but undeniably effective, modern-day variation on the medieval mace. Basic or not, over the weeks he'd used it to get rid of literally hundreds of these vile, germ-infested bastards and he was thankful for it.

With vast swathes of disintegrating corpses advancing from all sides it didn't seem to matter which direction he chose. Hoping to buy himself a few precious seconds' breathing space he yanked the loose helmet off the withered head of a dead motorcyclist which lay at his feet. Like an Olympic hammer thrower he spun around through almost a full circle before letting go of the helmet. It flew toward the store, smashing through what was left of an already broken window and filling the air with ugly noise. The nearest of the shambling cadavers began to shuffle toward the building, their movements in turn causing more and more of the dumb fuckers to follow like sheep. Webb held his position as the crowd surged predictably, then ran the other way.

He could still just about hear the bike in the distance. Its power-ful engine was louder than the two vans combined and he knew he'd probably be able to hear it until it reached the flats. It was only just over a mile. If the streets were clear he'd probably be able to run there in around ten minutes. Problem was, the streets were never clear any-more. Between here and home were thousands upon thousands of corpses, crammed together shoulder to shoulder, and one of the nearest had just lifted its bony arms and begun lurching forward in his direc-tion. With a grunt of effort Webb lifted the baseball bat and swung it in a loose arc above his head. He thumped it down into the side of the creature's chest, sweeping it off its already unsteady feet. Another swing, this time in the opposite direction, and two more swaying corpses were hacked down. Three gone, he thought to himself as he started running again, just a few thousand more to go.

Christ, he hated the smell of these bloody things. It was always there, hanging in the air like an ever-present fug, but it was a thousand times worse at close quarters. With his shoulder dropped he charged into the middle of the crowd straight ahead. Most of the bodies were too slow to react and they toppled like dominos, each one causing more of them to fall. Webb kept moving, leaping over their slow, grabbing hands and holding his weapon out in front of him like a battering ram, using its rounded end to smash them out of the way. A sudden unexpected gap in the crowd opened up, allowing him to slow momen-tarily and get his bearings. He was running away from the petrol sta-tion, but he was heading back toward the center of town. He needed to be moving in the opposite direction. Forced to make an instant deci-sion, he changed direction and headed back toward the main road, the way the others would have gone.

The repulsive remains of a forty-eight-day dead traffic warden angrily threw itself at him. Still dressed in the ragged scraps of its black uniform it moved with a sudden burst of unexpected speed and ferocity.

Webb had seen more and more of them attacking like this recently and he didn't like it. The faster ones scared the hell out of him, although he'd never admit it to any of the other survivors. He couldn't understand how something which had been dead for weeks could be getting stronger. For a split second he looked up into what was left of the traffic warden's hideously decomposed face before swinging the baseball bat around again and burying the points of two six-inch nails deep in the side of its skull.

Stuck.

Shit. He'd hit the body with such force that he couldn't get his weapon out. The sharp metal spikes were wedged tight into bone. He yanked hard, but only succeeded in pulling the thrashing body over onto the ground. It lay squirming at his feet as more and more of them closed in on him. He could feel their fingers on his back now, clawing and scratching as he tried to free the nails from the skull. Still stuck. *Stay calm*, he thought to himself, struggling to keep himself from panicking. *They're dead. I'm alive. I can do this . . .*

Webb stamped his boot down across the throat of the writhing corpse. The dead traffic warden, now flat on its back with its arms and legs flailing wildly, glared up at him with a single dark eye, the other having been gouged out of its socket by the force of the baseball bat impact. Webb began to twist the handle of his bat in his hands, still keeping the pressure on the corpse under his foot. Moving with frantic, frightened speed as the other corpses pressed against him, Webb twisted the bat backward and forward, from side to side and around and around in a desperate attempt to sever the head. Long-dead flesh, muscle and cartilage began to tear and brittle bone snapped. The body finally lay still and he stomped angrily on its neck until the final few troublesome connecting sinews gave way. Relieved, he took a deep breath of dirty, germ-filled air, then lifted the bat (with dead head still intact) and swung it out in front of him as he ran on.

8

Pushing his way through an impenetrable forest of cadavers, Webb forced himself to keep moving. He'd overheard a conversation between Hollis and Lorna on their way out to the petrol station less than an hour earlier. Much as Hollis annoyed him, he knew he'd been right and the other man's words now rattled around his head. "If you're surrounded," he'd said, "do anything but stop. Stand still and you'll have a hundred of them onto you in seconds. Keep moving and they can't get you. You've got speed, strength and control on your side; you can be gone before they've even realized you're there." Panicking again, Webb tried to work out how he was supposed to keep moving when suddenly all he could see in front of him was a brick wall. He changed direction and dived to his left, circling around the back of the petrol station now. *Just keep moving*, he told himself again, willing his already tired legs to continue working. Another swipe of the baseball bat (and impaled head) knocked a trio of bodies off their feet and down onto the concrete. Those immediately behind fell over the fallen corpses in their hopelessly uncoordinated attempt to get to Webb. *Stupid fuckers*, he thought as he pushed another two of them away with a determined hand-off before dropping his shoulder, increasing his speed and scrambling up a slippery grass bank toward the road. He cursed as he pulled himself upright and started to sprint again, muscles burning with effort. The wide carriageway ahead was packed solid with corpses. *Maybe it's not as bad as it looks*, he tried to assure himself as he barged into the nearest few. The dead had such a lack of color about them that it was sometimes difficult to make out any detail. Weeks of decomposition had eliminated almost all their distinguishing features. Different skin tones and colorings had been bleached away by decay so that the endless crowds now seemed to have mutated into a single dead race. Their ragged clothing was stained with so much dirt, dust, mold and seepage that they all now appeared to be wearing a kind of gray-green uniform. The upshot of all this, Webb decided as he threw a pretty decent punch at another one which had shown a little control and lashed out at him with gnarled, twisted hands, was that he couldn't tell whether there were a hundred of them up ahead or a thousand.

Just keep moving.

Webb found himself in a narrow sliver of space, just room enough to be able to swing the baseball bat around again. He struck out in an aimless arc, not knowing what, if anything, he'd hit. He made contact with the neck and left shoulder of an awkwardly advancing dead pensioner, hitting it with sufficient force to throw its skeletal frame up into the air like a rag doll. The traffic warden's head, still impaled, was loosened by the impact. Webb's second swing, even lazier in aim but stronger than the first, was enough to dislodge the decapitated head completely. He looked up and watched in amazement as he scored a bizarre home run, the head spinning up through the gray sky high above the massive crowd. Distracted, he followed its flight until it crashed back down to earth. A sudden surge of bodies forced him into action again.

Keep moving . . .

The ground beneath his feet was unexpectedly slippery and uneven now. He looked down and saw that he was virtually ankle deep in a foul-smelling, sticky slurry of human remains. His nerves and adrenaline prevented his stomach from reacting to the gross stench of the bloody mire. He knew that this appalling mudslide of rotting flesh and dismembered body parts was, perversely, a good sign. This was the gruesome wake of the bike and two vans which had abandoned him. The group had made their base in a block of flats just over the next ridge, and this grisly trail would lead him home. If he could just keep his footing and keep moving forward he knew he'd probably be okay.

Another unexpected rush of movement from the restless crowd on his right sent Webb tripping over. He landed on his backside, deep in the obnoxious mess, and gave silent thanks for the heavy motorbike leathers he wore whenever he was outside. The thick, waterproof material gave him some protection from the germs and disease which were no doubt thriving in the disgusting quagmire. All around him a seemingly endless number of cadavers slipped and scrambled to get closer, ignorantly trampling the remains of their brethren. Webb struggled to get back to his feet, the soles of his boots sliding in the greasy muck. He managed to roll over onto all fours—doing everything he could to avoid looking down and seeing exactly what his knees and gloved hands had just sunk into—before leaning on the baseball bat for support and forcing himself back up. Panting heavily, he threw himself into the next wave of bodies and ran toward the top of the hill.

Not far now. He just had to get over the rise, down the other side, then keep following this road until he reached the narrow track which snaked around the dilapidated garages behind the flats. Christ, what he'd give to be back there now. Thankfully the frantic physical exertion seemed to be taking the edge off his fear. He didn't have time to be scared. He had to concentrate on moving forward and smashing his way past body after body after body. A thing which used to be a school teacher, another which once was a chef, a car mechanic, librarian, gym instructor . . . it didn't matter what these hideous things used to be any more. He didn't give any of them more than a split second's thought before destroying them with as much force and venom as he could muster. He was getting tired swinging the bat around, now. The muscles around his shoulders and neck were aching but he knew he couldn't stop yet. The climb to the top of the hill was taking forever and his speed seemed to be reducing. Gravity and the slippery slope of the road were slowing him down while at the same time helping the corpses to hurl themselves at him with unprecedented force. *Almost there*, he thought as he finally neared the top of the climb. *Maybe the other side will be clear and I'll be able to stop?*

Wrong.

Webb didn't stop running when he reached the summit, choosing instead to try and make the most of the velocity he'd finally achieved and power down the steep descent on the other side. Still holding the baseball bat out in front of him, he ploughed into an even deeper sea of constantly shifting undead flesh, silently repeating the mantra to himself over and over:

Just keep moving. Just keep moving . . .

The crowd which now engulfed him, although huge, was almost completely silent. These creatures didn't speak or moan or groan, and the only sounds came from their heavy feet dragging along the ground and the constant buzzing of the thousands of insects which continually gorged themselves on a seemingly never-ending supply of decaying flesh. His labored breathing and the sound of his squelching footsteps were as loud as anything.

But wait—what was that? Just for a moment he was sure he could hear something else. He swung the bat into the chest of a peculiarly lopsided corpse, then stopped for a fraction of a second when he heard the sound in the distance again. It was an engine. Thank God, the others had realized they'd left him behind and come back for him. With renewed energy he threw himself forward yet again, knocking a half dozen scrambling bodies down like skittles.

The noise was definitely getting closer. Two engines this time—the bike and just one of the vans perhaps—and they were fast approaching. He sensed a change in the behavior and direction of the fetid crowd around him. Suddenly he was no longer the sole focus of attention. Easily as many bodies turned and staggered away from him now as continued to move toward him. Desperate to let the others know exactly where he was—if he didn't there was a good chance they'd drive straight into the middle of the crowd looking for him—he stopped using the baseball bat as a weapon and instead shoved it into the air above his head as a marker.

"Over here!" he screamed at the top of his voice as he anxiously barged through the dead, fighting past them as if he was the sole passenger trying to get off a train that everyone else wanted to get on to. He heard the van and bike stop.

"We can see you," Hollis's distinctive voice yelled back. "Now get your fucking head down and get over here!"

Webb knew what was coming next. They'd had to do this kind of thing numerous times before. He dropped to the ground and started crawling furiously away on his hands and knees, weaving around countless lumbering pairs of rotting feet. Speed was suddenly more important than ever. He had to get as close as he could to the others before—

A sudden searing blast of light and heat tore through the crowd just a few meters behind him. He allowed himself the briefest of glances back but kept moving forward, ignoring the pain in his knees and wrists. All around him the bodies began to converge on the area into which Hollis had just hurled a crude, but very effective, petrol bomb. They were attracted to the sudden burst of light and heat. Stupid things walked closer to the epicenter of the blast, many of them oblivious to the fact that they themselves were also now beginning to burn.

The crowd finally thinned sufficiently for Webb to risk getting up and running again. He could see the van and the bike waiting behind the gutted remains of a burned-out coach, parked at such an angle that the dead were prevented from getting too close. He pushed through the final few awkward figures, then slipped between the side of the coach and the front of the van. Hollis lobbed another two bombs directly over his head and watched them detonate deep in the heart of the maggot-ridden mob.

"Let's get out of here." Jas, on the bike, sighed wearily as he climbed back onto the saddle of his machine. Webb moved toward him. "Piss off," he spat. "You're not getting on here like that. Look at the state of you. You're covered in all kinds of shit."

Webb looked down at his blood- and pus-soaked leathers. Gore dripped onto the ground around him. With his face screwed up in a grimace he bent down and picked a piece of scalp—complete with a clump of lank brown hair—out of a crease in his trousers at the top of his boot. He tossed it away in disgust.

"You're not coming in here either," Hollis snapped, looking him up and down. "Hold onto the back of the van."

Too tired to argue, Webb picked up his trusty baseball bat from where he'd dropped it at the roadside, then climbed wearily up onto the footplate at the back of the van. Jas pulled up alongside him and shouted over the roar of the bike.

"And when we get back you make sure you wash yourself down before you take one step inside. I don't want to be stepping through your shit all night, okay?"

Webb didn't respond. He wasn't interested in anything Jas or any of the others had to say. He tightened his grip on the van roof bars as they began to move away, then looked back over his shoulder, watching the smoke rise up from the burning crowds. One of the dead, its clothes and hair aflame, broke free and staggered after the van like the last firework on bonfire night, eventually dropping to the ground when its remaining muscles had burned away to nothing.

Is that the best you can do? Webb thought. *Is that all you've got left?*

2

Cold, tired and angry, Webb stormed up to the third floor and headed straight for the communal flat where most of the small group spent much of their time. He barged into the living room, almost tripping over Anita, who was asleep on the floor.

"You left me!" he yelled when he found her. "You bloody well left me!"

Sitting on a threadbare sofa in the corner of the room, Lorna barely lifted her eyes from her magazine. Anita groaned at him to shut up.

"Yeah," Lorna mumbled, her voice devoid of any sincerity, "really sorry about that, Webb."

"You stupid bitch," he continued, her apparent lack of concern only increasing his anger, "I could have been killed."

"Now there's a thought."

"Didn't you even notice I wasn't there? Didn't you realize the seat next to you was empty?"

Lorna sighed and finally lowered her magazine.

"Sorry Webb," she said, her voice now overly sincere. "Truth was I *did* notice that you hadn't made it back. Problem was I was trying to drive a van filled with cans of petrol through a crowd of dead bodies. I could either turn back to get you and risk being blown to kingdom come, or just keep going. We both managed to get home in one piece, didn't we? I'd say I made the right decision."

"Bitch. You wouldn't be so cocky if it was you that had been left behind. If I'd been in the van—"

"Two things to say to that," she interrupted, pointing her finger at him. "One, I wouldn't have gone mooching around for fags when I'd been given a job to do. And two, you can't drive."

"You always have to bring that up, don't you? You've got a problem because I—"

"No, *you've* got the problem. I couldn't care less if you could drive two cars at the same time. I just think you need to start—"

"Will you two shut up arguing?" Caron demanded as she entered the room carrying a pile of recently looted clothing. "You're like a couple of kids. For crying out loud, look out of the window will you? The whole world's dead and all you want to do is fight with each other."

"We don't have to look out the window, Caron." Lorna sighed. "We've just been outside, remember?"

"And we're all very grateful," Caron replied calmly, refusing to allow herself to be drawn into the same pointless argument they had on a regular basis. "Thank you, both of you. Now will you please stop fighting and start trying to get on with each other?"

"Yes, Mom," Webb mumbled.

Insensitive prick, Lorna thought. Caron had been a mother up until just over a month ago; until the day she'd spent almost an hour trying to resuscitate her seventeen-year-old son Matthew, oblivious to the fact that the rest of the world outside her front door had died too. Still, she thought, at least Caron was trying to come to terms with what's happened, which was more than could be said for some of the others. She glanced over at Ellie, who was sitting in an armchair beside the door, cradling a plastic doll—a replacement for her seven-month-old daughter who had died in her arms on the first morning of the nightmare. Everyone knew it was wrong, yet Lorna couldn't bring herself to say anything. Webb watched her too, scowling at the way she talked to the damn thing, and how she kept checking it was warm enough, planting kisses on its cold plastic cheek. Fucking nutter.

Caron dumped the pile of clothes over the arm of the sofa and gazed out the window. This was one of the rare apartments in the block which was still fully glazed. Most of the others had either been smashed by vandals or boarded up in the weeks leading up to the infection. She still couldn't believe she'd ended up here. She'd driven past these flats hundreds of times before the world had fallen apart, and they'd always seemed to her to be the last place on the planet she'd ever want to live. Three grotesque concrete constructions that had both dominated and blighted the local landscape for years; dated, two-winged buildings which had once housed literally hundreds of underprivileged families. The decision to pull them down had finally been made by the housing authority more than a year ago, but—no doubt as a result of delays caused by pointless local government bureaucracy, bickering and red tape—they'd only demolished one and a half of them before everything had been reduced to ruin.

As quickly and angrily as he'd entered, Webb left the room, muttering and cursing under his breath, slamming the door behind him. The sound echoed around the flat like a gunshot. Ellie held her doll closer and soothed her. Lorna shook her head and continued to read her magazine. Caron cringed at the noise and looked out over the dead world outside—beyond the ever-shifting (and, it seemed, ever-growing) sea of bodies on the other side of the blockade of cars and rubble at the foot of the hill, and stared farther into the distance. She seemed to find herself doing this at least ten times every day, pretty much every time she looked out of the window in fact. Moving just

17

her eyes she traced her route home along suburban roads which were now barely recognizable. From her hilltop position she could see Wilmington Avenue, and from there she counted the rooftops until her eyes settled upon number thirty-two. Her house. Her pride and joy. Her precious home which she'd tended for years and where her dead son still lay on his back in the middle of the kitchen floor. At least that was where she hoped he was. She didn't allow herself to think about the alternatives. She couldn't cope with the thought of her boy endlessly dragging himself along the streets like the rest of those vile creatures out there.

"So how was it today?" she asked, her breath misting up the cold glass in front of her face. She wiped it clear.

"Same as usual," Lorna grunted, still flicking through her magazine.

"The neighbors seem a little more restless today," Caron said. She couldn't bring herself to call them bodies or corpses, or use any of the thoughtless and disrespectful expressions the others used. At least none of them used that ridiculous Z word. She found it easier just to refer to them as the neighbors. Then, in her mind at least, she could shut the door and close the curtains on them and forget they existed, just like she'd done with that awful man Gary Ross who'd lived and died over the road from her on Wilmington Avenue.

"Some of them were a bit wild. Nothing we couldn't handle."

"So what happened with him?"

"Who—Webb?" Lorna replied, looking up momentarily. "Just what I said. He decided he'd go off looting, and I decided to teach him a lesson. I'm sick of the rest of us having to risk our necks because of him. Bloke's a bloody idiot."

"Sounds like he was nearly a dead idiot."

"Maybe. He always makes things sound worse than they are. Anyway, serves him right."

Caron closed her eyes and leaned against the glass. What had her life become? What had she done to deserve this? Trapped in this horrific place, surrounded by these horrific people. She looked up again and focused once more on the gray slate roof of her house in the distance. She squinted, hoping to block out the thousands of cadavers and make them disappear.

Wilmington Avenue was five minutes away by car, but number thirty-two and the world she'd left behind felt a million miles away.

3

On a fifth-floor balcony, illuminated only by a three-quarter moon hanging high in the empty sky above them, three men stood together, drank beer, and watched the dead.

"Is that a corpse?" Stokes asked, pointing down into the shadows below. Hollis peered into the darkness, momentarily concerned. The figure was moving with coordination and control and he relaxed.

"Nah," he yawned, "it's Harte."

Hollis watched as the tall man walked over to the left side of the building and looked through the motley collection of buckets, bathtubs, wheelbarrows and paddling pools the group had left out front to gather rainwater. He half-filled a jug from a large plastic plant-pot then wandered back inside. For a moment everything was still and quiet again.

"So what exactly happened with Webb today?" Stokes asked, disturbing the silence.

"He's a liability," Hollis said quietly, leaning over the metal veranda.

"He's a fucking idiot," Jas said, standing just behind him. Stokes shuffled forward, maneuvering his sizable bulk around the limited space of the balcony so he could reach another beer. He snapped back the ring-pull and held the can out in front of him as the gassy froth bubbled up and dribbled over the edge. He shook his hand dry, took a long swig, then bustled back to his original position next to Hollis.

"He's just a kid, that's all," he said, stifling a belch. "He's all right."

"He's got to learn to keep himself under control and not get distracted." Jas sighed. "We've all got to get smarter when we're out there." He stamped on an empty can, flattening it with a satisfying crunch, then picked it up and pushed his way to the front of the veranda between Stokes and Hollis. He flicked his wrist and hurled the can out into the darkness like a Frisbee, the moonlight allowing him to track its curved path downward. It clattered against a half-demolished wall near to the remains of the second block of flats a little farther down the hill. The sharp and unexpected sound caused a noticeable ripple of inquisitive movement within the ranks of the dead nearby. He could see a sudden momentary swell of interest among the tightly packed corpses on the other side of the wall of rubble and wrecked cars they'd erected to keep the hordes at bay.

"We've just got to be sensible," Hollis said. "Just keep doing what we're doing until they've rotted down to nothing. We're not prisoners here. We'll keep going out and getting what we need, when we need it. We're in charge here. Those things will only ever be able to get to us if we let them."

"Maybe we should leave Webb here next time," Jas suggested. "He's going to get someone killed."

"He's just a loose cannon," said Stokes. "Don't write him off. He just needs to learn how to keep himself under control, that's all."

"I've seen dead bodies in the streets with more control than him," Jas grumbled as he stomped on another empty can.

"Don't joke about it," Hollis said, leaning over to one side as the second crushed can flew past his ear. "Did you see that one today?"

"Which one?"

"The one with the branch."

"What are you talking about?" Stokes asked, confused.

"It was just after we'd filled the first van," Hollis explained. "One of the dead came marching out through the middle of the crowd dragging half a bloody tree behind it."

"Must have got itself caught up," Jas suggested, sounding only half-interested.

"That's what I thought," he continued, "but I was watching it and . . ."

"And what?"

Hollis paused, not entirely sure what he was trying to say. "And I swear it was trying to pick it up and use it."

"Use it for what?"

"A weapon, I guess. Maybe it was going to attack us with it."

"You're worried about being attacked by a corpse carrying a branch?" Stokes said, smirking. "Christ, mate, you're going soft. There's thousands of them out there, and they're all ready to gouge your bloody eyes out. I don't think we need to lose any sleep over one that thinks it's going to kill you with a bit of tree!"

Christ, Hollis thought, Stokes could be a pain in the backside at times. He was an insensitive, uneducated prick.

"You fucking idiot," he cursed, amazed that he was having to spell out his concerns, "it's not what it was carrying that bothers me, it's the fact it was carrying anything at all. Have you seen any of them carry anything before now?"

"No, but—"

"Exactly. The last thing we want is for them to start picking stuff up and starting to—"

"Are you sure it was carrying the branch?" Jas interrupted.

"I was only looking at it for a few seconds," he admitted, "and there were loads of them around us."

"Don't get wound up about it, it was probably nothing. Like I said, maybe it just got caught up."

"Maybe, but what if—"

"Never mind what-if," Stokes snapped, "let's just concentrate on what we know they're capable of."

"And what's that?" Jas asked.

"Fuck all!" he laughed, his bellowing voice echoing around the desolate estate, bouncing off the walls of empty buildings.

"What I think," Webb suddenly announced from the darkness behind them, "is that we should go out there tomorrow and start burning them again. And this time we should keep at it until there's nothing left of any of them."

"You're a bloody pyromaniac, Webb. You're the reason we had to go out there to get fuel again today," Hollis reminded him.

"It's got to be worth it to get rid of a few hundred of them, though, hasn't it?"

"Problem is, you don't get rid of hundreds, do you? How many was it you managed last time?"

"Fuck off," Webb said, helping himself to the last can of beer. "At least I'm trying to do something."

"Seven, wasn't it?" Stokes laughed. "He takes two cans full of petrol right down to the edge of the crowd and he only manages to get rid of seven of them! You've got to try hard to be that useless!"

"Wasn't my fault," he explained angrily, "the wind changed direction before I could—"

"Funniest thing I've seen since all this started," Stokes howled, "you running away from that fire with all those bodies just stood there watching you! Bloody priceless!"

"Shut up. It wasn't my fault. At least I stopped them getting any closer."

"No, you didn't," Hollis said quietly. "They stopped getting closer long before you started with your party tricks. It's been days since any of them tried to get over the barrier."

"Why is that?" Jas asked, suddenly more serious. "Why do you think they're holding back?"

"They're waiting for Webb to go back out there," Stokes said, still laughing. "They're waiting for you to entertain them, mate! Or maybe they want you to light another fire to keep them warm!"

"Fuck you, Stokes."

Webb slumped against the wall and swigged his beer.

"Thought you were going to show us how to keep him under control," Hollis said quietly.

"I am," Stokes whispered back. "He needs putting in his place. If we tell him he did a great job getting rid of seven of them, he'll be back out there tomorrow morning trying to do it again like he's the fucking Terminator or something."

Hollis could see Stokes's point of view, but he wasn't convinced Stokes continually put Webb down for any reason other than to make himself feel better.

"No one answered my question," Jas said.

"What question?" Stokes mumbled ignorantly.

"Why do you think they're holding back?"

"Who?"

"The bodies, you moron."

"Well it ain't because of Webb!"

Hollis stared out toward the vast crowd of corpses in the near distance. In the low light the thousands of individual figures seemed to have merged together and formed a single, unending mass of decaying flesh.

"No way of knowing for sure, is there?" he finally admitted.

"But what do you think?" Jas pushed. "What's your gut feeling?"

"That they're either too scared to come any closer or they're biding their time."

"Biding their time?" Stokes protested. "What the hell are you talking about?"

"Maybe they're waiting for us to drop our guard. Maybe they're waiting for us to come out into the open so they can make their move and attack. They've got us outnumbered by more than a thousand to one."

"Bullshit," Stokes said. "They're not waiting for us."

"Like I said, we should just go out there in the morning and get rid of the whole fucking lot of them," Webb shouted from the shadows. "And if we can't get rid of them then we should just keep pushing them back until there's at least a mile between the nearest one of them and me."

4

"Where are we going?" sighed Driver. He picked a lump of dried food out of the end of his untidy month-long beard and flicked it under the table. Hollis held his head in his hands, then jabbed his finger down onto the map.

"Kingsway Road," he sighed. "Halfway down going towards town, just before you get to the station. Haven't you been listening?"

"That's the old twenty-three route," Driver answered, suddenly marginally more animated. "I know where you mean now."

"Thank God for that."

Hollis made momentary eye contact with Harte, who seemed to share his concerns about Driver. Christ, they didn't even know his real name. He'd turned up at the flats in the bus he'd been driving when the infection had first struck. He'd picked up several other survivors along the way but had been disturbingly lapse and vague about everything that had happened. Lorna, one of his passengers, had told Hollis she'd found a woman's carcass wedged under one of the seats. The smell of the decomposing grandmother had been strong enough for her to notice long before she'd spotted her tan-suede-booted foot sticking out. He'd been driving around with her rotting in the back of the bus for days and hadn't even noticed.

Less than forthcoming with any personal details, they had simply christened him with the unimaginative label of "Driver" because of his preapocalypse vocation. Good job they'd not adopted the same naming strategy for any of the others, Hollis thought to himself. Jas could have got away with "Security," as could Harte with "Teacher." Caron would probably have been quietly pleased to have been given the mantle of "Housewife," although Gordon, the short and repressed warehouse manager, would probably have insisted they call her "Homemaker" in a pointless effort to be politically correct. He decided he would have christened Webb "Young Offender" and Stokes "Failed Store Manager and Alcoholic." With few other distinguishing characteristics or traits, Ellie, Lorna and Anita would have all been labeled "Unemployed" and that, he decided, would have just been confusing. He didn't like to group Lorna with the other two girls, although they were all of a similar age and background. He liked her. She had more about her than the rest of them.

"What's the name of this place we're looking for again?" Harte asked, leaning over the map to get a better view. Caron looked at the business phone directory in her lap and ran her finger down the page.

"Shaylors," she answered, finally finding the right advert. " 'Wholesale cash and carry for retailers. Over twenty thousand lines including a wide range of fresh and frozen food, groceries, beers, wines, spirits, tobacco and nonfood items.' "

"Sounds perfect," Stokes chipped in. "Maybe we should move in there. It'd be a hell of a lot easier than going out looting all the time."

Sitting across the table, Jas shook his head. "You been down the Kingsway Road recently?"

"You know I haven't."

"Place was bad news before any of this started. It's going to be a nightmare today. It'll be crawling with corpses."

"Isn't everywhere?"

"Can't we find anywhere safer to go?" Gordon piped up from his usual position by the window. "Do we really need to risk going so deep into town just to get booze and cigarettes?"

"Last time I checked you weren't risking anything, Gord," Stokes said. "How long's it been since you last went out?"

"I've got problems with my hip, you know I have," he answered quickly, rattling off his stock excuse. "Seriously, I'd just hold you all up and slow you down. I've been on the waiting list for a replacement for more than two years."

"Well, you're not going to get your operation now, are you, mate? You might as well get used to the pain and start pulling your weight."

"Let it go," Hollis sighed. He wasn't in the mood to referee yet another slanging match. Truth be told, he didn't want to risk being out in the open with someone as weak and useless as Gordon anyway.

"Sounds good," Ellie said, sitting on the windowsill, cradling her doll and kicking her legs. "Get me some fags, will you? Me and Anita are down to our last couple of packs."

"Think about your baby," Stokes said with a smirk. Webb bit his lip and looked away, trying not to laugh.

"Where is Anita, anyway?" Jas asked, glancing around the room.

"In bed," Ellie answered.

"In bed?" he repeated. "Bloody hell, it's like a holiday camp here. What's she doing in bed?"

"Says she feels sick. Says it's something she's eaten."

"I reckon it's just another one of her excuses, lazy cow," Stokes said, for once putting into words what just about everyone else was

28

thinking. Anita seemed to be able to find a way of getting out of doing practically anything.

The bickering continued around him, but Hollis concentrated on the map on the table, doing his best to shut out the constant, pointless noise. They'd been systematically working their way through all the large supermarkets and stores on this side of town. Once they'd cleared a store out and stripped it down to bare bones, they crossed through it on the map and moved on to the next. Their strategy had worked well so far, but the danger was increasing. Their trips outside were now taking longer and thorough planning was necessary. Problem was, he thought, with this shower of tossers the risks were dramatically increasing too. He knew he could count on Jas, Stokes (despite his obvious faults), Harte, and Lorna, but as for the rest of them . . .

"I said, when are we going to do it?" Stokes asked, slapping his hand down on the table when he didn't get an answer, making Hollis jump.

"What?"

"Do we go now or leave it until later?"

"We should just get it done," Hollis replied. "Let's get out of here, get back, and then have a bloody good drink."

5

Jas pushed his bike out of the front lobby of the flats and wheeled it over toward the other vehicles. Hollis acknowledged both him and Harte, who climbed onto the back of the bike to ride pillion. Next to Hollis in the larger of the group's two vans sat Lorna, quiet and pensive and chewing her lip nervously, unaware he was staring at her. He often found himself watching her. She had a spark of energy and life about her. Even now, about to head out into the grim, dangerous and unpredictable ruin of their world, she remained remarkably positive. She was wearing a trace of makeup and had tied her hair up neatly. She did something different with her hair almost every day. It said something about her that she still took pride in her appearance. He, on the other hand, hadn't brushed his teeth for more than a week.

The hydraulic hiss of the doors of the bus opening on the other side of the car park distracted Hollis. He watched as Driver let Stokes and Webb on board. Before disappearing inside, Webb glanced along the length of the bizarre-looking vehicle. Once just like any other double-decker bus, over the weeks the group had cannibalized and fortified it to the best of their limited abilities. Barbwire had been spooled along both sides in an attempt to make it as difficult as possible for the dead to reach the survivors inside. Sheet metal had been bolted to its otherwise flat front to form a rudimentary pointed plow, perfect for cutting through the incessant crowds which gathered around them whenever they left the relative safety and calm of the flats.

The air, so eerily quiet and still most of the time now, was suddenly filled with noise as, one by one, the engines were started. Lorna shuffled forward in her seat and peered through binoculars down into the gray sea of cadavers. Even from this distance she could see that they were already beginning to react to the rumble of the machines.

The geography of the area around the block of flats had made the ugly concrete building a surprisingly effective base. Its location, perched three-quarters of the way up a steep hill, made it difficult for the bodies to get close easily. Some of them, those less damaged or decayed than the rest, were occasionally able to drag themselves through the desolation and get closer to the survivors, but were easy pickings. Webb in particular seemed to take great pleasure in destroying them, although Jas, Harte, and Hollis were always ready to take their turn. Behind their building, a myriad of tracks and roads led through an empty, mazelike housing estate which had also been scheduled for demolition before everything had ended. Many houses were boarded up, and the group had created makeshift road blocks and barriers, leaving only the most inaccessible roads clear and making it all but impossible for even the most determined of corpses to reach them.

No one was sure how much of a difference it made anymore, but it had become standard practice to create a distraction whenever anyone left the flats. Regardless of how much control the bodies had begun to exhibit, they could still be fooled. Fire was usually the best diversion. A little heat, light and noise were usually enough to take some of the pressure off whoever it was heading out into the open.

"Ready?" Ellie yelled from Hollis's right. He gave her a leather-gloved thumbs-up. On his signal she ran over to where Caron and

Gordon were standing and started working. Hollis wiped sweat from his brow. Christ, he was hot. One of the worst things about going outside—apart from the unwanted attention of the remains of the local population—was the regulation uniform they had each decided to adopt. Bike leathers, wet suits, over-trousers—anything that might protect them from the layer of germs, slime and decay which was gradually coating every square inch of the world outside.

Ellie lit a petrol-soaked rag and tossed it through the open window of a small, box-shaped silver car. A puddle of fuel on the driver's seat and in the foot-well immediately burst into flame. Moving with sudden purpose and speed, she ran around to the back of the car and, with the other two, began to push it away from the flats. They could hear the crackle and pop of the fire taking hold inside; dirty black smoke was already beginning to belch out through the window.

"Come on," Gordon grunted, his face flushed red with effort and his dodgy hip feeling like it was about to pop out of his pelvis. Ellie took a step back then ran and launched herself at the car, finally feeling its wheels beginning to turn and pick up some speed. Its interior now completely ablaze, it rolled down the hill with increasing velocity, running away from the three people pushing it. Breathless, she stood with her hands on her hips and watched as it raced down the slope, bobbling up into the air as it hit the curb. It juddered along a little farther, then thudded into the barrier.

"Could have done with that being a little more dramatic," Hollis grumbled, disappointed. "It'll have to do."

"Should be okay," Lorna said. She watched through the binoculars as bodies swarmed around the part of the barrier closest to the burning car. Worryingly, she was sure that one or two of them were actually trying to climb over the blockade to get closer to the flames.

"We'll just need to make sure we—" Hollis began to say before the quarter-full fuel tank of the burning car exploded in a swollen, incandescent mushroom of flame, showering the ground with shrapnel. The sudden burst of energy caused huge numbers of diseased creatures to surge toward the epicenter of the blast. "That's better," he said to himself, slamming his foot down on the accelerator.

"Here we go, then," Driver announced to his two passengers in his monotone, emotionless drawl. "Hold tight." He instinctively checked his mirrors and even indicated before pulling out. Stokes and Webb held onto the handrail inside the bus as if they were rush-hour commuters on their way to work.

Jas paused before following on the bike. The visor on his helmet still raised, he watched the bodies swarming around the fire. Many had been drawn to the flames, some had been crushed in the confusion and others had even found themselves close enough to the heat to be set alight. Others, he noticed, had changed direction. He could see six or seven of them actually trying to move away from the burning wreck. Damn things, it was almost as if they'd realized the fire was nothing more than an unsubtle decoy. Harte tapped his shoulder.

"Come on," he shouted, his voice muffled by his helmet. Jas flicked his visor down and powered after the bus.

6

"Almost there," Lorna said, glancing up from the notepad and map she gripped tightly in her hand. The windscreen of the van was covered in an almost opaque film of greasy stains and dripping gore and she couldn't see much up ahead. Hollis repeatedly tried to use the wipers but all they seemed to do was make the problem worse, smearing the foul muck from side to side in a bloody rainbow arc of insipid yellows, browns, and grays. He frantically used the screen-wash, managing to clear just enough of the glass to be able to see through. "Turn left and we're on the Kingsway Road."

Hollis swerved around a tight corner, then put his foot down again as the Kingsway Road stretched out in front of them. Apart from the fact it was crowded with the dead, it didn't look anything like he remembered.

"What next?"

She looked down at her notes again like the co-pilot in a surreal, obstacle-strewn rally. Her assistance was vital. The almost never-ending waves of bodies made it virtually impossible to navigate by sight alone anymore. They were frequently packed so tightly together that it was hard to see where the road ended and the curb began.

"Keep going for half a mile, go through a set of lights, then Shaylors should be on our right."

"Should be on our right?"

"*Will* be on our right," she corrected herself. A sudden thump made her jump and catch her breath as a dismembered arm (it may even have been half a leg) spiralled up from a ruckus in the crowd and thudded against the windscreen, leaving a bloody stain—a sudden splash of crimson red in the midst of the putrid yellow grays.

"Nice," Hollis mumbled. "They're virtually falling apart now."

"Just wish they'd hurry up and get on with it."

Hollis glanced into his rearview mirror but couldn't see anything clearly.

"Are they still behind us?"

Lorna turned around in her seat and peered along the length of the empty van to look out through the rear window. She struggled to focus—the ride was increasingly uneven as they powered through and over the dead—before finally seeing the bright lights of Jas's bike between the crisscrossing corpses. Farther back still, the bus continued to trundle sedately through the carnage. Its size and strength were such that it could move at a more pedestrian pace. It didn't matter at what speed Driver drove, nothing was going to stop him.

Harte was transfixed by his surroundings. Everything seemed so different from when he was last here: instantly familiar and yet completely different, like looking at the world he remembered through a filter of grime. He held onto the back of the bike as Jas jolted up the curb, mounting the pavement and skillfully weaving through a gap between an overturned hot dog stand and the front of a furniture store, then leaning the bike the other way to avoid the grabbing hands of a corpse. Harte hadn't seen as many of them this morning as he'd expected—hundreds, not thousands. His theory was that they'd gradually spread

35

out from here like blood on tissue paper. This godforsaken place had always been busy, always heaving with too many people. He'd taught at a school just a few miles away and had always done all he could to avoid coming here. The Kingsway Road ran right through the center of some of the poorest parts of town, and the squalor and ruin here today appeared uncomfortably familiar. He could see some of the pitiful residents of this densely populated hellhole trapped behind the doors and windows of buildings as they passed. Some still moved incessantly as if they might be about to find some miracle escape route which had eluded them for the last couple of months. Others stood slumped against the windows, pointlessly pounding their fists against the dirty glass.

Less than fifty meters in front of the bike and bus, the van had slowed down. Lorna wound down her window, stuck her hand out, and pointed over to the right. Knowing that was his cue to take the lead, Jas accelerated, roaring past the van toward Shaylors. The group of survivors, although frequently argumentative, unhelpful, and volatile, were occasionally surprisingly organized. They had developed a well-rehearsed routine for times such as this. The van dropped back, leaving Jas and Harte to get closer and suss out the surrounds of the building they were planning to loot.

After dodging a small group of cadavers which had lurched perilously close, Jas drove across the wide car park at the front of the building at speed. Harte spotted a signpost marked DELIVERIES. Perfect. He pointed toward it and Jas accelerated again. A straight length of road, no more than one hundred meters long, stretched all the way along the side of the building down to a fenced-off loading bay. Jas drove into the bay, turned a tight circle, then drove back the way he'd just come and gestured for the others to follow. Another tight full turn and he disappeared again. Hollis put his foot down, then braked hard and skidded around the corner after him. A short distance behind, Webb and Stokes held on for dear life as they approached the turning in the bus. The swarming bodies suddenly seemed the least of their worries. How the hell was Driver going to get the bus around the corner and along the gap between the side of the building and the fence?

"Bloody hell, are you going to get this thing down there?" Webb asked. Driver nodded confidently, checked his mirrors, and gently swung the bus around to the right to follow the others down the track.

"We'll be fine. They used to get trucks down here, didn't they?"

Driver carefully shunted the massive vehicle a few feet farther forward, then hard-locked the steering wheel. He took his time. A man who'd spent his life driving according to timetables and working regulations, he wasn't about to start hurrying for anyone or anything. With a total lack of urgency or any visible emotion he continued to inch forward, craning his neck and lifting himself up on his seat to be sure the farthest forward corner of the bus didn't clip the fence. He seemed oblivious to all other distractions—to Stokes and Webb, who cursed and mumbled incessantly behind him, to the endless stream of cadavers which had caught up with the bus and began hammering against the back of it, and to the rattle and whip of the coils of barb-wire which were scraped off the sides of the vehicle by the tall fence on one side and the brick wall on the other. Many of the bodies immediately became entangled in the spools of vicious wire. Their flesh, already ravaged by decay, was lacerated, virtually stripped from their bones by countless, pin-sharp metal spikes.

Hollis had turned the van full-circle as soon as he'd reached the loading area. Face-to-face with the oncoming bus now, he waited for it to complete its short journey, ready for the crowd of corpses which would no doubt be close behind.

"You get out," he told Lorna. "I'll plug the gap."

Having driven with before him on numerous occasions, Lorna knew exactly what he was planning. She grabbed her weapon—a claw hammer—then jumped out of the van and ran across the tarmac toward Harte and Jas. Hollis gripped the steering wheel tightly as the bus thundered past him. The moment his view of the track was clear he powered forward again, hurtling back down the narrow alleyway and annihilating the few pathetic carcasses which had somehow managed to avoid the barbwire and stagger closer. He slammed on the brakes when he had almost reached the front of the building, and the wet remains of several bodies slid to the ground with the sudden stop. The track was a foot wider than the van on either side, maybe a little more. Hollis steered to the right and edged forward, wedging the vehicle across the full width of the road and preventing any more of the dead from getting through to disrupt their precious looting time.

Hollis scrambled over the back of his seat, then climbed out of the van and sprinted down the track.

"Watch yourself," he heard Harte shout as a solitary body slipped out from behind an overflowing, rat-infested Dumpster in the farthest corner of the enclosed area. He watched it as it moved toward them with inexplicable intent. Just two months ago it had been a night worker here at the warehouse, a happily married father of four. Now it was a pitiful, bedraggled, bloodstained shell of a human being. A fall on the first day after reanimation had shattered the bones in its right arm, leaving the useless limb hanging heavily at its side, swinging like a pendulum with every uncoordinated trip and stumble.

"I'll do it," Lorna volunteered, striding toward the body with confidence. She took a step back with surprise as it lurched angrily toward her, arm flapping, then moved forward again and caved in its head with her hammer. The corpse dropped motionless at her feet, the contents of its shattered skull slowly leaking out over the ground, glistening in the sunlight. She nonchalantly shook the hammer clean and returned to the others.

"We ready then, ladies?" Jas asked as Stokes and Webb finally emerged from the bus. Driver remained in his cab, door closed, reading his newspaper.

Everyone carried their weapon of choice. Hollis unsheathed a machete he'd brought with him from the van. Jas also had a machete, Webb his trusty spiked baseball bat, Harte a hand ax and Stokes, bizarrely, a garden spade.

"Just do it," Stokes said. "I need a drink."

Jas pushed the door open and waited for a second before entering the dark building. He held his breath and listened. Nothing at first . . . then the sound of something moving close by . . . sliding, shuffling footsteps. He took another step forward and heard a clatter and crash just ahead. Several bodies at least. Impossible to tell how many.

"Anything?" Harte yelled from outside.

"There's something in here," Jas replied, inching forward slowly. "Can't see very much . . ."

"Be careful, mate."

Sensing movement in the darkness to his right, Jas glanced up and, with a single well-aimed flash of his blade, sliced through the neck of a cadaver which had been about to attack. It fell at his feet and he stepped over it to reach a second door. He could definitely hear movement on the other side. He banged his fist against the wood and, almost immediately, felt something thump back against it in angry response. Taking another deep breath he pushed it open and shoved a body back as it immediately launched itself at him from the gloom. Ignoring the unwanted attentions of the corpse he propped the second door open with a fire extinguisher and began making as much noise as he could.

"Come and get us," he shouted, his voice echoing through the vast, mausoleum-like building. There was an almost instant reaction to his words. From the shadows all around cadavers began to appear, all gravitating toward him. He quickly backed out through the open door.

39

"Any idea how many?" Lorna asked.

"Nah," he replied, "couldn't see much." He cleared his throat and shouted again, "Come on, you fuckers! Get a move on! Get yourselves out here!"

The first two bodies appeared quickly, almost fighting with each other to get through the door. A dead security guard tried to push past the awkward bulk of a badly decayed but still grossly overweight female shopper. The shopper's slobbering mass prevailed and it heaved itself forward, sending the smaller corpse crashing to the ground then trampling over it as it moved toward the survivors.

"Fuck me," said Stokes, "look at the size of that thing!"

The group stood together in silence and watched the body as it waddled toward them. Its massively distended, discolored belly hung heavy over the top of a pair of brown-stained leggings, little shock waves running up through its saggy, curiously lumpy flesh with every ungainly step it took. Huge, pendulous breasts swung down like bags of grain, almost reaching its waist, a tear in its shapeless T-shirt revealing dark-veined skin like blue cheese. For a moment no one moved, everyone waiting for someone else to take the lead and dispatch the enormous cadaver. The appearance of another six bodies from the building in quick succession forced them all into action.

"Watch yourselves," Hollis warned as his colleagues lifted their weapons and began to attack.

Harte was first to strike, grunting with satisfaction as he sunk the blade of his ax into the neck of the body of a teenage girl, the force of the strike knocking it to the ground. It reached up for him and he hauled it back to its feet, then yanked the ax free and swung it down again at its now lopsided head, this time managing to hit the back of its neck and almost completely cut through its spinal cord. Suddenly limp, the body slumped against him and he tossed it away as if he was throwing out a bag of rubbish. He stepped back, almost falling over the legs of the huge corpse which Stokes was now doing his best to destroy. The other man was ramming his shovel repeatedly into the creature's grotesquely swollen stomach, slicing through its flesh and splattering its rancid guts everywhere. The damn thing continued to fight, its arms and legs thrashing.

"Go for its head, you moron," Harte suggested, looking around for his next kill. Stokes was too engrossed in his work to hear him.

Lorna dragged another body into space in the middle of the tarmac, spun it around and slammed it down on its back. Keeping a tight grip on its neck, she dropped down onto its exposed rib cage, feeling bones crack and rotten flesh slide beneath her leather-clad knees. With her gloved left hand she grabbed hold of the corpse's chin and shoved its face over to the side before smacking the hammer down onto its temple, causing enough damage to its putrefying brain to immediately and permanently incapacitate it.

Still more of the hellish things dragged themselves out of the darkness and into the open, drawn out of hiding by the noise. In the time that Harte and Lorna had taken to deal with one body each, both Jas and Hollis had disposed of several more. The two men were now stepping cautiously through the bloody carnage, dragging the dismembered remains of their kills out of the way and dumping them against the back fence. Hollis was watching Stokes struggling with his obese victim when he was distracted by a sudden yelp of surprise from Webb.

"What's the problem?" Hollis yelled. The idiot had managed to get himself backed into a corner by two of them. He swung his baseball bat wildly but wasn't making contact. It was almost as if they were keeping their distance.

"Nothing," he shouted back breathlessly. "I'm all right."

"We don't have time for this," Jas said angrily as he marched across the loading bay and grabbed hold of one of the bodies by its shoulder, dragging it over. It kicked and flailed on the ground furiously.

41

Without a flicker of emotion he raised his machete and chopped down just above the creature's vacant eyes, hitting it with such force that the blade sliced right through the skull, taking the top of its head off. Taking advantage of the distraction, Webb angrily shoved the remaining corpse against the fence. He stepped back and swung his bat around, burying it in its face.

"I said I was all right," he said as he yanked the bat free and let the body drop to the ground.

"You two finished?" asked Lorna. Jas looked around and saw that the only person still fighting was Stokes, struggling with the massive corpse by the entrance door. The body's arms and legs continued to move wildly, and Stokes was still shredding its grossly oversized torso with his shovel. Much of the surrounding area, and his own legs, had been drenched with a layer of dark brown blood and slime.

"You fucking idiot," Webb spat as he stormed past Stokes. He stamped down hard on the face of the hideous aberration, crushing its features under his boot. It immediately lay still.

Jas was waiting at the door into the building, peering inside and banging his fist on a metal storage cabinet. The noise rang through the entire building, echoing around the loading bay and surrounding area outside.

"Any more of them?" asked Hollis, standing just behind him and peering over his shoulder.

"Probably. Bound to be a few of them stuck in there."

Hollis pushed past and disappeared inside, struggling to see anything in the suddenly low light. The others followed, matching his every move as he weaved along a gloomy passageway, pushing open doors which had remained closed for more than six weeks. More through luck than judgment they soon entered the main section of the warehouse. Grimy skylights let in just enough light to illuminate most of the vast space. They were immediately aware of movement around them again, but such was the size of the shop floor, most of the creatures were still some distance away.

He marched purposefully toward the nearest of the bodies and raised his machete, knowing they were all that stood between him and a decent-size stash of liquor, food, and other supplies.

"Fuck me," Webb laughed as Harte dragged a heavy trolley through to the back of the store. "Just look at all that . . ." He stared with eyes wide like a child's on Christmas morning at the boxes of cigarettes, crates of beer, and bottles of drink piled up on the trolley.

"Instead of just looking at it," Harte said, panting, "you could try helping."

Bemused, Webb shook his head, then moved around to the back and started pushing. Groaning with effort, the two men managed to guide the unresponsive trolley down an aisle strewn with rubbish and the skeletal remains of several shop staff. They pushed it through a pair of swinging double-doors out into the loading area, then hauled it toward the waiting bus. Hollis and Lorna were already unloading another similar trolley. Stokes was standing a little way back, leaning against the side of the bus, trying to convince the others that he was, in some strange way, helping. Hollis picked up a tray of food but stopped before climbing on board.

"You might want to try getting something we actually need while you're in there," he said as Harte staggered toward him carrying more beer.

"There's plenty of room," he replied, indignant.

"Don't forget about the others. Not everyone drinks, you know."

"We *are* thinking about the others. Look!" Webb smirked, holding up a bumper-size pack of disposable nappies. "For Ellie's plastic baby!"

Stokes let out a roar of laughter. Hollis was not impressed.

"You know what I mean."

"There's plenty of room," Harte said again, clearly irritated. "When those lazy bastards actually come out here and start taking risks like we do every week, then I'll start giving what they need a little more consideration. Until then, we'll get the essentials, but I need booze. Me and Stokes are having a competition to see whose liver rots first."

"He's got a point," Lorna said quietly as she slipped past and dumped the food she'd been carrying.

"I know," Hollis admitted.

"There's loads of clothes and bedding back there," Jas said as he stumbled toward them, his arms laden with bags. "They've got everything."

"Then we should get everything," Stokes suggested, still keeping his distance from the workers, "and quick. The population are starting to show an interest."

"What?" Lorna asked, immediately concerned. "Where?"

He pointed toward the back fence. There was a hole where several wooden slats had broken over time. Lorna crouched down and peered through the gap. Stokes was right. She could see a mass of spindly, unsteady legs on the other side of the fence. Hollis jogged back to where he'd left the van parked at the other end of the track. There was an unsurprisingly large crowd of corpses gathering outside the front of the store too.

"Many?" Stokes asked when he returned.

"Enough," he answered, picking up more food. "We should get this lot shifted and get home."

7

It was just after three in the afternoon, but it felt much later. The sun was beginning to sink lazily below the horizon, drenching the flats with hazy, warm orange light. The unexpected brightness and heat indoors was almost enough to give the illusion of it being an August afternoon, not postapocalyptic late October.

The frenzied activity of earlier in the day had slowed to a virtual standstill. Since the looters had returned the group had scattered themselves throughout the building, each person taking a little treasure for themselves—some food or drink, clean bedding or fresh clothes. Jas sat alone in the corner of his room. Next to him the remains of the best meal he'd eaten in days was spread over the dirty carpet. It had all been cold, processed, high-sugar, nutrition-free crap but he didn't care. It tasted relatively good and it filled his stomach and that, he decided, was all that mattered. He couldn't remember how long it had been since he'd last felt this full.

The room was becoming dark save for a few slender shards of incandescent light which squeezed between the boards, covering a single narrow window just above his head, illuminating strips of peeling, water-stained wallpaper. Despite its shabby appearance, Jas liked the isolation of this particular flat and retreated to it often. One day he might make an effort and drag some sticks of furniture in here, he decided. Until then he was happy to relax on an inflatable camping mattress. He yawned, stretched, and rubbed his eyes. The effort of the morning had worn him out. Six weeks on and he was still finding it impossible to get used to this stop-start, stop-start existence. Life either ran at a snail's pace or hurtled along at breakneck speed and there didn't seem to be any in-between. Truth be told, he preferred it when things were moving quickly. He found it easier to lurch from crisis to crisis than to sit alone in cold, empty rooms like this and think. Because thinking, he'd discovered, inevitably meant remembering, and that still hurt as much as it had on the first day. He slipped his hand into the inside pocket of his jacket and pulled out his wallet. He carried it everywhere with him, even though he had no need for it anymore. He took out the last remaining photograph of his wife and children, sandwiched between useless credit cards and redundant bank notes. There they were: Prisha, Seti, and Annia, still beautiful despite the horizontal crease in the picture which ran across their smiling faces. And just behind them, sitting with her arms around them all, was his Harj. God, how he missed her.

"Bloody hell," a voice yelled suddenly from one of the other flats nearby, distracting him from his darkening thoughts. It sounded like Driver or Gordon, and it seemed to have come from the general direction of the shared apartment. Jas jumped to his feet and ran toward the source of the sound, tucking the photo back into his wallet as he moved. What had happened now? He guessed it was probably a fight, most likely Webb and Lorna at each other's throats again.

Jas burst into the shared flat and immediately stopped and screwed up his face in disgust. The stench hit him like a punch in the face. Anita was leaning over the side of the sofa, spitting and retching.

On the pale yellow carpet beside her was a puddle of vomit, the color and consistency of red wine. Most of the others who were in the flat were now standing around the edges of the room, backs pressed against the walls, as far as they could get from the foul-smelling, bilious mess on the floor. Only Caron was brave enough to get any closer, but even she was forced to quickly scuttle out of the way as Anita lunged forward and threw up again. The sound of her heaving, followed by the splatter and splash of vomit, made the bile rise in Jas's throat and he struggled not to be sick himself. He leaned out of the door he'd just come through, desperate to get some air.

"Can somebody get me something to clean this up with?" Caron asked as she scrubbed at the floor with a strip of sick-soaked rag. No one moved. "Come on!" she snapped, the tone of her voice finally prompting Gordon to start looking through some of the boxes of supplies which had been collected earlier. As Anita began to retch again Jas took the opportunity to get out. He stepped back out into the corridor and walked straight into Harte, who was coming the other way.

"What's going on in there?" he asked, concerned.

"Anita's chucking up," Jas answered. "Must've eaten something dodgy."

"Something we brought back with us?"

"How am I supposed to know? Go and have a look for yourself if you're that interested." He sighed, grimacing. His stomach was still churning.

"No thanks," Harte replied, gingerly peering around the edge of the door. "She's probably just gorged herself like the rest of us. I'm not feeling too good . . ."

"What's all the noise?" Webb shouted, appearing at the end of the corridor with a can of lager in one hand and three more in the other. "Jesus, what's that smell?"

47

"Anita's sick," Harte replied. He watched Webb stop and consider his options. It didn't take him long to decide what to do next.

"Fucking stinks in here," he said over his shoulder as he turned and walked away.

8

Webb clattered down the stairs, spinning quickly around as he reached the bottom of each flight, desperate to get out of the drab concrete building. Having spent some time outside today he felt more confined by his gray-walled surroundings than ever, and the stench of Anita's vomit just now had been the final straw. If he'd been able to drive he might even have risked getting into a car and disappearing for a while. Sometimes there wasn't much to choose between spending the evening with the dead outside or the morbid, miserable fuckers inside. The last thing he wanted was to sit there and listen to their tedious conversation going around and around in circles until someone got upset or started a fight—that was inevitably what happened. He felt trapped. The whole world was empty and he was free to leave at any time, but he still felt trapped.

In the shadows of the block of flats, near to the area where they collected rainwater, Webb kept his pride and joy. To the others it was just another car but to him it was an escape. Sure, it wasn't much of an escape given that he couldn't drive it, but it was something. It wasn't what he'd have chosen if he'd had more of a choice, and he knew his mates would have laughed at him if they'd seen its color and the engine size, but it was where he was able to find a little sanctuary. He climbed in, shut the door and turned the key in the ignition just far enough around so that he could switch on the stereo. A CD clicked and whirred in the player. After a few moments of silence the inside of the car was filled with the relentless thump, thump, thump of high-speed dance music so deafeningly loud that it made the windows and door panels rattle and vibrate.

Webb pushed himself back into the driver's seat and looked out into the distance, hoping for a while that the beer and the noise would enable him to fool himself into believing this was a normal night in a normal world.

After three and a half cans of lager and more than an hour's sleep, Webb woke up in darkness. The CD had finished and everything was silent save for a high-pitched ringing in his ears. He felt nauseous and so drank the last of his beer to make himself feel better.

He was sure he could see movement up ahead. Who was it? It was rare for any of the others to come out looking for him after dark. Struggling with the controls, he eventually managed to switch the headlamps on full-beam. Just a few meters in front of him, dragging itself forward on unresponsive feet, a single rotting body had some-how managed to break free from the crowds below and find a way over the blockade. He'd only seen a handful of them climb this far up the hill before. The repulsive creature's movements were painfully slow, and yet it seemed to have an undeniable air of determination about it. It had altered direction and sped up slightly when he'd switched on the lights. Curious, Webb got out of the car and went around to the boot in search of a weapon. He'd stupidly left his baseball bat in-side, figuring the less he took out with him, the more beer he could carry. He grabbed the short metal handle from the jack and walked over to the swaying cadaver, which was still illuminated by the light from the car. He stopped a short distance away and waited for it to haul itself closer.

"Come on, then," he said, loud enough that the corpse reacted to his voice. The monstrosity obliged, taking another few awkward steps forward until it was little more than a meter away. Webb lifted the metal bar, ready to smash in what was left of its face.

And then it stopped.

The corpse stood face-to-face with Webb. What the hell was it doing? He'd never seen one of them stop like that before. They always kept moving, even when there was nowhere for them to go. For a few seconds he stared deep into the black, emotionless pits of its eyes. It had been male—he could tell from what was left of its clothing—and it had been of similar height and build to him when it had died. Its bottom lip was swollen and split down to its chin, revealing a gaping black hole with a few remaining yellow tombstone teeth inside which jutted out at unnatural angles. Its discolored, disfigured face was unrecognizable but who knows, he thought, maybe he'd known this person. Perhaps this was all that remained of someone he used to hang out with, or maybe it was—

The creature threw itself at Webb, abruptly ending the bizarre standoff. Clawed hands held high, it grabbed at his face. He responded with a single, well-aimed swipe of the metal bar to the side of its head, strong enough to hack it down to its knees. His second swipe did more damage, the third and fourth even more. By Webb's fifteenth strike, little of the head remained save for a mass of bloody pulp and shattered fragments of skull and jaw. Breathless, Webb looked around anxiously, worried that more bodies might have managed to follow this one up the hill. There was nothing. Everything was clear.

9

Both Stokes and Webb were up unusually early the following morning.

"Where are you two going?" Jas asked as they began to walk down the hill away from the flats. He shielded his eyes from the early morning sun which climbed over the ruins of the dead city in the distance. He always felt nervous when they were together like this.

"Therapy," Stokes answered, his voice sounding surprisingly cheerful. "Webb's feeling a little tense today. Thought it might do him good to take out his frustrations on a few of our friends down below."

He kept walking, forcing Jas to have to shout to make his next question heard.

"And what exactly is it you're going to do?"

"Still smells indoors," he said, being deliberately vague and holding up a plastic bag bulging with food and drink. "We thought we'd have breakfast outside this morning."

"Nosy bastard," Webb grumbled. Jas was still shouting after them, but they both ignored him and carried on walking down the hill.

"Ah, don't worry about him," Stoke said. "He's just trying to let us know he's in charge. Him and Hollis are like a pair of bloody mother hens. They nag me more than my old missus ever did!"

Webb smirked as he swung his baseball bat around, loosening his shoulders in preparation for the fight. Stokes glanced back over his shoulder. Jas had disappeared. Probably gone back inside to moan to the others about them, he thought.

The sweeping hill in front of them resembled a series of interconnected bomb sites. Hardly anything remained of the lowest block of flats and over time the bodies had managed to encroach on most of the uneven land where the building had originally stood. The sudden apocalypse had abruptly halted work on the second building midway through its demolition. One wing had already been completely leveled, the other reduced to a windowless, skeletal frame. The rubbish-strewn area had been enclosed by a wire-mesh fence, originally erected to keep vandals and other timewasters at bay. Two large diggers had been abandoned nearby and, once the group had worked out how to drive them, the powerful machines had proved useful in shifting tons of debris, beaten-up cars, and other wreckage to construct the ugly but effective barricade between the ruins of the first two buildings. Uneven and improvised it might have been, but it had successfully kept the ever-growing mass of corpses at bay for weeks now.

Webb and Stokes reached the wire-mesh enclosure. Stokes lifted a loose section of fence and Webb ducked down and went through like a fighter entering the ring through the ropes. Together they walked out into the center of the large patch of waste-ground, dotted with piles of masonry and the occasional sprouting of weeds. They used this area as a training ground of sorts, a place where Webb could flex his muscles and the older man could flex his vocal cords. Webb fancied himself as a welterweight champion. Stokes fancied himself as his coach.

"How many you going for today?" he asked. Webb stared back through the wire mesh at the hordes of bodies a short distance away.

"I'll start with five. Way I feel, though, I could get rid of the whole fucking lot of them."

"Just see how you get on," Stokes suggested, perching himself on a seat of crumbling brickwork and opening his first can of beer of the day. "Take your time. There's no rush."

Webb continued to look deep into the endless mass of loathsome figures, eyeing up potential opponents for the one-sided sparring session he was planning. He knew it didn't matter which monstrosity he plucked from the crowd—one worthless, maggot-ridden, decaying piece of shit was the same as the next. Running forward, he peeled a previously prepared section of the wire fence back in on itself, scrambled through the hole he'd made, and then jogged out toward the corpses. He climbed up onto the crumpled bonnet of an old black taxi, then reached down and grabbed the shoulders of the nearest body. He lifted its light, withered frame and, in a single movement, threw it over the taxi and back toward the hole in the fence through which he'd just emerged. It landed in an undignified heap in the dust, arms and legs everywhere, then immediately dragged itself up and began to stagger back in his direction. He paid it little attention, concentrating instead on plucking more writhing creatures from the crowd. Many vicious, thrashing hands reached up into the air as if volunteering for slaughter. He ignored them as he quickly hauled another four diseased figures over onto the other side of the blockade. He herded them back toward his arena. For the most part they conveniently followed him and he shoved each of them down through the gap when they were close enough. If they tried to retaliate or resist he simply threw them to the ground, then kicked and punched them through to the other side of the fence.

"Fuck me, look at that one!" Stokes laughed as Webb forced the last cadaver through the hole in the mesh. "No arms!" Howling with laughter he pointed at the naked remains of a middle-aged woman which stumbled back toward Webb as he closed and secured the fence. The pitiful carcass had somehow managed to lose both arms, one at the shoulder and the other just below the elbow. The longer of its two stumps twitched angrily. "Christ, Webb, fighting a dead woman with no arms? You really know how to pick them, don't you! You bloody idiot!"

"Piss off," Webb snapped as he sized up his wretched opponents. He picked up his baseball bat and watched the five empty shells as they slowly lumbered across the wasteland toward him. Their already awkward and unsteady gait was worsened by the uneven ground beneath their decaying feet. Several of them fell as they moved toward him, hitting the dirt with force and immediately hauling themselves back up again, not a flicker of emotion showing on their grotesque, deformed faces. Stokes watched closely as he slugged back his beer, lifting his legs out of the way as one of the creatures stumbled uncomfortably near.

"Take your time," he instructed, stifling a gassy belch and lowering his voice when the body that had just passed him turned back and shuffled toward him again. "Nothing clever, son, just take your time."

Webb wasn't listening. He'd already chosen his first victim. He advanced quickly toward the shell of a six-week-dead firefighter. It looked vaguely comical in its oversize protective jacket. It might have fitted once, but weeks of emaciation had reduced the size and bulk of the body considerably so that it now looked like a child that had stolen the jacket from a dressing-up box. Its helmet had slipped off its shrunken head and now hung around its neck by the strap. With a sudden roar of exertion Webb swung his baseball bat around in a climbing arc, thumping it up into the dead firefighter's chin. The force of impact flung the body up into the air. It crashed down at the feet of another shambling corpse. Webb rushed toward both of them with predatory speed, planting his boot on the chest of the body on the deck and swinging a wild punch at the other creature. More through luck than judgment he caught it full-on square in the face with maximum force. His leather-gloved hand sunk deep into its flesh. He quickly pulled it back again and shook it clean as the faceless cadaver crumbled.

"Not bad, eh?" He grinned breathlessly as he lifted his boot and stamped on the head of the firefighter on the ground. Two down.

"Not bad at all," Stokes agreed, enjoying the show. "Watch out, here she comes!"

Webb spun around to see the dismembered, armless aberration shuffling closer. It had a lopsided walk and an unusually sad and melancholy expression fixed on its frozen face. Save for its almost translucent skin and myriad of prominent dark purple and blue veins, its torso appeared relatively untouched by decay and he found himself staring at its surprisingly pert, bouncing breasts as it lumbered toward him. When it got too close he rammed the rounded end of the baseball bat forward, hitting it right between the eyes and sending it sprawling back. He viciously lashed out again, the second hard shunt splitting the paper-thin skin which was stretched tight across its forehead. A third smack briefly exposed bare bone before Webb lifted the bat and hammered it down, splitting its skull and permanently stopping it from moving.

"Too easy," he said, wiping his brow. Without stopping he marched on toward the fourth putrid carcass. This time he used the long shaft of the bat to attack, smashing it into the monster's right arm with a satisfying thud, then swapping hands and swinging it in the opposite direction, hitting the left side with enough force to shatter bone. The body continued to advance, not able to understand why it suddenly couldn't use its arms. Webb allowed it to get a little closer, knowing that the worst it could do was stumble into him. He finally shoved it back away then swung the bat around again, smashing into its pelvis. He'd already done more than enough damage to completely disable it but he continued to attack. The corpse found itself on its back, unable to move and looking up at the sun. Webb landed more brutal, bone-cracking blows across its ribs and legs, taking care not to damage it above the shoulders. When it had been completely incapacitated he stepped back and stared at his handiwork. Its head still moved constantly, just as inquisitive and curious as it had been seconds earlier, unable to work out why it couldn't get up. Rather than end its miserable existence, Webb instead decided to leave it where it lay to watch him. He liked an audience.

Last one. He sized up his final opponent.

"What are you waiting for?" Stokes shouted.

"Watch this," Webb yelled back. He ran toward the last corpse, swinging the baseball bat again and timing his strike to the head perfectly. Weak flesh tore and withered sinews snapped. Partially decapitated, the diseased creature staggered back, then collapsed on the ground, flat on its stomach but with its head still looking up.

"Nice one," Stokes said, throwing away his empty beer can and giving Webb a slow handclap. "Here you go, get this down you." He threw a can over to him, then opened another for himself. Webb drank thirstily.

"Going to do a few more," he said between gulps.

"Might as well," Stokes agreed. "Nothing else to do."

With adrenaline from the satisfying but one-sided fight still coursing through his veins, Webb finished his can, then scrambled back out through the wire mesh. Moving with more speed and confidence now, he jumped back onto the wreck of the taxi again and unceremoniously snatched four more corpses from the edge of the heaving crowd. He rammed them back through the hole in the fence.

"Take your time," Stokes suggested, standing on the pile of rubble now so that he could get a better view. "Fifty points for a kill, double if you do it with one hit."

Webb glanced over at him and grinned as he picked up his weapon again.

"Easy. Watch this."

His next victim was hunched forward like an old crone. Its physical deterioration was such that it was impossible to be sure what age it had been when it had died. Six or sixty, it didn't matter; it only had seconds left now. Using the cadaver's top-heavy gait to his advantage, Webb lifted the baseball bat high and brought it down hard on the back of its skull as if he was trying to hammer it into the ground. Facedown in the dust, the corpse twitched for an instant then lay still.

"One hundred points!" Stokes announced. "Good lad!"

Webb turned and moved toward the next shuffler, ready to repeat the maneuver and double his score. Maybe he'd knock this one's head clean off its shoulders, he thought. A sudden flurry of movement from another body on his right caught him off guard. He spun around to defend himself but was too late and he lost his balance, tripping over a pile of broken bricks as the corpse of a boiler-suited garbage collector grabbed hold of him. Stunned by the sudden, unexpected attack he struggled to shake the creature off. He lifted his arm to push it away and watched in disbelief as the horrifically decayed monstrosity sank its few remaining yellow teeth into the leather sleeve of his jacket.

"Jesus Christ!" Stokes shouted, jumping down from the pile of rubble and knocking his beer over. Although he usually did all that he could to avoid physical contact with the dead, he immediately grabbed the corpse and yanked it back, throwing it to the ground. Webb turned and unleashed a furious attack on the body, kicking its face repeatedly with his steel-toed boots.

"Damn fucking thing," he seethed. "You stupid fucking thing!"

The bloody body on the ground stopped moving almost instantly. Webb immediately turned and dealt with the remaining two corpses which, bizarrely, actually seemed now to be trying to move away from him. He ran at the first and grabbed a handful of greasy, wiry hair. In the same movement he continued forward, slamming its face down hard into a mound of broken concrete and twisted metal. He felt none of the usual satisfaction, just fear.

A short distance away, Stokes was gingerly pushing the last body away, trying to summon up the courage to attack. Full of words but usually very little action, he couldn't begin to match Webb's ferocity. Webb grabbed a length of narrow gauge metal pipe which was sticking out of the rubble at his feet.

"Get out of the way!" he screamed at Stokes as he ran toward him. Stokes obediently did as he was told, leaving the last corpse standing alone, swaying unsteadily. Webb speared it with his lance, sinking the pipe so deep into its chest cavity that it burst out through the other side, its decayed innards slopping down in a puddle on the ground behind it. Unbalanced, its legs gave way. Webb made certain of the kill with a single stomp of his boot to its vacant, emotionless face.

"Did that thing bite you?" Stokes asked, standing over the bulk of the fallen garbage collector.

Webb answered only with a nervous nod of the head before running back up the hill toward the flats. Stokes followed close behind with uncharacteristic speed, sheer terror keeping his out-of-shape body moving forward.

10

"It bit me!" Webb yelled as he flew into the communal living room, his voice close to breaking. "Fucking thing bit me!"

Hollis and Gordon were playing cards. Gordon looked up from the table momentarily but then looked down again, disinterested. Driver was asleep in an armchair with his newspaper over his face. Lorna had headphones on and was listening to music. Only Ellie showed any interest.

"What bit you?" she asked as she changed her doll's nappy.

"One of those fucking things out there!"

"What?"

"One of the bodies bit me!"

Hollis glanced up from his cards. Was Webb on something? None of them bothered taking drugs anymore, mainly because they couldn't find any. But had he found something in the warehouse yesterday? Was he still drunk from last night? Stokes's sudden appearance in the doorway derailed his train of thought.

"It's true," he gasped, red-faced and fighting for breath. "One of them bit him."

"Did it cut you?" Ellie asked. Webb shook his head and held up his arm, using his other hand to show where he'd been bitten.

"It just grabbed hold of me and bit me here," he explained. "It couldn't get through my jacket."

"So what's the problem, then?"

"The problem is it *bit* him, you stupid bitch!" Stokes yelled. Ellie shrugged off the insult; she'd been called much worse recently. "Are they going to start trying to eat us now?"

"You've watched too many crap films," she announced, putting the doll over her shoulder, then getting up and walking around the room, gently patting its back.

"Are you sure it bit you?" Hollis asked, finally putting down his hand of cards, knowing they weren't going to get any peace until Webb had his say.

"Of course I'm sure, you fucking idiot!" he screamed, his normally cocky voice filled with genuine panic and fear. "It had its teeth wrapped around my fucking arm!"

"But did it really bite you? Are you sure you didn't just put your arm in its mouth?"

"Are you having a laugh?" Stokes said in disbelief. "It bit him. What don't you understand? The bloody thing bit him."

Hollis looked at him for a moment longer, then picked up his cards again.

"It didn't really, though, did it? Why would it? Think about it. As far as I know they don't eat, so it wasn't trying to take a chunk out of you because it was hungry, was it?"

"It bit me," Webb snarled, his fear now giving way to anger.

"Put anything in their mouths and chances are they'll bite down on it. It's an instinctive reaction, isn't it? Just the same as walking or—"

"It fucking bit me!"

The volume of Webb's voice had reached such a level that everyone stopped to listen. Even Driver moved his newspaper slightly so that he could see what was happening. Jas and Caron appeared from the flat next door. Only Anita, who hadn't yet got out of bed today, was absent.

"What's the matter?" Caron asked, concerned. Hollis couldn't be bothered to recap.

"Calm down," he warned Webb, who seemed poised to erupt again.

"Calm down?" Stokes gasped having finally got his breath back. "Calm down? For Christ's sake, man, just listen to yourself, will you? One of those things out there tried to take a chunk out of his arm and you're telling him to calm down? Can't you see what—"

Hollis sighed. "It was just an instinctive reaction."

"You weren't even there!" Stokes yelled at him.

"But like I said, they don't eat," he protested. "They're not controlled enough to be able to attack like that. Like Ellie said, this isn't some stupid horror film. You're not going to become one of them because you've had contact with infected blood or anything like that."

"How do you know?"

Hollis rolled up his sleeve to reveal a seven-inch-long zigzag cut running along his forearm from his elbow to his wrist. The cut had been deep and sore but was beginning to scab over and heal. "One of them did this to me last week."

"How?" Jas asked from the other side of the room. "You told me you did it trying to move a car."

Hollis shook his head. "I said it happened while I was moving a car. I got scratched, that's all. Just a lucky hit from a body that had lost a lot of flesh on one of its hands. Caught me with a sharp edge of bone."

"Did you clean it up?" Caron quickly asked, her motherly instincts coming to the fore again. Hollis sighed. Did she think he was stupid?

"Of course I cleaned it up. Look, this really isn't anything like the films you used to watch or the books you read. Those things out there are just dead bodies. They're not flesh-eating monsters. They don't want our brains or anything like that."

"No, but they *do* attack us and they *are* getting smarter," Lorna said. In an instant the focus of everyone in the room switched to her. "I don't know how or why, but they *are* getting smarter, aren't they?"

"What's she talking about?" Gordon asked nervously. He turned around and repeated his question directly to her. "What are you talking about?"

"If you'd actually come outside with us and done something useful you'd know exactly what I was talking about."

"My hip . . ." he began, immediately making excuses.

"Fuck you and your hip," Webb said angrily. "Fucking waster."

Gordon looked down and shuffled his cards again. He couldn't handle confrontation.

"Is that right?" Caron asked, her voice suddenly tight and unsure. "Are they really getting smarter?"

"Not all of them," Harte answered, "but some seem to be."

"And did it really bite him?"

Hollis made eye contact with her and shook his head, the movement subtle enough for Webb not to see.

"I don't think it's anything to worry about," Lorna continued. "Doesn't matter how hard or fast they come at you, they're still falling apart. It'll still take a shitload of them to cause you any problems."

"What—a shitload like the fifty thousand or so we've got camped out at the bottom of the hill?" Stokes grumbled unhelpfully.

"You know what I mean."

"But what if they get up here?" Gordon asked anxiously.

"They're not going to get up here," Harte answered quickly.

"Who says?" Webb snapped. Driver fully removed the paper from over his face and sat up in his seat. Gordon put down his cards. Caron moved farther into the room.

"Shut up, Webb," Hollis said. "You're winding everybody up. For the last time, that thing didn't bite you, and none of them are going to get up here, okay?"

"One of them did last night."

"What?"

"While I was out in the car," he explained, "one of them managed to get almost all the way up here."

"Must have just got lucky."

"What happened to it?" wondered Ellie, looking nervously out of the window.

"I beat the shit out of it, that's what happened," he replied.

"So one of them managed to get over the barrier," said Hollis. "So what? The rest of them haven't. They're still stuck down there."

"At the moment," Stokes said. Hollis looked up at the ceiling in despair.

"For crying out loud, will you please stop trying to wind everyone up? We're safe here. Nothing's changed."

"You reckon?"

"Yes."

"Hollis is right," Lorna agreed. "We just need to keep a close watch on things. If something does happen then we'll deal with it straightaway."

"I'm ready," Webb said purposefully, a mask of machismo hiding the mounting fear he was feeling. "I'll fucking deal with them."

"I know you will," Lorna said quietly. "And that scares me more than the bodies do."

11

"Pass it!" Harte screamed at Webb. Webb looked up and kicked the ball wide to Jas, who made a diving run forward and booted it at Stokes in goal. The ball hit his belly with a loud slap and bounced away. He ran toward it and kicked it back across the car park. Harte scuttled after it.

"You won't get anything past me," Stokes boasted.

"That's because you fill the fucking goal," Webb laughed.

"Cheeky bastard!"

Harte reappeared and curled the ball to Jas on the wing. Jas dummied and swerved around Webb, who ran at him at speed.

"That's out!" Webb screamed. "You're off the pitch. We said the line was level with the front of the van."

"Piss off, Webb," Jas gasped as he sprinted toward the goal. Stokes readied himself for the shot. Did he shoot high or aim low? Try and swerve it around the side or just kick it straight at him? Jas lined himself up for the shot, only for Webb to slide along the tarmac and take his legs out from under him. The ball rolled away, Webb chasing after it furiously.

"Go on, Webb," Harte yelled. "Shoot!"

"You little bastard," Jas seethed, running at Webb again, grabbing his shoulders and hauling him down. Webb stuck his foot out and managed to get a shot in before he fell. The ball bobbled up in front of Stokes, who ran forward and booted it away again. It soared over Harte's head and bounced down the hill.

Jas and Webb stood face-to-face in the middle of the pitch.

"You do that to me again and I'll—"

"You'll what?" Webb jeered. "You'll let me get past again?"

"You little shit," he said, lunging forward and grabbing hold of Webb's collar. Webb squirmed but couldn't get away.

"Go on, then," he said, still writhing. "Hit me."

"You blokes are pathetic," shouted Ellie, pushing a pram across the car park. "Doesn't matter what else is happening, there's nothing like football to bring you closer to each other, eh? Bloody pathetic."

Jas let go of Webb and pushed him away. They continued to stare at each other for a second, both realizing the pointlessness of the argument, but neither prepared to be the one who backed down. Harte eventually broke the deadlock, pushing his way between them both to fetch the ball.

"Sort yourselves out, boys," he shouted as he ran toward the bodies.

Sliding tackles and bad challenges were forgotten as quickly as the final score of the ill-tempered kick-around. Although it was virtually dark, the footballers and Ellie, their sole spectator, remained outside. Webb sat on the bonnet of his car, his legs dangling down between the headlights which shone out into the darkness, providing them with a little illumination. The others sat on what was left of a filthy red corduroy three-piece suit which they'd dragged out of a damp ground-floor flat several weeks earlier. Ellie was sandwiched between Harte and Jas on a sofa on one side of the car. Stokes sat slumped in an armchair without a cushion on the other.

"So what are you suggesting?" Jas asked, leaning forward so that he could see Stokes.

"Hollis reckons they're not a problem," he said, his teeth chattering with the cold, "but I think they are. Like someone said, you're okay if you're up against one of them, but we've got thousands down there."

"We could move on," Ellie suggested, bouncing her doll on her knee. "Find somewhere else."

"No point," Stokes said quickly. "It's going to be the same wherever we go, isn't it?"

"So what are you thinking?" Jas asked again. Stokes paused before answering.

"Me and Webb have been talking about this. We think we should try a little crowd control."

"Haven't we been here before? Didn't you try and wipe them all out once, Webb?" She laughed sarcastically.

"Piss off," he hissed. "The wind changed direction. It wasn't my fault . . ."

"Crowd control?" Jas said, ignoring their bickering.

"We think we should just try and push them back a little bit."

"And how are we going to do that?"

"A bit of brute force and coordination. We'll take our time. Torch the ones at the very front, then use the diggers to shunt the barrier back."

"And you think that'll work? Problem solved?"

"Not quite, but problem reduced, anyway."

Jas slumped back in his seat, looked into the distance and gave serious consideration to what he'd just heard. He couldn't see anything past the limited light which came from the car's headlamps. Beyond their reach the rest of the world was drenched in an impenetrable shroud of never-ending darkness. Given the scale of the problem they faced at the bottom of the hill, he decided that not being able to see was probably a good thing.

"It's a hell of a job you're planning," he finally said, sniffing and wiping a drip from the end of his nose. "It's going to take time."

"We've got plenty of that," Harte said quickly. "No one's saying it's all got to be done by this time tomorrow, are they? Might be worth giving it a go."

"Why now?" Jas asked. "We've been here for weeks and—"

"Because they're changing, aren't they?" Stokes interrupted. "You heard what happened when we were out there earlier."

"One of them bit me, for fuck's sake," Webb interrupted energetically as if it was breaking news. Truth was, it was all he'd been talking about since it had happened.

"Look, are you sure you're not getting this out of proportion?" Jas wondered. "Hollis said that—"

"I'm sick of hearing about what Hollis says," Webb snapped. "He's full of shit. You know what he's like, he doesn't want to do anything until he's got no choice. If we sit and wait for him to make a decision we'll have corpses knocking on the front door before he's even agreed there's a problem."

"So are they really changing?" Ellie asked.

"Go down and have a look," Webb said.

"We know they are," Stokes interrupted, "and the longer we leave it, the worse it's going to get. We need to get in there now and sort them out before they're capable of fighting back. We should get down there tomorrow and get rid of as many of them as we can."

12

"I didn't think you wanted to play," Harte said to Hollis as he followed him out of the lobby and walked across the car park. Hollis covered his mouth and stifled a yawn. He'd given up wearing a watch several weeks ago but he guessed it was sometime around six in the morning, maybe even as late as seven. It was a cold, wet, and miserable day. Long overdue rain was finally filling the buckets, pots, and pans they'd left outside to gather water.

"I don't. I'll be keeping an eye on you silly bastards from the window," he said quietly as he filled a jug from the rainwater which had puddled at the bottom of a plastic paddling pool. "For the record I don't know if this is going to work, but I guess it's probably worth a try."

Harte nodded, surprised that Hollis seemed so positive. He watched him wander back to the flats, then pulled on a spare motorcycle helmet and ambled across the car park to where Jas stood checking the bike. Jas looked up as Harte approached.

"You ready?" he asked. He sounded subdued.

"Suppose," Harte mumbled, adjusting the straps of a small rucksack which he hoisted onto his back. "Let's just get it done."

It had seemed like a sensible plan last night, but now, standing here in the cold, low light of morning in full view of the endless devastation once again, they were both beginning to wonder what they'd agreed to. They were going out to try and create a distraction to reduce some of the pressure at the front of the crowd, but Jas suddenly felt less like a decoy and more like bait. Forcing himself to move, he turned his back on the huge expanse of rotting flesh which stretched out below him then climbed on the bike and started the engine. The spitting roar of the powerful machine disturbed the uneasy silence. Harte picked up a can of fuel and got on behind him, holding onto the back of the bike with his free hand as they drove away.

Stokes and Webb watched the bike disappear from the dubious comfort of the now rain-soaked sofa where they'd sat and talked last night.

"We should make a start," Webb suggested. "Get down there and get ready."

Stokes shook his head and opened a can of lager.

"Plenty of time, son," he said. "Plenty of time."

Jas weaved around the back of the building, cutting between the rubble and ruin and swerving around mountainous piles of rubbish which had been discarded by the survivors during their incarceration here. He drove the bike through a narrow alleyway, then powered across an empty rectangular yard lined with lock-ups and garages on either side. Through a gap in a chain-link fence, up a steep grass verge and they had reached the road without coming across a single body. There were always fewer of them on this side. Gravity, the overall geography of the land, and the mazelike layout of the dilapidated housing estate meant that the dead were naturally channeled down toward the foot of the hill rather than being allowed to gather in numbers up here behind the flats.

The plan this morning was simple. Get far enough away from their base to be safe, yet stay close enough to create a distraction that would attract the attention of some of the huge crowds gathered around the bottom of the hill. They figured their work would be easier if the corpses were looking in the opposite direction when they mounted their attack.

Navigating through the dead world was becoming more and more of a problem for Jas, particularly at such high speeds. He didn't want to drive any slower, despite the relative lack of corpses on this particular stretch of road. Traveling at this rate he knew that he'd be able to get past any of the bodies foolish enough to get in his way. If he reduced his speed at all the dead would have a chance, albeit just a slight one, of knocking him off-balance.

Harte maintained his one-handed grip on the bike with all the strength he could muster as the powerful machine dipped from side to side. Jas steered skilfully around the occasional wandering cadaver and other random obstructions, trying hard to fathom his way through the bizarre and chaotic landscape. He'd been here many times before, but the myriad streets all looked broadly the same, and as the world decayed so everything seemed to be becoming less defined. He powered down a long, sweeping, tree-lined road and finally spotted a landmark which helped him focus and make sense of his surroundings again. They drove parallel with a long gray-stone wall which ran the length of one edge of a massive reservoir, then passed the shadowy shell of a once-thriving college. Even now, weeks after they had died, the imprisoned corpses of students pressed their decayed faces against the windows when they heard the bike approaching, looking for release from their dormitory and lecture-room tombs.

Now Jas knew exactly where he was and where he wanted to be. They'd driven in a large loop which took them right around the back of the immense crowd at the bottom of the hill. Two sharp left-hand turns in quick succession and they were almost there. Harte looked up and could see the flats above them in the distance—a dark, imposing structure silhouetted against the ominous gray-white sky. Although their distance from home was unsettling, he was reassured by the fact that, from here, the building looked like an impenetrable gothic castle or fortress. He was distracted from his thoughts when Jas suddenly turned left again, nearly wrenching his shoulder out of its socket as the bike dipped to the side. They stopped and he flicked up the visor of his helmet.

"What's the matter?" he asked, glancing anxiously around. There were more bodies here, and he was already aware of several creeping, twisted figures which were emerging from the shadows on either side of the road.

"Need to work out how we're going to get out of here," Jas replied, his voice muffled and quiet.

"Don't you think we should have thought about that before we came out?"

Harte stared at a grotesque creature which limped closer to them. A huge chunk of flesh was missing from the right of its torso, as if something had taken a bite out of its side. It wore a pair of soiled pajama bottoms and slippers, and its awkward, lethargic movement caused more of its putrefied guts to spill out of the hole in its chest.

"Are you listening to me?" Jas said angrily. Harte shook his head, cursing himself for being so distracted by the monstrosity he'd been watching and the trail of guts it had left on the road.

"What?" he mumbled.

"We'll go around the back," Jas yelled, driving a little farther forward, then stopping midway down what had once been an ordinary suburban street lined on either side with unremarkable, semidetached houses. He looked up to make sure he could still see the flats—no point creating a distraction that can't be seen from up there, he thought—then gestured toward the nearest house. More bodies were hauling themselves toward them now. A group of three seemed to be moving together. "Open that gate!" he ordered, pointing to the narrow passageway which ran down the side of the house.

Harte immediately jumped off the bike and ran down the driveway, pausing only to barge a lanky and particularly unsteady body out of the way, sending it tripping over onto the tarmac. He tried to force the wooden gate open but it wouldn't move.

"It's locked," he shouted to Jas, who had driven down the drive after him.

"Of course it's locked, you idiot!" he shouted back. "Just climb over and get the bloody thing open!"

Inquisitive bodies were beginning to swarm down the driveway now, almost completely blocking the way out. Still holding on to the fuel can, Harte hauled himself up over the top of the tall gate and crashed down into the passageway on the other side, immediately picking himself up, turning around and sliding the bolt. As soon as the gate was open Jas drove toward him, barely giving him chance to get out of the way. Once he was through, Harte ran back and pushed the gate shut again, slamming it in the rotting face of a once-pregnant cadaver. The creature's distended belly—still filled with the partially-developed remains of its dead child—slapped against the wood like meat on a butcher's slab.

"Now what?" Harte asked, returning to Jas, who'd parked his bike on a patio. Weeds sprouted between the slabs they stood on.

"On foot," he said. "We'll cut through a few more gardens, then do it. It should disorient them. Once we start the fire they'll lose track of where we are. It'll give us a better chance of getting back out."

Harte didn't argue. He followed Jas deeper into the long garden, moving away from the back of the house and looking for a way through to next-door. Jas found a broken fence panel two-thirds of the way down the narrow lawn. He pushed it over and clambered through to the other side. Harte stayed close, running across the second garden and checking back over his shoulder to make sure he'd remember where they'd started out from.

"Bloody hell," Jas cursed as he crawled through a gap in a laurel hedge into the third garden, then stood up and walked straight into the dead arms of something which, from the look of its blood and paint-stained overalls, might have been a builder or decorator when it had been alive. It had been on the right side of the garden at exactly the wrong time for Jas and had managed to grab hold of him with its clumsy, outstretched arms. He pushed the corpse away. It stumbled back, then pivoted around on heavy, uncoordinated legs and lurched toward him again.

"I've got it," Harte said. Jas stepped out of the way as Harte plunged a garden fork up into the creature's face, one prong drilling through the side of its cheek and into the roof of its mouth, another gouging an eye, then sinking deep into what was left of its brain.

"Cheers," Jas grunted, stepping over the body and continuing through into garden number four. In no time he'd managed to get through gardens five, six, and seven. Still struggling to get across garden six, Harte, who was nowhere near as fit and was lagging behind, yelled for him to stop.

"Come on," he wheezed as he clambered over the final low fence. "Surely this'll do."

Jas stopped and rested with his hands on his hips. He cleared his throat and spat a lump of phlegm into a stagnant fish pond just ahead of him. His spit settled on the surface, barely even causing a ripple in the murky water, which was dark green, almost solid with algae and silt. He could just make out a few shards and slivers of orange and white among the sludge—all that remained of someone's pet goldfish.

Harte was already walking toward the house, moving around

74

the edge of a large, circular children's trampoline. The center of the trampoline sagged heavily. A puddle of rainwater had gathered over weeks, steadily distorting the once taut elastic sheeting. He climbed four low steps up to another weed-infested patio, then paused at the back door before entering the building. Jas peered in through the cobweb-covered kitchen window.

"Can't see anything in there," he said, unaware that he had suddenly started to whisper. Harte tried the door, which was stiff and hard to open. A shove with his shoulder and it moved. He pushed it fully open and stepped into the house. The building was filled with the suffocating and disturbingly familiar stench of death. His concern was not how many bodies he'd find inside, however, just how many were moving.

Speed was vital. Not needing to discuss the routine, the two men immediately began moving at pace. Jas checked downstairs while Harte worked through upstairs, briefly looking into every room, ready to react if anything moved, grabbing anything he thought might be of use later. Apart from two motionless, skeletal bodies curled up in bed together, the building was clear.

"All clear," he shouted as he ran back down the stairs. "Couple of stiffs up there, that's all. Nothing moving." He paused for a moment to look out a small window just to the right of the front door. There was an uncomfortably large number of bodies milling about in the road outside, most of them gravitating around the house the men had originally entered. Their numbers were nothing they couldn't handle, but something they could still do without. He found Jas in the dining room, piling furniture up against one wall. He had pushed a long, rectangular table over onto its side and was stacking chairs up against it. As Harte watched he pulled down the curtains and began to stuff them into the gaps between upturned wooden chair legs.

"Where's the fuel, Harte?" he asked as he worked. Harte disappeared again, leaving him alone. Jas ran around to the other side of

75

the upturned table to look for more to burn. He stopped immediately when he saw the body. How he hadn't noticed it before, he didn't know. Slumped in the corner of the room under the bay window was the curled up body of a child. Two years old when it had died, three at the most. For a moment the small, defenseless, withered husk was all that he could see and think about. It had died lying on its back, its tiny hand held across its face as if it had been trying to hide from whatever it was that was killing it.

"What's the matter?" Harte asked, returning to the room and finding him standing over the corpse on the carpet. He threw down a pile of coats he'd grabbed from the hallway and started to pack them around the table and chairs. Jas continued to stare at the child. The small boy looked about the same age as his little girl Annia had been when she'd . . .

Don't do this, he thought. *Please don't do this*. He could feel the pain of the family he'd lost welling up inside him. Most of the time he managed to keep this suppressed, but like everyone else there were moments when he was caught off-guard. He couldn't allow himself to break down. Not here, not now. He had to forget about everything he'd lost and—

"Jas!" Harte snapped. "Now's not the time. Come on, mate, get a fucking move on!"

Still nothing.

The last time he'd seen his children alive they'd been at home in their house, which was similar in design to the one they stood in now. He hadn't been back there since he'd lost them. Were they still there, lying motionless like this poor little creature, or were they moving? Was Annia up on her feet, staggering around hopelessly, aimlessly and tirelessly? Were the kids alone or had—

A corpse slammed against the window directly in front of him, distracting him and bringing a sudden, thankful release from his increasingly dark thoughts. He turned around and acknowledged Harte.

"Sorry," he mumbled, "I just . . ."

"Doesn't matter," Harte said quickly, doing all he could to avoid getting involved in another awkward conversation. He opened the fuel can and began to empty its contents over the pile of furniture. Jas pushed past him as the acrid smell of petrol filled the air and ran back to the kitchen. Harte followed, slowly shuffling out backward, carefully spilling a trail of petrol through the house behind him. Once the can was empty he kicked it across the kitchen floor; it clattered noisily on the hard tiles.

"Keep still," Jas mumbled as he ferreted around in the rucksack on Harte's back for a box of matches. As soon as he had them they both barged out through the back door, Harte not stopping until he was on the far side of the trampoline again. He shielded his eyes from the light drizzle and watched as Jas crouched in the doorway.

Jas almost allowed himself to think about the body of the child again before he struck the match; almost, but not quite. Just at the last second he managed to distract himself and, before his mind could wander again, he lit the flame. The vapor in the air caught light immediately. He turned and ran.

By the time the two men had worked their way back through seven gardens and were ready to get on the bike, the house down the road was well ablaze. The crackling, spitting flames, the noise, the belching black smoke and the dancing orange, red, and yellow light were enough to distract virtually all of the bodies out in the street. Jas and Harte were away before the dead had even realized they were there.

13

"They're coming," said Stokes. "I can hear them."

"About bloody time," grumbled Webb. He looked at the house in the near distance and watched it burn, incandescent orange against the dull gray of everything else. "We might as well get started."

"Give it a few more minutes," Hollis suggested. "Go in too fast and they'll forget about the fire and turn back at you."

"Doesn't bother me," Webb sneered. "Bring it on. I've been looking forward to this."

Pumped full of adrenaline, Webb marched down the hill, ignoring Hollis's warning. He glanced back as the motorbike finally returned, watching it sweep around the front of the building behind him. Their distraction seemed to be working. From here, halfway down the slope, he could see that the fire in the distance had spread along to several other nearby houses. As the size of the blaze had increased, so more and more bodies were being drawn to it. Although many thousands remained pressed up against the barrier of cars, rubble, and other obstructions, toward the back of the huge gathering hundreds more had begun to peel away and stumble toward the heat and light.

He stood and watched the dumb crowds below, and waited for the others.

To her surprise, Lorna found that, for once, Webb was right. The thought of destroying as many of the dead masses as they were able to was strangely appealing. As she walked down toward the foot of the hill with Hollis, Harte and Stokes at her side, all of them dressed in their standard-issue bike leathers, she decided that she too was in need of what Webb called therapy.

"So is there a plan?" Jas asked as he caught up with the others.

"Of sorts," Hollis replied. Although he'd originally planned to stay indoors and have no part of this massacre, the thought of allowing Webb free rein outside with weapons was enough of a concern to force him outside too.

"And?" he pressed.

"Lorna's going to use one of the diggers to start shifting part of the barrier back," he explained.

"And we're going to get rid of every single one of those fucking things that manages to get through," Webb added as they finally reached him. They lined up in silence alongside him and squared up to their decaying foes. Most of their usual encounters with the dead happened at speed, with the living doing their upmost to destroy any corpses they came up against in the shortest time possible. Here, however, the rules of engagement were suddenly very different. Here, standing just a short distance away across the no-man's-land of the barrier, they had an unexpected opportunity to stop and study their horrifically disfigured opponents. The bodies writhed and surged continually, but they weren't going anywhere. After six weeks their grotesque appearance had become less immediately shocking, but being face-to-face with thousands upon thousands of them like this was a daunting and unnerving prospect for even the most hardened fighter. There were just so bloody many of them. Harte found himself wondering whether he and Jas should have torched several streets full of houses, or even the whole town to distract the apparently endless crowds. Their small fire seemed a painfully insignificant distraction now.

Webb moved slightly farther forward, stopping when he was less than two meters away from the nearest cadaver. He locked onto one particular creature and stared deep into its ravaged face. It was hard to believe that it had once been human. Not a single centimeter of unblemished skin remained. Gross yellow and brown pus-like fluids had seeped and dribbled from every visible orifice. Its ill-fitting skin appeared mummified and hard in some places, unnaturally pliable in others. And the damn thing's jaw moved continually. Was it getting ready to sink its teeth into him? He wasn't going to give it a chance. *As soon as this one gets through*, he decided, *I'm going to rip its fucking head off.*

"You sure you're okay with that thing?" Jas shouted to Lorna, who had climbed up into the cab of the larger of two yellow diggers nearby. Truth was, he was nervous and had wanted the seat for himself.

"Been practising," she answered quickly, annoyed that he'd questioned her ability. For several weeks she'd been messing around with the diggers and with various other pieces of machinery they'd found lying around the ruins of the partially demolished second block of flats. Her interest in the machines had originally been for no other reason than to temporarily alleviate her boredom, but she was glad to have finally found a practical use for her newfound skill.

"Shift this one," Webb shouted to her, slapping his hand against the wing of a small, two-seater car. "Don't want to give them too much space to get through, do we?"

"He's good, isn't he?" Harte laughed sarcastically. "Got it all planned out in that tiny brain of his, he has!"

"Fuck you," Webb spat. "Your problem is you're too—"

No one heard what he said next. His moronic moaning was drowned out as Lorna started the digger's engine and then by Hollis as he pulled the starter cord on a chain saw. Webb shut up and focused, holding his baseball bat ready in one hand and an ax in the other. The bodies on the other side of the low wall of twisted metal and concrete seethed and surged forward, reacting to the noise. They were beginning to get riled.

Lorna accelerated and shunted the digger forward, lowering its heavy scoop and cringing as the metal scraped along the uneven ground. She raised it slightly and punched it into the door of the blue car, shoving the vehicle back. From her position in the cab it was difficult to see how far the car had moved. Another hard shunt and she'd pushed it too far, leaving a slight gap on either side.

And then they came.

Driven forward by their unnatural anger and by the weight of many thousands more bodies pressing behind them, the corpses at the front of the crowd began to slip around both ends of the small blue car which had helped keep them at bay for so long. Like a sticky, oily sludge they spilled forward. Hollis was the first to react. As Lorna reversed the digger and readied herself to try and block the slender gaps she'd left and shove the next section of the barrier back, he covered his face with a protective plastic visor, then raised his weapon and marched toward the advancing dead. The first of them walked face-first straight into the chain saw's powerful churning teeth, disintegrating most of its head on impact. Hollis continued to push the blade forward, dealing the exact same fate to a second body lurching too close behind. Webb stood back and watched, transfixed by the waterfall of crimson-brown gore which was soaking the ground like red rain around Hollis and the pile of body parts mounting at the other man's feet. One of the cadavers lunged to the side and slipped past him, moving toward Webb and forcing him into action. He dispatched it with a single ax blow to the forehead, the blade leaving a deep, dark groove between its eyes. The satisfying crack and splinter of the creature's skull was reassuring.

Lorna pushed the next car back as she had the first, taking care this time to make sure she plugged any gaps. There were still corpses pushing their way through the opening on the other side of the first car. She decided she'd deal with that problem next. Stokes, meanwhile, had found himself uncomfortably close to the fighting for once and had scuttled back out of the way, heading for the other, much smaller digger. He started the engine and slowly drove it back toward the front line, making a slight detour to crush a single spidery corpse which had managed to sneak past the others. Although he was now protected, from his elevated position in the cab the size of the job which lay ahead of them seemed even more daunting. Judging from the number of dead heads he quickly counted—some lying on their own in the mud like footballs, others still attached to bodies—he estimated that in the few minutes since the barrier had been breached, the survivors had destroyed somewhere in the region of ten to fifteen corpses. It was difficult to estimate with any degree of accuracy because of the continual frenzied movement all around him and also the fact that much of the mottled dead flesh had been butchered and sliced into a single detail-free layer. However many of them they'd managed to get rid of, there were many, many thousands more lining up to take their place and it was going to take hours to make any kind of impression on them. Not for the first time he found himself silently questioning what they were doing. Was this as bloody stupid an idea as it suddenly seemed?

"Pile 'em up over there," Hollis yelled in a pause between kills, struggling to make himself heard over the combined noise of the fighting, the two digger engines, and his chain saw. He gestured wildly toward an area of land close to the fenced enclosed where Webb had been bitten yesterday. Stokes moved toward the mass of fallen bodies, trying to familiarize himself with the controls of the digger. Satisfied

82

that he'd worked out how to move the shovel down, forward, and then back up again, he clumsily scooped a bucketful of flesh—some inert, some still twitching—then turned around and drove it over toward the area Hollis had pointed to. He tipped the shovel out, emptying its contents onto the rough ground with a reassuring slop and splatter. Even now as the last dregs dripped down, some of the dismembered creatures he'd scooped up continued to move. His stomach churned as he watched the half-torso of a cadaver, which had been hacked in two by the chain saw just below its nipple line, reach out with its one good arm and try desperately to drag itself away.

Lorna moved another car, closing one gap but inadvertently opening another. The digger's shovel had become entangled with the door of the car and she struggled to knock it free. She concentrated on the mechanical claw, trying to ignore the wave of corpses which now surrounded her, all of them pointlessly fighting to get even closer. A sudden flash of light overhead distracted her momentarily. She looked up and watched as Harte hurled petrol bombs into the front of the crowd, hoping to dissipate their numbers and make it easier for her to shunt the barrier back. The bombs flew through the gray sky above them in beautiful arcs of spiraling flame before smashing down into the bodies and exploding.

Hollis noticed the crowd growing around the digger and marched toward it. They were preoccupied with the machine and disposing of them was a simple matter. He simply held up the chain saw and walked into them, carving them up before they'd even realized he was there, the noise from the digger drowning out the powerful grind of his weapon. Lorna looked down and acknowledged him, then pointed behind, desperate to get his attention. He spun around to see a group of three corpses moving toward him. They attacked at the same time, surging at him with spindly limbs flailing. He lashed out with the chain saw and succeeded in cutting down the nearest two. He then ran toward the third—which, incredibly, now seemed to be retreating—and, with a flick of his wrist, sliced a jagged diagonal cut across its bony chest. The body fell to the ground, legs going one way, head and shoulders the other.

Just inches away from Hollis, Webb smashed his ax into the ravaged face of a body which reminded him of a social worker who had once been assigned to him. Concentrating on the satisfying splinter and crack of the creature's skull, he was unaware that the digger being driven by Stokes was close behind until Hollis grabbed him by the shoulder and yanked him out of the way. Webb turned to attack but then lowered his weapons when he saw that there was no danger. They stepped back to allow Stokes to collect another scoop full of bloodstained remains.

"You having fun?" Hollis yelled over the noise. Webb grinned. As perverse as it seemed, Hollis was enjoying himself too.

"You?" Webb asked back as he shook a lump of flesh off the end of his baseball bat and readied himself for his next victim.

"Wonderful," the other man grunted.

"They're fucking stupid," he laughed as he swung the bat at the head of another corpse, sending it flying into the side of Lorna's digger. "Look at them! They're just lining up to be wiped out!"

"Is that what you think?" Hollis said, shaking his head.

"'Course it is," he answered.

"You're really dumb at times, Webb," he said as he lifted his chain saw and readied himself to move forward again. "It might look that way, but just watch them. More to the point, watch yourself."

"Why?"

"Because if you look closely," he continued, pausing to cut another body in two from its groin up to its neck, "you'll see that some of them are actually trying to coordinate themselves and attack."

Webb laughed out loud at Hollis's comment, but he found himself watching the next cadaver more closely. It was slow and weak but Christ, he was right, it was moving with a very real purpose and intent. He expected it to leap straight at him aggressively, but it didn't. Instead it watched him with dull, unblinking eyes and chose its moment, suddenly lifting its spindly arms and increasing its speed and force. Whether it had been a considered attack or not, Webb destroyed it with a dismissive thump from the baseball bat to the side of its head.

After hours of virtually constant fighting, it was time to stop. Lorna dropped a car diagonally across the bonnet of another she'd moved previously, plugging the last remaining gap and stemming the flow of bodies toward the survivors. Exhausted and soaked with a layer of mud, blood, and gore, Webb, Hollis and Harte quickly disposed of the last few loose cadavers before dropping their weapons. Jas cleared the area with the smaller digger, dropping larger body parts onto a smoldering pyre, then scraping the metal shovel along the ground and dumping a scoop full of once-human slurry over the other side of the wall of cars and rubble, onto the heads of the unsuspecting crowd. Job done, he switched off the engine and climbed out of the cab. Without the constant mechanical drone of the two machines the world was suddenly eerily silent, so quiet that the loudest sound remaining was the trickle of liquefied flesh dripping from the metal scoop behind him into a muddy puddle.

Webb was the first to speak. Still buzzing with excitement from the kill, he babbled breathlessly as they began to walk back up the hill.

"How many do you reckon, then?" he asked.

"What?" Hollis asked.

"How many did we get rid of? Couple of hundred?"

"Something like that," Harte replied quietly, shaking something unpleasant from his right glove.

"Christ, I'm tired." Jas sighed wearily.

"I could do more," Webb continued.

"Be my guest," Hollis said. "You carry on."

"I could spend all day getting rid of those bloody things. There's nothing better than wiping out a load of them when you're pissed off and wound up."

"Most of us seem to be pissed off and wound up all the time," Harte said. "I've been like that since this all started."

"Well, at least we're doing something positive now. Taking a stand. Letting them know who's in charge . . ."

Webb shut up when he realized that Hollis had stopped walking. He turned around to look back at him.

"Problem?" Harte asked, concerned. Hollis was gazing back down the hill toward the crowd. Thick smoke was rising from the smoldering heap of charred flesh by the diggers and drifting out over the heads of the dead.

"Look what we did today," Webb said excitedly. "Look how many of them we got rid of."

"That's exactly what I was looking at," Hollis said.

"And?" Webb pushed, sensing that the other man still had more to say.

Hollis pointed back toward the area where they'd worked. "That," he said, "took six of us a few hours to clear."

"So what's your point?"

"It took us the best part of a day and a shitload of fuel and effort just to take out a hundred or so bodies. Bloody hell, there are hundreds of *thousands* of them down there—how long's that going to take? We haven't cleared one percent yet. We haven't even scratched the surface."

"You're a miserable fucker," Webb snarled, annoyed. "Tell me it doesn't make you feel good when you stand down there and rip those fucking things apart."

"I'm not denying that."

"So what's your problem?"

"There's too many of them, that's all. You're never going to get rid of all of them, are you?"

"No one said we were trying to do that," Harte said.

"Wiping the floor with a few dozen stiffs might make you feel like you've done something worthwhile," Hollis continued, "but do me a favor and let's not pretend it's going to change the world. I don't want to spend all day, every day, down there fighting. There's got to be more to life than that."

"Has there? Seems to me this is just about all we've got left."

Hollis shook his head and carried on up the hill, leaving the others standing in silence. They stared down through the smoke at the insignificant gray scar they'd left on the landscape below.

14

Hollis and Lorna sat at the bottom of a dark staircase, their faces illuminated by the flickering light from half a dozen candles. Gordon stood in a doorway opposite, arms folded. It was late and although they were tired, no one wanted to sleep. Stokes, Harte, and Webb were standing out on the balcony at the front of one of the flats on the floor below, making plans to continue their cull at first light. Their muffled voices could be heard echoing around the large and predominantly empty building.

"I like your hair," Hollis said unexpectedly. Lorna looked up and smiled momentarily before looking down again. She didn't like it when he commented on her hair. She didn't do it for anyone but herself. When Hollis paid her a compliment it made her feel like she was being chatted up by her uncle. She didn't tell him. She didn't want to upset him.

"Thanks," she mumbled, hoping that would be the end of the conversation.

"You always make an effort," he said. "You always look good."

"Why shouldn't I?"

"No reason," he quickly backpedaled, worried he'd offended her. "I'm down to one shave a week."

"Just because I feel like shit, doesn't mean I have to look like shit, does it?"

"Sorry," he said. "I didn't mean that you should . . ."

Nearby, Gordon looked away, embarrassed for Hollis. He was relieved when Caron appeared at the top of the staircase, carrying another candle. Taking care with her footing she slowly made her way down.

"How's she doing?" Hollis asked, his whispered words amplified by the silence. Caron had spent the evening sitting with Anita. She shook her head and sat down.

"Not good," she replied, her voice weary and low. "She's worse than ever tonight."

"What is it?" Lorna asked, knowing full well that Caron knew as little as she did. "Is she still being sick?"

"Nothing left for her to throw up," she answered, "and she hasn't eaten anything today. I tried to get her to take some water but she couldn't."

"I don't like this," Gordon said nervously. "It's like a tropical disease or something. It's come from the bodies, it must have. There are flies and maggots and germs out there and—"

"Shut up, Gord," Hollis snapped, silencing him. "You're not helping."

"But it could spread. We might all end up catching it. For all we know she might—"

"I mean it. Shut up, Gord," he warned again.

"I read something in a magazine once about outbreaks of disease after natural disasters," Caron said, cutting across them both. "Can't remember exactly what it said. Someone did a study after an earthquake or something like that when there were lots of bodies lying around."

"And?" Lorna pressed.

"Didn't pay much attention to it at the time," she admitted. "I didn't think I needed to. Wasn't the kind of article I usually read."

"Well, do you remember anything useful?"

"I think it said most germs were spread through direct contact with the bodies or through contaminated water. They weren't airborne, I don't think."

"That's just perfect," Lorna moaned. "We've spent most of the day ankle deep in their shite."

"Yeah," Hollis said quickly, "but most of it was on the suits, and all of it got washed off, didn't it? And we collect rainwater, don't we. We should be okay."

"Yes, but—"

"But nothing. I doubt if any of us have caught anything."

"How do you know? Anita has."

"So how did she get it?" Gordon asked, clearly agitated. "She hasn't been outside for ages. She's been drinking the same water we have."

"She might have had it before she got here," Hollis replied, clutching at straws. "Maybe it takes a few weeks to show itself? Or she could have just got unlucky and eaten something that was contaminated."

"I don't like this," he grumbled. "What if we catch it off her?"

"Then we'll just have to deal with it, won't we."

"And how are we supposed to do that?"

"We'll try and get her some drugs and keep her isolated. That's all we can do for now."

"But what if that doesn't work?"

"For Christ's sake, what do you expect me to do about it? Do you want me to go down to the edge of the crowd and see if any of the bodies used to be a doctor? Bloody hell, Gordon, just get a grip!"

"He does have a point, though," Lorna said.

"I know he does," Hollis admitted.

"We can't just let her lie up there like this, can we?"

Hollis shook his head and stood up. He slowly paced away along the corridor, but then stopped and walked back. He stopped a short distance away where the light from the candles was just strong enough to catch the outline of his tired face.

"Maybe a couple of us should go out tomorrow and try to find her some drugs," he suggested again. "Get some antibiotics or something. Hopefully that'll do the trick."

"And if it doesn't?" Gordon shouted after him as Hollis walked away and disappeared into the darkness.

"We'll cross that bridge when we come to it," his fading voice replied.

15

The early morning sun unexpectedly broke through the layer of dull gray cloud which smothered the land. Hollis waited in front of the flats for Lorna. Down below them, the cull had begun again. It was before seven but neither the early hour nor their tiredness after yesterday's exertion seemed to have put a damper on Jas, Webb, Stokes, or Harte's enthusiastic desire to try and obliterate another swathe of bodies. This morning, to his great surprise, Hollis noticed that Gordon too had found himself an ill-fitting set of bike leathers and joined the others at the edge of the crowd. Dodgy hip or no dodgy hip, he finally seemed to have overcome his pathetic fears and inhibitions and was facing the bodies head-on. Either that or he found the prospect of sitting waiting inside the flats more nerve-wracking today. Every conversation he'd overheard since waking up seemed to have been about Anita and her worsening condition.

A wash of golden sunlight dappled the heads of thousands of the writhing bodies at the foot of the hill. He wasn't sure why, but the one-sided battle unfolding below him somehow seemed different from yesterday, more ferocious. Maybe it was nothing more than the different perspective from which he was watching the fighting. Perhaps the bodies yesterday had been just as violent and animated as these, but they'd seemed less so because he'd been dealing with them at close quarters. Maybe it was just because people like Gordon and Stokes were less experienced and less capable when it came to hand-to-hand combat? Or were the bodies more animated, ready to retaliate after yesterday's slaughter?

"You ready?" Lorna asked, startling him. He turned around and saw that she was standing just behind him. He grunted and climbed into the grime-splattered van he usually drove. He'd spoken to Lorna again briefly late last night and they'd taken it upon themselves to go out searching for drugs. If they didn't do it, as she'd quite rightly pointed out, no other fucker would.

"So where to?" he asked as she sat down next to him and slammed the door shut. She knew the area far better than he did.

"There are three pharmacies near here," she replied quickly. "Head for the one at the bottom of Bail Hill first. That was a pretty big one. There should be plenty of stuff there."

"Okay."

"You got any idea what we're looking for?"

"No," he replied as he started the engine and drove toward the maze of garages, tracks and streets behind the flats. "I suggest we just get in there and empty the shelves into the back of the van. We'll worry about what we've got when we get back."

Hollis slammed on the brakes outside the pharmacy, leaving the van parked on the pavement, as close to the door at the far right of the front of the building as he could get.

"Five minutes," he told her, "that's all."

Lorna quickly disappeared inside. He paused for a second before following, stopping just long enough to look up and down the road to see what effect their sudden unannounced arrival had had. He counted around ten creatures crawling slowly toward them from both directions. No doubt there'd be hundreds more by the time he and Lorna were finished.

Lorna was already working when he got inside, collecting bottles of medicine and packets of pills in wire shopping baskets. She was nervously sweeping entire shelves clear with her arm and doing her best to catch what she could. She'd already filled three baskets. Hollis grabbed them and ran back out to the van.

Twice as many bodies as before now, maybe more. Christ, they were going to have to be quick.

"How are we supposed to know what any of this stuff is and what it does?" Lorna shouted across the shop as he returned. "Maybe there's a book or something we could take?"

"Doubt it," he said, grabbing the next two baskets and heading for the door again. "They'd have had it all on computer, wouldn't they?"

"Suppose. Might be something, though. It's worth having a look."

He threw the baskets into the back of the van. Many more bodies now. Getting close. Too close.

"No time," he shouted, collecting the final baskets. "We need to get gone."

Lorna pulled open a heavy white door next to where she'd been working which, she presumed, would lead to an office or another drugs store. Maybe she'd find some information in there which would help her to—

A body lunged out from the shadows into the light, missing Lorna and throwing itself at Hollis, who stood in front of it, completely unprepared. Wearing the once-white coat of a pharmacist, now yellowed and soiled by seepage, the dishevelled corpse hurtled toward him with unexpected force and venom. Trapped behind the door for more than fifty days, its sudden release seemed somehow to energize and invigorate it. Its weight was insignificant, but its speed and velocity were enough to knock Hollis over. He tripped and fell back, smashing the side of his head against the back of the wooden counter. The pain was excruciating.

Lorna grabbed a fire extinguisher from a bracket on the wall and brought the base of it crashing down on the back of the cadaver's skull with a sickening crunch. It collapsed on top of Hollis, black clots of blood and other foul-smelling gunk dribbling out of its mouth and nose. Hollis kicked and scrambled underneath it desperately, more aware than ever of the germs and disease which might be thriving in the stodgy liquids dripping over him. Finally free, he dragged himself back up onto his feet, gagging in disgust as the remains of the pharmacist slid onto the floor. He angrily put his boot through its face.

"Fucking thing," he cursed, gingerly touching his left ear. When he drew back his fingers he saw blood.

"Let's go," Lorna said, carrying another basket and moving toward the door. She stopped when she saw that almost the entire width of the glass frontage of the pharmacy was now a solid mass of dead flesh which reacted violently as she approached. Parts of the crowd appeared to try and recoil from her; others pushed harder against the dirt and cobweb-covered windows.

"Bloody hell," Hollis moaned under his breath. "How the hell are we going to do this?" They were used to being hounded by huge crowds of corpses wherever they went, but this felt different. Had they just managed to spook themselves by talking about the bodies getting smarter, or were some of the creatures on the other side of the glass really demonstrating behaviors which appeared conscious and controlled? It felt like they were waiting for the two of them to come out into the open, almost as if they knew they'd have to leave sooner or later.

"Are we going to stand here waiting for Christmas, or are we going home?" Lorna asked, trying to hide her mounting unease.

"No such thing as Christmas anymore," he replied. "Ready?"

"Think so," she mumbled, sounding far from sure.

"Get closer to the door."

Without questioning him she moved forward. The bodies were just inches away now, separated from her by a single sheet of glass. One of them seemed to be pushing at the door. Fortunately it was pushing the hinged side and it was never going to open, but its intent was clear.

Hollis disappeared back into the shop and picked up the bloodied fire extinguisher Lorna had used moments earlier. Still wincing with the pain behind his ear, he lifted the red metal canister above his head and threw it at the section of window farthest from the door. It thumped against the toughened glass, cracking it but not breaking through, then dropped to the ground with a sonorous thump and rolled into a display rack. Many of the bodies immediately began to shuffle nearer to the noise. Hollis picked up the extinguisher again and this time slammed it into the glass like a battering ram, doing enough damage to shatter it and causing huge, jagged shards to fall out of the metal frame. The dead immediately began to force their way inside, ignorant to the daggers of broken glass which sliced their feet.

Without stopping to look back Hollis ran over to Lorna, pulled the door open and pushed her through. She dropped the basket of medicine she'd been holding, sending packets and bottles flying. With the bulk of the crowd distracted, pouring through the broken window, they barged their way through the rest of the bodies. Hollis dropped his shoulder and waded into them as Lorna crouched down and wormed her way through, managing to scramble back into the van first.

Hollis was surprised by the dead's dogged resistance. Most of the dumb creatures had fallen for his ploy and were still pushing and jostling to get into the shop through the smashed window. Others were standing firm—still weak, still clumsy and still uncoordinated, but undeniably more determined than they ever had been before. He struggled with a particularly aggressive cadaver with a huge black hole in its face where its right eye should have been, until Lorna grabbed hold of his collar and yanked him back into the van. Many more bodies were shuffling toward them again. They needed to go.

"What the hell are you doing?" he jabbered nervously with surprise as he fell back into his seat. He knocked another rancid figure back onto the street and slammed the door shut. It was dark inside the van. Emotionless faces were pressed up against every window.

"We need to go," she replied, watching through a gap in the bodies as the pharmacy quickly filled with dead flesh. "We need to get out of here."

He started the engine—the noise immediately causing the still-growing crowd to become even more animated—and drove forward, dragging several of the rotting shells beneath the wheels of the van and churning them into the ground. Lorna turned around in her seat and watched as a smaller section of the crowd marched after them lethargically.

16

A frantic, unscheduled stop at a previously forgotten and well-sheltered medical center north of the flats allowed Hollis and Lorna to collect more drugs and pick up several medical journals and reference books. They didn't know if the information would make any difference, but just having it made them feel marginally better. Caron, who hadn't had any medical training other than a basic first-aid course at work some twenty years ago, gratefully took everything that was offered to her and shut herself away in the flat next to Anita's. She found descriptions of numerous conditions and diseases which Anita might have been suffering from, but next to nothing in the way of treatment advice or guidance.

Just after midday Hollis appeared in the doorway of the flat, carrying with him more drugs which he'd found rolling around in the back of the van.

"Any good?" he asked hopefully. Caron put down the text book she'd been reading and rubbed her tired eyes.

"Not really," she admitted.

"How's she doing?"

"No better."

"Is she still being sick? Has she eaten anything?"

She shook her head.

"She's not doing anything. Her temperature's sky-high and she's barely conscious. It's probably for the best."

"Have you managed to find anything that might help?"

She looked around the room at the piles of drugs surrounding her.

"I've got no idea what I'm looking for," she answered honestly, "and even if I could find the name of a drug which might help, how am I supposed to know what it looks like? I wouldn't even know if it was a pill in a packet or a medicine in a bottle. And some of this stuff is out-of-date."

"Point taken," Hollis said quietly as he walked across the room and stood at the window. "Do you know what I think?"

"I know what *I* think," she interrupted abruptly. "I think I should just force as much of this stuff as I can down the poor cow's throat and put her out of her bloody misery. Honestly, Greg, is it even worth her getting better?"

Hollis didn't answer. He was staring out the window, trying to remember the last time anyone had called him by his first name. Natalie used to call him Greg, and his mom and dad, and Mark and all the others he'd lost.

"What the hell is that idiot doing now?" he said suddenly, glad of the distraction.

"Which idiot?" Caron asked, standing up and walking over to him. "There's more than one around here."

"Webb. Just look at the silly little bastard!"

Webb was walking precariously along the top of the uneven barrier of cars and rubble which was somehow still succeeding in keeping the dead at bay. As he walked, he emptied the contents of a fuel can over the heads of the repulsive carcasses which grabbed at his feet incessantly.

"He scares me when he starts playing with fire," Caron admitted, her voice low.

"He scares me whenever I see him."

As they watched, Gordon passed another can of fuel up to Webb, who immediately began tipping it out over the crowd, drenching some cadavers which had already been soaked once.

"Careful with that stuff," Hollis muttered under his breath.

"He'll set fire to himself if he doesn't watch what he's doing."

"I'm not bothered about that, I just don't want him to use up all our fuel. I'm the sucker who'll end up out there fetching more."

They watched as Webb finished emptying the second can, then jumped down to stand with the others a short distance back from the corpses. There was no denying the fact that they had worked hard again this morning—an area of land had already been reclaimed which almost matched the size of the patch they'd taken all day yesterday to recover—but their methods seemed to have become even more haphazard and less effective as time progressed. The diggers, which had previously been used to carefully move one abandoned car or lump of masonry at a time, now sat unused a short distance back. It was clear from Webb's actions that the people remaining outside now were in the business of finding shortcuts. Safety and planning had been forgotten. It was now all about destroying the maximum number of corpses with minimum amount of effort.

"I can't watch," Caron said, half-turning away but then looking back when curiosity got the better of her. Hollis stared intently as Stokes, Jas, Gordon, and Webb scuttled away to a safe distance, leaving Harte on his own trying to light the limp rag-fuse of a petrol bomb with the intermittent flame coming from a frustratingly unreliable cigarette lighter. A sudden flash of orange appeared which made him jump back with surprise. Realizing that the rag was finally lit, he hurled it toward the wall of cars. It ricocheted off the roof of a beaten-up

4×4 before exploding into flames. A chain reaction spread instantly across the petrol-soaked crowd, an arc of fire racing to the right and left and back out over the decaying hordes. Harte ran for cover.

"Looks like it worked," Caron said, relaxing again. The people down below congratulated each other and laughed and pointed as the bodies burned.

"Thank God for that," Hollis sighed. "They're lucky it's not them that's on fire. If the wind had caught the fumes like last time they would have—"

A sudden explosion tore through the air outside. Fuel had leaked from the damaged petrol tank of a hearse (complete with coffin and body) and the resulting ignition blew it up into the air, flipping the long, box-shaped vehicle up and over. Its charred chassis clattered back down to the ground several meters behind the spot it had originally occupied, crushing scores of unsuspecting corpses.

Outside, the survivors ran for cover.

"Bloody hell," grinned Stokes, "that was close. You could have been standing on top of that, Webb."

"I *was* standing on top of it a couple of minutes ago," he replied, subdued. "Good job Harte took his time getting the fuse lit."

"Piss off," Harte snapped. "It was your lighter that slowed things down, nothing to do with me."

"I think we've got a problem here," Jas said ominously, taking a few tentative steps forward and peering through the heavy cloud of dense black smoke which was drifting low across the scene from the burning bodies and the blazing hearse. He shielded his eyes and looked down into the gap in the barrier where the hearse had originally been. The flames there had died down and now he could see movement.

"What is it?" Gordon asked nervously, moving a little nearer but being careful not to get too close. At first Jas didn't answer, instead pointing at the wide gap which had appeared in their defenses. A mass of furious bodies was beginning to quickly scramble through.

"Block it up!" Jas screamed, his voice suddenly hoarse with panic. "Block the fucking hole up!"

Webb and Stokes peered into the haze, still not sure what was happening. Harte immediately realized the danger and sprang into action, sprinting over to the nearest of the two diggers and hauling himself up into the cab. He started the heavy machine and rumbled toward the lumbering bodies, trying to work out how best to stop, or at least stem, the flow of dead flesh pouring through the ruptured barricade. Suddenly forced into action, Webb swung his nail-skewered baseball bat around with scant regard for his own, or anyone else's, safety. Even Gordon was forced to fight. He battered a single crippled creature to the ground with a bloodied fence post, standing over it and repeatedly slamming the wooden post into its face, continuing even when the decaying monster had stopped moving. Stokes scampered out of the way and climbed into the other digger, hand on the ignition, ready to get involved only if he had absolutely no alternative.

Harte blasted the digger's horn. Still fighting, Jas looked up and stepped back out of the way as the vehicle moved toward him, rolling relentlessly over the dead and squashing them into the mud. On the other side of the breached barrier, a short distance into the advancing crowd, he could see the roof of the wreck of another car which he could use to block the hole left by the still-burning hearse. He accelerated again, carving another deep and bloody furrow through the sea of cadavers, then shunted his way out through the gap and into the crowd. He concentrated on the car just ahead, doing his best to block out the fact that now, for the first time, he was completely surrounded by corpses on every side. Shutting out the noise of their, tireless hammering on the sides of the digger, he stretched out the vehicle's scoop, then smashed it down and punched a hole through the roof of the car. He slammed the digger into reverse and powered back, slipping out through the gap again, then veering over to the right and wedging the wreck across the breach.

All around the digger the chaos continued. The smoke and constant movement made it almost impossible to see what was happening clearly. Looking down from the flats, Hollis estimated that more than fifty corpses had managed to push their way through the barricade before Harte had blocked the gap. Around half that number had already been destroyed, most of them obliterated by the digger.

"I should go down there."

"They can take care of themselves," Caron said. "They made the mess, let them clear it up. Idiots, if they'd just slow down and think before they . . ."

Her voice trailed away to nothing as she watched the fighting continue. Several cadavers had surrounded Gordon. It might have been bad luck or inexperience on his part, but he'd somehow allowed himself to be cornered. His back was pressed up against a section of wire-mesh fence and he cowered as the dead approached.

"Get out of the way!" Jas shouted, noticing the other man was trapped. "Move!"

Terrified, Gordon looked for a way out. He was about to drop to his knees and try crawling away through the mud when the bodies attacked. Their movements were sudden, surprisingly controlled and inexplicably coordinated. It was almost as if they were working together.

"Get down!" Jas screamed again. Running forward, he unsheathed the machete he'd been carrying on his belt and began to lash out at the twisted creatures. He sank the blade into the small of the back of the first of them, cutting deep into its already partially exposed spinal cord. He then yanked it free and immediately struck out at the next nearest corpse. It was much smaller than the first, disarmingly child-like. He looked away as he slammed the blade down onto the top of its head, center-parting what remained of its lank, greasy hair and split-ting its skull.

Now that he found himself facing only one opponent again, Gordon managed to force himself back into action. He fumbled around for the fence post he'd been using as a bludgeon, then picked it up and swung it into the side of the third corpse's body, smashing its pelvis and giving it a far more serious hip problem than the one he himself suffered with. It collapsed into a puddle of bloody rainwater.

"You okay, Gord?" Jas asked, wiping his blade clean on the back of a slumped body lying next to him. Gordon was standing over the corpse he'd just crippled, pounding its face with the fence post.

"Fine," he said between angry grunts of effort. "Nothing to worry about."

Stokes watched from the safety of the stationary digger. Webb continued to hack down those cadavers unfortunate enough to find themselves within striking range of his baseball bat. Jas too had returned to the fray and was chopping at the remaining figures which lum-bered toward him. Harte continued to operate the other digger, stretch-ing the articulated arm out over pockets of attacking corpses, then dropping the heavy metal scoop on their unsuspecting heads, crushing them instantly. Stokes might have found their slapstick demise funny if he hadn't been so bloody terrified.

Hollis and Caron looked on from the safety of the flats.

"Looks like they've got everything under control now," Caron said optimistically.

"I know, but I really don't like this."

"What's the problem?" she asked. From where she was standing the survivors on the ground seemed to be doing well. The sudden surge of dead flesh through the barrier had been stopped and those which had made it through were being destroyed quickly and with very little effort.

"Watch him," Hollis answered, pointing at Gordon again. "He's not used to this. He's not as quick as the others."

He was right. Rather than move toward the corpses and attack, Gordon instead held back and waited for them to come to him, perhaps hoping that someone else would take action before he had to. Four decayed figures closed in on him now.

"Look!"

With remarkable coordination the four bodies suddenly increased their pace and launched themselves at Gordon. At the last possible moment he lifted his fence post and skewered the creature immediately in front of him through the abdomen. In a desperately defensive action he swung the post—with the limp body still impaled on it—from side to side, knocking two more of the foul figures clean off their clumsy feet. To Caron's relief, Jas returned to his side to help him finish off his rotting assailants.

"Did you see them?" Hollis asked.

"Yes, but—"

"Did you see the bodies?" he asked again. "Did you see what they were doing? The fucking things were moving together like pack animals."

"That's impossible."

"I tell you, they're working together!" he insisted. "It's like they're starting to realize they're no match for us on their own. Damn things are fighting in packs!"

17

"You okay, Webb?" Hollis asked as the two men met on their way to the communal lounge. It was just before nine in the morning, much later than most of them usually dragged themselves up out of bed. The effort of the previous two days of fighting had exhausted everyone and an early, relatively undisturbed night had followed. Webb's eyes were glazed. He still looked half-asleep.

"Slept like a fucking log," he answered with his usual lack of tact. "I'm still fucking knackered."

"You were out there for a long time yesterday. Those things might be falling apart, but they still take some getting rid of when they're coming at you."

"Didn't see you out there much."

Hollis shook his head.

"Didn't feel like it," he replied evasively. "Smacked my head when I was out with Lorna yesterday morning. Still hurts."

"You know," Webb said as they walked, gradually becoming more animated, "someone needs to go out there and tell those things that they're dead. You should have seen how they were going for us. I swear they're getting faster. I mean, they're still slow compared to you and me, but they're quicker than they used to be."

"You're right," Hollis agreed. "It makes no sense, but you're right. We've just got to be careful and not take any chances. It's like—"

"One of them bit me!" Webb interrupted. "Don't forget that! Fucking thing tried to take a chunk out of my arm!"

"Yeah, you've already mentioned that."

"We just need to keep doing what we're doing. If we can get rid of a load of them every day then we can keep pushing them back, and if we can do that we'll— Christ, can you smell that?"

As the two men neared the door of the flat Hollis suddenly became aware of the smell of food being cooked. He couldn't tell what it was but that didn't matter. He was starving and the smell made his mouth water and his belly growl. Stokes appeared from the other direction, moving with more speed than he had for weeks. The powerful aroma was like an alarm call.

"Morning, boys." He grinned cheerfully. "Grub's up!"

Stokes and Webb barged into the crowded flat and Hollis followed close behind. Harte and Lorna were in the small galley kitchen cooking on portable gas burners. Driver sat on his backside re-reading the same two-month-old newspaper he always read. Jas and Gordon stood at the window. Only Caron, Ellie, and Anita were missing. Jas glanced back over his shoulder to see who had arrived.

"Morning," Hollis said as he walked over.

"Morning," Gordon mumbled.

"What are you looking at?"

Jas sighed dejectedly. "The bodies, same as always. I was just trying to see if we actually achieved anything yesterday."

Hollis peered over his shoulder. The morning had been misty so far but the sun was gaining strength and was beginning to burn away the haze. At the foot of the hill he could see where the battles with the dead had taken place over the last two days. There was a definite scar of dark discoloration where the bodies had been butchered and brutally battered back but, from this distance, it was hard to see how much land had actually been reclaimed. The reason for Jas's lack of enthusiasm, however, was painfully obvious: no matter how much ground they'd gained, there was still an incalculable amount of work left to be done. Hollis lifted his eyes beyond the barrier and looked deeper into the crowd of corpses. It looked no different: still as large as ever, maybe even bigger. There were tens of thousands of bodies left to destroy, maybe more. For every one they'd hacked down, hundreds seemed to have taken its place.

"Going to take a little while, isn't it?" he said, deliberately understating the scale of the problem.

"Going to take forever," Gordon agreed, leaning his head against the glass.

"Is it worth the effort?" Hollis asked. No one answered.

"I busted my balls yesterday," Jas complained, "and risked my neck. And for what? Wasn't worth shit."

"Of course it was," Webb shouted across the room as he waited for his food. "Look how many of them we got rid of."

"Yeah, but look how many are left."

"Thousands," Gordon said quietly. "Millions, even."

"Less than yesterday, though," Webb continued, grabbing a plate and filling his mouth with breakfast. "And we ain't got to get rid of the lot of them, just enough so we can push what's left back some more."

"It's not worth it," Hollis announced. "Forget it, it's not working. Don't go back out there today."

"Has that bang on the head knocked you stupid?" Webb asked. " 'Course we're going back out."

"What else are we gonna do?" Stokes added, helping himself to food. "If we're not out there killing them, all we'll be doing is sitting in here watching them."

"Haven't actually seen you take one of them out yet," Jas sneered.

"Piss off," he spat, sending a spray of partially chewed food splattering over the kitchen worktop.

"Watch what you're doing," Lorna protested, screwing up her face in disgust and wiping away his greasy spittle with a damp cloth.

"At least I'm out there," Stokes protested, picking up his plate and carrying it over to the window, still chewing. "There's some folk here who've done nothing to help. At least I'm out there."

"Okay, okay . . ." Jas said.

"Look at him," Stokes ranted, pointing accusingly at Driver. "Lazy bastard sits and reads the same bloody newspaper all day, every day. We have to force him to do anything useful."

Driver glanced up from his paper but didn't react.

"You've made your point," Jas sighed, "now shut up."

"And there's Caron," he continued, still eating and still ranting. "Can't remember the last time she went out and did anything worthwhile. Spends all her time sitting with Anita, and she's no good either. Christ, how much looking after does she need? Just another fucking excuse if you ask me."

"Well, maybe I'll be able to do more to help now," Caron said. The others turned as she walked into the room. She looked drained, her face ashen.

"What do you mean?" Harte asked. Caron tried to answer but she couldn't. She slumped into the nearest chair and held her head in her hands. "What do you mean?" he asked again, crouching down in front of her. "What's happened?"

Caron cleared her throat and wiped her eyes.

"She's dead. Anita's dead."

"You're joking," Stokes said stupidly.

"Like she'd joke about that, you fucking idiot," Harte snapped angrily.

Hollis turned back to look out of the window, trying to absorb what he'd heard. Even when the world was so full of death, this sudden loss was almost impossible to accept. He could hear the others talking, some crying, but he kept his emotions locked tight inside. He didn't want them to see that he was completely fucking terrified at the prospect that whatever had killed Anita might still be hanging in the air he was breathing now. *The next gulp of air I swallow*, he thought, *might be the one that kills me.* He could see the reflections of the others behind him in the glass, and he sensed that they were all thinking exactly the same thing:

I might already have it. We all might. And there's fuck all any of us can do about it.

18

He had to get out. It was always hard being trapped inside with the others but it was worse than ever this morning. He understood why, of course, but that didn't make it any easier. He just had to get out.

Webb walked down the hill toward the fenced-off area where he'd previously fought with the dead for sport. He didn't feel like fighting today. He had his baseball bat with him as always, but he now carried it for protection only. As dumb and insensitive as he frequently was, in his own way Webb had taken the news of Anita's death as badly as anyone. He wasn't the sharpest tool in the box, but even he'd quickly made the grim realization that what had killed her could probably kill him too. He could cope with thousands of decaying bodies, but this was something else altogether. A germ or a virus. Something invisible and undetectable which he couldn't punch, kick, or smash into oblivion.

He'd left the others talking about the body. They were arguing about what they should do with it. None of them, him included, wanted to go anywhere near the corpse. Stokes had been saying that he thought Caron should deal with her, because she'd already spent so much time in the same flat and chances were she already had the germ inside her. Caron argued that they'd all got as much chance as each other of catching it, and that just scared everyone even more. Gordon said they needed to do something quick in case she got up again and started walking around. Harte told him to shut up and get a grip, that that was never going to happen. Gordon became hysterical, ranting about how Harte didn't know that was the case and how they couldn't afford to take chances. Harte threw him an ax and told him to go to her flat and chop her body into pieces. Gordon had started panicking and threatened to attack Harte before he went anywhere near Anita's body, and . . . and that was when Webb had got up and walked out.

He'd been sitting cross-legged in the dust for almost fifteen minutes when he realized he hadn't even looked up at the dead today. It said something about both his state of mind and the state of what was left of his world, that a sea of tens of thousands of reanimated cadavers no longer interested him. He picked up a stone and threw it lazily toward the featureless mass of flesh, smirking to himself when it clattered against an old car door and the resulting sound caused a sudden ripple of excitement and animation on the other side of the barrier. He threw another stone, then another, each time taking pleasure in the way he seemed to almost be controlling the corpses and making them dance to his tune. Marginally more interested, he got to his feet and walked closer, pausing to swing at a small rock with his baseball bat, using it like a golf club. The bodies trapped just in front of him were reacting angrily to his presence. They were slamming themselves against the blockade now, shuffling back as best they could, then throwing themselves forward again.

"Look at you," he announced pointlessly. "You're all fucking pathetic."

Now just a couple of meters away, he looked deep into the wall of gnarled, putrefied faces which stared back. He glared at one in particular which reminded him of his older sister. It was wearing the soiled shreds of a revealing pink summer dress and the stupid fucking thing still had a fucking ribbon in its hair! For Christ's sake, he thought, everything that corpse must have gone through and it's still managed to keep its fucking hair tied up! That was so like his sister, the silly bitch. She'd been arrested after a fight in a club once when she'd put some poor bastard in hospital. He'd watched the police shove her in the back of their van. Stupid cow, he'd seen her checking her makeup in her reflection in the window as they'd driven her away to the cells.

When Webb thought about his sister, he began to think about everyone else who had been a part of his life before the world had been turned upside down. He swung his baseball bat and thumped it into the side of the nearest car door, the shock wave rippling back through the crowd like a pebble dropped into water. He hit the car door again, now wanting the dead to react. How many of these wretched, dumb, stinking pieces of shit were the same wretched, dumb, stinking pieces of shit that used to give him a hard time and make his life difficult? He hit the door a third time, the metallic clang ricocheting around his empty world. How many of these things gave him grief or caused him pain or—

Webb was suddenly aware of movement to his right. What the fuck?

Bodies.

There were bodies on *his* side of the blockade. The first one was almost upon him before Webb, stunned momentarily, was able to react. He swung the bat into its groin, sending it flying. Another one lunged. He jabbed the end of the bat into its face, knocking it back into two more. What the hell was going on here? Where were they coming from? Yet another body hurled itself forward, its arms reaching out for him. He grabbed it by the collar and dragged it over onto its back, then stamped on its emaciated face until it was still.

More of them coming. Too many.

113

Terrified, Webb turned and ran from a crowd of almost twenty cadavers which slowly lumbered after him. Through a momentary gap between their constantly shifting shapes he thought he saw more climbing over the barrier—but that was impossible, wasn't it? He ran farther up the hill, the slothful dead no match for his speed, then turned back and looked again. His eyes hadn't deceived him; the bodies were dragging themselves up and over the blockade. Helped up by the countless corpses crushed under their rotting feet over time and by the relentless pressure of others constantly pushing them forward, the damn things were managing to clamber over the cars and rubble and were heading straight for him.

"Help!" he screamed as he scrambled up the hill, not knowing if anyone could hear him. "Get out here, now!"

Hollis, Harte, Lorna, Jas, and Gordon were already on their way down toward the surging bodies before Webb had even made it back to the flats. They thundered past him, leaving him standing alone at the top of the slope. He stopped to spit and catch his breath before heading back down after them.

"Did you see them?" he started to say to Stokes, who pounded after the others at his usual slow pace.

"We all saw," he answered quickly. "It's your fault for winding them up, you fucking jerk!"

"What?" he protested. "I didn't do anything to . . ."

His words were wasted; Stokes was already out of earshot. Still panting, Webb ran back down the hill. In the distance he could see that Harte and Lorna had reached the diggers.

"Just push them back," Jas shouted. He pointed deep into the growing crowd. "They're getting through over there. Build the wall up!"

Lorna was the first to get her digger started. She drove it across the uneven ground at full speed, heading straight for the mass of bodies which were still spilling over the top of the barrier. It didn't look as bad from down here. When they'd first spotted the breach from their high vantage point in the flats there had seemed to be hundreds of spindly figures pouring over. The reality was their numbers were far fewer but that was academic; one corpse on the wrong side of the line was one too many. Scoop down, she thundered into the center of the crowd, forcing many of the advancing grotesques up into the air and back over the blockade. Unsighted, she collided with the very car they were managing to clamber over and the sudden shock jolted her back in her seat.

"Block it up," Hollis shouted to Harte, gesturing at the point where the dead had managed to get over. It was hard to see clearly through the continual, frantic movement, but they appeared to be getting through by dragging themselves over the low bonnet of a small black, family-sized car. Once he was sure that Harte had heard him he returned his attention to those foul aberrations which had already crossed over, chopping and hacking at them with his machete.

Harte turned the digger around and moved away from the corpses. Behind him Lorna was now driving furiously from side to side, obliterating hordes of defenseless figures with every pass. He drove toward a pile of rubble, collected a huge shovelful, then turned back to face the barrier. It looked like they were beginning to regain control. Lorna had quickly dealt with an unquantifiable number of the dead, leaving Jas, Gordon, Webb, and Stokes to wipe up the few that had managed to get away. Hollis, unusually, was standing a little way back from the center of the chaos, the dismembered remains of a blood-soaked police officer twitching at his booted feet.

A loud warning blast on the horn and Harte powered forward. He stopped just short of the blockade—ploughing down six more cadavers on the way—lifted the digger's articulated arm and dropped several tons of crumbling masonry onto the front of the black car. When the dust settled it immediately became apparent that he'd hit the spot perfectly. The dead were shut out again. He felt a sense of smug satisfaction when he jumped down from the cab and saw that when he'd dropped the rubble, he'd also managed to crush a handful of bodies as they'd been trying to get across. Arms and legs jutted out from the confusion at awkward angles. The head of a trapped corpse, wedged at the shoulders between the bonnet of the car and a block of concrete, watched him until he ended its unnatural existence with a well-aimed punch to the face.

"Come on, you fuckers!" Webb screamed at the top of his voice, fighting to make himself heard over the noise of Lorna's digger and the chain saw which Jas was using. Suddenly pumped full of adrenaline again, he braced himself as yet another body hurled itself at him, its decayed face and gnarled lips almost seeming to sneer as it lurched forward. He shoved it back toward Jas, who sliced it in half with a single swipe, the whirring chain-saw blade sliding through its torso. Two more foul, dripping bodies edged toward Jas. He shoved the chain saw into the face of the nearest, angling the whirring blade away from him and down and wincing in disgust as a thick spray of blood, brain and rotten flesh soaked the ground. The other body of the pair seemed to have a little more sense, if that was at all possible. It suddenly veered off to the left, evading the next swipe of the chain saw. It turned its head back to watch Jas over its shoulder as it moved awkwardly away, then staggered straight into the path of Lorna in the digger.

"One behind you, Gordon!" Jas yelled.

Gordon spun around and waited nervously for the dishevelled remains of an elderly woman to attack. He gripped his hand ax tightly, wishing he could fight with the confidence and speed of the others. He felt hopelessly inadequate despite the obvious strength advantage he had over this particular corpse, but the monstrous thing was upon him now and he had no alternative but to take action. Go for the head, he silently repeated to himself, remembering what the others had told him. He swung the ax around and smashed it into the side of the corpse's face, shattering its cheekbone and splitting its ear in half. He wrenched the sunken blade free, then panicked as the creature continued to stagger forward, unperturbed. He swung the ax again, this time wedging it deep into its neck. It took another stumbling step closer, then dropped to the ground in front of him, dark crimson gore slowly dribbling out of its open wounds.

As quickly and as unexpectedly as it had started, the teeming movement around the edge of the barrier wound down to a halt. The diggers and the chain saw were silenced. On the other side of the barrier the bodies continued to surge forward, ripples and aftershocks of movement still running through the huge crowd in response to the sudden carnage and noise. Satisfied that the job was done, the group began to move back toward the flats. Only Hollis remained behind. Lorna walked over to him when she noticed he wasn't following.

"Problem?" she asked, anxiously surveying the scene, worried that he'd spotted something the rest of them had missed.

He shook his head.

"Doesn't matter."

"What is it?" she pressed, concerned. Hollis angrily kicked the corpse lying at his feet.

"This thing caught me off-guard," he reluctantly admitted. "Didn't know it was there until it got hold of me."

"So? You sorted it out, didn't you?"

"Yes, but . . ."

"But what?"

It was obvious there was something he wasn't telling her.

"I didn't hear it coming."

"So what? I'm not surprised. You know, with the diggers and the chain saw and Webb's mouth it's no wonder you didn't . . ."

He was shaking his head. She stopped talking.

"It's not that," he said.

"What, then?"

"Remember when we were out yesterday morning? You let that body out in the pharmacy and it went for me?"

"Yes."

"I hit my head when I went down."

"I know. Is that why you're . . . ?"

"I've damaged my ear," he said, his voice suddenly unusually emotional. "I can't hear a fucking thing on my left side, and that's why this fucking thing nearly had me."

He kicked the corpse at his feet again, sending its bloodied head skidding across the ground like a football, then walked away from her and began to march up the hill.

19

"What are we gonna do?" Harte asked, slumping in a chair and holding his head in his hands. Four hours had passed since the bodies first breached the barrier. They'd broken through three more times since, smaller advances which had been quickly contained. "Those damn things out there are learning! They're copying each other, for Christ's sake!"

"The obvious answer is to try and make the barrier stronger," Hollis replied, "but I don't think that's going to help."

"Of course it's going to help, you prick. How can it not help?"

"I don't think we're looking at the problem the right way."

"What?" Harte grunted. He wasn't in the mood for riddles.

"Are you talking about the bodies?" Jas wondered.

"Thing is," he explained, "I don't think it matters how they got over the barrier or if they're going to do it again, I think we need to be working out *why* they're doing it."

"That's bloody obvious," Lorna interrupted. "It was Webb. We saw you standing out there, throwing stones at them."

Hollis shook his head dejectedly.

"That's not it." He sighed. "Didn't help, though."

"What, then?" she snapped.

"I don't think it's just because of what you were doing today, Webb. I think they were reacting to what we've all been doing down there this week."

"Still don't understand," said Harte.

"For the last two days we've been pushing them around and smashing them up and burning a few hundred of them at a time."

"So?"

"So, they're running scared. Except they can't run, because there's too many of them and they can't get away. The only option they've got left . . ."

". . . is to fight," Jas said, finishing his sentence for him.

"Exactly. They reacted when you got down there today Webb because they thought you were about to start laying into them again. And they're climbing over the barrier now because they know that they can. They've seen others doing it."

"No way!" Stokes laughed from the other side of the room. "Is anyone falling for this bullshit? You've got to be fucking kidding me."

"Think about it," Hollis continued. "They're adapting to what's happening around them. It makes sense."

"None of this makes sense," Gordon said.

"So what are we going to do about it?" asked Harte. "I hear what you're saying, but can't we just build up the barrier and sit tight?"

"That's what I think," Stokes said.

"First off, how? We don't have enough stuff to build it up with— and anyway, I don't think we can risk doing it. You saw what effect Webb going down there had on them this morning. If we start throwing our weight around again, even if we're not directly attacking them, we're going to push them over the edge and we'll end up with a full-scale-pitch invasion."

"So what are our alternatives? Sit here and do nothing?"

"There's no way I'm just gonna sit in here, waiting for them to give up and keel over," Webb protested. "No way am I going to spend all my time shut in this fucking building, waiting. There's a fucking corpse in here too, don't forget."

"No one's forgotten, Webb," Hollis sighed. "I know it's not ideal, but what's the alternative? It's either that or leave. We pack up and get out of here."

Webb turned and looked out the window, not wanting to make eye contact with anyone. He didn't know which was worse—the idea of staying put, or the prospect of heading out for good. The flats might have been cold, uncomfortable, and right on the edge of the biggest cesspit of rotting human remains imaginable, but they'd been relatively safe here until now. None of them had any idea what they'd find elsewhere.

"There's something else you need to know," Caron said, standing in the doorway. Everyone looked around. No one knew how long she'd been there.

"What's that?" Hollis asked, immediately concerned.

"It's Ellie. She's sick."

"What do you mean?" he asked anxiously, fearing that he knew the answer to his question already. "Is she . . . ?"

"Same as Anita," she answered abruptly. "She said she felt sick last night but I didn't think much of it. It's early days, but her symptoms are just the same."

"This thing's going to wipe the whole fucking lot of us out," Stokes said, putting into words what everyone was thinking.

20

Late afternoon. Another wave of bodies had managed to scramble over the barrier. Between them, Harte, Jas, Stokes, and Webb had fought back the ninety or so cadavers which had forced their way over during the fifth breach and had worked quickly to strengthen the blockade at the weak point which had been compromised. Stokes and Webb had been left outside to mop up the last few scrawny figures which had escaped the initial cull and encroached closer toward the survivors' base.

"Five left, I think," Stokes wheezed as he moved toward the remaining corpses. Webb shielded his eyes and surveyed the area around them. The sun was setting and was now framed in a narrow strip of clear sky between the horizon and a band of heavy gray cloud just above. The brilliant orange disc drenched the world in light, casting long, eerie shadows across the rubble. He soon saw the bodies that Stokes had spotted—trapped between a skip and a pile of masonry. One of them had fallen and become wedged in the way of the others. He swung his spiked baseball bat up onto his shoulder and headed down after Stokes. Tonight, more than ever, he was in need of therapy.

Stokes was already fighting by the time Webb reached the dead, doing all the damage he could to the trapped corpse with a chisel and a lump hammer. He'd found them in a tool box in the back of a car and was now using them as a makeshift dagger and mace. It was an indication of how the day's events had altered the individual perspective of each of the survivors that a man as lazy and normally reluctant to fight as Stokes had, through sudden necessity, become remarkably aggressive. He yanked the fallen corpse up onto its feet and dragged it out of the way, immediately allowing the remaining bodies to move again.

"Let's get this done and get back inside," he suggested. "I've had enough for one day. I need a drink."

Webb nodded, watching the bodies wearily haul themselves back out into space. Unexpectedly and, he thought, unfairly, they moved toward him *en masse,* leaving Stokes to deal with just the solitary corpse he'd already got hold of. Probably for the best, he decided as he chose which of the pathetic creatures he'd go for first.

Panting with effort, Stokes shoved the lone figure away, then readied himself for its attack. It moved closer, lunging forward angrily with alternate steps, its unsteady movements the result of a broken right tibia which jutted out from an angry wound in its leg. He gripped his weapons tight, expecting it to throw itself at him like so many others had already done today. But instead it held back, rocking clumsily on its feet. It seemed to be sussing out its opposition—if, of course, it was capable of actually seeing anything through those dark, unfocussed eyes. The delay made the already anxious man feel even more uneasy. He decided to take the initiative, thrusting forward and swinging the lump hammer at the foul thing's head. He caught its chin, wrenching its jaw bone out of its socket and leaving it dangling and deformed. Part of him wished he'd started fighting like this earlier because Webb was definitely right—getting rid of these abominations so aggressively was strangely therapeutic. It made him feel alive. It re-enforced the fact that he was so much better than these useless lumps of decaying gristle and putrid flesh.

"How you doing, Webb?" he yelled as the body fell at his feet. He stamped on its chest, feeling satisfaction as its ribs cracked beneath his boot.

"All right," Webb replied, continuing to fight a short distance away. He'd already got rid of one body and had incapacitated another. It was on its knees just behind him. He'd broken both of its ankles and smashed its pelvis. Unable to fight back, it desperately tried to reach out for him, clawing wildly at the air. He ignored it, choosing instead to concentrate on another corpse which he'd just shoved face-down in the dirt. He repeatedly slammed the baseball bat down onto its back, ripping its flesh apart and sending a fountain of dark rivulets of blood and slimy scraps churning up into the air. Stokes looked around for his next victim. The fifth body actually seemed to be trying to keep out of sight. It moved behind the large yellow skip. Stokes simply went around the other way, then dragged it back out into the open and threw it to the ground. He dropped down on its exposed rib cage and hammered the chisel through its left eye.

Webb was still attacking the same corpse. He'd long since incapacitated it, but the urge to continue to violently disembowel the creature was strong. Battering it into oblivion and splattering its guts over the dust and rubble was helping him deal with the fear he'd felt since hearing that Anita had died and Ellie was ill. Stokes noticed the incapacitated cadaver behind Webb was still moving and he strode toward it purposefully, ready to put it out of its misery.

Concentrating on the carcass on the ground but suddenly aware of another figure approaching at speed, Webb turned into the sun and swung his baseball bat around with massive force. Stokes let out a whimper as it hit him square in the chest, the nails piercing through his skin and muscle and puncturing his lungs. He dropped to his knees, clutching his wounds.

"What did you do that for?" he asked, stunned with surprise, only just starting to feel the pain. Webb's legs turned to jelly as he realized what he'd done.

"Sorry, Stokes . . ." he stammered pathetically. "I didn't mean to . . . I didn't know it was you . . . I just . . ."

"It really hurts," Stokes groaned, tears of agony running down his face. He looked at his hands and saw that they were soaked with blood. His jacket and shirt were already drenched too. "Go and get the others," he wheezed. "Get Caron . . ."

Webb crouched down next to him. What the hell was he going to do? He reached out his hand but stopped before he touched him. Stokes looked at him again, his eyes wide with hurt, then slumped heavily over onto his side. He breathed a few labored, gurgling breaths and then stopped. Everything was silent save for the corpse scrambling around in the dust just out of reach.

"Stokes," Webb said, getting as close to the other man's face as he could without touching him. "Stokes, come on! Don't die . . ."

He reached out his hand again, this time forcing himself to touch Stokes's shoulder. He shook it but there was no response. He couldn't be dead. He just couldn't be . . .

The creature behind him managed to drag itself far enough forward to reach his boot with outstretched fingers. Webb turned and grabbed the corpse by the shoulders and threw it several meters away into the dust where it flopped back over onto its chest and began to drag itself toward him again. He didn't even look at it, concentrating instead on Stokes. He still hadn't moved.

Jesus Christ, Webb thought, his panic mounting, *what have I done? It was an accident. It wasn't my fault. If the stupid idiot hadn't crept up on me like that it never would have happened. The rest of them will understand, won't they? They'll know I didn't do it on purpose . . .*

For a few desperate seconds longer he weighed up his limited options; turn and run or go back and face the others. Much as he wanted to quickly disappear, one look at the thousands of corpses still gathered around the flats and he knew he'd never get away in one piece. If he'd been able to drive then maybe things would have been different, but the fact of the matter was that he couldn't. He was stuck here.

"What's the matter with you?" Hollis asked as Webb burst into the communal flat. Bloody Webb, why did his heart always sink when he saw him?

"They got him," he gasped.

"What are you talking about? Who got who?"

"Stokes. They got him."

"Who got him?" he repeated.

"The bodies. He's dead."

21

"I'm going," Harte announced, his face pressed against the window. "They're coming over the barrier again. Fuck this, I'm going."

His words were met with silence as the rest of the survivors thought about what they'd heard. Several others had reached the same decision individually, but no one had found the courage to stand up and say as much. Harte hadn't any courage either; he was entirely motivated by fear.

"Are you sure there's no other option?" Caron asked. The room was dark. She couldn't see how anyone else had reacted.

"I'll listen to anything anyone else has got to say," Harte replied anxiously, "but I can't see any other way forward. For Christ's sake, Anita's dead upstairs, Stokes is dead down there, Ellie's dying and the bodies are climbing over the barrier again. You tell me if there's any better option than getting the hell out of here."

Silence.

"We could go down there in the morning and clear them out again," Jas suggested. "I'm not going out there tonight."

"How many will be down there by then? I've seen half a dozen get over in the last couple of minutes. At that rate that's almost a hundred an hour. There'll be a thousand of them by the time the sun comes up."

Hollis got up and walked over to the window where Harte was standing. He was right—in the pale moonlight outside he could see that the corpses had found another weak point in their increasingly ineffective blockade. They were scrambling over the back of another car like cockroaches scuttling across a dirty kitchen floor.

"But is it going to be any different anywhere else?" Gordon asked. He was sitting on the floor in the farthest corner of the room, knees pulled up close to his chest. "It's not going to be any better, is it?"

"Couldn't be any worse," Lorna mumbled.

"Don't count on it," Jas said quickly. "We thought we were doing well here."

"I don't understand what's happened," Caron said. "Why's it all gone so wrong so quickly?"

"Bad luck," Hollis answered.

"It's a bit more than bad luck, you fucking idiot," Harte said nervously.

"We couldn't have planned for any of this," he continued.

"No one could have planned for anything that's happened since September."

"I know that, but we thought we'd be able to sit this out here, didn't we. I thought we'd be okay here until they'd decayed away to nothing. And maybe we still would have been if Anita hadn't got sick."

"But why now?" Caron asked. "Why are they climbing over the barrier today?"

"Because they're scared," Jas replied. "Because they've seen us down there beating the shit out of several hundred of them at a time, and we've scared them. They can't get away because there are so many of them, so they're fighting back like caged animals. What's left of their brains is telling them to get us before we get them."

"Do you really believe that?"

"I do," Hollis said quickly. "He's right. We've brought this on ourselves."

"So is there any point in leaving?"

"Well, yes," he responded with a blunt and irritating matter-of-factness. "Of course there is. Anita's dead and Ellie's dying. If we stay here then there's a strong chance more of us will go the same way."

"But like I said," Gordon whined from the corner, "aren't we just going to end up in as bad a mess somewhere else? We'll end up with another bloody huge crowd of them gathered around us."

"Maybe, but it probably won't be as big a crowd as we've got here. It's taken more than a month for that many of them to drag themselves over here. It's going to take time for things to get this bad if we're starting again from scratch, isn't it?"

"Yes, but—"

"You've seen what kind of a state they're in, haven't you? So, logically, by the time we get to this stage again with these kind of numbers, the bodies should be pretty much incapable of harming us, no matter how many of them there are."

"I'm sold," Lorna said quietly. "Makes sense to me. I'm going."

"Anyway," Caron protested, "this is all irrelevant."

"Is it?" she grumbled. "Why?"

"Because we can't go anywhere with Ellie the way she is."

"Yes, we can," Harte quickly replied.

"We can't just leave her here . . ."

"Yes, we can," he said again. "We can't take her with us, can we? Kind of defeats the object if we take her and whatever she's got with us, doesn't it?"

"But we can't just leave her."

"Are you sure she's got the same thing that killed Anita?" Jas asked.

"Well, her symptoms are the same and she's been getting worse as quickly as Anita did."

"So she's probably going to die, isn't she?"

Although she knew the answer, Caron didn't want to say it.

"She . . . she might not," she stammered awkwardly. "Anita might have had some other medical problem that we didn't know about. She might have—"

"I think she's going to die," Hollis said, "and a few more of us probably will too if we don't leave here."

"But you can't just abandon her!"

"Does she say anything when you walk into her flat?" Jas asked.

"No, but—"

"Does she sit up in bed? Does she look at you and talk to you? Does she even know you're in there with her?"

"Sometimes. Most of the time she's asleep or—"

"By the time we're ready to leave here that poor cow won't have a clue what's going on. She won't know if she's on her own or if we're all in the room with her. More to the point, she won't give a shit."

"We can't just leave her here to die. It's inhuman!"

"Then maybe we should put her out of her misery?" Hollis suggested. "If what's going to happen to her really is inevitable, speeding it up is only going to help."

"Christ, she's not a dog!" Caron screamed, crying now. "You can't just put her down!"

"I'll do it," Harte said, surprising the others. "Give her some dignity . . ."

"*Dignity*?" she yelled in disbelief. "Where's the dignity in being murdered?"

"There's more dignity in dying quickly and quietly at the hands of one of us than there is lying in a dirty flat, surrounded by thousands of dead bodies and in so much pain that you lose your mind."

"No one's trying to force you to do anything, Caron," Jas said, his voice a little calmer, quieter and less emotional than the others. "All we're saying is that we can't afford to take Ellie with us. If you want to stay here and nurse her then that's up to you."

Caron didn't answer at first. She stared angrily into the darkness, her mind filled with so many painful thoughts and impossible decisions that she couldn't make sense of any of it.

"When did you last check on her?" Lorna asked. Again, Caron didn't answer. She tried asking another question. "Have you seen her this evening? Did you go up there after the bodies first got through this morning?"

"I haven't seen her for hours," Caron eventually replied, having to force herself to spit the words out. "I haven't seen her since early this morning."

"Why not? I thought you'd—"

"I'm too scared," she admitted. "I don't want to go in there anymore after what happened to Anita, all right? I don't want to catch what she's got."

"Then there's your answer," Harte said under his breath as Caron's sobbing filled the room.

"The longer we leave this, the worse it's going to get," Jas said. "If the germs don't get us then those bastards outside will. Look what they did to Stokes."

"Poor bastard didn't know they were there until they'd got him," Webb said from where he'd been sitting on the floor next to the arm of the sofa. He swallowed hard and hoped that the others were sufficiently wrapped up with their own problems not to notice his sudden nervousness.

"You're right," Hollis agreed. "We've all seen it. Their behavior is changing. They're more aggressive, and they're working together."

"So where would we go?" Gordon asked, begrudgingly

beginning to accept that leaving now looked like their only option. Silence.

"In the summer," Driver suddenly announced, "I used to drive the two-twenty-two out of Catsgrove."

"Fuck me, Driver," Harte gasped. "I didn't even know you were in here!"

"He's always in here," Lorna muttered angrily. "Lazy bastard never goes anywhere else."

"What were you saying?" Hollis asked, trying to pick out Driver in the darkness.

"I used to drive the two-twenty-two," he repeated. "Day trips to the coast."

"What? You want to go to the seaside? You're a fucking idiot," Webb cursed.

"On the A197 out of town," he continued, unfazed, "you pass this bloody huge exhibition center. Make a good place to go, that would. Out in the country. Loads of space. Nothing else for miles."

The room was suddenly, completely silent. Even Caron had stopped crying to listen to Driver and think about his suggestion. Hollis wondered why he'd waited until now to speak up. Whatever the reason, he was glad that Driver finally had.

22

After a sleepless night and an hour spent collecting her belongings from her flat, Caron climbed the stairs to the room where Ellie laid. Her nervousness increased with each step she took. She couldn't believe she'd allowed herself to be coerced into doing this. She clutched a polyethylene bag full of drugs in her hand but didn't know whether she'd be able to use them. She didn't even know if she'd be able to go into Ellie's room this morning. The stench had been appalling when she'd last checked on her. She'd made a halfhearted attempt to clean her up but the mess had been too severe. Ellie's bedding was heavily soiled but, as Hollis had pointed out, the poor girl was bound to be long past the point of caring now. It would have caused her more distress to get her up and clean her than to leave her lying in her own shit.

The cold wind blew through an empty window frame, gusting into Caron's face like a slap across the cheek. She walked down the final long, dark corridor and reached the door to Ellie's flat. She was too scared to go in, too scared to stand outside and too scared to go back downstairs without having seen her. She could hear the others out in the car park, loading their supplies into the bus and one of the vans. She didn't want to leave, but she definitely didn't want to stay either. When she'd looked out the window first thing this morning the barrier at the foot of the hill had all but disappeared, obscured from view by hundreds of bodies which had managed to drag themselves across during the long hours of the night just ended. Only the steep slope had so far prevented them from getting any farther.

Closing her eyes and struggling to hold her nerve, Caron cautiously pushed the door open and looked inside. No movement. No sound. She tiptoed into the flat and peered through the bedroom door. Still no movement. Christ, the smell was worse than she remembered: the stagnant stench of sweat, vomit, and excretion mixing with the ever-present wafts of death and decay drifting in from outside. Was Ellie dead? She wasn't moving. Maybe it would be better for all concerned if she'd gone in her sleep. Caron took a few steps farther into the bedroom, the drugs gripped tightly in one hand, a handkerchief held over her mouth and nose with the other.

"Ellie," she whispered lightly. "Ellie, honey, are you awake?"

Ellie still wasn't moving. Caron crept a little closer, not wanting to get too near. Her foot kicked Ellie's doll, sending it spinning across the floor. She cringed at the noise and squinted into the darkness. Ellie was on her side with her back to her and her torso uncovered. She still couldn't see any movement. Was she breathing? Maybe she should try and touch her and check for a pulse or—

"Jesus!" she screamed with surprise as Ellie threw herself over onto her back with a sudden, painful groan of effort. Caron immediately felt disappointed that she was still alive, and then felt massive guilt that she'd actually wished the girl dead. She wasn't sure whether it was because she'd hoped she'd been put out of her misery, or whether it was because she didn't want to have to do it for her.

Ellie groaned again, half-opened her eyes and mumbled something unintelligible. Without realizing she was doing it, Caron backed away.

"I'll get you some water," she whispered, her eyes filled with stinging tears. She went through into Ellie's living room and found a half-empty plastic water bottle sitting on a windowsill. Unable to take her eyes off the girl's bedroom door, she crushed as many pills and capsules as she could manage, added them to the water and shook the bottle. For half a second she considered drinking it herself. That was stupid. She couldn't allow herself to think like that. She looked at the bottle in her hand and wondered whether it would actually have any effect at all. Would it just make Ellie even more ill? Caron didn't seem to be able to look after anyone anymore—would she be any better at killing them? She'd lost her son, then Anita, and now Ellie . . . What kind of a mother had she turned out to be?

Despite being high up, she could hear the others outside again, and that forced her into action. She wasn't sure what she wanted any more but she definitely didn't want to be left here. With nervous determination she walked purposefully into Ellie's room, ready to get her to take the drugs. But she couldn't do it. She found Ellie lying motionless on her back again, naked and soaked with sweat, staring up at the ceiling with wide, vacant eyes. Caron knew what she had to do, but she just couldn't do it.

"Ellie, sweetheart," she said quietly, gingerly putting her hand on the girl's cold shoulder and shaking her slightly. "Take this, it'll make you feel better."

She raised the water bottle to Ellie's chapped lips but couldn't make her drink. In desperation she began to pour it into Ellie's open mouth, but most of it simply ran down her cheek and onto the already drenched bedding. She didn't even react to the temperature of the water. Caron knew she was as good as dead already.

The easiest option—the cowardly option—was to put the bottle in her hand and leave.

With tears running down her face, that was exactly what Caron did.

23

The barrier at the base of the hill had gone now, swallowed up by an unstoppable yet slow-moving tide of cold, dead flesh. Thousands of restless bodies, pushed ever forward by thousands more, had surged silently over the vehicles and rubble through the night. The stronger cadavers—those which had somehow so far avoided suffering any major physical damage—now crushed their weaker brethren beneath their rotting feet. The fetid remains of countless fallen figures had pooled and been compressed over time, allowing other corpses to trample over them and use them like an access ramp to scramble up over the blockade, following the lead of others. Whether driven by curiosity, fear, instinct, or hate it didn't matter, they were moving ever closer to the living. And, as Hollis, Harte, and several of the others had noticed, while now compromised and able to allow bodies in, their barrier also acted like a valve, preventing those creatures inside from getting back out. Although none of them had, as yet, managed to climb the hill, it was inevitable that they would. Staying put and doing nothing was no longer an option.

Driver folded up his tattered newspaper and shoved it into the gap behind the steering wheel of the bus. He leaned out of his cab and watched as Jas and Harte struggled to load up the last few bags and boxes. They were already out of breath, having just stowed Jas's bike in the back of the van after he'd decided he'd be safer traveling on four wheels with the others.

"You could get off your backside and help if you wanted to," Harte sneered sarcastically.

"You've almost done it now," Driver mumbled.

"Thanks for nothing," he said as he stormed back off the bus. Harte's bad mood was worsened not only by the panic and concern they all felt this morning, but also by the fact that they had managed to pack pretty much everything they owned into the bus and one van and there was still plenty of space to spare. They'd even decided to leave the other van behind. It was unreliable and had an oil leak, and the truth of the matter was they just didn't need it. He suddenly felt hopelessly underprepared and ill-equipped for life away from the flats.

Hollis was walking away from the tall gray building, his arm around Caron's shoulder. Gordon followed close behind looking typically awkward and uncomfortable. Jas moved to one side to let the three of them onto the bus. He waited for Caron and Gordon to disappear upstairs before speaking to Hollis.

"What happened in there?" he asked.

"Don't know," he replied abruptly. "Don't want to ask. Are we ready to go?"

"Think so."

"Reckon she did it?" Harte whispered.

"Did what?"

"Finished her off?"

"Christ, you're an insensitive prick," Hollis said. "For Ellie's sake I hope she did."

"I'm not insensitive," Harte protested. "I just want to know what happened."

"Doesn't matter what she—" Jas began.

"Just leave it," Hollis interrupted. "We need to get going. Are you ready?" he asked, looking at Driver, who nodded but didn't answer. Hollis got off the bus and jogged over to the van where Lorna and Webb were waiting for him. He climbed in and started the engine, keen to get moving.

"I reckon we should torch this place before we go," Webb suggested, sitting in the back of the van behind the other two.

"What good's that going to do?" Lorna asked.

"You're a fucking pyromaniac," Hollis said sadly, shaking his head in despair.

"I'm not, I just think—"

"No, you don't," Lorna yelled at him angrily, sounding unexpectedly furious, "and that's the problem. You don't think at all. You just bulldoze and bullshit your way through everything. Ellie is dying in there, and we're leaving her behind. Isn't that enough for you? Do you want to make sure you finish the job off by burning her to death? Christ, do you know what I—"

"Will you both just shut up!" Hollis shouted, slamming his fist down on the steering wheel. "Bickering like a pair of fucking five-year-olds. Just shut up!"

He swung the van around in a wide circle, then waited for Driver to line himself up behind. One last look at the dead—the farthest forward of them now beginning to creep slowly up the hill—then one last look at the towering gray block of flats, the closest thing he'd had to home since they'd all lost everything weeks ago. Strangest thing was, he felt worse about leaving this place today than he had when he'd last walked out of his house the day his world had fallen apart back in September. Staying there had never been an option. It had been full of memories of people, places, and everything else he'd lost. For a while, though, these damp and uncomfortable flats had given them all some

138

security and a base from which they could try and rebuild their lives. All gone now. With Lorna and Webb still arguing he put his foot down and drove away.

Gordon pressed his face up against the glass, feeling his whole body shake with every rattling movement of the bus as it weaved through the carnage on the roads leading away from the flats. He sat on the backseat of the top floor. Caron sat opposite, her back to him, staring out the window on the other side. Harte was three seats in front, Jas another five seats ahead of him. Given the limited confines of their transport, they couldn't have been much more spread out, not that this was unusual. Gordon used to travel by bus regularly and he considered it an unwritten rule to put as much distance as you could between yourself and any strangers. Today, however, these people kept their distance to avoid sharing their fears and concerns. A couple of days ago everything had been relatively okay. How had it all gone so wrong so quickly? Gordon glanced over at Caron. What was she thinking? She still had a plastic bag full of pills gripped tight in her hand. Who were they for? Had she not given any to Ellie? Did she intend taking them herself? Surely things couldn't be that bad, could they?

Driver swerved left then right to avoid the blackened remains of a smaller bus which straddled the carriageway, dead passengers still visible inside. His own passengers were momentarily shunted up into the air as the cumbersome vehicle clattered up the curb then back down again. The sudden, jarring movement threw Gordon to the side and he banged his head against the glass. He rubbed the bump, closed his eyes, and tried to concentrate on the sound of the engine. Unexpectedly, and just for the slightest of seconds, everything felt reassuringly familiar. Just for a moment he allowed himself to believe that instead of driving away from the silent, skeletal remains of the city where he'd lived all his life, he was actually on his way home from work. He tried to convince himself that if he opened his eyes he'd see the comforting, familiar sights of his daily commute again. Any moment now the bus would slow down then stop as they joined the snaking queue of traffic escaping the city center. If he looked outside he'd see hundreds of people all making their way back home like him. Another fifteen minutes' drive and he'd reach his stop. A ten-minute walk after that and he'd be home. What would Janice be cooking for him tonight? A piece of fish or a chop with chips? His mouth began watering at the thought of it. Christ, he hoped she hadn't been experimenting. He hated it when she cooked what he called "exotic" dinners. He didn't like pasta or rice or curries or anything like that, but he always forced himself to eat it. Maybe he'd have to do his usual trick and take the dog for a long walk tonight. One of those walks that involved stopping off for a burger and eating it on his way back through the park . . .

Gordon opened his eyes and stared out at the dead world around him. Drained of color, raped by disease, and disintegrating almost as he watched, it bore little resemblance to the place he remembered. The bones of his fellow commuters were scattered on the ground, kicked aside by those horrific creatures which still dragged themselves through the streets. And Janice, his long-suffering wife of twenty-three years, was still suffering too—condemned to spend the rest of forever trapped in their living room behind the door he'd boarded up after she'd got up and started moving again.

24

The van stopped suddenly. Driver, following too close behind, slammed on his brakes to avoid crashing into the back of it.

"What's the matter?" Caron asked anxiously, getting up from her seat and running the length of the bus to the front where Jas was already standing at the window. They'd been on the move for less than an hour. The road they'd been following had meandered through open countryside for a time, but they'd now reached Cudsford, an unremarkable town nestled between two larger but equally uninteresting towns and the first relatively built-up area they'd come across. On balance they'd decided it was easier and quicker to drive straight through rather than skirt all the way around and add miles to their journey.

"Doesn't look like anything major," Jas said, looking down onto the street below. "There's a van blocking the road, that's all."

Harte was already on his way downstairs, hand ax at the ready just in case. Jas followed, pausing only to pick up the chain saw from where he'd dumped it on an empty lower-deck seat. By the time he'd stepped out onto the narrow backstreet, Webb, Hollis and Lorna were already out and surveying the scene. A single corpse staggered from behind the crashed van, tripped in the gutter and fell at Webb's feet. He nonchalantly smashed its skull with his spiked baseball bat.

"Well?" Harte asked, keeping his voice low. Hollis pointed at the front of the blue liveried van which had thumped into the front of an office block, leaving its rear end jutting out into the road and blocking their way. The dead driver—who was still trying to get out from behind the wheel—slammed its decaying face up against the glass as they moved closer.

"Problem is," Hollis explained, ignoring the corpse's frantic movements, "it looks like it's wedged in." He leaned over the front of the van and looked up. The impact had brought the low canopy of a porch crashing down onto its roof. There were visible cracks running up the face of the building and the glass in many of the first-floor windows had been smashed. "There's a chance if we move it that we'll bring the whole lot down."

"So?" Webb grunted, returning his attention to the crash.

"So we could end up blocking the road instead of clearing it," he replied, wishing that he wasn't stuck out in the middle of nowhere with someone as dense as Webb.

"I think it'll be all right," Harte said, carefully stepping under the canopy and looking up to try and assess the damage. "I don't think there's any other way of shifting—"

A sudden movement from Lorna distracted him. She rushed across to the other side of the narrow street and grappled with a bloody figure which threw itself at her. She grabbed its scrawny neck, forcing it back against the nearest wall before cracking its skull and beating it repeatedly with the claw hammer she'd been carrying. Sometimes she scared herself with her own brutality. She looked up and saw that the damn thing wasn't alone.

"Get a move on," she whispered, looking farther down the street and counting at least seven more bodies heading in their direction. "They're coming."

Webb, his appetite for violence clearly undiminished despite the events of the last twenty-four hours, ran forward to head off the approaching dead, swinging the baseball bat wildly through the air. He thumped it into the face of the cadaver nearest to him, catching it perfectly, almost laughing out loud as it tripped blindly back into two more bodies like an uncoordinated drunk, knocking them both over. He ran toward them with predatory speed, determined to finish them all off before they could pick themselves back up.

"So what do we do?" Jas asked hurriedly, seeing that even more bodies were closing in. "Move this thing, or turn around and find another way through?"

"Driver's never going to get the bus turned around here. He'll have to back it out . . ." Hollis's words trailed away when he heard the bus suddenly begin to move.

Jas started the chain saw and ran back toward the huge vehicle as the farthest advanced figures at the front of an uncomfortably large crowd of corpses began to surge past it, slipping down either side. He held the chain saw at waist height and waded into them, dragging the churning blade from side to side, scything down the creatures as if they were trees being felled. The road beneath his feet, until then relatively clear save for a little rubble and broken glass, was suddenly awash with blood and gore. As he sliced the legs off yet another body that foolishly stumbled toward him, the bus accelerated. Uncharacteristically alert and decisive, Driver shunted it forward and angled it across the street, reversing back to fully block the width of the narrow throughway and prevent any more of the dead from getting closer.

At the back of the top floor of the bus, Caron stood next to Gordon and looked down in disbelief as the entire street behind them quickly became clogged with dead flesh. She hadn't been this close to them for weeks, probably more than a month, and she was terrified, both of their appearance and their sudden vast numbers. Physically they had deteriorated to an incredible extent and were grotesque—decaying and literally falling apart in front of her. But at the same time, they continued to move with unquestionable intent. When she'd last been this close to them they'd looked relatively untouched by disease. Now their faces were hideously scarred and mutated, barely recognizable as human. Gordon was saying something, rambling incessantly about why he should stay up here with her and how he probably would just get in the way out there, but she wasn't listening. She hadn't realized how strong and safe the flats had been. *All that's separating me from them now*, she anxiously thought, *is this bus.*

Out on the street, Harte yanked open the door of the crashed van and grappled with the driver's corpse trapped inside. It threw its withered arms at him and he battered them away with the ax, unable to get the right angle to use the weapon properly in the confined space. The smell in the van was horrific and he gagged as he struggled to grab the squirming cadaver, undo its safety belt, and drag it out onto the street. He managed to get hold of its arm, his gloved hand easily wrapping right the way around its bony, emaciated wrist, and then yanked it out into the open. Its right foot caught between the gearstick and handbrake. Harte tugged at the struggling creature desperately, pulling with enough force to rip the foot off at the ankle. Finally out, he slammed its face into the pavement, then climbed in and settled himself behind the wheel. The seat was tacky beneath him. Screwing his face up with disgust, he reached down, picked up the dismembered foot from under the pedals, and threw it out of the window.

When Harte next looked up he saw that the number of bodies hauling themselves down the street toward them had increased massively. The bus had blocked the road one way, but the other direction was still clear and a relentless deluge of flesh was now approaching, channeled forward by the tall buildings on either side. Lorna, Webb, and Jas stood and fought, trying desperately to head them off. Jas was a couple of meters ahead of the other two, carving up as many of them as he could reach with the brutally efficient chain saw blade. Lorna and Webb worked behind him, mopping up any of the despicable figures that somehow managed to get past.

"Get it started!" Hollis yelled, hammering on the back of the van.

Harte turned the key in the ignition, willing the engine to fire. It groaned and whined but wouldn't start.

"Careful, don't flood it!" Hollis warned.

Harte tried again, turning the key and pumping the pedals with his feet, not knowing if that would help or make the problem worse. The engine almost caught.

"Come on!" he shouted in frustration, slamming his hand against the steering wheel angrily. One more try and the engine suddenly spluttered into life. He accelerated hard to keep it alive, the delivery van's exhaust belching dirty clouds of fumes into the street, then quickly reversed back. Hollis had said something to him about being careful and driving slowly, but all that was forgotten in the heat of the moment. He careered back, steering hard around to keep the van on the pavement, looking up at the canopy at the front of the damaged building and praying it would hold. It didn't. The sides of the porch collapsed inward, littering the ground with dust and rubble. The front of the building, thankfully, remained standing. He drove up onto the pavement, leaving the road clear, and parked.

"We need to go," Hollis said to him as he got back out of the van. "This isn't good."

Harte looked up at Lorna, Webb, and Jas, who were just about managing to hold back the tide. They remained in control, but the dead masses still herded toward them and their numbers were increasing.

145

They'd been carving them up for several minutes now and had reduced more than fifty to little more than a bloody pile of unrecognizable body parts. Easily as many again were still stumbling lethargically toward them, and more would undoubtedly follow when the next fifty had been hacked down, then more and more . . .

Harte ran back to the bus, distracted momentarily by a body which appeared to fall from out of nowhere, dropping facedown onto the street just in front of him and disintegrating on impact like bad fruit. He recoiled in disgust as dark, sticky blood and other foul substances splashed up at him from the splattered remains on the tarmac. He looked up at the office block beside him, bewildered. The sudden, constant noise and movement out in the street had alerted a number of corpses which had been trapped inside the building but which had now found a way out thanks to the damage he'd caused. Drawn out of the shadows by the chaos outside, the stupid creatures were now plummeting out from the first floor like lemmings. Ignorant to the danger and desperate to get closer to the living, the damn things were literally falling out of the sky around him. Another one fell nearby, its head somehow protected from the fall but its body irrevocably damaged. Regardless, it tried to pull itself along the ground toward him with its one remaining good arm.

"We're going," he announced to Driver. Not needing any further instruction, Driver straightened the bus again and moved it forward. Stumbling corpses began to slip through on either side, their speed increased by the pressure of others pushing from behind.

A short distance up ahead, Hollis moved their van up to where the others were fighting. Lorna climbed in quickly, shouting across at Webb and Jas for them to follow. Webb heard her and ran back, stopping when he realized that Jas was still out there, isolated from everything else that was happening by the noise of his weapon. He ran forward again and grabbed his shoulder, spinning him around and stumbling back as Jas lunged at him, chain-saw blade whirring angrily. At the last possible second he realized it was Webb and yanked the blade back.

"What the fuck do you think you're doing?" he spat furiously as unchallenged corpses began to hurl themselves at him. "I could have killed you!"

Jas immediately shut up when he saw what was happening behind him. Suddenly able to get through again, streams of cadavers were pushing ever closer. Sandwiched between two advancing walls of dead flesh, he followed Webb to the van and dived for cover.

"Get in!" Lorna screamed, her voice so loud that it hurt. Bodies slammed against the van. One of them, half of its face eaten away by rot, glared at her with its one remaining eye and hammered against her window with greasy, leaden fists. She turned away from it in disgust, but all she could see were more equally hideous dead faces staring back through every available square inch of glass. Hollis drove forward, knocking the monsters away and powering through the crowd, thankful that they'd decided to move before the corpses had been able to bunch up tight. The entire street, which had been empty just minutes earlier, was now teeming with death—infested with hundreds of decaying cadavers.

"What the hell just happened?" Jas breathlessly asked from the back. "That was so fast."

"I guess that's the reception we're going to get wherever we go," Hollis answered, holding the steering wheel tight as they juddered through the seething crowd.

"Five minutes," Jas said. "We couldn't have been out there any longer than five minutes."

"If we're all that's left," Lorna said quietly, "then this will keep happening. Back at the flats we'd got thousands of them gathered in the one place because they knew where we were. Out here they're running wild."

25

The van powered along quiet and relatively clear rural roads having easily outrun the last of the rotting population of Cudsford. The difference here on the other side of the town was stark; there were hardly any bodies and considerably fewer wrecks and ruins than they'd seen in a long time. Hollis noticed that there were still plenty of the telltale signs of the devastation which had blighted the country, he just had to look a little harder to see them. Moss and weeds were slowly taking over here and there, encroaching on everything with greens and browns. Buildings, abandoned vehicles, and dead bodies alike would eventually be completely swallowed up and absorbed back into the landscape.

"Where's the bus?" Jas asked, anxiously looking over his shoulder. Hollis glanced into his mirror. The road behind them was empty. He slowed down—not daring to stop, despite the relative lack of bodies around them—and waited. After a few seconds the lumbering, blood-splattered bus came back into view. The sudden freedom of the open road had caught Hollis off-guard and he'd simply driven too fast.

"Here they are," he announced, accelerating again.

The wide, tree-lined road curved to the left around the foot of a large hill. Several hundred meters ahead was a traffic island, sign-posted with names which didn't mean anything to Hollis, who searched for something familiar. He thought he could remember the route to the exhibition center Driver had talked about, but like everyone else his nerves were shattered and he needed reassurance.

"Any ideas?" he asked hopefully.

"Second exit," Lorna replied, her voice sounding nervous and unsure. Hollis steered the van around the roundabout, flinching slightly as he plowed into a lone body which had foolishly tripped into his path.

"I need a piss," Jas said, banging on the side of the van.

"What do you want me to do about it?" Hollis snapped.

"Well, you could stop the van and let me out," he answered, annoyed. "I'm not going to do it in here."

"And I'm not going to stop."

"Don't be stupid, Hollis, I'm bloody desperate."

"You've got to stop," Webb chipped in. "Come on, I need to go too."

"Just piss in a bottle or something and throw it out of the window. I'm not stopping. Look what happened back there."

"That was different and you know it." Jas sighed. "That was the middle of a town, for Christ's sake. There's nothing around here."

"You reckon? Look over there."

He pointed to an area of land over to the right of another roundabout. A number of corpses were gathered outside a dilapidated petrol station and service area, milling around between the pumps and outbuildings. When they heard the noise of the engines they immediately began to herd toward the road in a ragtag group.

"So what?" Webb protested. "There's fifteen of them, twenty at most. Bloody hell, Hollis, any one of us could sort that number out on our own back at the flats."

"Yes, but we're not at the flats now, are we?"

"A corpse is a corpse. Doesn't matter where it is."

"I know that, but we don't know the area."

"It's all fields, for fuck's sake. There's nothing to know."

"Things are different when we don't know the area. Look what happened earlier. You don't want to be caught out by a hundred of them when you're stood there with your dick in your hands."

"Come on, Hollis, stop making excuses. Just stop the van for a minute so we can have a piss."

"No."

Hollis put his foot down and increased his speed, making a point and powering toward the first of the group of cadavers which had staggered out into the road. He swerved around them and accelerated again, racing ahead down a long straight, leaving the bus trundling after them, struggling to catch up.

"You fucking jerk," Webb hissed. "Just because you're scared you're going to make the rest of us suffer. You know what I hate most about you?"

"I don't give a shit Webb. Just shut up!" Hollis ordered, silencing the whining little idiot in the back as he swung the van around a sharp right-hand turn. His speed was such that two of the wheels temporarily left the ground, then crashed heavily back down. "Jesus Christ," he cursed, slamming on the brakes, bringing the speeding vehicle to a sudden, lurching halt just inches away from the side of an abandoned truck which blocked the full width of the road.

Behind him Driver had accelerated to catch up and now struggled to stop the bus in time. Jas turned around and braced himself for impact. The distance was deceptive but there was no collision, just a bloody thump when a lone corpse stumbled out in front of the still-moving bus and was hit and thrown against the back of the van. He watched as it slid slowly down the glass. By the time it had dropped to the ground the vehicle behind was still. He could see the relief on Driver's normally expressionless face.

"Oh that's just bloody perfect," Lorna moaned, looking at the obstruction in front of them. "What the hell are we supposed to do now?"

Decayed figures immediately began to converge on the two vehicles, flinging themselves forward and hammering on their metal sides.

"Now do you believe me?" Hollis shouted, turning around to face Webb and Jas in the back. "You see, according to your logic there shouldn't be any bodies around here but look, there are loads of the damn things. Do either of you want to go for your piss now?"

He was right. Inexplicably the dead were again swarming all around them. Jas didn't want to look for explanations or prolong his argument with Hollis; the sooner he got this mess sorted, he decided, the sooner he could empty his bladder. He moved quickly, climbing out of the van and grabbing a crowbar on the way, not wanting to risk the noise from the chain saw again. He slammed the door shut behind him and swung his fist at the nearest body, knocking it into the back of the van, then battered the head of another corpse into a bloody pulp with the crowbar. Many more of the pitiful creatures lurched after him, hauling themselves along on weary feet. He slipped past the bulk of them, confusing them with his speed, and ran toward the cab of the crashed truck, quickly scrambling up onto the bonnet, then climbing higher and standing on the roof.

"Can you shift it?" Hollis shouted from the van, leaning out of the window and pushing a furious cadaver away with one hand. "Is there any way around?"

Something wasn't right. Hordes of wretched bodies clamored around the vehicles, reaching up for Jas incessantly. In no more than a couple of minutes the stretch of road they'd just driven along had become a seething mass of furious, baying corpses and still more were coming. Where were they coming from and how many more were there? More important, how would they get away if he couldn't get

151

this bloody truck shifted? They'd have to move quick if they wanted to—

Hang on a second, he thought as realization suddenly dawned. The ground on the other side of the truck he was standing on was clear. Absolutely empty. There wasn't a single damn corpse anywhere to be seen. The truck had stopped in such a position that it had blocked the entire width of the carriageway, left almost perfectly at right angles to the direction of the road. Its front was pushed up close to a brick wall and its back end overlapped with the side of another similar-sized vehicle, making it impossible for anything to get past. He dropped to his knees and pressed his face against the rain-streaked windscreen. There was no body in the cab. No driver. This truck hadn't crashed here, he realized, the bloody thing had been parked!

Suddenly revitalized with energy, he jumped down onto the clear side and pulled himself up into the cab. Christ, whoever had done this had even left the keys in the ignition! He'd never driven anything of this size before but he had to act fast and do what he could. He started it up, cringing inwardly as the machine shuddered into life and the throaty roar of its powerful engine drowned out every other sound he could hear. More through luck than judgment he managed to select a reverse gear and sent the truck juddering and kangaroo-jumping back, steering hard to swerve its tail around the other vehicle which had been abandoned directly behind. Up ahead Hollis drove the van through the gap as soon as he was able. The bus also squeezed through, as did somewhere in the region of thirty scrambling bodies. Jas searched anxiously for a forward gear now, aware that every second he wasted allowed more and more of the dead to flood through after the survivors. With relief he did it, sending the truck lurching forward again, stopping just inches short of the wall and blocking up the gap, crushing another handful of spindly figures which had managed to get halfway through. He stopped the engine and sat there with his

152

head in his hands, panting with exhaustion as if he'd just run a marathon.

By the time Jas got out of the truck, the job of destroying the cadavers which had made it through the gap was well in hand. Webb, Lorna and Harte were each standing in different locations, attacking the bodies with whatever weapons they'd managed to lay their hands on. The corpses grouped around each one of them, almost seeming to taunt them by delaying their attacks momentarily. Some stood back and waited. Others, sometimes moving in twos or threes, immediately launched themselves at the nearest survivor. Hollis remained behind the wheel of the van, driving around furiously, doing all he could to wipe out as many of the dead as possible without hitting any of the others. Gordon, who had finally plucked up enough courage to emerge from the bus, quickly realized what Hollis was doing. He offered himself up to a relatively quick-moving, long-dead shell of a man. As the repellent body stumbled toward him he stepped back out of the way and watched with smug satisfaction as the van powered forward, smashing it into oblivion.

"What the hell's going on here?" Jas yelled to Lorna as he ran toward her. He tripped a corpse, kicking its legs out from under it, then stamped on its face until it stopped moving.

"What do you mean?" Lorna shouted back between gasps and grunts of effort. She shoved the grotesque remains of a schoolteacher back into the path of the van. The button-less, tattered rags of the dead woman's blouse revealed her exposed torso. Her green-blue skin was severely lacerated and what was left of her intestines hung down like a bizarre adornment to her outfit. The van plowed into her at speed, the force of the impact hurling her high into the air.

"Look around you," Jas replied, waiting for the van to pass between them and the noise to reduce.

Lorna did as he said. Until now it had been difficult to see anything through the mass of constantly shifting bodies but there were only a handful of them left now, and Hollis was doing his best to chase them down. Ignoring the chaos, for the first time she allowed herself to stop and look around at her surroundings. She was standing next to a set of traffic lights. There were signposts and yellow-hatched markings on the road and . . . and she realized that this had once been a busy junction. The road they'd been following continued through the junction with turnings to the right and left making a crossroads. But, apart from the corpses they'd just hacked down, the area was completely clear. She couldn't understand—every other stretch of road she'd seen like this had been almost waist deep in wreckage and bodies. Surely the traffic would have been busy here when everyone had died back in September? The entire junction had been cleared and every available exit sealed off. Who had done this?

Webb swung his baseball bat into the chest of the last corpse standing, sweeping it up and smashing it back against a brick wall. He yanked out his weapon and the body dropped to the ground, a bloody, deflated mass. Driver and Hollis stopped their respective vehicles and suddenly everything was quiet and still. The only noise came from the muffled thumping and banging of countless dead hands hammering against the other side of the truck.

"Which way now, then?" Gordon asked as he carefully wiped blood off his boots on a patch of overgrown grass.

"Don't know," Hollis answered, looking around for inspiration. "Whoever did this must be around here somewhere. They wouldn't have gone to all this effort if they were just going to—"

His words were interrupted by the sudden slam of a door and the rumble of an engine starting. The vehicle up ahead—a long, white and blue coach—was slowly beginning to move out of the way.

Harte grinned. "There's our answer!"

26

Hollis waited impatiently behind the wheel of the van for the driver of the coach to move out of the way. He watched intently as the long, cumbersome vehicle trundled slowly and very carefully backward, leaving the mouth of a narrow, previously unseen road open. A solitary figure stood a short distance back up the track and waved his arms, beckoning them toward him. He began to jog away, occasionally looking back over his shoulder to make sure they were following. Behind them the driver of the coach parked it back into its original position across the width of the road, then got out and climbed onto a bicycle which had been hurriedly dumped in the tall hedgerow. He pedaled furiously after the bus and the van.

"Where the hell are we going now?" Jas asked, standing at the front of the bus next to Driver's cab, swaying as they moved along the twisting track. Tall, impenetrable, leafy hedgerows lined either side of the road, preventing them from seeing anything other than what was immediately ahead and behind them.

"The Bromwell Hotel," Gordon answered, standing at his shoulder, holding onto the handrail as the bus lurched from side to side. "I thought it looked familiar."

155

"How do you know that?"

As they reached a fork in the road, Gordon pointed toward a purple sign set into the tall hedge just ahead of them. Ornate white writing proudly proclaimed the name of the hotel they were approaching and an arrow directed them to the right. The person they'd been following had already jogged away in that direction.

"I came here a few Christmases ago for an office party," Gordon answered, his voice suddenly sounding flat and unenthusiastic as he remembered the occasion. "Bloody terrible night, it was. I didn't recognize the place today. I mean, I thought we might be close, but not this close . . ."

"So what's it like, this hotel?" Jas wondered, glancing back at him. Gordon shrugged his shoulders.

"Okay I suppose. Decent enough place. The facilities were good but the food was vile. It was all that horrible nouvelle cuisine stuff—a little pile of this, a dribble of that . . . Didn't fill me up. I had to stop for a kebab on the way home. You want turkey and all the trimmings at Christmas, don't you, not a few scraps of meat and a bloody vegetable puree."

"Fuck me," Harte gasped, ignoring him and pushing past to get a better view. "Look at the state of it. Fucking brilliant!"

The bus, followed closely by the van, slowly drove around the final bend in the road. The hedgerow on their right gradually tapered in height and then disappeared altogether, revealing a large car park and, beyond that, an open expanse of grass. Ahead of them now was the hotel itself. A fairly modern, off-white building, in comparison to the grim concrete surroundings they had left this morning it was an unexpected paradise. There was space to move around outside. The windows all had glass which hadn't been smashed. The grounds appeared clear of all rubble and dead flesh. This place was an oasis of normality.

"Jesus, this is fantastic," Gordon said, all memories of his disastrous office party now long forgotten. "How many people do you think are here?"

"Don't know," Jas replied, grinning. "Thinking about it though, there must be a fair few of them, at least. There's plenty of space and the way they'd got the entrance hidden back there was genius. I think we've landed on our feet here, lads!"

The lone runner, who had just about managed to keep ahead of the vehicles, finally slowed when he reached the steps at the front of the hotel. He bent over double with his hands on his knees and breathed in deeply, the effort of the sudden sprint obviously taking its toll. He looked up as the bus and van both stopped and quickly emptied. Jas and Harte walked over to him but neither could immediately think of what to say. These people were the first new survivors they'd seen for weeks, months even. Gordon broke the uncomfortable stalemate.

"I'm Gordon," he announced, moving toward the other man with his hand outstretched. He wiped his hand on his trousers before reciprocating.

"Amir," he replied quietly, standing up straight and shaking. "Where did you all come from? Was it your helicopter?"

"Helicopter?" Hollis asked, confused. "What helicopter?"

"Christ," Harte said, "this gets better by the minute."

"We've heard it a few times now," Amir explained, "a couple of times earlier this week and again this morning. We've been trying to attract their attention. I just assumed they'd seen us and you were with them."

"We don't know anything about a helicopter," Jas interrupted. "Christ, we didn't even know about you until we nearly drove into your truck back there. Bloody hell, that must mean there are even more people left alive."

"Well, they might not have found you, but we have," Hollis said. The man riding the bike finally caught up. He jumped off, letting the bike clatter over onto its side, then walked purposefully forward and shook Hollis by the hand.

"I'm Martin Priest," he said, not letting go of Hollis's hand, still shaking furiously.

"Greg Hollis."

"It's good to meet you Greg. It's good to meet all of you. It really is so good." He brushed a wisp of unkempt hair from his narrow, bearded face and then took off his glasses and cleaned them on his sweater. Martin was short, thin, and sweating profusely. His clothing was ragged and dirty with long gray socks pulled up to his knees. Harte smirked at his bizarre dress-sense, then looked down at his own wardrobe: a curious miss-match of bike leathers, skiwear, and other, more typical garments. There seemed to be something about the end of the world, he silently decided, that made everyone dress like complete fucking idiots.

Lorna stood a short distance from the others and looked around, eyes wide with a combination of surprise, tiredness, and relief. The hotel complex looked safe and welcoming, its faux-Mediterranean appearance out of place and yet somehow still reassuring and familiar. The car park was virtually empty with just a handful of vehicles parked here and there. Harte had noticed that too.

"This couldn't have been the most popular of hotels, judging by how many cars are over there."

"More than half the rooms were occupied when it happened," Martin said. "There were more cars than this."

"So what have you done with them all?"

"We used them to block the roads and entrances. They've been useful."

"How come everything's so . . ." she began to ask before losing herself in her question.

"Clear?" suggested Martin.

"Empty?" added Amir.

"Quiet?" said Gordon.

"No, it's more than that . . ."

"What have you done with all the fucking bodies?" Webb grunted, successfully putting Lorna's feelings into words with surprising perception and his trademark lack of tact. "You got rid of them all?"

"Couldn't do that," Martin answered. "I don't know what it's like where you've come from, but there are far too many of them around here for that."

"So where are they?" Lorna asked.

"The grounds of the hotel are enclosed," he explained. "We blocked up the entrances like you saw back there, then tricked them into going elsewhere."

"Martin used to work here," Amir added.

"Believe me, I know every inch of these grounds. Before all this happened I was chief groundsman and—"

"What do you mean, 'tricked them'?" Hollis asked, cutting across him.

"Well, they're not the brightest of sparks, are they? It doesn't take much to distract them."

"So what did you do?" he pressed, intrigued.

"Did you see the fork in the road just now? The road runs right the way around the western edge of the grounds," he explained, gesturing with his arm. "Over there and to the north is a golf course, a full eighteen holes' worth of empty space. We've blocked the other end of the road to stop them getting through and made a few gaps in the fence around the golf course to let them onto the greens."

"And how's that helped?" Gordon wondered.

"You know what those golfers are like," he explained.

"Were like," Gordon corrected.

"More money than sense, half of them," he continued. "They built

159

themselves a lovely clubhouse. Beautiful place, it is. Huge. There's a track leads from the road right around to the kitchens at the back of the building."

"Get to the fucking point," Webb grumbled impatiently.

"The point is we can get inside the building and they can't."

"Still don't understand how that makes any difference," Lorna grumbled, obviously unimpressed.

"It's simple, really. I play music to them and they think we're in the clubhouse."

"You play music?" Gordon said in disbelief. "Are you serious?"

"I don't stand there with a guitar serenading them, if that's what you're thinking. We set up a couple of portable generators and I leave CDs playing on repeat until the fuel runs out. They think we're sitting in the clubhouse so they crowd around it and stay away from here. Because there are so many of them and so few ways onto the golf course, once they get through the holes in the fence, it's almost impossible for them to get back. Might sound a little unusual, but it works."

"There's no doubting that," Jas muttered under his breath.

"I have to go up there two or three times a day to change the music and refill the generators, but—"

"Sorry, but can we get inside?" Caron asked nervously. "I don't care if there aren't any of them around, I don't like standing out here."

Martin moved first, picking up his bike and leading the way to the front of the hotel complex. He took them inside, up a few low stone steps and through a wide glass door with arched windows on either side into a long, open-plan reception area. Lorna collapsed onto a dusty brown leather sofa and gazed at her surroundings, still unable to take it all in.

"You okay?" Hollis asked, concerned. She looked at him and smiled.

"Just trying to get my head around everything. I never thought we'd find anywhere like this."

"If you could all just check in at reception," Martin laughed as he leaned his bike against the side of the ornate wooden desk, "I'll get your keys and have someone take you up to your rooms!"

Amir shook his head and sighed. "Silly bastard, he's been waiting to say that to someone since we first got here!"

Harte looked around anxiously. He could hear something. It was a *clack-clack-clack*ing sound coming toward them along a corridor on their right. It didn't sound human, but it was moving much too quickly to be one of the dead. He instinctively looked around for a weapon, but immediately relaxed when the source of the sound appeared. A scruffy, black and white, medium-sized dog with short, wiry fur and a tatty red collar poked its head through the doorway then walked forward again, its claws rapping against the terra-cotta floor tiles as it moved. It stopped and cocked its head to one side, then glanced back over its shoulder. More footsteps, heavier this time and much slower. A tall and stocky, red-faced man who was hopelessly out of breath entered the room and grabbed hold of the dog's collar.

"Wow," he said simply, shaking his head with disbelief when he saw the size of the crowd gathered in reception.

"This is Howard Reece," Martin said, introducing him. Howard shuffled forward.

"Good to see you all," he wheezed, relaxing and letting go of the dog again. It walked over to Lorna and began to sniff at her dirty, bloodstained trouser legs and boots. She leaned down and stroked its head.

"Beautiful dog," she said, ruffling its short fur. "What's its name?"

"I just call it Dog," Howard replied.

"Original," Jas said.

"She doesn't care. I never wanted her. Bloody thing just attached herself to me when all this started," he explained, "and now I can't get rid of her."

"She's good to have around," Martin continued. "She's got a good nose on her. She sniffs out the dead for us."

"What?"

"They freak her out, send her wild."

"They freak us all out," Harte mumbled.

"But she catches their scent earlier than we do. She lets us know when they're close."

"But what about her barking? Isn't it a risk having her around?"

"She's not stupid," Howard said as the dog padded back over to him and sat down at his feet. "She had a couple of close calls early on when they first started to react to us. She knows not to make any noise but she lets you know when they're near. You can see it in her face and the way she moves."

"Bullshit," Webb said. The dog just looked at him.

"So where's everyone else?" Jas asked, keen to get back to more important issues.

"In the restaurant," Amir answered. "Follow me."

He led the group across the reception area and into a corridor directly opposite the one from which Howard and his dog had just appeared. In silence they walked along a wall full of windows which looked out onto an enclosed courtyard—half-paved, half-lawn. Hollis noticed a sign on the wall at the foot of a glass-fronted staircase which pointed to WEST WING - ROOMS 1–42. He assumed that the similar-looking part of the complex on the directly opposite side of the courtyard—an identical staircase at either end, three floors, many equally-spaced windows—was the east wing, and that it almost certainly had a comparable number of rooms to the west. He looked up at the mass of rectangular windows he could see from ground level.

Christ, he thought, *more than eighty rooms. If just a quarter of them are occupied then we've more than doubled our number.* He remembered the disorientation, desperation, and cold fear he'd felt on the day everyone had died, and how much easier everything had felt when he'd finally found other survivors. *The more people I'm with,* he'd long since decided, *the easier the ride should be.* The potential of using the hotel as a long-term base was immediately apparent, as it surely had been for everyone else who had ended up here. It was strong, safe, secure, and a damn sight more comfortable than the flats where he'd spent almost all of his time since the infection had first struck. Proper beds, space to move around freely, kitchens, and no bodies . . .

"Swimming pool," Jas said, grinning as they passed another sign on the wall.

"Out of action," Martin immediately told him. "I'll show you around properly later."

"All this space," Caron mused, looking across the courtyard at the three-story block of bedrooms, trying to decide where she wanted her room to be. Now this was more like it. She'd become used to living her life surrounded by waste and rubbish. The interior of the hotel, however, appeared relatively well-kept. Sure it was dusty and everything smelled stale, and it might have only been a two-star hotel when she was used to three at least, preferably four, but the floors were clean and the rooms she'd so far seen were tidy and, if she really was condemned to spend the rest of her days suffering and scavenging with these people, at least it looked like she'd now be able to separate herself from them from time to time. Imagine that—the luxury of being able to close and lock the door behind her and shut everyone else out. She was sick of trying (and failing) to look after people and clean up for them and sort out their pointless, petty squabbles. Maybe now she could just stop and spend her time looking after herself.

At the end of the corridor a sudden sharp-right turn led the group along the farthest and shortest edge of the rectangular courtyard,

163

parallel with the reception area they'd originally entered. They passed an empty meeting room and a bar. The rows of half-full optics behind the wooden counter caught the attention of several of the new arrivals. Webb attempted to make a quick detour but was jostled back on course by Harte. They followed Amir through a set of swinging double doors into a restaurant. Two people—a middle-aged woman and a tall, thin, and much younger man—immediately got up from where they'd been sitting slouched around a table playing cards and walked toward them.

"Ginnie and Sean," Amir announced. Harte acknowledged them with a nod and looked hopefully around the large, empty room.

"Where are the others?" he asked.

"There are no others," Martin replied. "Just the five of us."

"And a dog," Webb added unhelpfully.

"That's all?" Jas said, surprised. "Just five?"

"Yes," he answered. "I was working here when it happened and Howard found me a couple of days later. We found Ginnie and Amir when we were out looking for supplies, and Sean found us when he heard us driving around."

"So that's it?"

Martin appeared perplexed. "You sound disappointed."

"I am," he admitted. "This place is great. I thought there'd be loads of people here."

"Well, we haven't exactly been broadcasting the fact that we are here very loudly. We don't want those things out there to start dragging themselves back over to us."

"But what about when you go out? Have you not looked for anyone else?"

"We don't go out," he answered abruptly. "It's too dangerous. We'll go back out there when the time's right."

"You need food, though."

"We've got enough."

"But how do you get—"

"We manage. We don't need to go outside or make any noise or do anything that might risk what we've got here," Martin said, sounding both aggressive and defensive at the same time.

"We do have one other resident," Howard said cryptically. "I think we should tell them about her, Martin. We don't want them stumbling into her in the dark, do we?"

Hollis felt the hairs on the back of his neck stand on end.

"Come this way," Martin said, his voice a little calmer. "I'll introduce you to the Swimmer."

27

Hollis and Harte followed Martin deeper into the hotel complex. Howard's dog walked alongside them, constantly sniffing at the air.

"You've got the pool, a gym, and a small sauna room down here," Martin explained. "None of it's any use without power, I'm afraid. We hardly ever come up here, actually, only to see her."

"I don't like the sound of this," Harte admitted, his voice low. His head was rapidly filling with all kinds of unsavory thoughts: necrophilia, torture, some other kind of weird perversion he hadn't even thought of . . . He had no idea what they were about to find going on in the dark and shadowy depths of the hotel.

"The dog usually follows when anyone comes down here," Martin continued. "She thinks she's protecting us—not that we need it, of course." He stopped walking as the cream-walled, windowless corridor began to curve away to the right. The smell here was noticeably worse—a noxious combination of stagnant water and dead flesh—and the light levels were uncomfortably low. He beckoned them farther forward and then gestured toward a narrow rectangular window set in the wall. He peered cautiously through the glass.

"What's going on?" Hollis demanded, his nerves getting the better of him. Martin scowled and lifted his finger to his lips. The dog padded forward, clearly agitated. They could see what Howard meant now—the animal was pacing up and down below the window, snarling but not making a noise. "Does that mean there's a body in there?"

On Martin's instruction he stepped up to the glass and looked into a dark office, illuminated only by a few slender beams of light trickling through a grime-covered skylight. Something was moving in the farthest corner of the untidy room. He couldn't make it out at first, but when it shifted again he saw that it was a corpse. In the low light its appearance was muted and indistinct: female, perhaps a little shorter than he was, short blond hair, wearing only a swimming costume discolored through weeks of putrefaction. He was distracted when Harte shoved him to one side so he could look in. The sudden movement seemed to agitate the corpse, which lunged forward and threw itself at the glass with surprising speed and aggression, slamming against the window and leaving a smeared, face-shaped stain. It took a few stumbling steps backward, then stopped and stood swaying on its unsteady feet, staring at Harte with dull black eyes.

"She likes you!" Hollis smirked, watching with equal amounts fascination and disgust as the cadaver stumbled back into the shadows. He felt a surprising sadness, perhaps even pity for the abhorrent creature. Who had it once been? Why had she been at the hotel? On holiday or business? Had she been here alone or were the bodies of her family nearby? He found it strange that he was suddenly asking himself so many questions about this one particular carcass when he'd seen thousands upon thousands of them before and not given a damn. Had he come across this poor bitch outside he probably wouldn't have wasted another thought on her—he'd have gone straight for her head with whatever weapon he'd had and he'd have beaten her until she stopped moving. Maybe it was because she was isolated and trapped here that he felt different? Perhaps it was because he could watch her without fear of attack?

As she moved away he noticed that she had a tattoo on her right shoulder blade, just visible next to the strap of her swimming costume. Her skin had an unnatural, mottled blue-green tone, but he could just make out the faded outline of Winnie the Pooh. He hadn't expected that. Seeing the tattoo increased the strength of his confusing feelings. It reminded him that the lump of dead flesh in front of him had once been a living, breathing human being like him with friends, family, likes, dislikes, passions, and vices. Now look at it . . .

"She was a guest here," Martin said quietly, gently forcing his way between the other two men. "I saw her the day before it all happened. Good-looking girl, she was."

"So how did you get her in there?" Harte asked.

"I didn't," he replied. "She got herself trapped. The changing rooms are on the other side of this office. Poor cow must have been getting ready to swim when it killed her. She must have been bloody terrified and dragged herself in here looking for help. Probably the last thing she did."

Hollis and Harte continued to stare at the pitiful creature in the shadows. Her movements were slow but appeared definite and considered. She was more coordinated than many of the bodies they'd come across previously. There had been others which had exhibited a similar level of control—some even more so—but they'd never had the opportunity to study any of them at such close quarters and without fear of attack.

"So why is she here?" wondered Harte. "Why haven't you got rid of her? Have you got a thing for dead women in swimming costumes?"

Martin ignored his cheap jibe.

"She's protected in here. She's useful."

"Useful? How exactly?"

"She's like a human barometer."

"What the hell are you talking about?"

"You know what a barometer is, don't you?"

"'Course I do," Harte said quickly, offended, "but what's a dead body got to do with the weather?"

"Absolutely nothing," Martin explained. "It's not about the weather, it's about their behavior."

"You can study them without going outside." Hollis said, beginning to understand. "You can see what they're doing without getting too close."

"Exactly."

"But what would you want to study them for?" Harte grunted ignorantly. "You're never going to find a cure, or a reason why it happened, or—"

"No, nothing like that," Martin interrupted, shaking his head and beginning to lose his patience. "That girl in there is protected from the elements. She's still decaying, but there's nothing in there to speed up the decay like wind or rain. That means—"

"—that she's probably stronger and in better condition than most of the corpses outside," Hollis said.

"Maybe not stronger, but she's certainly in better physical shape than most of them."

"So what you've got in there is the worst-case scenario?"

"Something like that. By watching her and how she reacts, we can get an idea of how the rest of them are going to respond next time we have to head out from here. We can see what they're going to start doing even before they've started doing it!"

"So what have you learnt?" Harte asked, still not taking his eyes off the corpse.

"That they're becoming more violent and they're starting to make decisions."

"Is that all? We could have told you that."

"And they think we're a threat."

"And?"

"And we're not going outside again until we absolutely have to. We're going to make our supplies last and sit this thing out."

28

Gordon, Webb, and Caron, along with Ginnie, Sean, and Amir, began to unload food from the back of the bus. With six uncoordinated people trying to get in and out through the bus and hotel doors, frequent bottlenecks formed. After working hard (by his low standards) for almost half an hour, Webb took advantage of one such brief and unexpected delay to disappear for a smoke, stopping only to grab a four-pack of beer from a cardboard box he'd been keeping a very close eye on. Sean noticed him leaving and followed him around the side of the building, out of view of the others. He found Webb sitting on a low wall, opening a can of beer and lighting a cigarette.

"Fuck me," he cursed as Sean suddenly appeared. "You scared the shit out of me!"

"Sorry, mate," Sean said apologetically.

"Thought you were one of the others come to find out why I'm skiving."

Sean shook his head. "Nah, I just felt like having a break and it looked like you'd had the same idea."

"Smoke?"

"No thanks. I'll have a beer, though."

Webb threw a can over to him.

"Cheers," he said, swigging on his drink. It was the first beer Sean had had for a couple of weeks since they'd run out. God, it tasted damn good.

"So how have things been here?" Webb asked.

"Boring," Sean replied.

"Boring?" Webb repeated, surprised. "You've got to be fucking kidding me! It's the end of the fucking world! There are millions of dead bodies out there trying to rip us apart—how can it be boring?"

"Do you see any bodies here?" Sean said, knocking back more beer and sitting down next to Webb.

"Fair point, but you must have had to deal with some of them? Christ, we've been surrounded by thousands of the fucking things for weeks."

"I got here before they really started to turn," he explained. "We've seen Martin's pet corpse and how she's changed, and we've seen others fighting from the window, but we've just stayed put."

"For nearly two months?"

"Something like that."

Webb couldn't believe what he was hearing. Next to him, Sean shivered with cold. He was dressed in a thin hooded fleece, T-shirt, jeans, and trainers. Webb, in comparison, was still wearing his heavy boots and blood-soaked biker trousers. He looked like he'd been fighting the dead for weeks on end without a moment's rest. Sean looked like he'd just got home from college.

"Don't know how you've done it, mate. I'd have gone out of my fucking mind."

"It's not the bodies that get to me," Sean quickly said, glad to finally have a chance to say what he thought, "it's that lot in there. They're so fucking cautious. It's sit here, do this, don't make a noise, keep your head down . . . I'm fucking sick of it."

"Can't you just walk?"

"What?"

"Can't you just get out of here for a bit? I did it when we were back at the flats. I either used to sit in the car or find a few bodies to beat up."

"You went looking for them?"

"Sometimes. It was pretty easy where we were. I'd get ahold of a few of them and batter the fuckers until there was nothing left but a pile of blood and bones."

"Don't know if I could do that."

"Don't be so fucking soft! Of course you could. It's not difficult. Bloody things are dead. As long as you don't do anything stupid you'll be fine."

"But they killed one of your people, didn't they? I heard someone say the bodies killed a man."

Webb took another swig of beer and looked out toward the horizon, avoiding eye contact.

"That's right," he answered, not wanting to say anything else about Stokes's death but feeling obliged to keep talking to cover his tracks. "I was with him when it happened, poor bastard."

"So is that why you're here?"

"Suppose. That and the germs."

"Germs?"

"Couple of the girls got sick and died. We got away before anyone else got ill."

"Shit, I didn't realize."

"And you're telling me you're bored?"

Sean looked down at his feet, feeling suddenly foolish and naïve. He couldn't deny his frustration, nor how the increasingly intense and relentless claustrophobia was getting to him. He'd risk putting his neck on the line just to get away for a while. Christ, what he'd have given to have seen some of the action Webb had described.

"They sit around at night and play cards, for fuck's sake," he moaned. "I tell you, it's like being on a day trip to the end of the world with your fucking grandparents!"

"What about when you go out for supplies?"

"You're kidding, aren't you? We don't. They *won't*."

"What d'you mean?"

"What do you think I mean? You've already heard Martin—he goes mental if you even mention it."

"So how long's it been since you last left here?"

"I haven't. Got here less than a week after it started and I haven't been anywhere since. I'm going out of my fucking mind."

"So just go!"

Sean didn't say anything for a few moments. He drank more of his beer, got up, walked away, and then stopped and turned back to face Webb.

"I can't," he reluctantly admitted.

"Why? Scared of what the folks will say?"

"No, it's not that."

"I tell you, mate, the whole fucking world is out there for the taking. If all you're gonna do is sit here and moan about it, you might as well roll over and end it right now."

29

Eight o'clock. Pitch black outside. Everywhere silent. The entire group sat around tables in the restaurant and ate. Howard's dog prowled up and down, sniffing the air hungrily and grabbing at whatever scraps happened to fall her way, but the amount of waste was negligible. Those who had been living in the hotel were starving, the meager rations they'd so far survived on were nothing compared to the relative riches the others had brought with them.

"I never used to like tomatoes," Ginnie said excitedly as she helped herself to another serving of lukewarm chopped, canned tomatoes, "but my God, this tastes good!"

Caron and Hollis exchanged glances across the table. What had these people been eating? Caron asked the question.

"Not much," Howard replied, just visible in the candlelight at the other end of the table. "I reckon I've lost a couple of stone." He lifted up his baggy sweater to reveal an equally baggy T-shirt. "Few more stones to go yet, mind," he added, patting his wide belly.

"I don't understand why you haven't just gone out for supplies," Harte said. "There's a town just down the road, you could have been there and back in a couple of hours. And you've got those trucks too.

If you'd filled one of them you'd have had enough to last you weeks, months even."

"We just haven't wanted to risk going out there," Martin answered. "Okay, so we've gone hungry, but none of us are starving and we've been safe so far. I know what I'd rather have."

"I'd have risked it," Sean said from a table a short distance away where he was sitting with Webb and Jas.

"We all agreed, Sean," Martin sighed. "There were only five of us here. We'd have been taking too much of a chance."

"*You* all agreed," he protested. "I don't remember getting to have much of a say. You'd decided before I even knew you were having a discussion."

"It was for the best, Sean. Come on, son, everything's worked out okay, hasn't it?"

Sean grunted and carried on eating. He found it a little easier to stay calm and not lose his temper now that he wasn't so hungry. Christ, it was good to taste so many different flavors again. It was all tins and packaged convenience food, but it was more than he'd had in a long time. And beer! Although the lager made the cold night feel colder still, the numbing effect of the alcohol was worth it.

"There are more of us here now," Amir said quietly. "Kind of changes things, doesn't it?"

"Does it?" Martin asked, thoughtfully chewing a mouthful of food.

"Of course it does. Now there's more than twice as many of us, maybe we could risk going out?"

"We don't need to. They've brought plenty of stuff with them."

"You think?" Jas interrupted. "We brought as much with us as we could, but it's not going to last forever. Seems to me we've got no choice but to go out some point."

"You don't understand. It's not as easy as that."

"I do understand. I understand perfectly well. I understand that

176

if we're all going to stay here then we're going to need a lot more food than we've got at present, and I also understand the bodies a lot better than you do too. We've dealt with thousands of them at a time."

"But it's not as black and white as you're making it sound," Martin protested. "Our safety relies on them not knowing we're here. If you go out there and start throwing your weight around, you'll attract their attention and before you know it—"

"I think we're talking about one trip outside, two at the most. Surely that's not going to have too much of an effect if you keep playing your music to them?"

"They're starting to work things out," Hollis warned. "You can't just assume that—"

"There's no need to go outside," Martin repeated, his voice tense but still low. "We just need to show some self-control. A little discipline. Make the food that we've already got here last—"

"One trip out and one busload of supplies will make all the difference." Jas sighed wearily, already growing tired of the conversation. At the mention of his bus Driver stirred in the corner. Jas glanced across at him. Bloody waster was fast asleep with his paper over his face, backside on one chair, feet up on another. He'd barely even eaten anything.

"Jas is right," Harte agreed. "The risks are small but the potential rewards are huge. We could set ourselves up here for months."

"Oh, so we're definitely staying, are we?" Lorna asked, disgruntled. She'd been following the conversation with disinterest. After spending the best part of two months trapped with most of these men she'd begun to find their relentless arguments and indecision incredibly tiring, and the men they'd found here seemed no better. Put more than two men in a room together and make a suggestion, she'd long ago discovered, and they'll spend hours debating the most obvious points before finally deciding you were right all along and claiming they'd had the idea in the first place. She'd grown tired of the way they seemed to feel obliged to take charge then blunder their way through every situation trying to convince themselves, and everyone else, that they knew what they were doing. "Not that I have a problem with staying here," she explained. "It just would have been nice to have been consulted, that's all."

"No one's decided anything," Hollis said.

"You see?" Sean interrupted angrily. "That's exactly what I'm talking about. They're doing to her exactly what you do to me all the time. You think you always know what's best and I can't stand it."

"Keep the noise down, Sean," Martin warned, cringing at the volume of his voice.

"No one's decided anything," Hollis repeated.

"I have," Caron said quietly. "I don't know about the rest of you, but I think I'll be staying here." The faces in the room all turned to look in her direction. "I don't mind going without much food until those things outside have disappeared. I'd rather starve and be safe, and if we're away from the bodies then there's less chance of anyone else catching whatever it was that killed Ellie and Anita. We've got space here and I can have my own room with four strong walls and windows which aren't smashed and—"

"Ellie and Anita?" Ginnie asked.

"They caught some kind of germ from the bodies," Hollis explained dismissively.

"All the more reason to stay inside," Martin quickly interjected.

"Are you sure it was from the bodies?" Ginnie wondered anxiously. "There's no chance you could have brought it here with you? The last thing we need is—"

"They caught it from the bodies," Hollis said firmly. "They must have. And if there are fewer bodies here, then there's little chance of anyone catching anything."

"Caron's right," Gordon agreed, yawning. "We'll struggle to find anywhere better than this. And the fact that you've kept the bodies at bay is an added bonus. The safety's got to be worth a little discomfort."

"You're just too scared to go outside, Gord," Webb said. "It's got nothing to do with the bodies or how much food there is."

"We'll keep watching the Swimmer," Martin said. "If she looks like she's going to start causing problems then we'll know it's time to change our plans."

"The bodies are falling apart. They're going to become less of a problem, not more," Ginnie said, helping herself to more food.

"Don't count on it," Harte started to say before being interrupted.

"One of them bit me," Webb said, suddenly animated, "and they killed Stokes."

"Christ, change the bloody record, will you?" Hollis sighed.

"Well, I'm staying put," Caron said again, standing her ground admirably. "You can all go back outside if you want to. I've got a suitcase full of books, a comfortable bed, and all the time in the world."

"What you've done here is incredible, and I think we'd be stupid not to stay," Hollis agreed, "but I also think we need to get out and get supplies. It's like Jas said—one properly coordinated trip out there and we could set ourselves up for weeks, maybe even months. Just think about it, safety *and* comfort."

"But it's taken weeks to get the bodies away from here," Howard protested. "You're just going to bring them straight back again."

"Sure, we'll excite a few hundred of them, but once we're back we'll batten down the hatches and sit and wait for them to disappear. Martin can keep playing his music to them and within a couple of days no one will be any the wiser."

"Makes sense. I'm in," Amir volunteered, surprising the other residents of the hotel.

"And me," Sean agreed quickly before anyone else had a chance to speak.

30

Martin stood outside at the back of the kitchens, sheltering from the wind behind an overflowing waste bin, and tucked his trousers into his socks. He pulled on a hat, zipped up his warmest coat and dragged his bike out of the passageway where he stored it. The world was reassuringly dull and gloomy and he was pleased. He liked it like that. It was early morning and no one else had yet emerged from the individual bedrooms they'd claimed as their own late last night. His breath condensed in icy clouds around his face as he straddled the bike and listened and waited. There it was. Thank God for that, he could still just about hear it in the distance. He always found it easier to do this when the music was still playing. His heart thumping in his chest and his mouth dry with nerves, he began to pedal away from the hotel.

He'd ridden this route so many times now that he'd carved a muddy furrow across the once well-tended gardens and lawns at the back of the main building, right the way over to the boundary fence. Slowing down as he reached the edge of the estate, he edged his front wheel forward through the gap he'd made, looked up and down the empty road on the other side, then pushed through and began pedaling again. It was easier now that the ground beneath his wheels was solid and even. He could move quickly and with much less effort here and he felt relatively safe, shielded from the rest of the world and the risk of attack by the thick, virtually impenetrable hedgerows on either side of the road. He could occasionally see them moving on the golf course through the gaps between the branches and leaves—those stupid, staggering, aimless creatures—but he remained invisible to them. They'd blocked both ends of the road with cars belonging to dead hotel guests and nothing was going to get through.

He could clearly hear the music now, a beautiful, lilting tune carried gently on the air, underscored by the steady belching *thump-thump-thump* of a generator. Only one of the stereos was still playing. The fuel must have already run out in the generator powering the other machine, he decided. Good job he'd got access to plenty more from the various vehicles abandoned locally. He and Howard had built up a store close to the back of the clubhouse. Enough, he hoped, for several trips a day for a few more weeks at least. *I have to keep the music playing*, he told himself as he filled two fuel cans. *It's vital.*

Up ahead, Martin could now see the turning in the track which led to the back of the clubhouse. His heart started to race again. Christ, he hated being this close to the dead. He didn't want to look at them, didn't want to give them eye contact for even a split second, and yet at the same time he had to keep watching. He had to stay alert and on guard, although he didn't know what he'd do if he found himself face to face with any of them. Clearing the hotel of stiff, mannequin-like bodies before they'd got up and started moving again had been one thing, but dealing with the obnoxious creatures they had subsequently become was a different matter altogether.

Originally a tradesman's entrance into the clubhouse for those who couldn't afford to walk through the front door, this sheltered way, fenced off and hidden from the rest of the building, had previously allowed deliveries to be made and refuse to be collected without the overprivileged club members being disturbed by the staff. Today it allowed Martin to get inside without being seen—and how he loved walking through the clubhouse once he was there. For too long this place had been the exclusive retreat of the overpaid and underworked, and he felt a deep, smug satisfaction knowing that he'd survived when the golf club members, no matter how rich they'd been, had almost certainly all died. A man who loved the outdoors and who couldn't understand why so many acres of beautiful land had been reserved for a select few to traipse around hitting little balls into holes, he used to hate golfers with almost as much venom as he now hated the dead.

Martin stood at the bottom of the staircase and listened to the stirring classical music blasting out from the floor above. The illumination downstairs was negligible, all of the windows having been blocked up and the doors shut and barred to prevent the corpses from catching sight of him whenever he was there. More important, it stopped him from having to look at them. He knew they were out there. Hundreds of them, probably thousands, their rotting faces pressed hard against the sides of the building, hammering continually on the walls with leaden, unresponsive hands.

He took a deep breath and quickly climbed the mud-splattered but luxuriously carpeted stairs, carrying the cans of fuel and passing the expensively framed portraits of numerous dead golf captains as he jogged along the landing toward the meeting room where he'd set up the first stereo. It was cold and damp in the large rectangular room, all of the windows having been propped wide open to spread the noise and fumes as far as possible. Working quickly, he refuelled the still-warm generator and fired it up again, drawing comfort from the volume of its constant chugging noise. Once power had been restored he moved over to the stereo which he'd left on a table just far enough inside to be sheltered from the wind and rain. With cold hands he restarted the disc, checked the volume was at maximum and switched it to repeat.

Martin stepped back as the music began to blare out from the stereo, the volume cranked to such a deafening level that the speakers rattled and the sound crackled with distortion. It didn't matter; as long as it was loud enough to attract the dead and keep them here he didn't care what it sounded like. For a moment longer he stopped and listened to the music—the first track of a country music compilation CD he used to listen to in his car. Sean had joked that his taste in music would probably drive the dead away rather than draw them closer. Cheeky little bastard.

Moving faster now, he ran across the landing to the administration office where he'd left the second stereo sitting on a windowsill. He repeated his well-rehearsed refuelling operation and leaned back against the wall once the music began to play again, feeling protected by the screeching, jarring, cacophony of noise which now filled the entire building. On their own each CD was, in his humble opinion, a masterpiece. Played together and accompanied by the generator noise, however, they sounded ear-splittingly awful.

Should he look?

Some days it was easy, other days he didn't want to do it. He wasn't sure today. He had been feeling a little more confident since the others had arrived yesterday, but at the same time their spontaneity, bravado, and noise made him feel uneasy and unsure. At least if he looked outside today he'd have an idea of the size of the crowd that had gathered on the golf course. He hadn't wanted to look for a week or so, maybe longer. In fact he couldn't remember when he'd last done it. Most days he preferred to try and convince himself that all he'd see out there would be the well-tended greens and freshly mown, rolling fairways. Maybe he should just have a quick look this morning . . .

"Been far?" Hollis asked Martin as he wheeled his bike back through the kitchens.

183

"Jesus Christ!" the older man gasped, holding onto a stainless steel worktop for support, "You scared the hell out of me. What are you doing down here at this time of morning?"

"More to the point," Hollis said, standing up and walking closer so that he didn't have to shout, "what are you doing out on a bloody bicycle at this hour?"

"I told you yesterday," he replied, his composure returning. "Playing music. First refuelling trip of the day."

"Many of them about out there?"

"Enough. Didn't hang around to do a head count. Can't stand the sight of them."

"You and me both. So is it working?"

"Seems to be. I guess the fact that there aren't any here indicates that it is."

"Fair point. Good plan, actually."

"I think so."

"You've managed to channel them away and keep them at a distance."

"Keeping them at a distance is just about the best we can do, I think. There are too many to try doing anything else."

"Try telling that to Webb."

"What?"

"Bit of a loose cannon, is our Webb. Where we've just come from we had crowds right around the front of the building. He seemed to think he had to get rid of them all, or at least enough to be able to push them back."

"That's never going to work, is it?"

"Suppose not. I thought it might for a while. Most of us got involved when he first suggested it, but it was obvious pretty quickly that it wasn't going to happen. It would have taken us years."

"All you're doing is winding them up. You're just showing them where you are and inviting them to come pay you a visit."

"Like I said, try telling Webb."

"Your friend's not very bright, is he?"

"He's not very bright and he's definitely not my friend," Hollis said, looking around at the empty racks and shelves. "I'll tell you something, though, Martin, at the risk of sounding like a broken record: we do need to get out of here and get supplies. We're going to sit here and starve if we don't."

Martin's heart sank. Not again, he thought. Since the others had arrived yesterday, and after the conversation they'd had last night, he'd thought about little else. As much as he didn't want to admit it, he knew that Hollis was right. For the sake of a few hours out in the open they could improve their situation here dramatically. The thought of having to survive on the pitiful scraps they had left in the hotel stores was depressing. Last night they'd eaten something resembling a proper meal. Sure, none of it was fresh and it had been thrown together, but it was the best food he'd had for weeks. He'd felt re-energized afterward and some company, a few glasses of wine, and a long-overdue cigarette had, for a while, made him feel almost human again.

"You're right," he begrudgingly admitted.

31

Caron sat on the end of her bed and held her head in her hands. She was exhausted. It didn't make sense: the most comfortable bed she'd had in almost two months, the safest surroundings, fresh faces, no crowds of dead bodies, and yet she still hadn't been able to sleep. Truth was she couldn't clear her head enough to switch off, not even for a few precious minutes. Every time she closed her eyes she pictured Ellie, Anita, her son Matthew, or any of the others she'd let down recently.

Caron's room was the first on the second floor of the west wing. Its corner position afforded her an impressive and expansive view to the front and side of the hotel. She stood up and walked to the window, keen to benefit from the limited heat of the sun which had just begun to peek out through a layer of heavy cloud. The carpet felt unexpectedly warm and soft under her feet. She couldn't remember the last time she'd been able to walk around barefoot. The view outside was clear and uninterrupted and allowed her to see for miles back in the direction from which they'd arrived yesterday. She couldn't see anything recognizable, just hills and fields and open space. She tried to look even farther into the distance, right out toward the horizon. Somewhere out there, she remembered sadly, was the dilapidated building they'd left behind and, inside it, the sick girl they'd abandoned. Sure, she knew that Ellie had been dying and there was nothing more she could have done to help her, but had she really deserved to be left alone like that? Had she even been alone? Had those godforsaken monstrosities which tirelessly dragged themselves along the streets somehow managed to force their way even farther up the hill and into the building? Had they found her and torn her limb from limb, ripping her to pieces as they had done Stokes? Even worse, what if she'd recovered from her illness? Imagine that, finally coming out of her feverish malaise and finding herself alone with no way of following the others or even knowing in which direction they'd gone. Whatever had happened to Ellie—and she hoped for her sake that she'd died a quick and relatively painless death—Caron felt like shit.

She turned away from the window and entered the small bathroom on the other side of the room. She switched the light on instinctively, despite knowing full well that the electricity had been off for weeks. She flicked the switch down again, feeling unnecessarily foolish and angry, and shoved the door open as wide as it would go, hoping that the sunlight would stretch far enough across the room to reach the bathroom. The sink and the mirror above it were partially illuminated by daylight. She wiped the dust-covered glass clean with an equally dusty towel which had been left draped over the edge of the bath by a long-since-dead housekeeper, then stared at her own reflection. Christ, she looked old this morning. Perhaps it was the light and shadow? Maybe it was the fact that she no longer used the creams and lotions and makeup that she'd treated her skin with for years? Maybe it was just because her life had become a relentless and unbearable nightmare that she looked so bad? Whatever the reason, she dumped the towel angrily in the sink and went back and laid down on the bed.

Caron's stomach was knotted tight with nerves. She'd last felt like this a couple of years back when she'd discovered that her husband had been sleeping with Sue Richards, the receptionist from the doctor's surgery. It hadn't been his deceit or lies which had hurt her—in fact, their sex life had already deteriorated to such an extent that it was something of a relief that he'd found himself an alternative channel to vent his pent-up sexual frustrations. Instead, Caron had struggled with keeping the secret and maintaining a façade. She'd found it almost impossible to carry the weight of the pretense when both she and Bob had decided it would be better for all concerned—particularly Matthew—if they just pretended his little indiscretion (actually numerous little indiscretions) hadn't happened at all. She'd hated sleeping in the same bed as him when she despised him, hated him touching her when he made her skin crawl, hated forcing herself to speak civilly to him when all she wanted to do was scream in his face and tell him to fuck off and die. Strange that she should feel so similar today. As she buried her face in her pillow she decided it was because, like her dead husband Bob, all these other people wanted her to pretend to be someone she wasn't. They all thought she was capable of things which, in reality, she couldn't do. Ellie and Anita thought she'd help them. Matthew thought she'd always look after him . . .

So this is it, she thought to herself, rolling over again and looking up at the ceiling. *This is your best chance—your last chance—to make something of what's left. Do you take it, or is it time to give up and admit defeat?*

It was a difficult decision. Her instinct was to continue to fight and try to survive, but her brain was saying something else entirely. Was there any point in fighting if there was no longer anything worth surviving for? If the events of the last few days were anything to go by then probably not. But here, out in the middle of nowhere in this unexpected oasis of corpse-free space and silence, there was the slightest chance that things might actually prove to be different. Yesterday evening Ginnie had alluded to her finally having someone to help her in the kitchen "looking after the boys." Caron had balked at the idea, telling her she was sick of playing mother hen all the time. And that, she decided, was the decision she would ultimately have to make: did she try and survive to make things easier for everyone else, or for herself? Without thinking, on the bedside table she'd arranged a symbolic representation of her ultimate choice. On one side was a bottle of cognac and a trashy romance novel, on the other the bag of pills she'd brought with her from the flats, enough to kill a horse.

Tired, irritated, and unable to relax or even get comfortable, Caron got up again and walked back over to the window. She could see people outside now. There was Howard Reece walking his dog across the overgrown lawns on the far side of the car park. She could also see Harte and Jas peering in through the windows at the swimming pool and poolside gym, then pulling open an outside door and disappearing inside. It certainly looked as if the others were going to give their new surroundings a chance.

I'll do the same, she decided. *I'll give it a couple of days and see how things are going. If it looks like everything's going to work out, I'll keep drinking the booze and reading the books. If I wind up just facing the same old problems, then maybe I'll have to think again.*

32

"Problem is," Jas sighed, "you need power to use most of this stuff."

Harte nodded and continued to walk around the collection of gym equipment at the side of the pool. It was just far enough away from the stagnant water to avoid the worst of the acrid stench which they'd tried to clear by propping open some of the outside doors. This place would have been quite nice in the summer, he thought as he gazed around through the dust and cobwebs. He'd never been much of a fan of exercise, but the prospect of finally having something constructive to do with his time was appealing. Providing they could get enough food and nutrition to replace whatever energy they used up while working out, the benefits of using the gym equipment were obvious. As well as keeping them in shape—or, in the case of most of them, getting them into shape—the physical exertion would also undoubtedly allow them to release some of their frustrations. Webb could continue with his therapy sessions without having to round up decaying corpses and batter the hell out of them.

"Weights are all right, though, aren't they?" he said. Jas looked up and nodded. He'd been wiping the dust off a screen attached to the front of some kind of rowing machine.

"Weights are fine," he replied. "I used to do a lot of weight training. I can show you a few exercises that'll help."

"I don't want to end up looking like a bloody bodybuilder," Harte immediately protested. "All the muscle turns to fat as soon as you stop training, doesn't it?"

Jas grinned.

"You've got to get the muscle first, mate!" He laughed. "You got any idea how much they had to eat to get like that? And there's the bulking up foods and the steroids and—"

"I get the picture."

"We only need to do enough to keep ourselves in shape—just in case."

"In case what?"

Jas shrugged his shoulders. "You know the score. If it's not the bodies, then there are a few people in here who look like they're ready to kick off."

"Such as?"

"Such as Webb."

"Oh, him," Harte said. "Don't need much strength to keep him in check. Kid's a bloody idiot. You shout at him loud enough and you can see his lips start to quiver. I tell you, mate, when I was in teaching I came across hundreds of kids like Webb. They're all talk and no action. He's no threat."

"You sure about that?"

"As sure as I can be."

"And how sure's that?"

Harte didn't answer. Instead he started looking at another piece of training equipment. It looked more like a medieval torture device than anything that might actually have been designed to do some good.

"What's this do?" he asked. Jas didn't answer.

191

"Just watch yourself around Webb," Jas warned, his voice low and deadly serious. "I've seen him in action and I don't like it. I've watched him when he thinks no one's been looking. I've seen him do some things—"

"Like what?"

Jas, now much closer, wouldn't be drawn. He continued past Harte and stood at the edge of the pool, looking into the murky water. They'd need to drain the pool, he decided. The glass doors, roof and walls made the place like a greenhouse.

"Doesn't matter now," he eventually replied, forcing himself to think about Webb again. "Just be careful, that's all. He's got himself a new friend now. We need to make sure he doesn't get carried away and start showing off."

"That kid Sean seems okay. He seems pretty sensible."

"He's like a coiled spring," Jas said. "Poor sod's been trapped in here with a bunch of old bastards who are scared of their own shadows. By the look of the dust in here he hasn't been using the gym to let off steam, so he's going to be full of frigging teenage angst and hormones. I tell you, he'll be itching for a chance to get out of here and see some action to prove he's a man."

"Looks like a strip of piss to me," Harte grunted. "I can't see him fighting his way out of a bloody paper bag."

"Keep your eye on the quiet ones."

"Whatever."

"I mean it. Just don't let him get carried away. If you see him getting out of control, jump on him hard. If he starts looking up to Webb and seeing him as a role model, then we're going to have all kinds of problems to—"

Jas stopped talking, interrupted by a sudden crashing noise.

"What the hell was that?" Harte asked anxiously. Jas disappeared back out through the nearest door and ran along the corridor.

Howard's dog pelted toward them from the opposite direction. The animal stopped beneath the window of the small office where Martin's pet corpse was kept. She looked up and snarled but didn't make a sound. Howard himself followed breathlessly at a distance. Jas peered through the glass. He could see the Swimmer scrambling about on the floor, slowly picking herself back up.

"Problem?" Howard asked.

"Stupid thing fell over," Jas answered. "Looks like it knocked itself into a locker."

"Was that all it was?" Harte asked, his heart pounding. He looked over Jas's shoulder. In the dappled light from the skylight he could see a metal locker lying on the ground that hadn't been there yesterday, but he couldn't see the corpse.

"She hates that bloody thing, don't you, girl," Howard said, leaning down and ruffling his dog's fur. The dog didn't move. "She gets all defensive when it starts making noise."

"You sure that was all it was?" Harte asked again, his whispered voice barely audible. "Where is it?"

"Over there," Jas replied, pointing toward a corner of the room. Harte squinted into the gloom but couldn't see anything. Then, just for a fraction of a second, he caught sight of an arm swinging clumsily behind a metal storage rack. "It probably heard us while we were by the pool. Fucking thing's hiding now!"

Feeling slightly braver, he took a step closer and pressed his face against the window. He could clearly see the outline of the side of the corpse now that his eyes were becoming accustomed to the light. For a moment he thought it was looking back at him.

"None of us like having that thing around," Howard mumbled. "I think Martin's getting too attached to it. I just tolerate it 'cause I know that when this one's rotted down to nothing and it can't get up again, it'll be safe to go back outside."

"How can you tell what condition it's in if it spends all its time hiding in the dark?" Harte asked. "Maybe we should force it out into the open so we can see exactly what it's up to."

"What do you want it to do?" Jas sighed. "A bloody tap-dance routine?"

"Stupid fucking thing," Harte said. He lifted his fist and hammered on the thick safety glass. "Come out where we can see you, you stupid fucking thing!"

"Give it a rest," Howard said. "Keep the noise down."

Harte ignored him and carried on hammering.

"Harte," Jas said angrily, "cut it out."

"Not until it comes out. No good having a pet you can't see, is there?"

The corpse suddenly lurched forward. It threw itself across the room, slamming into the window, the impact and recoil sending it tripping back into the shadows again. Harte jumped back across the corridor with surprise.

"Christ," he said, trying unsuccessfully to appear calm and unfazed. The creature in the office dragged itself back toward the window and stared out, its dull eyes constantly moving from face to face.

"What the hell are you doing?" Martin asked, rushing toward the noise like an overprotective parent. He pushed his way closer to the glass. Jas noticed that the trapped corpse almost appeared to relax when it saw him. It immediately backed off and returned to the shadows. Had it recognized Martin, or had he just imagined it?

"We're not doing anything," Harte replied, sounding like a guilty child who'd just been caught doing something he shouldn't.

"Leave her alone," Martin said, seething with anger and turning on the other men. "She's important. The day she finally drops is the day we're free to go outside again. We need her. We've managed perfectly well here so far and we don't need cretins like you coming along and screwing it all up. Understand?"

Harte didn't say anything. Martin didn't give him a chance to. Before Harte could open his mouth he'd turned his back and stormed away along the corridor.

33

"You must have got rid of one of them?"

"No, nothing."

"Christ, it's been almost two months and you haven't even fought one? You haven't got your hands dirty once?"

"No, I told you. Look, I'm not proud of it. I wish I could have been out there instead of being stuck in here, but you've seen what they're like. You've seen what I'm up against. This lot are scared of their own shadows."

"It does you good to get rid of a few of them from time to time. Me and Stokes used to call it therapy."

"Therapy?"

"Good for the mind and good for the body. You should try it."

"Maybe I will . . ."

"Come on, then."

"What? Now?"

"Why not? You scared?"

"No, it's just that I don't think we should—"

"Come on, you fucking wimp."

Webb and Sean sprinted down the twisting track which led away from the front of the hotel, glancing anxiously over their shoulders to make sure they hadn't been seen. It would be easier if they could get away without the others knowing—they'd just ask stupid, pointless questions and try to stop them. They wouldn't understand. Webb knew what he was doing. This was important. Sean was surely going to have to fight eventually. Better that he got used to it now than when it really mattered. More to the point, if it came to the crunch he didn't want to find himself fighting side by side with an amateur.

"Slow down," Sean moaned, "I've got a stitch." He was nervous and hot and was struggling with the sudden exertion after weeks of sitting around doing very little. Webb had also insisted he put on as many layers of clothing as he could find and he was feeling increasingly uncomfortable. Webb grinned at him without any sympathy.

"Not chickening out on me, are you?"

"No, it's just that—"

"Come on!" he shouted, still running toward the coach which blocked the end of the road. "Get a move on!"

Sean watched as Webb athletically pulled himself up the side of the coach using the wing mirror, then scrambled over the roof and lowered himself down the other side. With considerably more effort and less success he followed, clambering clumsily over the vehicle then half-jumping, half-falling to stand next to Webb in the middle of the desolate road junction where the survivors had fought yesterday. The carnage was incredible. He'd never seen anything like it. The carpet of blood and gore and dismembered remains which covered the ground was grotesque and yet he couldn't take his eyes off it. He'd seen some sights since everyone had fallen and died weeks back, but nothing like this. Sean also found himself watching Webb, who casually kicked his way through the mayhem, using his nail-skewered baseball bat weapon to sweep decaying guts and smashed bones out of the way. The violence he had imagined beyond the hotel walls suddenly felt uncomfortably close and real.

"Okay then," Webb announced, his voice cocksure and overly confident. "Let's get started."

Sean tried to say something but then realized that he couldn't. His mouth was dry with nerves and all he could do was watch as Webb looked around and then jogged across to the far side of the junction. He climbed up onto the roof of the cab of another truck, knelt down and watched the dead on the other side as they immediately swarmed toward him. Using his spiked baseball bat like a bizarre fishing rod, he hooked the back of one of the nearest corpses and dragged it up out of the crowd. Its emaciated weight was negligible and lifting it was easy. He stood up and paused momentarily to steady himself as it threatened to slip and squirm off the nails which had pierced its skin and become wedged between the bones of its neck and shoulder. Webb yanked the cadaver a little higher until its swaying feet were hanging above the heads of the other corpses, then flipped it over and threw it down onto the other side of the truck. It landed unceremoniously in the road close to where Sean was standing and immediately began to drag itself up onto its feet. He backed away nervously.

"Don't be so fucking useless," Webb said as he jumped back down and speared the back of the creature again. "There's nothing to worry about. One of them on its own won't hurt you."

Sean took a single tentative step toward the hideous remains of the man which writhed angrily on the end of Webb's bat. He was transfixed by its grotesque appearance. Could this thing have ever been human? The discolored skin on its face was ripped, blistered, and pockmarked. Blood, pus, and all manner of other seepages had matted the patchy beard which covered its chin and the curled, dark hair drooping over its forehead. Its mouth hung open, its jaw moving up and down constantly, giving the impression that the damn thing was chewing or mumbling or both. As he neared the corpse it lifted its arms and began to lash them through the air, trying to reach out for him but held in check by Webb.

"Are you sure about this?" Sean asked, starting to move back again.

"Completely," Webb replied. He twisted the bat around, wrenching it free from the creature's sinewy flesh. Suddenly finding itself able to move without restriction again, the body lunged forward with surprising speed, almost immediately colliding with Sean, who was desperately slow to react. As the obnoxious creature crashed into him he lifted his arms and shoved it away, feeling his gloved hands sink into its rotten flesh. Unbalanced, it tripped over its own clumsy feet and fell to the ground again, twisting around mid-fall and slamming face-first into the tarmac. Sean felt an unexpected rush of power, immediately silencing his earlier nerves.

"Fuck . . ." he mumbled as the grotesque figure began to pick itself up again.

"See?" Webb said. "Just like I told you. They're useless. Nothing to worry about."

The cadaver stood upright. Its movements were unsteady and it tipped awkwardly to the right, allowing the remains of its bowels to slip through a gaping hole in its abdomen and land on the tarmac with a nauseating splatter and splash. Sean put his hand over his mouth and gagged. He closed his eyes and desperately tried not to vomit.

"Can't do this," he said, his mouth watering, about to throw up.

"Yes, you can," Webb immediately told him. "Thing is, mate, you ain't got any choice."

"What?" he mumbled uselessly, still looking at the glistening puddle of decayed guts in the middle of the road. Webb didn't say anything else, he just threw his bloodied baseball bat along the ground toward the other man, then ran over to the far side of the junction, putting maximum distance between himself and the advancing corpse.

"Next time you face one of these," he shouted to Sean, "you might be on your own. You might not have anyone else to bail you out. You might have to get rid of it before it gets rid of you."

"But I . . . I don't know what to do," he stammered. "I don't know if I can—"

"You just hit it," Webb yelled, getting annoyed. "Just hit the fucking thing as hard as you can and if it gets up you hit it again. Keep hitting it till it stops moving."

The body slipped in its own entrails and stumbled. Sean jumped back but then stopped, Webb's words ringing in his head. What if he was right? What if he did find himself face-to-face with one of these things out in the open? Digging deep, he swallowed hard, then ran forward and shoved the cadaver away. It managed to keep its balance—just—then began moving back toward him. His confidence increasing, he shoved it back once more. Then again. Then again. The foul-smelling, maggot-ridden, rapidly decomposing aberration in front of him wouldn't give up. Each time he touched it, the physical gulf between him and the corpse became more apparent.

"That's it," Webb shouted in encouragement. "Keep going!"

Another brutal shove sent the corpse slamming back into the side of one of the trucks which blocked the junction exits. Feeling more confident, Sean stood his ground as it bounced back and came toward him. This time he thrust it back much harder, suddenly reveling in the unexpected satisfaction of the one-sided fight. After weeks of being held back and stifled he could understand why Webb thought of this as therapy. Problem was, what did he do next?

"What now?" he asked, feeling nervous again.

"Finish it," Webb replied.

"How?"

"The bat."

He looked over his shoulder. The baseball bat was on the ground a short distance behind him. Giving the body a final hard shove to keep it at bay, he picked up the bat, then turned back around to face his dead opponent. The weapon felt comfortable in his hands, reassuringly natural. As the cadaver began to stagger forward again he swung the bat around. Almost two months of pent-up anger, pain, frustration, fear, and grief added to the strength of his attack. He felt the bat slice through the air, heard it whistle as it flew past his ear, then felt it smash into the body, lifting it clean off its feet. An unexpected shock ran through his arms as the end of the bat drove straight through the dead man and thudded into the side of the truck, nails sinking into metal. He dropped his hands. The weapon remained stuck in the truck door.

"Fuck me," Webb said, getting closer again. "Good shot, mate."

Panting, Sean looked up and admired his handiwork. The remains of the bearded man were pinned to the truck, the bat having pierced its throat, almost flattening it. He looked down and saw that the force of his attack had been such that the creature's feet were swinging inches off the floor. With a a satisfied grunt, he pulled the bat free and the bloody carcass dropped to the ground.

"How you feeling now?" Webb asked.

"Get me another."

34

Bloodied and exhausted, Webb and Sean returned to the hotel hours later to find the rest of the group gathered in the Steelbrooke Suite—a large, bright conference room with floor to ceiling length windows along two sides, located toward the rear right-hand corner of the hotel complex, overlooking the grounds and the boundary fence. The two men stashed their soiled clothing in an empty bedroom before joining the others, hoping to hide the evidence of their excursion like naughty schoolchildren. They needn't have bothered. Hardly anyone looked up when they arrived.

"Where've you been?" Harte asked, only slightly interested.

"Exercising," Webb replied before Sean could say anything which might incriminate them. He walked toward the back of the room where Hollis, Lorna, Martin, and Gordon sat looking at a map of the area. He stopped first at another table, upon which a pile of food had been left. He helped himself to a bar of chocolate, threw one across the room to Sean, then began cramming food into his mouth.

"Take it easy," Martin complained as Webb almost immediately picked up a second bar and unwrapped it as he walked toward the others.

"Why?" he protested with his mouth full, showering the map in chocolate and spittle. "There's plenty left."

"We've only got one more box left in the stores," Ginnie piped up from where she sat nearby, sewing a pair of trousers.

"I'm not talking about what's in here," he explained. He pointed out of the window. "I'm talking about out there."

"I'm working on them, Webb, give me time," Hollis told him. Intrigued, Webb looked down at the map.

"Where's this, then?" he asked, still chewing.

"You are here," Hollis answered, tapping his finger on the top right corner of the page.

"So what's here?" Webb wondered, drawing a large circle in the air above the map. "Anywhere worth going?"

"Bromwell," Gordon volunteered, pointing out the small town a few kilometers east of their present location.

"So that's where we're heading?"

"We're not sure yet," Martin quickly interrupted. "That's what we were talking about, but no decisions have been made."

"Well, I'm sure," Harte said from across the room. "Forget all this bullshit, that's where I'm going."

"And that's what bothers me."

"What's that supposed to mean?"

"You know exactly what I mean. I saw how you were with the Swimmer this morning. If you go out there making as much of a disturbance you'll end up bringing thousands of bodies back here with you."

"Whatever," Harte mumbled, far from interested.

"We *are* going to make some noise," Hollis said. "It's inevitable."

"Yes, but I don't think you understand how dangerous that might be."

"I don't think *you've* got any idea how dangerous it might be,"

Harte said, obviously annoyed. "How would you know? You haven't been out for weeks."

"That's right, and we've done perfectly well so far. I'm starting to think we should just delay this and see how long we can last."

"But there isn't enough food," Harte sighed.

"You're right," Martin agreed, "but there is *some* food. If we ration ourselves properly we could make it last for a while. Then when we do leave here the bodies will be weaker."

"And so would we," he protested. "Why the hell should we ration anything? Christ, we're probably the only living people for hundreds of miles. There's never going to be a queue at the fucking supermarket, is there?"

"No, but—"

"You're out of your damn mind if you just want to sit in here and do nothing. Like we've already said, half a day's effort now and a little risk will make the difference between us living like beggars or living like kings."

The strength of Harte's outburst surprised the others, even those who had spent the last few weeks living with him.

"Nicely put," Hollis said.

"Well I'm not going back out there," Caron mumbled from behind the pages of one of her books. "I'd rather starve and be safe."

"Me too," Ginnie agreed.

"I'm going," Sean said defiantly. "I'm sick of sitting here doing nothing. This isn't living, this is just existing. We're no better off in here than those poor bastards out there. Christ, they'll have a better quality of life than us if we stay locked inside this bloody hotel any longer."

"Do you have any idea how stupid a comment that was?" Martin complained, belittling Sean and trying unsuccessfully to put him in his place.

"Piss off!"

204

"Don't you dare use that kind of language with me."

"You see," Webb interrupted, "that's half the problem here. You're not his fucking parents, you know."

"We're looking out for him."

"Yeah, well, it's all going to come to nothing if you starve to death," Harte said, silencing the argument. Hollis rubbed his eyes and wearily looked up from the map again.

"The way I see it," he began, "is we don't have enough food to last. We need to get more and I'd rather go out there now than wait until I'm half-starved. We've got a town just a few miles from here which has probably been left untouched. If we can get there and fill the bus, that'll do us. Harte's right, half a day's effort will make a massive difference to all of us."

"I know that," Martin reluctantly agreed, shaking his head sadly, "but I just—"

"No one has to go outside if they don't want to," Harte continued.

"I'm going," Sean quickly said again, desperate to secure his place. Harte glanced up at him, then carried on speaking.

"As long as there are enough of us then we should be fine. We'll get in, get what we need, then get out. We've done this loads of times."

"I know you're right," Martin said again, his voice suddenly frightened and quiet, "but just be quiet. For Jesus Christ's sake, be quiet. Make as little noise as you can."

35

The brightness of the early afternoon belied the low temperature. The sky was clear, uninterrupted blue and the sun held a position high above the red-tiled roof of the hotel. Despite pushing to go out for supplies sooner rather than later, last-minute nerves and tiredness had combined and the planned trip out had been delayed until the next morning. Most of the group found themselves outdoors, relaxing in the relatively fresh air and enjoying the luxury of being able to spend time out in the open. It wasn't long before the football had been found.

"Shoot, you idiot!" Jas yelled at Harte, who'd just dribbled the ball between Webb's legs and now had a clear shot at goal. Sean waited on the goal line, trying to guess which way he needed to dive.

"I've got him!" shouted Amir, sprinting toward Harte, ready to throw himself at the ball. Aware that he was there, Harte waited until the last possible second, then sold him a dummy, flicked the ball a couple of feet to his right, lined up his shot, and blasted the ball at Sean. To his credit Sean moved in the right direction. He just managed to touch the ball with outstretched fingers, but only succeeded in deflecting it into the corner of the goal he was defending.

"You're fucking useless!" Webb screamed across the makeshift pitch. "What are you playing at?"

Dejected, Sean dropped his head and jogged after the ball. He picked it up and booted it back into play. The sun was in his eyes and he sliced the ball off the side of his foot, sending it bouncing over the boundary fence, right over the road and onto the golf course.

"Sorry," he whined.

"You jerk," Webb yelled. "You complete fucking jerk. What did you do that for?"

"It was an accident."

"You can go and get it!" Jas joked, a wide grin on his face. "Don't worry about it, mate. We'll get another one tomorrow."

"You never know, they might throw it back!" Harte laughed, his mind filling with images of dead bodies playing football across the road. "I can see it now, there's bound to be a few of them that—"

"What's the matter?" Amir asked anxiously, unnerved by the way he'd suddenly stopped talking.

"Shh . . ." Harte said, lifting his finger to his lips and looking up. "Listen."

"What?" Webb demanded.

"The helicopter," Amir said, spinning around and scanning the skies. "It's back."

"Where?"

"There!" he said excitedly, pointing up into the distance.

"Is it the same one you saw before?" wondered Jas.

"Think so," Amir replied, following the flight of the machine through the air. It seemed a little closer today than it had been when they'd seen it previously. Maybe the pilot had seen them, he allowed himself to dream. Perhaps he's just scouting around trying to find somewhere safe to land?

Martin, Hollis, Ginnie and several of the others had rushed outside.

"How many times have you seen it now, Martin?" Hollis asked.

"This is the fifth, I think," he answered, standing on tiptoes to try and keep track of the tiny aircraft as it flew farther away.

"And which way has it been going?"

"Alternate directions each day."

"So it's flying between two sites?"

"Seems that way. No way of knowing for sure, but that seems likely."

"We've just got to hope it comes back again, and work out a way of making ourselves more visible."

"I don't know how. I don't want to do anything that's going to bring the bodies back."

"We might have to. We might not have any choice."

A handful of people remained out in the open long after the helicopter had disappeared, hoping it might return. Hollis and Caron sat together on a wooden bench at the front of the hotel and watched as Howard played with his dog. He threw a rubber toy as far away from the building as he could. The dog sprinted after it, skidding in the long grass, almost running too fast to stop. She grabbed the toy in her teeth and ran back, dropping it obediently at Howard's feet and waiting expectantly for him to throw it again. He hurled it up into the air and watched as it dropped back down.

"Doesn't she ever get bored of this game?" Hollis asked.

"No," Howard replied, rubbing his hands to keep them warm, "but I do. I don't mind, though. She doesn't get enough exercise. It's not like I can take her out for a walk or anything like that."

"Shame," Caron said, shielding her eyes from the sun and looking into the distance. "all this beautiful countryside and we're stuck here."

The dog returned, dropped the toy and looked up again hopefully. Growing weary, Howard stooped down, picked it up, and threw it again, this time hurling it farther than he had previously, out toward the hedgerow. The dog sprinted away at full pelt, covering almost half the distance before the toy had hit the ground.

"Nice throw," Hollis commented. Howard massaged his suddenly aching shoulder and cursed under his breath.

"I've had enough," he announced. "I'm going in."

He turned and began to walk back toward the entrance door. Caron stood up to follow him. Hollis didn't move.

"What's the matter?" she asked. He was still staring out toward the hedgerow which enclosed the hotel grounds. He stood up slowly and shielded his eyes from the sun. Then, when he still couldn't see properly, he stood on the bench. "Greg, what's the matter?" Caron asked again.

"Where's the dog?"

Howard stopped walking and turned around. His instinct was to call out but he knew that he couldn't. Any second now, he thought, and she'll come thundering back, her toy clamped tight between her teeth. Maybe she hadn't found it. Perhaps it had become stuck in a tree or in the hedge? Still no sign. Hollis jumped down from the bench and began to jog across the grass. Howard was close behind.

"Be careful," Caron urged, her stomach suddenly knotted with nerves.

Hollis ran up over a slight rise and then stopped. He could see the dog. She was standing perfectly still, ears pricked up.

"What's the matter with her?" he asked.

"That's not good," Howard replied ominously. "See how she's standing? That's what she does when they're near."

The two men continued cautiously toward the hedge. The dog hardly moved. Her ears twitched and she sniffed and turned her head momentarily as they approached, but otherwise she remained completely still. Hollis noticed that her teeth were bared. She was snarling but not making a sound.

"Must be on the other side of the road," he whispered. "I take it from this reaction that they don't usually come down this far?"

"Not seen them here for a long time," Howard replied.

Hollis edged closer to the boundary. Iron railings ran around the perimeter of the hotel which, over the years, had been swallowed up by thick laurel hedging. Beyond that was the road and, on the other side, the golf course, itself enclosed by another hedgerow. Despite the distance he could see flashes of movement through the mass of gnarled and twisted branches. He could see three or four bodies, maybe more. Their awkward, stumbling gait gave them away.

"What's brought them back?"

Howard looked at him incredulously. Didn't he understand? Christ, from what he'd seen Hollis was supposed to be one of the more intelligent of the new arrivals. Did he have to spell it out to him?

"You noisy bastards," he answered angrily, keeping the level of his voice low. "Them being here is the result of the noise you lot made when you got here yesterday and your friends playing football earlier. Now just imagine how much damage you'll probably do when you go out again tomorrow."

Hollis began to walk back toward the hotel. "Two hedges, metal railings and a road," he said. "They won't get through. I don't care how many of them there are, they'll disappear again in time."

"You reckon?"

He kept walking. Howard crouched down next to his dog, held her head in his hands and blew gently into her face, distracting her.

"Come on, girl," he said quietly, grabbing her collar and leading her away. "It's all right."

36

A long evening doing nothing, a relatively good night's sleep, the most substantial breakfast they could muster from their dwindling reserves, and they were finally ready to move. Eight o'clock in the morning and Hollis, Harte, Jas, Webb, Lorna, Amir, and Sean prepared themselves to head into town. They climbed onto the battered bus as Driver started the engine. Jas watched him intently. What was the unkempt and increasingly insular man thinking? Did he feel as nervous as he himself did? Could he taste bile in his mouth and were his guts churning with nerves too? As he slumped into the nearest seat he couldn't help wondering why he felt so damn uneasy this morning. As the doors closed and the bus began to move he put it down to the fact that the hotel had, unexpectedly, provided them with the most isolation they'd yet had from the nightmare world outside. And here they were, already on their way back out into the chaos and uncertainty again.

Driver edged his clumsy vehicle slowly along the track, past the fork in the road and back down to the junction. Howard, Gordon, and Ginnie were already waiting there. Somebody had to move the vehicles to let them through and, as that job seemed considerably safer than venturing into Bromwell, Howard and Ginnie had reluctantly volunteered.

Gordon, as probably the most experienced fighter remaining at the hotel, was there to mop up those few (he hoped) random corpses which managed to slip through as the bus drove out. He stood on one side of the junction, nervously swinging an ax in one hand and a crowbar in the other. He was dressed in as much protective clothing as he'd been able to find, enough to keep him safe from the germs and any slimy slugs of decaying flesh that an encounter with the dead might throw up into the air. He stood there wearing a pair of fisherman's waders, safety goggles, and a bright yellow construction worker's hard hat, but he didn't care how ridiculous he looked.

"Ready?" Ginnie shouted from behind the wheel of the coach, fighting to make herself heard over the rattle of the engine and, for once, not worrying about the volume of her voice.

Driver acknowledged her with a simple thumbs-up and stared straight ahead as the coach began to move to the side. He inched slowly forward before increasing his speed and driving out into the middle of the deserted road junction. He stopped to give Howard a chance to pull himself up into the driver's seat of the truck which blocked the exit they planned to use. Dog in tow, he settled into the cab and immediately peered down at the mass of bodies on the other side. There were too many to count. Not the biggest crowd he'd ever seen, but too many all the same. His hands suddenly trembling with nerves, he started the engine and waited for Driver to pull the bus closer. The dead began to thump and push against the exposed side of the vehicle. The dog sat in the passenger seat and silently snarled at them, her nostrils full of the smell of rotting flesh.

The truck that Howard was driving spanned the gap between a six-foot-tall brick wall ahead and another truck just behind. As the bus began to move toward him he slowly reversed.

"Get as near as you can," Hollis said to Driver, standing next to him at the front of the bus like a passenger waiting for the next stop.

"You want to try and push as many of them back and out of the way as you can, try and stop them getting through."

"Thanks, I'd worked that bit out for myself," Driver grumbled. He tightened his grip on the steering wheel and nudged forward as soon as there was room for him to move. Bodies began to pour through the gap, most of them immediately being dragged down beneath the bus or shoved away by the impromptu snowplow they'd bolted to its front weeks earlier. Driver accelerated, slicing through the crowd with ease. Hollis looked over his shoulder along the length of the bus. Through the small rectangular window at the back he watched as Howard immediately shunted the truck forward again, blocking the road and preventing any more cadavers from getting through.

"Well, that wasn't too bad," Harte said, relieved, standing just a little way behind Hollis and watching the rotting world rushing by through the windows on either side.

"Nowhere near as many of them as I thought there would be. Must be Martin's music," Hollis admitted. "Give him his due, I thought he was off his head, but maybe not."

"Crazy bugger says he's been playing music to them every day for more than a month," he laughed. "Damn things are probably sick of it!"

Hollis nodded and smiled, then turned to look ahead as the first buildings of the town of Bromwell loomed on the dull horizon.

Incredibly, just three bodies had managed to drag themselves safely through the gap and into the blockaded road junction while the truck had been out of position. All of the others had been swept up and crushed by the bus. Gordon, now feeling far less confident than he had been just a few minutes earlier, stood rooted to the spot, waiting for the first of them to get close enough to attack.

"You okay, Gordon?" Ginnie shouted from the relative safety of the coach. The bodies were instinctively moving in her direction now, distracted by the noise of the engine and her voice. He wanted to stop them getting any closer. He liked Ginnie. She reminded him of someone he used to work with, and that unexpected familiarity, no matter how tenuous, was welcome. He took a deep breath and swallowed hard. Time to fight.

Running forward, he swung the ax into the side of the nearest cadaver's neck, wedging it deep into its putrid flesh, just below its ear. The body, a stocky, awkward creature with only one arm and one eye, was overbalanced by the speed and force of the brutal strike. Gordon dragged it over onto the ground, then plunged the end of the crowbar into its exposed temple. A few seconds of twitching and kicking and it lay still. He yanked out his blood-soaked weapon, suddenly feeling like a gladiator, and turned to look for the next kill.

The body of a nurse was stumbling precariously close to the side of the coach. Gordon spun it around and, with another savage swing of the ax, ripped through the front of its throat, cutting so much weak flesh away that its head was largely unsupported but still remained attached. It flopped back on itself and dangled over its shoulders, now looking behind. Unbalanced, the corpse dropped to its knees and Gordon delivered another killer blow with the blade, this time strong enough to decapitate the corpse and send its head rolling away along the ground, eventually becoming wedged under the coach.

Howard's dog suddenly shot past Gordon, the unexpected speed and movement catching him off guard and making his pulse race. He knew there was still another body to get rid of, but he'd lost sight of it momentarily. He spun around and saw that the dog had come to his aid. It jumped up and wrapped its teeth around the forearm of what remained of a young garage mechanic. The animal was too strong for the corpse and pulled it over. It fell flat on its face and the dog leaped away, then scurried back toward Howard—who was keeping a safe distance, skirting around the edge of the junction and avoiding the violence.

Now feeling more confident, Gordon strode over to the creature on the ground struggling to pick itself up. It managed to lock its arms and raise its head and shoulders and it looked up at him. He stared back, studying what was left of its face. It had very little hair and a gold hoop earring in its right ear. The ear itself was almost completely detached, clinging to the side of its head by nothing more than a few slender strips of flesh and cartilage. The creature managed to lift its decaying bulk a little higher, its sudden movement startling Gordon and forcing him to take a few steps back. He stopped, knowing that the pathetic lump of flesh at his feet was no longer a threat to him or anyone else. It straightened its arms again and lifted its torso. Just above the breast pocket of its blood and oil-stained overalls, the name KEVIN had been embroidered. Strange to think that Kevin had once had a life and a home and a family and friends and . . . and so what? Gordon finally realized that today, almost sixty days after the world had been irrevocably scarred and changed forever, Kevin and every other corpse that still walked the face of the planet no longer mattered.

He sunk the crowbar deep into its half-open right eye, shoving it into its skull and twisting it around, reducing what was left of its brain to pulp.

37

"You ever been to Bromwell before?" Amir asked Lorna and Jas as they drove deeper into the dead town. He didn't care what their answer was or even if they didn't answer at all. He was just trying to distract himself; trying to settle his nerves and take his mind off the hellish, almost unrecognizable world they were now traveling through.

"Doesn't look like we missed anything," Jas said, not in the mood for conversation.

"I think my dad brought me here once when I was little," Lorna answered. "I wouldn't recognize anything now, though."

"Damn right." Amir smiled sadly. "Bloody hell, I drove down this road to work every day for more than twelve years and I don't recognize anything."

"If you're a local," Harte said, eavesdropping from the front of the bus, "come up here and tell us where to go."

Amir reluctantly got up and walked along the aisle, holding onto the passenger rail as the bus lurched from side to side and wishing he'd kept his mouth shut. He looked out through the dirty windscreen, trying to make sense of the carnage flashing past.

"Any suggestions?" Hollis asked.

"Give me a second," Amir said quietly, trying to take in their surroundings and wipe a tear away from the corner of his eye. He hoped no one had noticed. He hadn't realized how much coming home would hurt. In spite of the fact that everything looked so very different this morning, he knew exactly where they were and had done from the moment they'd set off. It was hard to concentrate and think about where to go next when everywhere he looked he saw the crumbling, dying ruins of places he used to know. They were just fading shadows now, gradually dissolving away to nothing. His whole world had been raped and ruined beyond repair.

"Well?" Harte pressed impatiently.

"Take a right here, then go straight up the high street."

"Think we'll be able to get through?"

"Should do. It was partially pedestrianized. There wasn't a lot of traffic around when it all kicked off."

"How do you know?" Hollis asked, holding on as Driver swung the bus around to the right. Amir wiped away another tear, unable to look away from the disintegrating world outside.

"Because," he explained, his voice suddenly full of emotion, "I used to live here and work here and I was here when it happened." The bus rumbled forward, then took a gentle turn and began heading up the high street. "And," he continued, pointing out of the window at the row of shops and businesses on the right hand side of the road, "because until all of this happened, the Bromwell Jewel was the best place to eat for miles around here."

"Was that where you used to work?" Harte asked.

"That was my business," Amir answered as they passed the blue-fronted building, its unlit signage now faded and dull and its windows covered with cobwebs and dust. "That place was my life."

What remained of the people of Bromwell were beginning to emerge from the shadows. They slowly spilled out from dark, hidden

217

corners and dribbled through doorways, alerted by the noise. Their numbers were surprisingly low.

"Why so few?" Harte asked as a gray-suited cadaver dragged itself out in front of the bus. He winced as the powerful vehicle slammed into it, its head smacking against the bottom of the windscreen and popping open like a blood-filled balloon. "Can't all be down to Martin's music, can it?"

"What else could it be?" Amir wondered. "I'm sure that's got something to do with it, but look out there. Some of them are holding back."

He pointed farther up the street. Harte and Hollis peered ahead, but the fact that the color seemed to have been drained from everything, bodies included, made it difficult to make out detail until one of the cadavers moved. Amir was right, though, some of the creatures in the shadows were definitely keeping their distance, staying out of the way until the bus had almost reached them and they had no option but to move. Harte turned and looked out the rear window. Behind the vehicle the scene was disappointingly familiar. The main street was full of corpses all dragging themselves after them.

"What's all that about?" Amir wondered, his eyes wide, nervous, and bewildered.

"We've seen it before," Hollis replied. "They're not as dumb as you'd think. Sometimes they keep out of the way if they think they're in danger."

"Seriously?"

"You just watch them," he continued. "When they're isolated or there are just a few of them they tend to keep out of the way. Now look behind the bus. The immediate threat's gone so they come out into the open and follow us."

"So is Martin making things better or worse? If they're easier to deal with on their own, shouldn't we be trying to keep them apart?"

218

"Don't know. There's no right answer. Even if you're only up against one or two of them, if they can't see a way out, they'll fight you whatever."

"Now where?" asked Driver. The end of the street was looming. Amir forced himself to concentrate and look ahead again. The far end of town had been redeveloped over the last eighteen months with several large buildings having been built on reclaimed wasteland the other side of a recently restored canal. There was a supermarket there, as well as the usual entertainment and fast-food outlets that always seemed to crop up together. He'd spent the last six months cursing the place, blaming it for draining the life from the town and dragging his customers away. Now he couldn't get there fast enough.

"Keep going to the end of the road, then take the bridge over the canal. We should find something up there."

The bus clipped the back corner of a burned-out car and sent the wreck spinning toward the buildings on their left. It crashed into the bronzed-glass frontage of a large social security office, releasing a previously trapped pocket of bodies which immediately began to pick their way through the rubble and glass, then lurched along the rubbish-strewn road. Harte walked the length of the bus, pressed his face against the back window and watched them. From all directions cadavers were now streaming out onto the main street and following the vehicle like a herd. There were still many fewer bodies than he'd expected to see, but more than enough to cause them problems.

Driver forced the bus up over the narrow bridge which separated the redevelopment from the rest of the town, the sudden jolting movement violently throwing his passengers about.

"Jesus," Hollis cursed, gripping the handrail tighter and struggling to stay on his feet. He looked out the door and peered down into the canal with disgust. The sides of the waterway were largely open with benches and shelters scattered along the tow path. Over the weeks vast numbers of dumb, uncoordinated bodies had fallen into the cloudy water. There were so many of them around the sides of the bridge that the canal had become a dark, murky quagmire filled with flesh. Bony, barely recognizable heads, limbs, and other body parts jutted out from the greasy green-gray sludge at unnatural angles. It occurred to him that the canal might actually help them in the same way that a moat protected a medieval castle. Some of the cadavers following the bus would no doubt manage to cross the bridge by chance, but many more would join the packed masses below already wallowing in their watery graves.

There were hardly any bodies on the other side of the canal. Harte was reassured by what he saw as he returned to the front of the bus. From left to right there was a large toy store, an electrical super-store, some kind of furniture and household goods outlet, a bowling alley, and a supermarket.

"Look for the loading bay," he suggested, hoping that their usual tactics would work. Driver was one step ahead of the game.

"Good idea," Amir said quietly.

"We've done this before," Harte mumbled.

The once-white supermarket building appeared dirty and decayed. Weeds and moss had sprung up around the entrance and had begun to climb the walls, their surprisingly aggressive growth rates no doubt increased by the plentiful nutrients supplied by the remains of the dead shoppers lying nearby.

"Fuel," Hollis said, nodding toward the supermarket filling station on one edge of the car park. This was an excellent find. There was a tanker on the forecourt. If they were lucky it would still be full. If they were unlucky the fuel would be in the tanks beneath the pumps. Wherever it was stored, this was good news. Maybe they could even drive the tanker back if it was still loaded up. Not today, but later in the week perhaps. Hollis forced himself to concentrate on getting the maximum amount of supplies today, that was why they were here. They could make plans for their next trip tonight as they rested in comfort back at the hotel and ate decent food and drank themselves stupid.

"Doors are closed," Harte said as they drove past the main entrance, wiping out another trio of curious cadavers.

"Is that good?" Amir asked. He thought it was a strange thing to say.

"Absolutely!" he replied. "You want to try going into one of those places when the doors have been left open? Swarming with those fucking things, they are. They're drawn to shops even after they're dead!"

"Are you serious?"

Harte laughed. "No, but it is easier when they're closed up. Thing is, they can get into buildings easier than they can get out."

"Like the golf course?"

"Exactly, and the longer you leave it, the more you'll find stuck inside. Just adds to the fun!"

"Fun?" Amir grumbled nervously. He was sweating profusely and trying hard to remain calm. The bitter sadness he'd felt since returning to Bromwell had now been replaced by absolute fear. He wished he'd stopped at the hotel. He couldn't believe he'd actually volunteered to come out here. It had seemed like a long-overdue opportunity to break the monotony of his prison-like surroundings, but now all he wanted was to be back in his "cell."

Driver skillfully coaxed the bus around a tight corner and into the loading bay, knocking down the "maximum height" warning sign which hung from a barrier overhead as he reversed into position. This place obviously hadn't been designed with double-decker passenger buses in mind.

"Bingo!" Jas said excitedly. "Look at that. Delivery!"

Hollis couldn't believe what he was seeing. The morning was

getting better by the minute. Straddled across the far end of the loading bay was a huge delivery lorry, decked out in the supermarket's distinctive orange, yellow, and white livery. The doors at the back of it were hanging open and they could see that it was still more than three-quarters full. It looked like they might be able to get what they need without even having to risk going inside the store. Perfect.

"Going to have to stop here," Driver announced. "Won't get out if I go in much further."

"Okay," Hollis agreed, grabbing onto the nearest handhold again as the bus lurched to a sudden stop. The doors hissed open, letting in a blast of cold air from outside, accompanied by the fetid stench of dead flesh and rotten food. Sean and Webb thundered down the stairs from the top floor, weapons in hand, ready to get rid of the first few bodies which were already inching closer.

"I'll keep those two in check," said Jas, picking up the chain saw and squeezing out between Hollis and Harte. He ran after the others, quickly catching up with Sean. Webb was already level with the first of the advancing cadavers, wielding his baseball bat with typical blundering force, making short work of any corpses unfortunate enough to stagger within range.

"Do we try and block them off from the bus or . . . ?" Sean started to ask, suddenly feeling incredibly nervous again, despite what he'd learned yesterday. Jas shook his head.

"Not worth it," he replied. "We might as well just get rid of them. Makes it easier in the long run. Look, we can cut them off if we get closer to the bridge. Most of them are going to end up in the canal, so we'll just be left with the ones that manage to get across. Dumb bastards."

He started the chain saw and marched forward purposefully. Machete in hand, Sean followed close behind, figuring that he'd stay back and deal with those few corpses which managed to evade both Webb's and Jas's attacks.

Lorna, who had been quiet and subdued since leaving the hotel, quickly sprang into action. Hollis, Harte, and Amir were at the back of the lorry, discussing what to take first and how to best organize themselves.

"Come on," she said, barging past them all and clambering up into the massive vehicle. "It won't empty itself."

Not waiting to hear their response, she grabbed the first thing she could lay her hands on—a tray of tins of beans—and slid it across the floor toward Hollis. He picked it up and carried it over to Harte, who had returned to the steps of the bus. He took the tray from him and took it down to the end of the vehicle where he stored it carefully in the foot-well just in front of the farthest seat back.

We need to pack this stuff carefully, he thought. *The better we pack it, the more we'll get in. The more we take now, the longer before we have to come out here again.*

It took less time than they'd expected to empty the back of the lorry and transfer its contents to the bus. Hollis mooched around in the darker corners of the loading bay, keen to check they'd taken everything of value before leaving. He shifted a pile of traffic cones, shovels and other bits of maintenance equipment, then walked over to the other side of the bay to investigate a few wooden pallets which had been stacked up against a wall. He glanced back at the bus as he worked. The others were sitting on the steps up to the rear entrance of the store, drinking, eating, and catching their breaths before they headed home.

The pallets were of little interest. Some were broken, others had just been piled up awaiting collection by the next—

A single cadaver suddenly threw itself at Hollis, grabbing hold of him and sending him tumbling over. His heart thumping, he struggled to right himself and get a grip on the rancid figure which had rushed him. Where the hell had it come from? He forced his hand up,

223

gripped the foul-smelling creature's neck and squeezed. His gloved fingers dug deep into its rotting flesh, ripping open its disintegrating trachea and allowing all manner of disgusting dribbles of decay to squeeze out and run down his arm. His composure quickly returning after the sudden surprise of the attack, he gradually managed to shuffle himself around and roll right over so that the corpse lay beneath him and he could use his weight advantage to the full. He stared into its revolting face—a mass of pus, dried blood, ripped skin, and an infuriatingly vacant expression which seemed to scream *so what?* at him—and wondered how something so pathetic and inadequate could catch him off-guard like that. Was it just the fact that he couldn't hear properly, or was he losing his touch? His confidence wavering, he angrily grabbed a long-shanked screwdriver which he'd been carrying and plunged it into the monster's left temple. In one side and out the other. He pulled it out again, stood up and gave the suddenly limp figure an angry kick to the gut to make sure it wouldn't get up.

"You okay, Hollis?" Jas shouted. "Having trouble?"

"I'm fine," he answered quickly, determined not let the others know what had just happened. He must have released the cadaver when he'd been scavenging around just now. He'd acted like a fucking amateur and he felt angry and scared. Angry because he'd been stupid and put himself at risk unnecessarily, scared because he hadn't heard the body until it had been too late. He'd got away with it today, but the outcome could have been much worse. He'd hoped his hearing would have improved by now but, if anything, it was deteriorating. How the hell was he supposed to survive if he couldn't hear? Hollis felt more exposed and vulnerable today than he had done when the rest of the world had first fallen dead at his feet. He wiped the gore off his screwdriver and put it back in his pocket as Jas approached.

"We're going to head off," he said. "You ready?"

Hollis nodded and followed him back toward the bus.

The lower floor and half of the top floor of the huge vehicle had been filled. Struggling to find a seat, Lorna wearily climbed the narrow stairs and flopped heavily into a chair right at the front, well away from everyone else. The bus began to rumble and shake as Driver started the engine, then it slowly trundled forward. She could already hear the crashing of badly packed supplies and excited laughter and conversation coming from her fellow looters standing in the aisle downstairs. By the sounds of things they'd be lucky if there was any booze left by the time they made it back to the hotel. She closed her eyes, leaned back in her seat, and tried to shut it all out for a while.

The bus turned around and powered back across the bridge over the canal. The sudden jolting movement threw her forward and she opened her eyes again. She gazed down over the dead streets of Bromwell. Even now, two months since it had first happened, it was hard to comprehend the full scale of the inexplicable devastation which surrounded her. She could see many bodies scurrying around in the shadows down below, dragging themselves around ceaselessly and tirelessly like busy worker ants but without purpose or direction. She couldn't imagine a worse existence—condemned to haunt this dead world until such time that their physical form finally failed them. What had any of these people done to deserve this?

Half an hour earlier, Lorna had watched Webb and Sean taunting a corpse. The pathetic, maggot-ridden creature had been sliced in half by Jas's chain saw but it had still been moving. She'd watched it pull itself along the ground, the stump of its spinal cord dragging behind, leaving a crimson snail trail on the gray paving stones. Like kids teasing a stray dog, Webb and Sean had taken turns to lie down directly in its path, taunting it and playing chicken; waiting until the last possible moment before rolling away, then tricking the corpse into crawling after them in another direction. Stupid idiots. Didn't they care that that used to be a person? Maybe they did. Maybe it just didn't matter anymore.

Maybe she was the one who'd got it all wrong.

38

Webb, Sean, Amir, and Harte were drunk. Their successful excursion into Bromwell, coupled with the news that the helicopter had been heard flying nearby yet again today, left them feeling temporarily invincible. They, it seemed, were fully in control. Hollis and Jas watched them from the other side of the Steelbrooke Suite. Their noise was beginning to make Hollis nervous. The rest of the group had gone to bed, but he wasn't going anywhere until these stupid, selfish fuckers had settled down. He didn't want to think about what they might do if they were left unsupervised and, although the hotel grounds and surrounding area were relatively corpse-free, he wasn't prepared to take any chances. Webb and Sean seemed more volatile than usual tonight, buoyed by the events of the day. Sean in particular had been unexpectedly aggressive when, less than an hour ago, Hollis had suggested to him that maybe he'd had enough to drink. Rather than antagonize them, Hollis had instead decided that the best approach was to give them what they wanted. Like leaving a fire to burn itself out, he planned on making sure they had enough booze to help them lose consciousness. It was the only way he could guarantee keeping them quiet.

He heard footsteps in the corridor outside. He picked up his torch and went out to investigate. It was Martin. He looked tired and preoccupied.

"Come to complain about the noise again?" Hollis asked.

Martin shook his head. "Would it do any good?"

"Probably not. What's up?"

"Just been down by the pool."

"And . . . ? Got a problem with your pet?"

"Don't take the piss." He sighed. "She's acting strangely."

"Stranger than usual?"

"It's the noise this lot are making," he explained, nodding toward the Steelbrooke Suite and cringing as Webb threw another beer bottle onto a pile of empties. "She's not used to it and it's freaking her out. We've survived here for as long as we have by keeping quiet and staying out of sight. What you're doing now is going to undo all of that."

"Don't be overdramatic. They're just letting off steam, they're not doing any harm. Listen, I'll talk to them in the morning and—"

"You don't understand," Martin snapped, his voice angrier but the volume still restrained.

"What don't I understand?" Hollis snapped back. "As far as I can see you've spent all your time locked in here with your head down. You haven't actually seen what's happening to the rest of the world. I have, and I know that we'll be safe here."

"Come with me," Martin interrupted. He turned and walked away, leaving Hollis with little option but to follow. He knew exactly where Martin was taking him, back to the body he kept trapped in the office so he could prove his point. But what point was he trying to make? Sure enough, they turned down the corridor which led to the swimming pool.

"Look, Martin," Hollis protested, "I promise you I'll speak to them tomorrow. I won't let this happen again. I'll make them see that—"

He immediately stopped speaking when they reached the window through which they usually watched the corpse. He shone his torch into the room and jumped back when the creature slammed against the glass. Its dead eyes followed his every move and its numb, unresponsive fingers clawed pointlessly at the window, leaving a criss-cross hatching of blood-tinged, greasy smears. It slid along as he approached, keeping as close to him as it could.

"Why's she doing that?" he asked, suddenly concerned. "She's never done that before, has she? She's always tried to get out of the way, not followed like that."

"You see what I mean? She's scared," Martin hissed, turning back and walking away, almost as if he didn't want the corpse to hear. He disappeared down the west-wing corridor. Hollis followed, breaking into a jog to try and catch up. Martin stopped when he reached the foot of the staircase which led to the rooms on the first and second floors.

"Thing is, Greg," he whispered, "I know you've managed to stay alive by doing things your way, and that's worked for you. Christ, the very fact that we're both standing here now is proof that we've all succeeded."

"What are you trying to say?"

Martin thought carefully for a moment, choosing his words and finally beginning to calm down.

"What I'm saying," he began, "is that our methods of survival have to be adapted to our surroundings. Where you were before, it suited you to make a bloody huge noise and to fight and destroy them."

"And what about here?"

"Here things are different," he immediately replied.

"How?"

"We're relying on the fact that they don't know where we are."

Rather than explain further Martin began to climb the stairs and beckoned Hollis to follow. He sprinted up each flight until he'd reached the top floor. Halfway down the corridor was room West

37—his room. He opened the door and went inside. Hollis walked with him into his remarkably clean, comfortable, and well-ordered living space. Martin stood at the window which overlooked the car park and the countryside below. Hollis moved closer. He couldn't see anything but the usual never-ending blackness.

"What exactly am I supposed to be looking at?" he asked.

"Down there," Martin replied, opening the window slightly and pointing. The air outside was cold. Hollis shivered as a blustery gust hit his face.

"What?" he asked again.

"Look down there on the other side of the road. What can you see?"

Hollis stared, his eyes slowly becoming used to the outside gloom. He could see the thick, protective hedgerow which enclosed the hotel grounds and the gap where the narrow road ran around its perimeter. Beyond that was the hedge on the other side of the road which bordered the golf course and surrounding fields. There was some movement in the field immediately opposite. Corpses. He couldn't see how many.

"There are a few bodies. Nothing out of the ordinary. Why?"

"Because that *is* out of the ordinary."

Hollis leaned forward again. He could see the tops of as many as fifteen, maybe twenty bobbing heads moving in the field on the other side of the road. He couldn't see what the problem was. A noise from downstairs—a sudden torrent of drunken, shouted abuse from Harte—distracted him. It affected the bodies too. As soon as they heard it they shuffled closer to the hedge.

"But there are still only a handful of them," Hollis protested. "They'll probably be gone in the morning." He was tired and cold and was beginning to get annoyed with Martin.

"You're not listening to me." Martin sighed. He shut the window and sat down on the corner of his bed.

"I *am* listening, I just don't see what the problem is."

"Christ, Greg, I thought you'd understand."

"Sorry . . ." he mumbled, shrugging his shoulders, not actually sure what he was apologizing for.

"You might be used to having that many bodies around. You might be used to having hundreds more, thousands even. We're not."

"But we can sort them out. They're not a concern, believe me."

"Thing is," Martin continued, "we did have that many here to start with, but we dealt with them. We distracted them and we fooled them. We tricked them into moving away with the music and we lit a couple of fires on the golf course, then we locked ourselves down and kept quiet and out of sight. From what I've heard, you did the opposite. You just carried on like nothing had happened."

"Well, not quite, but—"

"You did! As far as I can tell from what you've said, you kept going out to get your food and your fuel and your booze and whatever else you wanted."

"What's wrong with that?"

"I'm not criticizing what you've done."

"You sound like you are."

"Well, I'm not. I'm just saying that in your situation back where you were based, that approach worked. You can't do that here. You can't keep going outside and you can't keep making the kind of noise that those bloody drunks downstairs have been making all evening."

Hollis was struggling to understand.

"I still don't know why you're getting so upset—"

"I'm not upset," Martin protested. "I'm concerned."

"What about? Come on, spell it out for me. What is it that's bothering you tonight? We knew we were going to attract a few of them."

"I understood that, but I've been watching the bodies out there for a couple of hours now, Greg. Their behavior is changing. We've had them this close before, but they've always disappeared by now. Those things out there tonight aren't going anywhere. The music's still playing and there's still a big enough crowd to keep them on the golf course, but it doesn't seem to be working like it usually does. Christ, man, they're moving in the opposite direction!"

Hollis looked out again, carefully considering the frightened man's words.

"What about the helicopter?" he asked. "It flew over again today, didn't it?"

"Yes. What about it?"

"We need to do something to make them see us."

"Is this relevant?"

"I think so. How are we going to attract their attention without attracting the bodies too?"

"I don't know. I was thinking about marking a message on the lawns or something like that."

"Might work. Some kind of beacon would be better, though. They won't see your message unless they fly right over us and happen to be looking down."

"I know . . ."

"The point I'm trying to make is that we're going to have to risk making our presence known at some point. And we can deal with the dead, Martin. We've done it before. Bloody hell, Webb alone has torched hundreds of them."

"He might well have, but there are thousands more waiting out there."

"Waiting?"

"Yes, waiting. Waiting to find out where we are. Driving around in bloody trucks and buses, lighting beacons and making a bloody noise like you lot have done today is just going to bring them straight back to us. You're going to start a chain reaction. Once a few of them know where we are, the whole bloody lot will follow."

39

At first light, at Martin's request, Hollis walked with him up to the clubhouse where he set the music playing. It was the first time in weeks that Martin had walked rather than cycled along the track which ran around the western edge of the hotel grounds. Without his bike he felt as if he'd traveled much farther than usual, and the perceived increase in distance made him feel even more vulnerable and exposed. If he hadn't had Hollis with him he doubted he'd have dared make the trip on foot. Keen to gain a better appreciation of their location, Hollis had insisted they initially continue down the narrow lane to get closer to the bodies they'd seen last night.

Martin pointed through a gap in the hedge to help Hollis get his bearings. He glanced back over the wall of tall laurel bushes behind him at the hotel. He could just about see Martin's room on the top floor, the angle indicating that they were roughly level with the area they'd observed last night. Crouching down, he peered through the mass of tangled branches in front of him. On the other side of the hedgerow was a large, open field.

"Is this still the golf course?" he asked, his whispered voice barely audible. "Couldn't really see last night."

Martin shook his head.

"No, this field's part of a farm. The golf course starts another couple of hundred yards further up the road."

Hollis could see numerous bodies staggering around. There appeared to be at least as many as there had been previously, maybe even a few more. His view was limited and he looked for another gap.

"I've never seen this many here before," Martin hissed. "There's only ever been a handful here at a time, and they've always been moving towards the music, not away from it."

Hollis continued to watch the dead. Although some were clearly still trying to move toward the source of the distant sound, others were definitely traveling in the opposite direction. Some remained standing in the same place, constantly shuffling but never straying more than a few meters away at a time. He could only assume they were gravitating toward the hotel or at least toward the remains of the crowd which had been gathered in this area last night. Whatever the reason, their actions seemed to add weight to Martin's earlier argument. Hollis wondered whether he had really underestimated the effect of their arrival and the noise of the bus—and the drunks—yesterday. More to the point, maybe he'd underestimated the steadily increasing levels of intelligence and control which the dead seemed to be exhibiting here.

"There still aren't that many," he mumbled, taking care to keep his voice low but struggling to find the right volume because of the constant pain and muffled sound in his damaged ear. He shifted position again, not able to see as much as he wanted. "A few more hours of silence and I'm sure they'll disappear. It's not been that long. Once we explain to the others what's happening they'll—"

He stopped speaking immediately as a corpse rushed toward him. It crashed into the other side of the hedgerow and tried to stretch its gnarled hand out through the tangled undergrowth. He tripped back in surprise, and then moved closer again when the initial shock had faded.

235

"What is it?" Martin asked anxiously, keeping a safe distance.

"Got a lively one, that's all," Hollis replied. He looked into the dead monster's face through a gap in the branches, satisfied that it couldn't reach him. He couldn't tell if it had been male or female. Its skin was heavily pockmarked and decayed and its top lip had been torn away, exposing its yellowed teeth. A large flap of skin hung down from the side of its head, covering its ear. Its eyes, however, although dark and unfocused, appeared relatively undamaged. Hollis realized that the damn thing was staring straight at him. Its sight may well have been limited, but the creature in the field was watching his every move. It suddenly threw itself into the hedge again, reaching out as far as it could. He watched in disgust as savage thorns and branches stripped rotting flesh from its bones. Two now; another corpse, alerted by the sudden movements of the first, rushed forward also. Then another, then another. Within seconds at least five of the decaying monsters were clamoring at the hedge close to where Hollis was standing. Surprised and unnerved by their unexpected ferocity, he turned back and silently ushered Martin along the road toward the clubhouse.

Still uneasy, Hollis relaxed slightly when they reached the enclosed passageway which led up to the back entrance of the clubhouse. Martin led him inside, moving quickly through the pitch-black ground floor and up the stairs to the balconied landing. Both of the stereos were still working and the combined noise from the music and the generators was appalling, loud enough for Hollis to almost be glad that one of his ears had stopped working. He followed Martin into the meeting room, watched his well-rehearsed refueling routine, then crossed the landing to the office. He noticed that Martin was keeping his head down, looking at the floor as much as possible.

"What's the matter?" he asked, concerned.

"Nothing," Martin replied. "Just don't like to look at them, that's all."

He replaced the stereo and moved to one side. Hollis immediately stepped forward, his inquisitiveness getting the better of him. He leaned out the window, hanging onto the frame for support.

"Fuck me," he said, forgetting himself. The music drowned out his words. He glanced back at Martin, who looked away from him, not wanting to share the horror of what he'd just seen. Hollis turned back to face outside.

The sun was rising on the horizon. Incandescent yellow light was slowly seeping across the world, illuminating everything and burning away the shadow and shade. Below Hollis, stretching out for as far as he could see in every direction, stood the largest crowd of bodies he'd ever seen. Thousands of them—hundreds of thousands, even—filled every inch of the golf course. The size of the crowd was incomprehensible and terrifying. He couldn't compare it to the gathering outside the flats—there the dead had been free to wander, but here they were restricted and confined. In an instant, however, he completely understood why Martin had reacted so badly to the little noise they'd made over the last two days. If this crowd turned on them, he realized, there'd be no escape.

If this number of bodies get any closer to the hotel, he thought, *they'll either tear us apart or crush us. There will be no way out. No escape. And if they don't kill us, with that many of them so close it'll surely only be a matter of time before the germs that killed Ellie and Anita start spreading.*

40

With the rest of the group still indoors, Jas slipped out and crept over to the bus, which had been abandoned right outside the hotel entrance yesterday. In the sudden euphoria which had followed their successful looting expedition, they had simply unloaded enough food and drink to get them through the night with the intention of finishing the job in the morning. It was still early and nothing had so far been done. Lethargy, hangovers, and general tiredness seemed to have affected everyone. Everyone except Jas.

Feeling undeniably guilty and uneasy, he crept onto the bus and began to pick up boxes of food. He carried them back through the hotel, taking care not to be seen, and took them up to the middle room on the first floor of the east wing of the building: room 24 East. Hardly anyone slept over there and that room, he'd discovered, was one of the largest. The first floor felt safer than the others. He'd stopped on the glass-fronted staircase for a while and had studied the almost identical west-wing part of the building opposite and the enclosed grassy courtyard below. He knew that if anything happened and he ended up trapped in the room he'd just chosen, he'd have the security of being off the ground floor but would still be low enough to get out of a window should he need to make a sudden escape.

His plan this morning was simple: fill the room with supplies so that they had an additional stockpile which he could get to in the event of an emergency. The others could use it with him. Well, some of them, anyway. Whatever the reason, it made sense not to store everything they'd managed to scavenge in one part of the building.

He was getting off the bus for the seventh time when he got caught.

"What the hell are you doing?" Webb asked, stepping out from around a corner, early morning cigarette and beer in hand. Jas jumped back with surprise. The panic on his face was clear and Webb chuckled as he swigged from his can of lager.

"Nothing," Jas answered quickly.

"Like hell. Doesn't look like nothing."

"Just piss off, Webb," he said. "It's none of your business."

"Yes, it is. That's my stuff you're taking."

"It's *our* stuff," he corrected him.

"Whatever. Point is, it's not *your* stuff, you thieving bastard. I've been watching you for the last half hour. I know where you're stashing it."

Jas sighed dejectedly. How could he explain to this stupid little shit what he was doing without him thinking he was simply creaming off the best of their supplies for himself—which, if Jas was completely honest with himself, he was. Did he need to explain himself at all?

"Look," he began, deciding he should give it a shot and see how Webb reacted, "at the moment everything we've got is scattered around this place. Most of it's up by the restaurant and the conference room, lots more still out in the bus."

"So you thought you'd help yourself?"

"All I'm doing," he replied, determined not to give Webb

239

opportunity to argue, "is putting some of it somewhere else. What if there's a fire and half the building goes up in smoke? What if someone gets sick like Anita and Ellie and we have to shut ourselves away from them? What if the bodies get in here?"

"Bullshit," Webb spat, full of animosity. "You're a liar. You're not going to tell anyone else where you're putting this stuff. You're taking it for yourself, you fucker."

"Shut up," Jas said, struggling to remain calm and not overreact. *He's not worth it,* he silently told himself. Unable to suppress his anger, he dropped the box he'd been carrying and moved threateningly toward Webb.

"You're a fucking thieving bastard," Webb continued, his anger unabated and his confidence buoyed by booze. "Wait till I tell the others what you're up to."

Jas lunged for Webb and grabbed him by the neck. After checking that no one else was around he pushed him up against the nearest wall, knocking his head back with a satisfying thump.

"Do yourself a favor and shut up," he said, his voice disarmingly calm. "You're not going to tell anyone anything."

"Why shouldn't I?"

"Because if you do," he whispered, moving even closer so that his face was now just millimeters from Webb's, "I'll tell them what you did to Stokes."

Webb immediately stopped struggling. He mouthed a few silent words but, for a second, he was unable to respond.

"Didn't do anything," he eventually mumbled. "I didn't do anything."

"Yes, you did," Jas said ominously. "I saw you."

Not waiting for a response, he picked up his box and disappeared back into the building, leaving Webb standing useless and alone outside.

41

"If there's one thing we've got plenty of here," Ginnie said, her arms fully loaded, "it's white sheets."

Hollis moved to let her through and watched as she disappeared outside to find Martin and Caron. Gordon followed close behind. Those two seemed to be attached at the hip, he thought as he pushed past him, desperate to catch up. Finally Lorna came through, her hair tied up in a long ponytail, struggling with yet more linen.

"Here, let me," he said, holding the door open. She smiled briefly, but didn't say anything. Hollis ducked into the kitchen to pick up another pile of sheets, then followed the rest of them out.

The early morning cloud had remained but had steadily lightened from dark gray to a brighter white as the sun tried to break through. It wasn't much after eight but it felt much, much later. *Funny how our body clocks seem to have synchronized themselves with the sun and the moon,* he thought as he walked across the lawn toward the others. Previously he'd have got up when it was time to go to work and gone to bed when he'd finished watching TV or come in from the pub. Now the only thing which happened with any regularity was the steady progress

241

of the sun across the sky, and they'd all matched their daily routines to the light. Up at dawn, ready to sleep by dusk.

Martin was flapping like an overprotective mother hen. Caron seemed to have a better grasp of the task at hand.

"No, Martin," she protested, "we need to start over here and put the letters the other way up to how you're suggesting. Down the lawn, not across it, see? H . . . E . . . L . . . P . . ."

As she spoke she pointed to where she thought each letter should go.

"She's right," Gordon agreed. "We can make the letters bigger if we do it that way."

"Doesn't really matter which way up they go, does it?" added Ginnie enthusiastically, pleased to have finally found something to occupy her time.

"Keep your voices down," Hollis nervously warned. They were almost at the boundary fence, near to the gap he'd gone through with Martin earlier. They could hear snatches of music in the distance and he felt uncomfortably close to the dead. If only they knew just how many bodies he'd seen gathered on the golf course.

Lorna didn't speak. Ignoring the others as they fussed and argued, she began laying down the first sheet and opening it out. Using sand, soil, stones, and whatever else he could find, Hollis followed her around and weighed down the edges of the material.

"Think this is going to do it?" he asked as she unfolded the second sheet.

"We've got nothing to lose by trying, have we?"

Following her lead, Gordon and Ginnie also started to work. Ginnie lay two sheets down to form the cross of the H, Gordon secured them. Hollis was fetching more linen when a football bounced up off the grass and hit him in the face, knocking him back. Sudden, searing pain coursed through his injured ear. He looked up angrily to see Sean approaching. Webb wasn't far behind.

"Sorry," Sean began, jogging toward him. Hollis barged past.

"What the fuck do you think you're doing?" he yelled at Webb, the blinding pain and anger making him temporarily forget the volume of his voice. "Are you fucking stupid?"

"No, are you?" Webb goaded. Hollis ran at him but the younger man was too fast and sidestepped his clumsy attack.

"Come here, you little bastard," he seethed. "I'm gonna kill you."

"No, you're not. You can't even catch me!"

"Leave it out," Lorna pleaded, running after them both. "Come on, Hollis, this is pointless. He's just a little idiot. Not worth wasting your time on."

"You can fuck off too," Webb spat.

Hollis sprinted forward again and slid in the dew-soaked grass, much to Webb's amusement. He picked himself up and glared at him, breathing hard. Lorna held him back.

"Please," she said, "just ignore him. He's only doing it to wind you up. Come back and help us get this finished."

"Fucking idiot," Hollis shouted, forgetting himself again. "Why can't you do something useful instead of screwing around all the time?"

"You call that useful?" Webb shouted back, pointing at the sheets on the grass. "How is that useful? How's that going to help? Who's gonna see it?"

"What's going on?" Jas asked. He'd emerged from the hotel when he'd first heard the raised voices. "You lot got any idea how much noise you're making?"

"It's okay, Jas," Lorna told him as she tried again to pull Hollis away. "There's no problem. It's nothing."

"Come on, mate," Sean said to Webb, passing the football to him. "Let's go. No point standing here arguing about—"

He looked up at the sky. The others immediately did the same. One by one they heard the helicopter engine approaching. Webb was the first to spot it—a small, black, spidery silhouette crawling across the off-white sky several miles north of where they were standing.

"There it is," he said, pointing up at the aircraft, "and that's why what you're doing is stupid. How are they supposed to see your letters on the ground when they're not even flying overhead? They're fucking miles away. They'll never see it."

He was right and Hollis knew it.

"So what do you suggest?" he asked, sounding uncharacteristically desperate. "What else are we supposed to do? What we're doing is better than doing nothing at all."

"You need a fucking fire or something," Webb answered. "A great big fucking fire in the middle of nowhere. At least then they'll—"

"Shut up!" Jas interrupted. "Listen!"

Another engine, loud enough for them all to hear.

"There!" Lorna said excitedly. "Look at that! It's a bloody plane."

"Christ," Sean said under his breath as they stood and stared at the second, much larger aircraft. "There must be loads of them. It's a bloody mass evacuation."

"That's not good," Jas warned.

"Not good?" he protested. "How can it not be good?"

"Because you might be right—and if you are, then they're probably clearing out, aren't they? And if they're doing that, then they ain't going to be flying over here many more times."

42

"They're a bunch of fucking wasters," Webb cursed, finishing another can of beer—he'd lost count of how many he'd already had today—and throwing it onto the growing pile of empties in the corner of Sean's room at the back of the hotel. "They're going to sit in here and fucking rot, I tell you. Just fucking look at them."

He held back a corner of the curtain, letting a little light into the otherwise dark room. They were all still out there, writing their pointless message on the grass with dirty bedsheets.

"Don't let them get to you," Sean said. "You just have to ignore them. I've had weeks of that kind of bullshit since I've been here. They're always telling me you can't do this and you can't do that. Honestly, mate, it's been worse than living with your bloody parents!"

"What happens if that helicopter does see us and lands? Where are we going to end up? We'll still have them with us. Same shit, different place. Don't know how you've put up with it for as long as you have, mate."

"What else could I do?"

"You could have stood up for yourself. Could have told them how pissed off you were."

"And what good would that have done?"

"You could have left them. I would have if I was stuck here. At least back at the flats I could get out when I wanted to."

"But I didn't want to go out. They told me how bad it was and how we had to keep our heads down and I believed them."

"That was all bullshit! You saw it for yourself yesterday. It's no fucking walk in the park out there, but we did okay, didn't we?"

"I was scared because *they* were scared, I can see it now. Until yesterday I was fucking terrified of going outside, but you were right, it was an absolute fucking breeze."

"Thing is," Webb continued, the alcohol increasing his ire, "they don't actually want us here. We're just a pain in the backside to them. They wouldn't miss us if we went."

"So let's go, then."

"How?"

Sean opened the curtain fully. "See the road between here and the golf course?"

Webb nodded. "What about it?"

"Follow it back towards the front of the hotel."

Webb did as he was instructed. He followed the curve of the road right around the outer edge of the hotel grounds. All he could see was a field on the other side of the road, empty save for a few hundred bodies staggering around aimlessly. A ragged group of them— he couldn't see how many—appeared to be hanging around close to the hedge in an unruly mob.

"What am I supposed to be looking at?"

"See there?" Sean said, pointing down toward the front of the hotel complex. "There's a car parked in the road."

"Yeah, so?"

"Martin and Howard put that car there to block a gate."

"Into that field? So what? You thinking of going for a bloody picnic?"

Sean shook his head.

"Point is there's another gate on the opposite side of the field. We can get out that way without moving any of their bloody trucks and buses. Go the other way at the fork in the road, take the brakes off and shift that car, and we're out."

"But what about the bodies? I can see plenty, but aren't there supposed to be thousands of them 'round here?"

"Didn't think that bothered you."

"Doesn't bother me," Webb replied arrogantly, "but I'm not about to stick my bare arse out in the middle of a massive crowd of corpses unless I've got no choice."

"They're all on the golf course up there, well out of the way. Those are just the stragglers. Come on, you've told me you've dealt with bigger crowds than that before."

Webb didn't answer at first. He continued to stare out the window into the field that Sean had showed him. There weren't that many bodies; even the unexplained mass clumped around the hedge wasn't huge. Could they try running for it? Maybe that was too risky. There had to be another way of getting out.

"How did you say you got here?" he asked, a plan forming.

"Scooter," Sean replied, "but it's fucked. I've got a flat tire and hardly any fuel."

"Can you ride a bike?"

43

Almost eleven o'clock. Gordon, Ginnie, Lorna, and Caron were still unloading and sorting supplies from the bus. They were working deliberately slow, dragging out the job to keep themselves occupied and fill their empty day.

"Was there really any point in bringing back this much pickle?" Ginnie asked, looking down her nose through half-moon glasses at the three trays of sandwich pickle Lorna had just carried inside. "Horrible stuff."

"One day," Lorna replied, sweating and breathless with effort, "you might be grateful for that. And like I keeping saying, love, if there was something special you wanted bringing back, you should have got off your backside and gone out there with us, shouldn't you?"

"I'll eat it," Gordon said unhelpfully, ripping open the packaging, picking up a jar and studying the label. "I love this stuff. I could live on it."

"You might have to," she grumbled.

"Just the smell of it makes me feel sick," Ginnie continued to complain. "Makes me want to throw up. You know, I used to have a friend who—"

"We should all be thankful for what we've got and for the fact we're here at all," Caron interrupted, still working. "It's funny how perspectives change, isn't it? A couple of days ago, Ginnie, you'd probably have killed to get your hands on a jar of pickle, no matter how ill it made you feel. We need to remember that we—"

She stopped talking. The others looked at her expectantly.

"Remember what?" Lorna asked.

"Shh . . ." she hissed. "Listen. They're back."

In the distance they could hear an engine. Disagreements, differences, and pointless arguments over pickle were forgotten in an instant as they all dropped what they were doing and ran across the central courtyard and through to reception. They burst out of the front door and onto the car park. Hollis and Martin were already there, scanning the skies. Amir ran toward them from the other side of the building.

"No use looking up there," he panted. "That's no helicopter."

"What?" grunted Hollis. His ear was so bad that he was having trouble hearing anything.

"It's on the ground," he explained, "and it's moving away from us."

The entire group turned around as Jas came thundering out of the hotel.

"They've taken my bike," he shouted. "Those little bastards have taken my bike!"

Sean weaved through the staggering corpses which hurled themselves at him from all directions. The grassy ground beneath his wheels was dry but uneven, and a deceptively steep slope away from the hotel made it even harder for him to keep control of the powerful bike. He didn't dare do anything but aim for the gate in the farthest corner of the field and accelerate hard. Webb held on tight behind him, his arms wrapped around Sean's waist, feeling dangerously exposed. He looked up and saw through the confusion that they were almost there.

The gate was open, just as Sean said it would be. Martin had left it like that to make it as easy as possible for the dead to find their way through this field and onto the golf course. He tightened his grip on Sean as the bike powered through the opening, leaving the ground momentarily, then thumping back down onto the tarmac. Almost immediately a sharp left turn loomed. Sean dipped the bike over to such a sickening extent that Webb thought they'd never recover from the turn. He squeezed his eyes shut, held on, and waited for an impact which never came. To his amazement they were still moving.

Sean drove around in a large loop, bypassing the blocked-off road junction and eventually rejoining the route to Bromwell which they'd followed yesterday. They'd already decided on today's destination: the bowling alley alongside the supermarket they'd looted. The journey was faster this morning; despite the fact that there were many more bodies around than had been there previously, it was far easier to steer the bike through and around the carnage than the bus. The dead had no doubt been attracted by the noise they'd made the day before, Sean decided. Whatever the reason, it didn't matter. He knew how to deal with them now. They were no longer the threat he'd allowed himself to believe they were, just barely coordinated, germ-infested, vacuous bags of flesh and bone.

They raced down the main Bromwell high street, passing Amir's dilapidated restaurant and various other insignificant sights which had been pointed out yesterday. Webb—who finally felt brave enough to lift his head and look up—actually found himself silently thanking the others for once. Their day trip out in their lumbering, beaten-up double-decker bus had cleared the way for him and Sean today. The bus had blundered through scores of bodies and had forced masses of wreckage up out of the way leaving a relatively clear, yet still bloody and treacherous path through the mayhem. Up and over the bridge which spanned the flesh-filled canal—which seemed to be full of even more unfortunate corpses than it had been before—past the front of the supermarket and they were there. Sean stopped the bike outside the glass-fronted bowling complex.

"What now?" he asked, anxiously watching a group of seven bodies which had just turned around and were moving toward them. He glanced over his shoulder and saw at least double that number were coming up from behind. *Damn corpses must have dragged themselves up here to check out the supermarket after we left yesterday,* he thought. He suddenly felt nervous and uneasy, but he didn't dare let Webb see.

"Go around the back," Webb answered, his experience of both dealing with the dead and breaking and entering again proving invaluable. "there probably won't be as many of them there. It'll make it easier when we leave too."

Sean immediately did as he was instructed, swerving around the closest of the corpses and sticking a foot out to trip up the dumb creature. He turned right down the side of the building, focusing on avoiding another pocket of cadavers which had hauled themselves out from behind the building next door. They were everywhere. Surely they couldn't all be here as a result of the noise they'd made yesterday, could they? Momentarily preoccupied with the dead, Sean jumped with surprise when Webb shook his shoulder.

"Stop!" he yelled over the noise of the engine. "Turn around. Fire door."

Sean glanced over his shoulder, then stopped. Webb slid off the back of the bike and ran toward a dark blue fire exit halfway down the side of the redbrick building. The door was wedged open by a single skeletal arm which jutted up from the ground as if its dead owner was waiting to have a question answered. Insects gorged on its rotting fingertips, buzzing away as he yanked the door open and the arm flopped down. Sean immediately drove into the darkness, quickly abandoning the bike and running back to shove the body out of the way. Once they were both inside Webb pulled the door shut with a reassuring thump, plunging the entire building into darkness.

"Get a light on!" he screamed, immediately aware of sounds of movement somewhere near.

Sean panicked. "What light?"

"The bike! Use the fucking bike!"

Sean ran back toward the motorbike but was knocked off his feet by a corpse which, more through luck than judgment, smacked into him head-on. He recoiled at the appalling stench which immediately filled his nostrils, then tripped as the creature's unsteady head rocked back with the impact, then fell forward again, butting him in the eye. The sudden dagger-sharp pain was intense and he collapsed, dragging the body down with him.

"You all right, mate?" Webb yelled. "Where are you?"

"I'm okay," Sean hissed through clenched teeth, the sudden shock and pain now beginning to fade, "I've got it." Lying on his back, he reached up and wrapped his gloved hand around the body's throat, squeezing as hard as he could. He felt decaying skin and gristle give way as the pressure he exerted increased. Tighter and tighter he squeezed, putrefied flesh dribbling out through the gaps between his fingers, until the body stopped thrashing and slumped motionless on top of him. Webb managed to pick up the bike and turn on the headlamp, filling their corner of the building with light.

"Nice one!" he laughed as he watched Sean pick himself back up and kick the cadaver away to one side. "You're starting to get the hang of this!"

Sean said nothing. He brushed himself down as he looked around, shaking his head to clear the numbness which remained from his assailant's lucky head butt. His eyes were slowly becoming accustomed to the low light levels indoors. Some sunlight was seeping inside through the glazed front of the building, but most of the bowling alley remained disappointingly gloomy and dark. He'd hadn't expected any different, but as they'd approached it had been hard not to remember this place as it had been when he'd last visited. He'd been here on a team building event with the design company he'd worked for on the Friday night before everyone had died. The place had been full of noise, light, and people back then. Hard to believe that everyone he'd been there with was now dead . . . *Get a grip,* he ordered himself, feeling uncomfortable, long-supressed emotions beginning to rise.

"Looks like the place was empty," Webb shouted to him from the other side of the bowling lanes. "Can only find this one."

Sean moved forward to get a better view. Webb was dragging the body of a female cleaner behind him by its hair. Poor cow didn't look like she'd been any older than twenty when she'd died. The corpse's light blue pinafore, gray T-shirt, and jeans were stained with dribbles of blood, pus, and Christ alone knew what else. Its arms and legs thrashed about furiously as Webb bumped it down three low steps toward him. A clump of scalp came away from its skull, leaving him holding just a handful of greasy hair and skin. The body tried to get up but he was having none of it.

"Sorry, darling," Webb said as he put his arms around its emaciated waist, "your cleaning days are over." With that he swung the corpse around, clouting its head hard against a concrete pillar, shattering its skull and showering the ground with what was left of its brain. Disinterested, he dropped it like it was an empty beer can and walked away, looking for food and other distractions.

For a moment Sean stood and stared into the dead girl's face which, at this angle and in this light, appeared surprisingly untroubled by all that had happened to her. Poor bitch, he thought to himself sadly. It wasn't her fault. She didn't deserve that. He glanced back over his shoulder at the carcass which had attacked him just minutes earlier, then looked down at the girl at his feet again. He nudged her chin with his boot, hard enough to make her head roll and reveal the other side of her face, a bloody mass of fetid, blistered skin and dribbles of decay. *Get a grip*, he said to himself again, angry that he'd allowed himself to feel something for the grotesque corpse. *Can't afford to think like that anymore. Doesn't matter who or what any of these things used to be, they're not human now.*

The hours which followed were unexpectedly surreal. Sean continued to feel a bizarre mix of emotions—nervous, desperate, and scared one minute, elated and free the next. After collecting food and drink by smashing open vending machines—and disturbing a nest of squealing, fat, overfed rats in the process—Webb had suggested they try bowling. It didn't last long. The electronic scoreboards remained black and unlit and when the pins and the balls disappeared over the precipice at the end of the lanes, they never returned. But, for just a few snatched moments at a time, Sean was able to close his eyes and recall how everything used to feel and sound: the reassuringly familiar rumble of the heavy balls rolling down the alley filling the vast room, followed by the clatter and bang of the pins being knocked down.

They gave up on bowling when all the balls had disappeared, neither man relishing the prospect of disappearing down into the labyrinthine bowels of the alley to retrieve them. Instead they cleared a space in the carpeted area where rows of blank-faced arcade machines stood and then, between the two of them, dragged a pool table nearer to the tall windows at the front of the building. As the sun began to sink toward the horizon, and under the vacant but watchful gaze of several hundred dead faces pressed hard against the glass, they played for as long as they were able, finally accepting that it was time to return to the hotel when the light had all but completely gone.

"We could stay here, you know," Sean had suggested as they prepared to leave. "We don't have to go back."

"Nah," Webb had quickly replied. "I want my bed and my beer. We can come back tomorrow."

"We can go anywhere we bloody well want to tomorrow," Sean said as he climbed onto the motorbike, already planning his next escape. He wasn't looking forward to facing the bunch of miserable fuckers who would be waiting for them at the hotel. In many ways they worried him more than the crowds of grotesque cadavers swarming across the countryside. It didn't matter, he decided. If they gave him any trouble he'd just turn around and leave.

What was left of the world was his for the taking.

44

Sean drove back across the field, the bike's headlamp slicing through the darkness and illuminating the crisscrossing corpses which staggered out in front of him. Half way across he switched off the light, then turned off the engine just short of reaching the hedge. Largely invisible, they coasted toward the gate in the corner. He was off-course slightly, reaching the other side of the field a little low.

"Go and get the gate open," he hissed at Webb, who was still clinging on tightly behind him.

"What?"

"Get the fucking gate open!"

Webb reluctantly jumped off the bike. Using the hedgerow as cover he ran blindly forward along the farthest edge of the field, anxiously shoving corpses out of the way. He was panting with effort by the time he reached the gate. His hands numb with cold, he undid the latch and pulled the metal barrier open, aware that a mass of shadows was already closing in on him.

"Done," he shouted, hoping his voice was loud enough for Sean to hear. The starting of the bike's engine and the immediate flood of light across the field was confirmation. The bike roared toward him and burst through the open gate onto the road, collecting a single corpse along the way and sending it flying through the air like a rag doll. Webb shut the gate as soon as Sean was through. He struggled with the awkward latch again, fighting to concentrate on the lock and ignore the countless dark figures which were swarming ever closer. Two of them clattered against the gate, the force of their uncoordinated impact jolting him back and showering him with droplets of decay. Behind him Sean was already off the bike. He grabbed the cadaver in the road and snapped its neck, surprising himself with his brutality, then climbed into the car which had previously blocked the full width of the gate. He released the handbrake, then jumped out and, with Webb's help, pushed it forward a few feet so that the barrier was secure again.

"You all right?" he asked, looking into Webb's face, partially illuminated by a sudden glimpse of early moonlight. Webb nodded.

"Fine," he said, glancing back at the twenty or so corpses which were now smashing themselves relentlessly against the metal gate. He wished they'd stop. The noise was making him nervous. He climbed back on the bike and held on tightly as they powered down to the fork in the road, then sharply turned back on themselves and roared up toward the hotel. The building loomed large up ahead, silhouetted against the darkening sky. Sean could already see movement.

"Shit!" he cursed as the light from the bike illuminated the outline of a crowd of figures moving toward them across the car park. Three—no four—bodies were heading their way. How the hell did they get through? Had they left the gate open earlier? Had they somehow got in through . . . wait . . . they were moving too quickly, and their movements were controlled. It was Hollis and the others. He drove up to the front of the building and got off the bike, relieved.

"It's all right," he said to Webb, calmer now. "It's okay. It's just Jas and—"

Jas silenced him with a savage right hook which sent him spinning around and crashing down. Stunned, he didn't know where he was or what had happened. Jas then moved toward Webb, who cowered pathetically, covering his face with his hands.

"Don't hit me," he pleaded as Jas grabbed his collar and pulled him closer. "Please, I—"

"Leave it," Hollis warned, forcing himself between the two men. "Not out here."

"Fuckers took my bike," Jas seethed.

"Not out here," Hollis repeated.

"Never mind your damn bike," Harte said anxiously, "just get them inside before they do any more damage."

"What you talking about?" Webb stammered, trying to hide the fear in his voice and failing miserably. "We blocked the gate. We didn't let any of them through."

"Just shut up and get inside," Jas hissed, shoving him back toward the hotel.

"But we didn't—"

"Just get inside," he shouted, running forward and grabbing Webb again. Face-to-face, Webb found himself looking deep into the other man's eyes. The anger he'd expected to see wasn't there, just fear. He wrestled himself away and ran toward the safety of the hotel's shadows.

45

"I just can't believe you'd be so damn stupid," Jas ranted as Sean and Webb were frog-marched into the Steelbrooke Suite. "What the hell did you think you were doing? Are you out of your fucking minds?"

"Fuck you," Sean mumbled, his jaw still stinging and his head spinning with pain. One of his teeth felt loose and he could taste blood in his mouth. He cowered back as Jas lunged for him again.

"Stop it!" Caron screamed, lowering her voice immediately when she realized how unintentionally loud she'd been. "For Christ's sake, please stop. We've got enough to worry about now without you beating each other senseless."

"What's she talking about?" Sean asked, confused. "What's happened?"

"It's the bodies," Gordon said unhelpfully from the table where he sat with Ginnie.

"What about them?"

"Seems they're smarter than we've given them credit for," Martin began to explain.

"What?" Webb grunted.

"The noise you lot made coming here a couple of days back started it, and when you went out for supplies yesterday it just made matters worse. What you two did today might just have been the straw which broke the camel's back."

"I don't understand," Sean said. Martin sat down in the nearest chair and held his head in his hands. Howard explained further.

"They're coming back. There's a load of them gathered over the road."

"What about the music?"

"Not working anymore."

"That's not exactly true, it is still working," Hollis corrected him, "but like Martin says, they're getting wise to it. It fooled them before because they didn't know anyone was here."

"And now?"

"And now it's still drawing them in from miles around. Problem is, when they get close enough and hear us moving about or arguing or driving around on stolen fucking motorbikes, they understandably get more interested in us than anything else. They're starting to work out that the music is just a decoy and that we're the ones actually making the noise."

"Can't be . . ." Sean said.

"Can be," Harte quickly replied. "It's instinctive. It's exactly what started happening back at the flats. The more noise we made, the worse they got. A handful of them broke through our defenses, hundreds followed. They *learn*."

"So what are we supposed to do?" Ginnie asked, shuffling a little closer to Gordon. "Is there anything we can do?"

"What we should do now," Martin announced, unsuccessfully attempting to exert some authority, "is exactly what we were doing in the first place before you clowns arrived. We keep our heads down, stay absolutely silent, and wait for those creatures out there to disintegrate down to nothing. If we run out of food then we go hungry. If we start to—"

"No way!" Sean yelled, his voice furious, the fuzziness in his head clearing and being replaced with anger. "No fucking way. If you think I'm sitting here in fucking silence with you lot just waiting for the bodies to rot, then you can think again. You can stick your fucking—"

"That's exactly what you're going to do," Jas said, moving toward him again. Sean recoiled. "Because if you don't I'll break your fucking neck."

"Is that right?" Webb goaded.

"Don't you start. I'll kill you now if you want me to, you little piece of shit."

"Come on, then!" he yelled, jumping to his feet and squaring up against Jas. The others cringed, willing them both to shut up as the volume of their pointless argument continued to increase.

"Leave it, Jas," Harte said. "He's not worth it."

Webb stood his ground as Jas moved forward again. Their faces almost touching, he whispered loud enough for Webb alone to hear.

"Want me to tell them about Stokes?"

Webb pushed him away and slunk back into the shadows.

"Let's just keep things in perspective," Lorna said. She'd been watching the discussion deteriorate with disappointment. "There's no need to panic. They still can't get to us. Every access point is blocked. Like Hollis says, we just need them to forget we're over here."

"But what about the helicopter?" Caron wondered. "And the plane? How are we supposed to attract their attention if we're keeping our heads down? We don't know how many more times they're going to fly over."

"Have they been here again?" Sean wondered.

"Twice more," Gordon replied.

"Twice?"

"Flew over late afternoon," he explained, "then again just about an hour later."

"They're clearing out, aren't they? It's like you said this morning, Jas, they're evacuating."

"I think he's right," Gordon said.

"Then that's all the more reason for us not to lock ourselves down, isn't it?" Sean nervously continued. "If we don't let them know we're here now then they'll never find us. And I'm not just talking about writing love letters on the grass with bedsheets or playing music, we have to do something big that they're going to see and we have to do it now!"

"Sean . . ." Martin warned. His voice was getting louder again.

"Oh, just shut up, Martin. Will you get off my case? You haven't even—"

"Just calm down and be quiet."

"What if I don't want to? I know exactly what we have to do to get that helicopter or the plane to see us, and I'll do it if none of you have got the nerve to."

At the side of the room, unnoticed by anyone but Ginnie, Gordon stood up and cleared his throat. With great hesitancy but a definite need to act, he slowly walked forward into the middle of the argument, placing himself directly between Hollis, Martin, and Jas on one side, and Sean and Webb on the other. He looked Sean straight in the eye.

"Listen," he began, captivating the others with his unexpected and uncharacteristically positive involvement, "you have to listen. I know you're angry and you're probably just as scared as I am right now, but you've got to listen. Please don't do anything stupid. We've sat in here today and we've watched those things work out where we are. It's only a fraction of them at the moment, but if the rest of them catch on and end up down here we're going to have a real problem on our hands. I know you don't want to stay here, but I really don't think you've got any choice. None of us have."

Sean stared deep into Gordon's face and carefully considered his words. He knew he wasn't overstating the threat from outside, but were they really only limited to one option? He didn't think so. Being outside today had been such an unexpectedly uplifting experience. Could he turn his back on that freedom and everything he'd seen now? He couldn't stand the thought of being shut away in this hell-hole with these people any longer.

The silence in the room was deafening.

"Don't know," he said eventually. "I don't know if I can—"

"You have to," Caron said from the shadows to his left. Christ, he reminded her of her son at times. He was just like Matthew—so volatile and opinionated, yet vulnerable too.

"I don't have to do anything," he answered, glaring at her. "None of us do. You can all stay here if you want to but I think I'll take my chances out there."

"Just give it some time," she pleaded.

"I'd give anything for another day like today," he said, his voice suddenly wavering with emotion. "Do you know what I did today?" he asked, looking around at the few faces he could see. When no one answered he continued. "I lived," he explained, tears welling up in his eyes. "For the first time in weeks I actually felt like I was alive and it didn't matter what I did. And I come back here and everything feels wrong again, and it's not because of the bodies out there, it's you lot."

"What are you talking about?" Gordon asked.

"From where I'm standing there's no difference between the bodies on one side of the fence and the other. There's no difference between any of you and those things out there. You're all dead. You're all just sitting here rotting, waiting for the end to come. I don't really care if I've got one day left or fifty years. I don't care if I don't get through tomorrow. I just don't want to spend the rest of my time trapped in here with us all watching each other decay."

46

"How many?"

Startled, Martin spun around and saw Harte standing in the doorway of his second-floor bedroom. Hollis, who was standing next to him, hadn't heard a thing. He turned around when he saw that Martin had been distracted, then turned back to face the window.

"Maybe as many as five hundred or so," Martin replied. "Difficult to tell."

"Are more still coming?"

It was difficult to make out much detail in the late-evening gloom, but there still seemed to be plenty of movement in the field across the road. The dark mass of inquisitive corpses had grown steadily through the course of the day just gone and their numbers showed no signs of slowing.

"Plenty more," Martin answered, his voice tired and low.

"So what do we do now?" Harte asked, joining the other two at the window.

"Depends," Hollis grunted. He could hear him now that he'd moved closer.

"On what?"

"On them, mainly," he replied, nodding in the direction of the throng of constantly shifting figures. "It depends how responsive they are. If all they're going to do is just stand on the other side of the fence, then there's not much of a problem. If they decide they want to attack us then—"

"They won't," Martin immediately interrupted. "Why would they?"

"If they're threatened they will," Harte said quietly. "We've seen it happen loads of times."

"But who's going to threaten them?"

"What you see as a threat and what they do are very different things," Hollis explained. "Take those fucking jokers out on the bike, for example. We just see a couple of idiots escaping for a while. The dead react like animals would. They see the speed and hear the noise and sense the danger."

"Then try and attack before whatever it is can get them," Harte continued.

"So we stay here and wait for them to rot." Martin sighed. "Just like we were doing before you lot turned up here and screwed everything up."

"We haven't screwed everything up," Hollis corrected him. "Be honest, Martin, you were starving and you wouldn't have lasted much longer. Sean would have cracked eventually and you'd have ended up in this exact same mess. It's not completely our fault."

"We've just fucked things up a little quicker than you would have on your own," Harte said, his attempt at humor falling flat.

"But we've got supplies now, and Sean's had his moment. We can let him and Webb leave if they really want to."

"They won't go," Hollis said. "They haven't got the balls to do it. If they had they wouldn't have come running back tonight."

"Then we've got to keep them under control, Greg," Martin

added. "Stop them getting so wound up. Find a way to get them to let off steam."

"That might be difficult," Harte announced ominously. "We have another problem."

"What?"

"It's why I came looking for you two."

"What?" Hollis demanded impatiently.

"Driver's sick."

"Sick? What, like—"

"Yes, sick like Anita and Ellie," Harte said quickly, anticipating his question.

"The girls that died?" Martin asked anxiously.

"Yep," he answered. "So I for one don't actually fancy sitting in here for another couple of months anymore."

"Where is he now?"

"Packed him off to bed with his paper and enough food and drink to keep him happy for a couple of days. Told him we'd keep checking on him."

"And will you?"

"No fucking way. I might go back up there in a few days and see how he's doing. If he's still alive then he hasn't got what Ellie and Anita had and we're safe."

"Where's his room?"

"Luckily he's always been an antisocial bastard. He's up on his own on the top floor of the east wing."

"Good," Martin muttered.

"We've also got the plane and helicopter to think about," Harte continued, subdued. "I think Jas is right, and if they are evacuating from somewhere like he says, then they'll probably be done soon. The fact they flew over so many times today makes me think they must be close to being done now. We need to get them to see us."

"But we can't risk giving away our location." Martin sighed. "We've already been through this. That might be all it takes to tip the bodies over the edge."

"Well, we might just have to take that risk," Hollis said.

"We can't."

"We might have to."

"But—"

"He's right," Harte said. "We could torch this whole fucking place if we had to. Imagine that . . . there's the distraction you need. Every single one of those fucking things outside would drag their sorry backsides straight over here. We could just walk away."

"No, that'd be suicidal. No way."

"I'm not suggesting we do it, but it's an option."

"It's a stupid option," Martin protested, his voice getting louder.

"Let's wait until morning," said Hollis. "We can't make any decisions tonight. I think we should try and work out how the bodies are likely to react, then work out how to attract the attention of the plane, if it comes back."

"How are we supposed to do that?"

"Isn't this is exactly the kind of reason you've kept the body by the swimming pool?"

"Suppose," Martin said, sounding more subdued.

"Well, we need to see how your corpse reacts when we get up close."

47

The morning came too soon. Hollis's stomach grumbled with pangs of hunger but he was too nervous to even think about eating. He waited for Martin at the end of the corridor which led to the swimming pool. Lorna, Harte, Howard, and Gordon waited with him.

"You okay?" Lorna asked, picking up on his obvious unease. He nodded but didn't answer. He didn't want to talk. Others didn't seem to want to shut up.

"Remind me what we're supposed to be doing again," Gordon mumbled nervously.

"Stop being such a fucking drip," Harte said. "You know exactly what we're doing."

He was right, Gordon understood completely, but like the rest of them he didn't relish the prospect of being face-to-face with one of the dead, even if they did outnumber it six (and a dog) to one. He wished there was an alternative, but none of them had managed to come up with a safer way of being able to properly gauge the strength of the creature's reactions. It had seemed like a sensible idea when they'd talked about it late last night. Now they were actually here, however, they were all having serious doubts.

Martin appeared from the direction of the Steelbrooke Suite. He tried to hold back, but the others made it abundantly clear that he should go first.

"She's your baby," Howard whispered.

The group walked down the curved corridor, stopping just before the window into the office. Martin peered in but it was difficult to see anything through the layer of grease and rotten flesh which had been smeared across the glass. After having spent so much time hiding in the shadows, the increased amount of staining on the window indicated that the behavior of the corpse had indeed changed. Had it been looking for them? Howard's dog stood beneath the window looking up, her sharp white teeth bared in a silent, sneering growl.

"So how are we going to do this?" Howard asked. He jumped back as the corpse's rot-eaten face appeared at the window. Its dulled eyes looked around at the six people who stared back at it. Perhaps sensing it was outnumbered, it took a few awkward, uncoordinated steps back into the darkness.

"There's not enough room here," Martin answered. "We should get her out onto the side of the pool."

After a few seconds of nervous inactivity, Lorna pushed past the others and followed the corridor around to the entrance to the pool. She shoved the heavy door open, wincing with disgust when the smell of the stagnant water hit her. The air was icy cold and a sudden smacking, clattering noise made her catch her breath. A door on the other side of the pool was blowing open in the strong wind, then slowly closing again when the breeze died down. She hadn't actually been in here before, she'd just glanced in from outside. It would have been lovely, she thought sadly to herself, just the kind of place she could have imagined spending her pre-Armageddon time if she'd ever been able to afford to stay in a place like this. On one side of the pool were the various items of gym equipment which she'd heard Jas and

Harte talking about previously, and over in the far corner a scattering of wooden deck chairs and sun-loungers, all draped with a shroud-like layer of dust and cobwebs. The large, open windows and the glass ceiling, had they not all been covered with dust and dark, moss-green stains, would normally have allowed the whole area to flood with sunlight. Her daydreams were interrupted by the noise of Hollis yanking open the changing room door. He disappeared into the darkness momentarily to prop open the door to the office, giving the corpse a clear passage out to the pool.

"Come on," he yelled. "You've been in there too long, sweetheart. It's time you came out to see us . . ."

The rest of the group stood a safe distance back and waited. For a moment nothing happened but then, very suddenly and very definitely, low sounds of shuffling movement came from inside the office. A loud clatter and bang sent Hollis scampering back to the others.

"Can you see her?" Lorna asked quietly. Howard's dog took a couple of padded steps forward and then stopped and bared her teeth again. Normally completely silent, she emitted the faintest low growl as more noises came from the darkness.

"Nothing yet," Hollis replied, shuffling tentatively forward again. "Hold on, here she comes . . ."

The corpse dragged itself out into the light, and it was an abhorrent sight. Despite the filth, the sloping glass roof above them meant that the light levels in the swimming pool were better than in much of the rest of the hotel complex, certainly better than the office in which the loathsome carcase had been held captive for almost two months. This, Martin realized, was the first time he'd seen her in her full glory, and her dishevelled appearance fascinated him. He felt an instant revulsion but also genuine pity as she lumbered clumsily forward. A guest at the hotel on the day that she and almost everyone else had died, he remembered again having seen her just before the infection had struck.

Transfixed, he walked over to where Hollis was standing, finding it hard to believe that the grotesque creature he was looking at now was the same woman he'd seen previously. Her figure—and she'd had a great figure, he remembered that clearly—was all gone. Where her body had been pert and tight before, it now sagged and drooped. Gravity had steadily drained the contents of her bowels down. Her feet were swollen and blue, her belly and buttocks distended and her heavily stained and discolored swimming costume had been stretched completely out of shape. The straps of the one-piece outfit had cut into the skin on top of her shoulders, wearing little grooves where they'd continually rubbed against her deteriorating flesh.

"Careful," Lorna whispered. Without realizing it, both Hollis and Martin had continued to move closer to the corpse.

"It's okay," Hollis said, keeping his eyes firmly fixed on the body. The cadaver, in turn, kept what was left of its eyes trained on the figures which surrounded it. Although labored in its movements, it was definitely looking around the group. It slowly moved its rotting head from left to right, then turned back again when Gordon slipped in a puddle and lost his footing for a moment. Howard's dog growled again, an ominous low rumble of warning, and the body reacted, dropping its head and looking down at the animal standing its ground just meters in front of it.

Then it stopped.

It began to move backward.

With even less control than it had demonstrated before, the body slowly began to retreat, leaving behind it a trail of smudged, slimy footprints. It shuffled back across the tiled floor, bumping into the frame of the door through which it had just emerged. Then, more through luck than as the result of any conscious decision making, it shuffled left and slipped back into the darkness of the room where it had spent the last sixty days.

"Fuck me," Hollis said.

"Where's it going?" Gordon asked, unnerved by the creature's unexpected behavior and hoping that someone would have a plausible explanation.

"She's trying to get away from us," Lorna suggested.

"This is great," Harte said from his position a little farther back. "Damn thing knows it hasn't got a hope in hell."

"Did you see her checking us out, though?" Howard said, standing next to him. "I reckon she saw there were too many of us and decided it wasn't a fair fight."

"I think you're right," Hollis agreed. "If it's got any sense left in its head, it's got to know that it's got no chance on its own against six of us."

"And a dog," Howard added.

"It knows it's safer back in there than out here," he continued.

"So what do we do now?" Martin nervously asked. "Have we actually proved anything? If we go outside, do you think all those bodies are going to start backing off when they see us?"

"They haven't so far," Lorna said, moving slightly and trying to peer deeper into the changing rooms. Hollis did the same.

"The difference is it's still got a choice at the moment," he said. "Most of the bodies left out in the open don't have anywhere to hide. We need to see what happens when we take away its options."

"Force it out into the open?" Lorna wondered. Hollis nodded.

"Martin, why don't you go through to the corridor and try to force her back out here. Then close the door behind her so she can't get away again."

"I-I don't know . . ." he stammered anxiously. "Do you really think we should be doing this?"

Lorna sighed. "Oh, for Christ's sake, stop being so pathetic. I'll do it."

"Be careful," Hollis warned.

"It's no big deal," she said flippantly as she walked away. "Just a half-rotted sack of shit."

Hollis watched her leave, then returned his attention to the corpse in the shadows. He could see it hiding just behind the door. It was standing still—or at least as still as it could—but the uneasy swaying of its body gave the game away. An arm would swing out into the light momentarily, or its head would droop down lazily before it pulled itself back out of sight again.

Lorna stood in the corridor outside the office and composed herself before going in. The handle was stiff and she needed to shove the door hard with her full weight to get it open. She paused again before going any farther, letting the cloying stench of the captive corpse's decay dissipate. She felt unexpectedly nervous. Christ, what was she worried about? She'd dealt with hundreds of these creatures before now, and this one wasn't any more of a threat than any other. And besides, she reminded herself, this is one corpse against six of us. Damn thing doesn't stand a chance.

She entered the dark room, picking her way through the waste and rubbish which had accumulated over weeks, trying not to slip in the dark puddles of offensive-smelling gunk which had seeped and dribbled from the cadaver over time. She moved toward the light coming from the pool. The corpse in the doorway was still preoccupied with the men lying in wait for it outside and didn't notice her approaching. She'd never been this close to one of the dead before and not been about to destroy it. It was a grotesque, yet morbidly fascinating sight. The nearer she got, the more unpleasant detail she could make out. The various lesions and open wounds on its torso and legs were filled with teeming movement—thousands of maggots and worms gorging on its decaying skin. A chunk of flesh hung loose from the side of its right calf. She could see bones and what was left of its muscles and sinew under the skin. Although for a moment her nerves threatened to get the better of her, she forced herself to stay focused and keep going.

"Get ready," she shouted.

At the sound of her voice the cadaver began to slowly try and turn itself around, but it was far too slow and clumsy. Lorna lifted her hands and shoved it firmly in the small of its back, taking care to handle its swimming costume and not make contact with bare flesh. Knocked off-balance, the corpse tripped back out into the open again. She followed it through to the poolside, slamming the door behind her and sealing off its escape route. It instinctively lurched toward Hollis and Martin, the closest of its aggressors. Howard's dog bolted forward and he dragged her back, just managing to grab her collar as she leaped at the Swimmer. Her claws dragged along the raised floor tiles at the side of the pool as she scrambled to break free and attack.

"Watch it!" Gordon yelled as the dead woman heaved its disfigured bulk toward Martin. He put his arms up to protect himself, but Hollis shoved him out of the way. The body acted with remarkable speed, almost immediately turning its full attention toward him instead. It crashed into him with unexpected momentum, shoving him back and over.

"See," he said as he picked himself up and struggled to grab hold of the hideous figure which writhed and squirmed relentlessly, "it has no choice now. We've made it fight. All it can do is attack."

The monster's loose, greasy skin seemed to slip and slide around its bones as he held it. It managed to free itself from Hollis's grasp and immediately lurched toward Harte, the next closest. He could see that it had already been damaged as a result of its brief skirmish with the other man. The flesh at the top of its right shoulder had been torn away and now appeared to be falling down its arm like a loose-fitting sleeve. He looked deep into its vile face as it neared. Harte knew nothing of the creature's past. He knew only that it was time to end its pitiful existence. He jumped toward it, grabbing a fistful of hair and slamming its face onto the tiles at the edge of the stagnant swimming pool. Still it continued to try and fight, hopelessly overpowered but stubborn and relentless to the end.

"Fucking thing won't give up," he said anxiously as he fought to keep hold of it. No one else moved. Howard, in particular, had seen far fewer corpses than the others and was overwhelmed by the full extent of this cadaver's grotesque appearance. Every movement it made caused more damage but it didn't stop. He could see rotten flesh literally peeling away from its bones; the more it fought, the more damaged it became. But what else could it do? The enormity of what they were witnessing was not lost on Lorna. More used to being this close to the dead, she could ignore the shock of the grime and gore and concentrate on the implications of the creature's actions.

"So those bodies outside," she said as Harte dragged it back up onto its unsteady feet, "are all going to react like this?"

"We've got to assume so," Hollis answered.

"Dear God," mumbled Martin, covering his mouth in disbelief.

"Get rid of it," Gordon said, backing off. "Please . . ."

Harte let go of the corpse and it staggered away for a few steps farther. He watched it for a moment, long enough for it to clumsily turn back around and start moving toward him again, then he barged it into the pool. The Swimmer waved its arms furiously, its frantic, uncoordinated movements keeping it afloat for a final few seconds before it was sucked below the surface. Martin watched until it was just a dark, unfocused shape on the bottom of the pool. Damn thing was still moving. Even down there, the damn thing was still moving . . .

48

"Helicopter," Sean said simply, pointing out of Jas's bedroom window, then turning and heading for the door.

Jas looked up. He was right. There, crawling across a dull sky peppered with gray and white clouds, was the helicopter again. He was sure it was the same one they'd seen previously. He scanned the skies behind it, desperately looking for the plane which had followed every time they'd seen it yesterday, hoping he'd see it again and disprove his evacuation theory. He stared up into the sky for what felt like forever but it wasn't there. His heart sank. He was certain that meant they were running out of time.

"Aren't you coming down?" Harte asked. Sean had already disappeared. Jas shook his head and remained sitting on the end of his bed, cradling a drink in his hands.

"No point," he replied sadly. "I can stay up here and watch them fly away, no need to waste energy running downstairs to do it. Anyway," he said, taking another swig of his drink, "they'll be back later."

"How do you know?"

"I've been thinking about it."

"And?"

Jas wearily got up and walked over to the window just in time to see the helicopter bank left before completely disappearing from view. "And the fact that the plane hasn't come back this time tells me I'm probably right. First time it flew over yesterday it went from east to west, then it came back, then it did the same again. I said from the start I thought these people were packing up and moving out. Maybe two plane loads was enough to get them all away, and the fact they made so many trips so quickly yesterday kind of proves the point. I think the helicopter's back to mop up anyone or anything they left behind."

"So what are you saying?"

"What I'm saying is I think this might be the last time they'll pass by. Another couple of flights at most, but I think this is it. They'll fly back when they've done what they need to do and we won't see them again."

"You might be wrong."

"I hope I am."

Harte paused for a moment to consider the other man's logic. His explanation seemed feasible. "So do you think it was the military or the government?"

"No idea. Probably neither. I doubt there's anything like that left anywhere. No, I just think it's a bunch of lucky fuckers who've struck gold. They've got someone who can fly so now they're off to find somewhere where there are no bodies, no germs, and no arseholes like Webb and Martin."

"I get the idea."

Jas finished his can of beer and leaned against the window. Martin, Ginnie, and the others were outside now, standing around their pathetic message on the lawn, trying not to feel completely fucking useless. He turned his attention to the ever-growing crowd of bodies in the field over the road. Even now, even after they'd all done as they'd agreed and kept quiet since Sean and Webb had returned yesterday evening, still more of them were continuing to drag themselves back from the golf course. There had to be almost a thousand there now, maybe double that number, and they showed no signs of reducing. Who was to say the whole damn lot weren't about to turn tail and start moving away from the music in some kind of bizarre slow-motion stampede? A few hundred breaking away weren't a massive concern, but a few thousand . . . now that was a different matter.

"We need to do something," he announced, the tone of his voice suddenly more positive and definite. "Sitting here and doing nothing isn't an option anymore—we've tried that and it hasn't worked. We've got to get that helicopter to see us next time because it might be our last chance."

"Let's be realistic about this for a second. Even if they do spot us, are they going to risk landing here?"

"Who knows? There's enough space, but you're right. Maybe we need to think about getting away altogether? We're no better off here than we were at the flats. Exactly the same bloody problems, in fact— there are crowds of bodies getting closer and one of us is sick."

"But we've isolated Driver."

"Good. That lazy bastard did nothing for me while he was fit and well, I'll be damned if he's going to kill me with his bloody germs now he's sick."

"We don't know if he's got the same thing yet. It might not be—"

Jas sighed. "Come on, don't be soft. Of course it's the same thing."

Harte leaned back against the wall so he didn't have to look out at the dead. "So now we've got all the usual questions to answer. How do we do it? How do we get away and where would we go?"

"If it comes to it we could just drive out of here the same way we came in," Jas suggested. "And what about that exhibition center everyone was banging on about before we got here? Sounded like a pretty good place to aim for to me."

"Still don't know how you reckon you'll get the helicopter to see us."

"Fire!" he answered simply.

"What? You thinking of setting fire to the hotel?"

"No, you idiot, there's no point doing that. I think we need to get out there and cause a bit of carnage in the fields. We need to start a few fires, maybe an explosion or two. Think about it. It'll take the pressure off this place again, because those dumb dead fuckers will head for the fire, not the hotel. And if the helicopter pilot does come back, when he sees three or four decent-sized fires in close proximity to each other but out in the middle of nowhere, he'll have to realize that there are people down here. If he looks hard enough, that'll be when he spots their message on the lawn."

"And if he doesn't?"

"Then we get in the bus and the van and we take advantage of the fact that the bodies are distracted to get the fuck out of here."

49

Hollis had fallen asleep on a bench in the courtyard in the middle of the hotel. He'd only planned to sit down for a minute, but by his watch that had been a couple of hours ago. He was having trouble sleeping at night and was grateful that he'd managed to snatch some unexpected relaxation, even though it had left him feeling disoriented, nauseous and cold. He shook his head clear, sat up, and looked up into the cloud-filled sky above him. Disgruntled and uncomfortable, he got up and went inside to look for something to eat.

In many ways the long and empty hours like this were worse than the frantic, desperate times when they were running, fighting or both. At least dealing with crisis after crisis kept him feeling alive. Sean's words yesterday evening had rattled around his head. *"You're all dead,"* he'd said. Was he right? Was the gap between the living on one side and the dead on the other really narrowing as much as he'd suggested? *If this is the quality of life we've got to look forward to,* he thought sadly, *then maybe he's got a point. At least the dead can move around freely and without fear.* Was it better to feel and think nothing, he wondered, than to have your head filled constantly with the kind of desperate, nightmarish thoughts which seemed to constantly plague him?

"I said, are you okay?" Lorna said, tapping his arm. She'd walked right up behind him and he hadn't even noticed. Either he'd just been preoccupied, or his hearing was getting worse. He tried to convince himself that his thoughts had just been elsewhere, although the reality was that he could now hardly hear anything through his damaged ear. That terrified him. In a world where the slightest sound could make the difference between remaining undetected or being surrounded by corpses, how would he survive?

"I'm fine," he replied, trying unsuccessfully to hide his depression. Lorna was getting to know him too well.

"I'm just going to steal a couple of bottles of wine and some food," she told him, very matter-of-factly. "Come up to my room if you feel like a chat."

"Okay," he mumbled, watching as she turned and disappeared into the kitchens. For half a second he stupidly allowed his mind to wander. Why was she inviting him up to her room? Was it just to share a bottle, or was there more to it? He'd long looked at her and wished that he could have her, but he'd never got the impression that she felt the same way. *Don't be such a fucking idiot*, he thought, angry that he'd allowed his mind to wander, *you're old enough to be her father. She's only interested in you as a friend. That's the only kind of positive relationship that exists now. There's no room in this fucked-up ruin of a world for sex, love and lust and—*

Car engines. Coming from outside. He could hear several of them.

Hollis immediately sprinted through to the front of the hotel, bursting through the main reception doors and running down the steps into the car park. He jumped to one side as a silver estate car careered toward him and tried to flag it down. Harte, behind the wheel, accelerated and swerved past. A blue executive saloon driven by Amir with Webb in the passenger seat beside him followed close behind, then a third car, a beaten-up, dark green family-sized hatchback

281

driven by Sean, powered past. Where the hell were they going? Did they realize how much noise they were making? He turned around and saw Jas moving toward the van. He ran to stop him, trying desperately to get to him before he opened the driver's door.

"What the fuck are you doing?" Hollis said, slamming the door shut as Jas tried to pull it open.

"Just leave it, Hollis," he replied, barging him out of the way.

"You're not taking the van," he yelled, throwing himself forward again. Jas, a good eight inches shorter but much stronger, wrapped his arms around Hollis's waist and swung him around, throwing him down onto the gravel. Before he could pick himself up Jas had climbed into the van, locked the door and started the engine.

"Just get inside and keep out of the way," he shouted through the half-open window.

"You fucking cowards!" Hollis screamed, hammering on the side of the vehicle as it started to move. "Why are you running? All you're going to do is let them in here."

"We're not running," Jas hollered back. "Not yet."

He put his foot down on the accelerator and drove away from the hotel. Hollis ran a few meters after him, but it was pointless. As the van disappeared around the curve in the track he turned and sprinted back inside to warn the others.

Jas stopped at the fork in the road. The three cars traveling ahead of him were having to shunt themselves around to take the tight turning and follow the other branch of the track up past the fields and toward the golf course. He waited anxiously for them to get out of the way. Despite the length of his car Harte had already managed to complete the tight maneuver with the minimum of effort. Amir, however, was struggling. He shunted his car backward and forward, backward and forward, making inches of progress at a time. Jas tried not to think what effect the sound of his over-revving engine would have on the crowds of dead bodies gathered nearby. As he waited to move he reached into his jacket pocket and took out his wallet. He unfolded the photo of his beautiful wife and children, long dead but still a huge part of him, and kissed it. He hadn't looked at them for a couple of days, and that made him feel guilty. But he'd thought about them, he reassured himself. He'd thought about Prisha, Seti, Annia, and their mother almost every waking hour since he'd lost them.

"Have I got this right, Harj?" he asked, looking into the last remaining image of his wife's deep brown eyes. "Or are we just about to fuck everything up?"

Sudden movement caused him to quickly put the picture away. Amir had finally made it around the corner. Sean wasn't far behind—a textbook three-point turn and he disappeared behind the fence. Jas put his foot down again and followed, roughly yanking the van around the tight bend, crashing into the hedge on either side, no longer concerned about the noise. The three other cars had stopped again a short distance ahead. Harte was out and was running to the car which Sean and Webb had moved yesterday to get into the field. With Webb's help he managed to shunt it far enough out of the way to leave the gate clear. Even from his position at the back of the queue Jas could see that a huge gathering of bodies had almost immediately amassed on the other side of the gate. They pushed forward angrily, rattling the low metal barrier. Webb sprinted for cover and climbed back into the middle car with Amir as Harte flicked the latch and shoved the gate open, knocking the cadavers at the front of the group backwards. They immediately surged forward again but it didn't matter. Back behind the wheel of his car, Harte accelerated into the field and sent them flying. Amir and Sean followed, both cars crunching through gravel then pounding over the uneven mud. Jas brought up the rear, glancing back in his mirror momentarily and watching the gate swing shut again. It wasn't locked, but it would have to do for now. Hopefully the sudden arrival of the four vehicles in the field would be enough to distract the crowds of slothful figures. Judging by the vast numbers of them already stumbling toward him, that certainly seemed to be the case.

As they'd arranged, Harte veered off to the left, plowing into a wave of corpses and driving down the slope of the field toward the very bottom, right-hand corner, diagonally opposite to the gate they'd just entered through. He looked back over his shoulder to make sure that Jas was following. Behind him the van thumped through the sea of lethargic figures, wiping out many of them. There were hundreds of the fucking things here, many more than he'd expected and far more than had been visible from their vantage point back at the hotel. Jas accelerated again, following the curve of the blood-soaked scar Harte had left across the field.

"That's got to be far enough," Harte said to himself, anxiously trying to work out where he was. His brief had been to drive as far as he could across the full width and length of the field, but he hadn't accounted for just how little he'd be able to see from behind the wheel. His driving position was low and all that he could see around him now was a relentless forest of constantly shifting corpses. *Better to stop and do it here*, he decided, *than end up driving into the bloody hedge and killing myself.*

He slammed on the brakes, skidding to a juddering halt, the rear end of the car spinning out and smashing into a handful of soggy, rag-doll-like cadavers. Jas pulled up alongside and watched him frantically scramble out of his seat. He leaned over into the back and emptied out half a can of fuel, then looked up to make sure that Jas was ready for him. He tried to shove the door open and almost immediately a mass of emaciated, clawing hands thrust back at him. Jas reversed, then accelerated forward, turning into the car and driving alongside it, scraping a layer of bodies away. In the short-lived moment of space which followed Harte threw himself out into the open, lit a match and dropped it into the back, then ran over to the van. He hauled himself up into the passenger seat just as the inside of the car was filled with a scorching whoosh of billowing flame. Job done.

"Nice one," Jas said, turning the van away and forcing it in the opposite direction back up the incline, its engine groaning with effort. The bodies around them temporarily reduced in number, the fire in the car proving to be a more interesting distraction. Harte twisted around and hung back over his seat to watch as the ragged gray figures surged toward the light. The boot of the car—packed with several plastic canisters full of fuel—exploded, showering the dead with flames and red-hot shrapnel. The car itself flipped over on its end and landed in the middle of the hordes, crushing untold numbers of them. Despite being steadily consumed by the heat and light, those which were alight but still able to move continued to stagger around until their already weakened muscles had burned away to nothing, setting light to more of the stupid creatures they blindly stumbled into.

"Can you see the others?" Harte asked, panting with a heady mix of nerves, effort, and exhilaration.

"We'll find them," Jas replied, sounding less than confident. Not only were they still surrounded by a seemingly unending mass of rancid flesh, but the gradient of the hill was also proving difficult. They were driving up, but they couldn't yet see what was happening at the top of the climb where the ground leveled out closer to the golf course.

Less than a hundred meters away but out of sight of the van, Amir and Webb were also struggling. The sheer number of bodies which had surrounded their car had completely disoriented both men. Throngs of disintegrating cadavers filled every available scrap of space, making it difficult to see in any direction and impossible to navigate. Amir kept the car moving forward, but had little idea where he was heading and was certainly not traveling at anywhere near a fast enough speed. His relative inexperience with the dead was painfully apparent. Rather than accelerate into them he frequently swerved or just ground to a halt and tried to nudge them out of the way. Webb was beginning to get desperate.

"Hit the fucking things!" he screamed. "Speed up, for Christ's sake!"

"But I don't know where we're going," Amir protested, wrenching the steering wheel hard around to the right and turning them in a tight circle, wheels skidding in decay.

"Neither do they."

"But we might end up in the fence or too close to the gate."

"It doesn't fucking matter." Webb shouted, his voice hoarse with panic and exacerbation. "We're about to blow the bloody car up!"

"Why don't you drive, then?" Amir suggested. Webb just glared at him.

"There!" he said suddenly, pointing over to the far left where he'd just spotted the roof of the van whipping past above the heads of the corpses. Amir slowed again, then turned around and accelerated. "Keep moving," Webb moaned, terrified that they were about to come to a sudden stop, stranded and surrounded. They burst into a muddy track of open, gore-soaked space, a sure sign that the van or one of the other cars had been there just a few seconds earlier. Amir followed the bloody route through the crowd until it disappeared again, swallowed up by another group of lurching figures.

"Where now?"

"Let's just do it here."

"But the van's not here. We can't do it until the van's here to pick us up."

Webb seethed, holding onto the side of his seats as the car bounced over a particularly uneven stretch of ground and clattered into another swell of rotting flesh. "You bloody idiot, it doesn't matter where the van is. Once we set fire to this thing they'll see us quickly enough."

Amir couldn't think straight. What did he do? Did he keep driving or was Webb right? Should they just stop now? He winced as the front of the car sliced the legs out from under a ragged body, cutting it in two and sending its head and torso spinning into the windscreen directly in front of him, leaving a large crack and a slimy smear of black blood. There were more bodies than ever up ahead of them now, so many that they looked like a solid black mass, no longer recognizable as individual cadavers. Behind the corpses he could see trees rising up on either side. Webb realized what was happening before Amir could react.

"You're gonna drive us into the fucking fence!" he screamed, covering his head.

Amir finally recognized where he was, but it was too late to do anything about it. He'd been here with Martin and the others way, way back when the nightmare had first begun. He'd spent hours out here as they'd struggled to channel the unresponsive bodies away from the hotel. There was a gap in the trees which marked the position of a break in the fence he and the others had made, and on the other side of the fence was the golf course. It was too late . . .

He had to make a snap decision. With so many corpses coming toward him he knew he either had to hit them at full speed or stop and turn back again. *Too close to the fence now,* he thought as the trees loomed up above them, *only one option left.* He jammed his foot down on the accelerator pedal.

"Hold on," he said pointlessly as he struggled to keep hold of the steering wheel. The car bounced and clattered through the hole that he, Howard and Martin had hacked through the fence weeks earlier. Webb braced himself for the impact he felt sure would come at any second.

The wheels thumped back down onto the hard ground. A sudden swerve to the left, then to the right, and the car burst out of the rough and onto the fairway. Too terrified now to make any rational decisions, Amir simply kept the car moving forward as far as he could, driving head-first into the largest crowd of dead flesh that either of them had ever seen. A relentless storm of decay and dismembered body parts was thrown up into the air as the blood-soaked vehicle blasted into the lifeless masses.

"Where the hell are you going?" Webb yelled, terrified. Amir didn't answer. He didn't know. He no longer had any idea what he was doing. The plan that Jas and Harte had come up with was in tatters. Maybe if he could find a way of turning around they could get back.

The car veered off course as it dipped down a sudden steep incline, hidden from view by dense swarms of dead bodies. Amir tried to compensate by steering straight back up into the climb, but the angle was too sharp. He'd almost made it up onto the seventeenth green when his tires, their grooved treads already filled with mud and rotting flesh, lost all traction and began to slip and slide back down the bank again. He frantically tried to steer himself back into control but it was no good—the drop away was too severe and the car leveled off. The engine straining and screaming with effort, he managed to keep moving forward at speed for a few more meters, until the front driver's-side wheel thumped into a low tree stump, forcing it up into the air. The battered blue car spiraled over and over and down, finally coming to rest on its crumpled roof in the middle of a stagnant stream.

Sean had spotted an opening, a way to still be able to do what he'd agreed to do for the others and then get the hell away from this godforsaken place and the fools and cowards he'd found himself trapped here with. He'd driven around haphazardly for a while, waiting for Harte and Amir to do what they had to do and taking a welcome opportunity to obliterate as many corpses as he was able. He drove in circles three-quarters of the way up the field, keeping an eye on the van up ahead as Jas tried unsuccessfully to track down Amir and Webb. The majority of the bodies in the field were still stumbling toward the burning wreck of Harte's car, attracted to it by the ferocity of the flames which were continuing to spread through scores of tinder-dry corpses. A sizable number of other cadavers, he noticed, had somehow managed to swing the gate at the top of the field open and were beginning to work their way along the road, spreading out in both directions. He wasn't unduly worried. The van would wipe them out on its way back to the hotel.

Through the crowd he caught sight of Jas again and decided it was time. He didn't know what the delay had been, or why he hadn't seen Amir's car set alight. Whatever the reason, there was no point waiting any longer. He stopped the car just short of halfway up the field, almost parallel with Harte's burning wreck, and gave a loud blast on the horn. Many cadavers immediately turned, shuffled toward him and began to thump their decaying fists against the windows. More important, the van also turned in his direction, smashing the lethargic creatures out of the way as it thundered along. It was almost completely covered in blood and gore. Scraps of skin and bone had wedged themselves into every available crease and crevice of its metal body. Flesh dripped off its headlamps and down the grill of its bonnet. When it was close enough that he could see Jas and Harte inside, Sean turned around and, as agreed, soaked the back of the car with fuel. The van pulled level and Harte beckoned him to move faster. He opened the sunroof and hauled himself out through it.

"What are you doing?" Jas yelled, winding down his window.

"Go," Sean replied.

"What?"

"Just go! I'm not coming back."

"What do you mean? Come on!"

"What do you think I mean?" he shouted. "I'm sick of that fucking hotel. I'm getting out of here."

"Are you stupid?"

"Might be," he answered. "Anyway, when you find Webb, tell him I'll wait down at the road junction for an hour, then I'm going."

"Going where?"

"Back into town."

"You *are* stupid."

"I just don't want to go back inside," he said, "that's all. Now piss off so I can torch this bloody car."

Before Jas could say anything else Sean lit a match and dropped it through the sunroof into the back of the car. As the vapors ignited he slid down onto the bonnet, then pushed himself away and sprinted into the crowd. He was out of sight almost instantly, swallowed up by the constantly swaying figures which filled the field and surged toward the light and noise.

Jas shoved the van into gear and motored away, willing the tired vehicle to move quickly through the swarming hordes. Just a few seconds later and the stockpile of fuel in the back of Sean's dark green car behind them exploded, turning it from an ordinary vehicle to a deadly weapon in an instant.

"You going after him?" Harte asked, craning his neck to look for Sean in the carnage.

"Fuck him," Jas grunted angrily.

"What now, then? Do we look for Amir and Webb?"

As with the first explosion, the sudden ball of smoke and flame that had just belched up into the sky was proving to be more of a distraction than the van. The dead converged on the remains of Sean's car like a hunting pack.

290

"Five minutes," Jas announced. "That's all we can give them." He wasn't interested in what might have happened to Amir and Webb, he just wanted to know why they hadn't done the job they'd been sent to do. Pair of useless fools. He cursed himself for leaving the two of them together.

50

"Shit," Howard cursed as the second car exploded in the distance. Hollis didn't hear anything but jumped up when he saw the other man's reaction. Sensing trouble he ran back outside, leaving the others standing dumbstruck in the courtyard in the middle of the hotel. He sprinted down the steps and out into the car park to see a dark cloud of smoke belching up into the sky above the top of the tall hedgerow. A distance to the left—at least several hundred yards, he estimated— the dirty pall from the first blast continued to climb into the air.

Back in the courtyard, Caron sat down at the edge of the overgrown lawn and poured herself a large glass of wine.

"Idiots," Martin muttered nervously. "What in Christ's name do they think they're doing?"

"Helping," Lorna insisted.

"Helping? How the hell is this helping?"

"At least they're doing something," Gordon said from the opposite side of the courtyard.

"Doing nothing is better than something," Martin protested. "Doing nothing is exactly what we all should be doing. All this is going to do is bring the bodies back here to us."

"They might bring that helicopter as well," Caron mumbled, knocking back her wine, already half-drunk.

"Just give them a chance," said Lorna.

Martin paced up and down anxiously.

"Think about it, Martin," Gordon continued, desperately trying to calm him and diffuse his increasing panic. "This might actually help. They're drawn to fire. Someone said yesterday that they were getting used to the music—well, maybe this will keep them occupied for a while longer and get rid of a few hundred of them at the same time."

"A few hundred?" he barked furiously. "A few hundred? Do you have any idea how many of them are out there? There are thousands and thousands crammed onto that bloody golf course."

"And you've said yourself that they can't get off it."

"No I haven't. I said we'd made it difficult for them, not impossible. The music's kept drawing them in until now, and the fact there have been so many of them moving in the same direction has kept them penned in. If they start turning back in large numbers we're screwed."

"But they're still on the other side of the road, behind two fences that they'll never manage to get through."

"If there are enough of them alight they could burn their way through," Martin suggested, his logic suddenly screwed by his nervous fear.

"That's hardly likely," Caron grunted, sniggering into her wine glass.

"If it comes to it I'll stand on a ladder chucking buckets of water over them," Gordon said, irritated.

"We haven't got enough water," Martin immediately answered back. The conversation was becoming ridiculous.

Howard's dog, which had been sitting at Lorna's feet, stood and pricked up its ears.

"What's the matter?"

The dog sniffed the air. As Lorna leaned down to stroke its head, it suddenly bolted. It ran at full speed across the courtyard, weaved through the marbled-floor reception area and jumped down the steps. Hollis spun around when he caught sight of it out of the corner of his eye, then watched as it hurtled toward the track leading away from the hotel. It stopped just short of the mouth of the road, barking. Hollis ran over and tried to shut her up. "What's the matter with you, girl? All this noise freaking you out?"

There were bodies coming up the track. From where he was standing Hollis could see at least four, but he knew that many more would probably be following close behind. The dog hurtled forward again, jumping up at the first cadaver and knocking it flat onto its back. It stood with its front legs on the creature's torso, pinning it down, biting and tearing at its clothing with its vicious teeth. The body on the ground—unable to understand what was happening to it—attempted clumsily to push the animal away but it was too strong and determined. Four other corpses wearily dragged themselves past the frantic melee near their feet and stumbled on regardless.

"Bodies!" Hollis yelled, immediately running back into the building to find a weapon. He met Gordon and Lorna coming the other way, already alerted by the barking of the dog.

"Many?" Lorna asked as they passed on either side of the reception desk.

"Enough," Hollis replied, grabbing a fire ax and turning back again. He glanced up to see Howard disappearing upstairs. Fucking coward, he thought.

By the time he'd made it back into the car park Lorna was already poised to batter the closest body with a machete. The corpse— the lopsided, rancid husk of a fourteen-year-old schoolgirl—advanced toward her imperiously. Gripping the machete tight she swung it upwards and grunted with effort and satisfaction as it connected with the underside of the creature's chin and sliced through its diseased face. A second strike and its head exploded like a watermelon, showering the ground and the other corpses nearby with blood.

Gordon sprinted forward with screwdrivers held high in either hand, all talk of dodgy hips and excuses now long forgotten. With a yell of savage, guttural rage he launched himself at the dead shell of a jogger, still dressed in full running kit. He plunged the screwdrivers into the creature's temples, feeling them hit each other as they crossed in the middle of what was left of its brain, then yanked them free, wiping them on the back of his trousers and moving straight on to the next kill, narrowly missing Hollis, who had just swung his ax up into the groin of a hideously decayed vicar.

Howard came pounding back down the stairs, looking for the others. He struggled to catch his breath and tell them what he'd seen. Caron, Ginnie and Martin waited anxiously at the bottom of the staircase.

"It's not that bad," he began.

"Not that bad!" Martin pointed outside. "There are bodies out there! How can it not be that bad?"

"Shut up, Martin," Howard gasped, leaning up against the wall. "Jas and the others have gone into the field through the gate we blocked with the car," he continued, gesturing back over his shoulder. "They've left it open so they can get out again."

"But they're letting them through!"

"Not that many," he answered quickly, still panting. "Believe me, there's enough going on out in that field to keep most of them occupied. I only saw about twenty of them on the road, thirty at the most."

"Thirty!" Martin screamed. "There are only six of us left here now!"

"It'll be fine," Caron assured him, the skinful of wine she'd had filling her with false confidence. She put her hand on his shoulder. He recoiled and pulled away. "Thirty is nothing," she continued, unperturbed. "Believe me, I've seen Greg deal with more than that on his own before now."

The carnage continued outside. Fighting close alongside each other Hollis, Gordon and Lorna had managed to inch slowly down the track. The ground was now littered with blood-soaked carcasses and dismembered bodies, some still twitching, and the dead were being pushed back. Hollis prayed that they could keep this progress up without being seen or heard by too many more cadavers. This number he could deal with, but he'd seen just how many more of them were amassed on the golf course less than a quarter of a mile from where they now stood fighting. It wouldn't take much to open the floodgates and bring thousands of them trudging back here.

Howard jogged down from the hotel, meat cleaver in hand. He stopped short of the others, reached down, and pulled his dog away from the corpse it continued to attack. Although ferocious, all she was doing was savaging the creature's innards. Its arms and legs moved regardless.

"Out of the way, girl," he said as he pulled her back by the collar and dropped to his knees. Squeezing his eyes shut—he didn't want to see what he was about to do—he slammed the cleaver down, cutting through the cadaver's neck. A sudden shock jarred his arm when the edge of the blade hit the tarmac. The body on the ground immediately stopped thrashing, and he let go of the dog and scrambled back out of the way. She bounded forward again and leaped up at another corpse. Howard remained where he was, finding it strangely hard to accept that he'd just decapitated someone. Something, he forced himself to remember, not someone . . . *something*. He stood up and looked for the others.

"Greg!" he yelled, watching Hollis as he neared the bend in the track, getting closer to where the road forked. Hollis stepped back when he heard his name being called.

"What?" he shouted back, eyeing up his next victim as a corpse in a blood-encrusted shirt and tie stumbled dangerously close.

"There are only about thirty or so of them. They're coming in through the gate."

"What did he say?" Lorna asked, stamping on an upturned face which stared up at her from the ground with cold, sunken eyes.

"Don't know," Hollis grunted as he returned to the fight. "Something about a gate."

"There's a gate," Gordon explained breathlessly between kills. "Ginnie showed it to me earlier. That's how they got the cars through."

"So if we can beat them back far enough . . ." Hollis began.

"Then we can get the gate blocked up again and stop them getting out," Gordan said.

Standing at his side, Lorna cracked the skull of another cadaver with her weapon, then shoved what was left of the corpse into the hedge. She nodded to show that she'd heard him and that she understood their position, then began to swipe and hack at the dead with renewed energy and speed.

"It's no fucking good," Jas snapped angrily. Next to him Harte continued to scan the area, desperately looking for Amir's car.

"Bet they've gone back," Harte said. "The no-good fuckers have lost their bottle and turned back."

With one last burst of acceleration Jas drove back up the incline and onto level ground again. For the first time since entering the field he stopped. All around them now was total carnage. An unprecedented number of bodies had been destroyed by the vehicles, the explosions, and the fire, and countless more still hauled their withered frames toward the two burning wrecks. Even now, after the initial effects of the explosions had died down, the inquisitive creatures continued to drag themselves closer to the flames and heat. All around them charred remains had been churned into the ground, mixing with the mud to form a single unidentifiable mire which covered the entire area. More bodies began to slam and hammer against the sides of the van and Jas drove away again, heading toward the gate.

"Screw them," he said. He accelerated out onto the road and began thumping into the backs of the unsuspecting cadavers which had escaped the field and were staggering down the track.

"The gate," Harte reminded him.

Annoyed by his oversight, Jas stopped the van, then reversed back, destroying another batch of corpses which had stumbled out into the road after them. He braked again and Harte begrudgingly jumped out, pulled the gate shut and locked it. Out in the open the acrid stench of burning cars and burning flesh stung Harte's throat and made his eyes water. He coughed and stepped back from the barrier as more bodies crashed against it and reached out for him with numb, grabbing hands. Forget the car, he thought, not wanting to spend another second out in the open.

"That'll do," he said as he got back into the van, still coughing.

Jas couldn't be bothered to respond. He needed to get back to the others and plan their next move. It was either up or out, he decided. If they couldn't attract the attention of the helicopter pilot this time—and if everything they'd just done didn't do it, he thought, what would?—then it would probably be time to say good-bye to this hellhole hotel and get away. His mind was made up. It was down to the rest of them to decide if they wanted to go with him.

Howard's inexperience was showing. The other three were way down the track and yet he still remained at the mouth of the road, standing and looking at the mass of bloody limbs and shredded flesh which lay all around him, attacking incapacitated corpses which were no longer a threat. He didn't want to go down and fight with the others but he knew that he had to. Christ, even the dog was doing more than him. He watched it jump up at yet another cadaver and sink its razor-sharp teeth into the corpse's arm, dragging it down to the ground. He tightened his grip on his meat cleaver and began to run forward again, determined to get involved. Then he stopped. What was that? He could hear another engine. Was it the van coming back? At first he couldn't locate the source of the swirling sound. Was it coming from the road running between the hotel and golf course, or from the road junction at the end of the track or even the field? It sounded like it was behind him . . . He spun around to see the bus careering around the front of the hotel with Martin at the wheel. He turned sharp left and hurtled down the track toward Howard, who ran for cover as fast as his tired, heavy legs would carry him.

"Move!" he screamed at the top of his voice to anyone who could hear him. Farther down the track Gordon looked up.

"Christ," he mumbled, grabbing hold of Lorna by the waist and pulling her away from the corpse she was carving up with her machete. She struggled to release herself from his grip, terrified for a second that it was one of the dead who had her trapped in its decaying arms. A little farther ahead Hollis continued fighting. He hadn't heard anything.

"Greg!" she screamed, looking around and quickly realizing what was happening. "Get out of the way!"

Howard's dog raced back toward its owner at full pelt, carrying half an arm in her mouth. Gordon pulled Lorna behind him, dragging her back up as she tripped over a bloody, headless torso, then pushing her into the hedgerow as the bus thundered past. It missed them both by the slenderest of margins, temporarily filling the world with deafening noise and a sudden hot blast of choking exhaust fumes.

"Hollis!" she screamed again as the back of the bus filled the width of the road and he disappeared from view. She stood in the middle of the tarmac strip with Gordon and watched helplessly as the bus raced away, instantly wiping up the last few cadavers which had made it this far along the road, smashing them like flies on its windscreen. Wrestling herself free from Gordon's well-meaning grip she ran down after it, stopping when she reached the area where Hollis had been standing.

"Hollis!" she screamed.

"Fuck me, that was close," she heard him say from somewhere to her left. She looked around with relief and helped him up as he disentangled himself from the undergrowth. "Who the hell was that?"

"Martin, I think," she answered.

"What does he think he's doing?"

"Trying to block the road or get rid of the bodies," she replied. "Or both."

The van blasted down the other side of the track at breakneck speed. Jas looked for the sharp, almost complete 360-degree turn that he needed to take the fork in the road back up to the hotel. At this pace it was difficult to see much—the hedgerows merged to look like a single, uninterrupted border around the hotel. Wait . . . there it was. He could see the back of the hotel sign now, and he could also see the sign to the golf club pointing up along the stretch of road they'd just come down. He slammed his foot hard on the brake and yanked the wheel around to the right, planning to make a three-point turn in the narrow space. Now facing the hedgerow, he crunched into reverse.

"Shit," Harte cursed, suddenly covering his head and diving over toward Jas. Jas looked up and, for the briefest of moments, was aware of the front of the bus thundering toward them.

The massive vehicle and its makeshift, blood-covered snowplow punched into the side of the van, the force of impact sending it crashing into the hedgerow and showering the road with broken glass. The bus itself continued forward, its front wheels ramming up the muddy bank at the bottom of the hedge. Harte shook his head and checked himself for injuries. Jas, who could already see that they were both unharmed, shoved him back over into his seat.

"Come on," he said, jumping out onto the road. He rubbed his aching neck and turned back to look for Harte, who was struggling to get out, unable to open his badly buckled door. "This way," he shouted.

Disoriented by the jolting shock and speed of the crash, Harte continued to try and get the passenger door to open for a second longer, unable to understand why he couldn't do it. Distracted, he looked up when he saw more movement out of the corner of his eye. The front of the bus was just a couple of meters away from where he sat, forced up at an unnatural sloping angle, and someone was trying to escape from inside. It was Martin. What the hell was he doing driving the bus? And what had he done? Blood was pouring down his face and he was banging on the glass.

"Come on," Jas yelled again, reaching back into the van and dragging Harte out onto the road. His head clearing, he picked himself up and ran around to the front of the bus. Martin was hammering frantically on the windscreen now, desperately trying to free himself.

"Keep still," Harte shouted. "Shut up and keep still!"

Martin was panicking. He was kicking and screaming and trying to get himself out of the driver's seat with no appreciation of how precariously balanced the bus was. Harte could see that all of the wheels on one side had been forced up the bank. Again he tried to stop Martin moving, but his words had no effect. The wiry little man finally freed himself from the seat and stood up to get out, scrambling up the steeply inclined floor. His desperate, clumsy movements were enough to upset the delicate balance of the bus and force it completely over onto its side. Jas yanked Harte back out of the way as the huge vehicle crashed down into the road. Martin was thrown across the cab, thumping his head again as he went down. This time he didn't get up.

"Do you think he's . . ." Harte began to ask.

"Probably," Jas said, his voice cold and devoid of emotion. "Stupid bastard. What the hell was he doing?"

Harte hauled himself up the front of the box-shaped vehicle and stood on its uppermost side, the top edge of the folding door at his feet. He dropped to his knees and pushed against it, managing to force it half-open.

"Martin!" he shouted. "Martin . . ."

Six feet below them, Martin began to groan.

"We'll come back for him," Jas said as he pulled himself up. "Stupid, bloody fool." He glanced down again at Martin's slowly stirring body, then turned and ran along the side of the bus.

"Looks like he was trying to clear the road," Harte said, stopping when he reached the back end of the vehicle and looking down at the track, completely awash with blood and unrecognizable heaps of fetid remains.

"Fucking idiot. All he's done is block it."

"Come on, he didn't know we were coming around the corner, did he?"

"I don't care. Fact is he's blocked our way out. How are we supposed to shift this thing now?"

"No idea. Come on, we'll sort it out later. We should get back to the others."

He was about to move when he heard the distant whine of another engine. He remained where he was, completely motionless. Where was it? Who was it? It had to be Webb and Amir. Where the hell had they been?

"Helicopter," Jas said, immediately recognizing the noise and pointing up at the aircraft he'd just spotted. His heart began to thump in his chest and his legs felt heavy with nerves. *Come on*, he thought, *this is it.*

He glanced over to his left. Two huge black columns of smoke were still rising high into the sky—surely they had to see them. Surely they'd fly over here to investigate . . . There was hardly any wind and the smoke was rising straight up like hundred-story-tall arrows pointing down at the hotel. He willed the helicopter to change course and fly closer.

"They'll see it," Harte said under his breath. "They have to . . ."

Jas stared unblinking at the single speck of black crawling across the white clouds. He watched it until it disappeared, praying it would bank around and come back.

Minutes passed before he stopped looking.

"That's it, then," he said dejectedly, his voice weak with emotion. "I don't think they'll be back again. We're completely fucked now."

51

Webb was upside down and he could taste blood in his mouth. The light was low and he struggled to make sense of his surroundings. Was it night already? Had he really lay here unconscious for hours, wherever here was? He could hear running water, and he could smell its pungent, stagnant odor too. What the hell had happened? He tried to move but a sudden sharp, jabbing pain in his gut made him stop. With cold, swollen hands he reached out and disentangled himself from his baseball bat. One of the nails was sticking into him. Fortunately several thick layers of clothing had prevented the point from piercing his skin. The pain immediately stopped and he let the bat fall from his hands. It landed with a thump on the upturned roof of the car, right between Amir and himself.

"Amir," he said, managing to tilt his head slightly so that he could see the other man's face, "are you okay?"

Amir didn't respond. Webb looked around again, confused, his eyes gradually becoming accustomed to the gloom. Amir was also upside down, still anchored in his seat by his safety belt. What kind of an idiot wears a safety belt these days? Webb wondered. And why am I lying on my back on the roof? The car, he slowly deduced, his head still cloudy, had turned over in the middle of a stream. He began to remember a few fleeting flashes of how they'd ended up here—plowing into the bodies on the golf course, Amir panicking and steering the wrong way, the sudden stomach-churning drop and the flashing of light over dark again and again as they rolled down the bank—but little else. Still not yet daring to move, he worked his way back through events to try and make more sense of his predicament. He remembered the reason why they'd been away from the hotel. The others would all probably have made it back by now and they'd have given him and Amir up for dead. But wait . . . maybe it wasn't as late as he'd first thought. He angled his head around again so that he could look out the window at his side. The glass was almost completely obscured by mud and a corpse which had its legs trapped under the car and was trying unsuccessfully to get away. When the corpse moved its leaden arms he could see definite flashes of daylight.

Got to get out of here.

"Amir," he said again. He managed to reach across and shake Amir's shoulder. He felt cold to the touch. Was he dead? He shook him again but still there was no reaction. What did he do now?

Webb slowly moved his legs and found that he was able to work them around the edge of the back of the seat he'd been sitting in when they'd lost control of the car. Now able to move with a little more freedom, he stretched out and shuffled along the roof up toward the engine. The car had come to rest at a slight angle. The front of it was out of the water, propped up on the bank, while the back end was submerged. If he could smash his way through the windscreen, he'd be able to crawl out under the upturned bonnet and get out. What he'd do after that was anyone's guess. The most prevalent of the snatched memories he had of the moments just before the crash was the incredible size of the crowd they'd managed to drive into. It was fucking huge.

"Amir," he whispered for a third time, "come on." When there was still no response he reached out to touch his neck and try to find a pulse. Amir's skin felt warm but clammy. He noticed that there was a puddle of blood on the roof below his upside-down head and he carefully turned his suspended head to face him. There was a deep gash across Amir's forehead and, when Webb looked back, a corresponding bloody smudge in the middle of the cracked windscreen. Ironic that Amir was the one who had been strapped in, he thought. Poor bastard.

Webb moved again and his outstretched foot kicked the fuel can which had also dropped onto the roof. Burn the car and distract the corpses, he remembered, that had been the plan. It might still work. He had no idea where he was in relation to the hotel, but anywhere on the golf course would be far enough away from the others not to matter, not that he cared about them and their plans anyway. Never mind getting that helicopter Jas had been constantly banging on about to see them, setting fire to the car would cause enough of a distraction to give *him* a chance to get away.

"Oi, Amir," he said, this time a little louder. He shook his shoulder again but still there was no response other than a sudden sickening dribble of blood where before there had been only drips. Time to move. There was nothing he could do for him. Even if he got him out of the car, he was going to have enough trouble getting himself off the golf course.

Struggling in the confined space, Webb spun around on his back through a slow 180 degrees and kicked at the windscreen. A series of three good, strong boots to the already weakened glass was enough to shatter it and kick it through. He turned back around again, grabbing the can of fuel and his baseball bat as he moved, and then crawled out of the car.

The appalling sight which greeted him was almost enough to send him scuttling back under cover but he forced himself to keep going. For as far as he could see ahead the stream was nothing more than a sicken-

306

ing stew of decay, packed solid with incalculable numbers of corpses which had fallen into the mire over time and been unable to get out again. Strangely cushioned and protected in the ditch, however, they continued to move constantly, never stopping but never getting anywhere either. The water he'd heard under the roof of the car was little more than a pathetic trickle. Filled with unidentifiable lumps and chunks and with a disgusting putrid brown-green hue, it reminded him of vomit.

The nearest bodies were trapped, either by each other or by the upturned car, and he found that he was able to move around them with surprising freedom. Working quickly he opened the fuel can and set it down under the bonnet. He tore a strip of rag from the back of a corpse which was stuck facing away from him, soaked it with fuel and jammed it into the mouth of the can. Taking out his lighter from under several layers of clothes, he lit the rag and furiously scrambled away.

"Webb . . ."

What the fuck was that? He spun around anxiously. It sounded like Amir, but he was dead, wasn't he? Jesus Christ, what if he was wrong? What if Amir was still alive; if he'd just passed out because of the blood? Webb could see him through the cracked windscreen. He didn't look like he'd moved. He must have imagined the noise. Amir's eyes were still closed and the blood was still dripping and . . . and the rag was still burning. Webb jumped to his feet and hauled himself up the steep bank, grabbing at random corpses and using them as leverage, stamping his feet down onto flesh and bone and whatever else he could get a grip on. He threw himself over the top of the bank, straight into a solid mass of bodies the size of which he couldn't even begin to appreciate, and then dropped to his knees as the car behind him exploded. Like unprotected trees around a bomb blast, hundreds of cadavers were flattened in a rough circle around the epicenter. Webb found himself buried under a mass of dark figures dripping with decay.

Keep moving.

No time to think. Make the most of the delay before the rest of them start moving toward the blast. As he climbed back to his feet and began to trip through a quagmire of flesh and body parts several inches deep, he glanced back over his shoulder. The car, or parts of it at least, had been blown back out of the ditch. He could see twisted chunks of its blackened frame burning fiercely. If Amir wasn't dead, he thought, then he is now.

All around Webb, hordes of bodies were turning and advancing toward him. They staggered and stumbled unsteadily through the gruesome slime which coated the once-pristine golf course. Thousands of continually moving feet had churned the remains of countless fallen creatures with the cloying mud to cover everything with a layer of dark, sticky, foul-smelling sludge. *Keep moving,* he told himself, *it's the fire they're heading for, not me.* As those corpses which had made the most progress lurched nearer he instinctively dropped to his knees and began to crawl through the slurry around and between their emaciated feet, hoping that remaining low would be enough to keep them from reacting to him. Stupid things never look down, he tried to reassure himself. If they looked where they were going, there wouldn't have been so many of them stuck in the bloody stream. He lowered his head and held onto his baseball bat as he began to move through the sea of spindly, unsteady legs which slipped and slid through the once-human soup all around him.

Which way now?

Time to make another decision. He couldn't keep crawling like this indefinitely—although he continued to do so as he tried to decide what to do next. Lifting his head momentarily, he glimpsed the trunk of a large, twisted tree up ahead and to his right. He altered his course and moved toward it, intending to use it as cover as the crowd continued to gravitate toward the fire. If he stayed on the blind side of the tree they probably wouldn't see him. In less than a minute he was there, and he cautiously raised himself up behind it, holding onto its rough bark and pulling himself back up onto his feet with gloved hands. It was surprising how much more he could see and hear now that he was upright. Down at ground level the sheer bulk of the bodies above him had blocked out much of the natural light, and they were so tightly packed that they'd acted like a canopy, muffling the rest of the world. Now that he was finally up straight again he could see over the heads of the dead. Almost all of them stooped, walking with their heads bowed as if the weight of their skulls were too much for their weakened bodies to support. He hadn't appreciated that before, but he hadn't been this deep in corpses and dared to stand still before now either.

Music.

He had to be imagining it. Could he really hear Martin's music? He was sure he'd imagined hearing Amir's voice just a few minutes earlier—was this just another cruel trick of his tired and increasingly confused mind? No, he could definitely hear it. His ears suddenly seemed to lock onto the frequency of the tune playing in the distance and it gradually became clear. A god-awful, screeching country and western tune was echoing around the golf course. Thank God for Martin Priest, he thought. He cautiously allowed himself to peer out around the side of the tree, quickly pulling his head back in again when a particularly grotesque figure raised its emaciated arms and lunged toward him. Christ, for a second in the confusion it looked like Stokes, but he knew that was impossible. It was just the low light and his nerves playing games with him. He looked again . . . slowly . . . carefully . . . forcing himself to concentrate . . . and then he saw it. The clubhouse. A couple of hundred meters away. Reachable.

I'm going to get out of here.

Webb dropped back down to his hands and knees and began to crawl.

52

Hollis and Gordon carefully lifted Martin out of the bus, hauling him up through the door.

"You stupid bugger," Gordon cursed as he struggled with his heavy legs. Martin groaned but didn't respond.

"He just panicked," Hollis whispered, putting his hands under his shoulders and lifting, "That's all. He was just trying to protect this place."

"Just trying to protect himself, more like."

"Doesn't matter now, does it?"

They reached the end of the bus. Hollis jumped down and called Howard over to help lift Martin down. Groaning with his awkward weight, between them they lowered him to the ground. There was movement all around them as Harte, Lorna, and Ginnie cleaned the drive—scraping up what was left of the dead with shovels, then transporting it in wheelbarrows and buckets away from the hotel.

"Mind out," Hollis said, almost backing into Harte and knocking him into a waist-high pile of fetid corpses and dismembered limbs.

"Watch what you're doing," Harte grumbled, realizing who they were carrying. "You going to chuck him on this pile? Stupid bastard nearly got us killed just now."

"No, he didn't," Hollis said quickly. "*You* nearly got yourselves killed. You were the ones who drove into a field full of dead bodies and started blowing cars up. Nothing to do with Martin."

"Suppose it was our fault he crashed into us as well," Harte said.

Hollis shook his head, refusing to be drawn into yet another pointless argument. "Whatever."

The road clear again, Harte threw down the shovel he'd been using and walked back toward the hotel. Howard, Hollis, and Gordon followed carrying Martin, who continued to moan. Ginnie and Lorna were close behind. They found Caron sitting on the steps outside the main entrance. She looked up as Harte stomped past her, then moved to the side to let the others through. It had started to rain—just a light mist—but it was refreshing and cool. Caron decided she'd rather sit out and get wet than go back indoors, no matter what dirt or germs were being washed down by the water. Lorna stopped and sat down next to her.

"You all right out here?" she asked.

"Fine."

"Aren't you cold?"

"I'm fine," Caron snapped.

"Sorry," Lorna mumbled, surprised by the strength of her reaction.

"It's all right," Caron replied. "Don't want anyone fussing, that's all."

"That's your job, isn't it?" she said sarcastically.

"I've given all that up," she said quietly, taking a swig from a bottle of wine. She offered it to Lorna, who took it gratefully.

"Shame," she said, wiping her mouth. "You were good at it."

Caron shook her head and stared out toward the edge of the hotel grounds. "I don't think so."

"What makes you say that?"

"Because all the people I've tried looking after recently are dead."

"In case you haven't noticed, love," Lorna whispered secretively, "pretty much everyone's dead, and it had nothing to do with anything you did or didn't do for them."

Caron thought for a moment.

"Suppose," she said, drinking more wine and shivering with cold. "Do you know what we need to do now?"

"What?"

"Absolutely bloody nothing."

"Nothing?"

"I might be drunk," Caron blathered, "but I know what I'm talking about. The more you try these days, the less you get. Those boys went outside today and tried too hard, now we've lost Amir, Sean, and Webb."

"Webb's no great loss."

"No, but the others were," she replied angrily, slurring her words slightly as she became more emotional, "and we didn't have to lose them. Now if we all just sit still, be quiet, and do nothing, we'll be okay."

The rain began to fall with more persistence. Lorna stood up, then reached back down and held out a hand to Caron.

"Come on," she said, hauling her up onto her unsteady feet. Together they walked through the cold and quiet building, along the glass-fronted corridor which ran along the edge of the courtyard. She glanced up and saw Howard pounding back down the staircase at the end of the opposite wing. Gordon was following close behind.

"More trouble," Caron said dejectedly. "It's always trouble when people like Gordon and Howard start moving quickly."

Lorna sighed as they walked toward the restaurant. "You don't

312

know that, but you're probably right." She braced herself for bad news but was surprised by the self-congratulatory smiles which greeted her.

"It worked," Hollis said as she walked over to him and took a can of beer.

"What worked?"

"Jas's little stunt outside today," he explained. At the mention of his name Jas turned around and grinned.

"You should see it!" he enthused. "We've just been watching upstairs. We shifted thousands of them today, and the rest are more interested in the fires we started than anything we're doing here."

"Congratulations." Lorna smiled, not exactly sure how she felt. Was it even worth reminding him of the pointless sacrifices which had been made? Perhaps it was better just to shut up and not burst his bubble.

"I don't think we should do anything else today," Harte said, picking up where Jas had left off. "But maybe we should think about getting out of here tomorrow or the day after that. We could take one of the trucks from the road junction."

"Are we going to gain anything from that?" Lorna asked cautiously, remembering Caron's earlier words.

"You can just stay here if you want to," he snapped.

She sighed. The arguments were becoming disappointingly stale and familiar around here.

"I'm not going anywhere," Caron announced, her drunken voice louder than intended.

"Shut up, Caron," Jas laughed. "You're pissed."

"I might well be," she replied. "but I'm not stupid."

53

Webb had almost reached the clubhouse. His progress over the final few meters of the once perfectly maintained golf course had been painfully slow. The number of cadavers around him seemed to have increased as he got nearer to the building, as had the depth of the repugnant sludge through which he continued to move. The sickly sea of decay, almost a foot deep in places now, had built up over weeks. Many hundreds of corpses had gravitated here over time, and a huge number of them had been dragged down and trampled underfoot. Their remains, along with the obnoxious juices which had dripped, dribbled, and seeped down from the masses still standing, had combined to become this unholy gray mire. Webb was covered in it. The damn stuff was in his hair and his eyes. It was in his nose and he could taste it at the back of his throat. He could feel it on his skin, cold and repellent. It had soaked him, permeating through his many layers of protective clothing. He tried to convince himself that it was just mud, and when he looked too closely and saw the occasional eye, or ear or other equally distinguishable shape floating by, he forced himself to look away and concentrate on the music still playing in the distance.

What now? He tried to keep his head down as much as he could but he allowed himself to glance up momentarily and saw through the forest of tripping, sliding legs that the front of the building was now only a couple of meters ahead. The music was uncomfortably loud now, although it continued to be muffled down at ground level by the increased number of corpses swarming above and around him. They walked over him, oblivious to his presence, frequently standing right on top of him and not realizing. Damn things didn't even know he was there.

It was impossible to see with any certainty, but the congestion around the door up ahead didn't look as bad as he'd expected. Sure, there was a huge number of corpses congregating around the building, but a decorative low wall or fence on either side of the door seemed to be channelling many of them away. Regardless, he was going to have to get up to get inside. He paused and lay still for a moment longer, collecting his thoughts and trying to steady his nerves. He'd managed to drag his baseball bat along with him. His only option now, it seemed, was to get up, smash his way through the crowd, and then batter the door—and any corpses that got in his way—with all the strength he could muster. Hopefully the speed and surprise of his attack would be enough to confuse the cadavers for a few seconds. By the time they realized what was happening, he hoped, he might already be inside. And what after that? He wished he'd listened more closely to Martin's explanation of the layout of the building. From what he could remember there was a back entrance which he used to get in and out. An entrance which was connected to the road and which would enable him to get back to the hotel. Back to safety and food and drink and his room and then—

Another decaying foot pressed down on the small of his back, pushing his face closer to the foul stench beneath him. He closed his eyes and tried to focus on what he was about to do, his guts churning with nausea and fear. Try and get a little closer, he decided, then just go for it.

Webb slithered through the mud and grime until the ground dropped away slightly. He'd reached the top of a gradual low slope which had remained invisible until now, disguised by the number of bodies tightly packed around the building. The slope led directly to the wide double-door into the clubhouse. Taking a final deep breath of noxious-smelling, germ-ridden air, he hauled himself back up to his feet, knocking several cadavers down into the mud as he did so. Dripping with the odious, rotten slime, he lifted his baseball bat high and swung it around his head, hacking down a wide circle of disoriented creatures. Before any others could react he ran to the door, slipping and sliding precariously down the slope. For the moment it seemed to have worked, and it was immediately apparent why: in the fading light the dead could hardly see him. Their eyesight was poor and he looked almost the same as they did, just another indistinguishable gray blur. Camouflaged by the thick, sludgy layer of mud and decomposed human remains, he now wore the same gray-green-black uniform as the rest of them and had become virtually invisible. With the bodies so tightly packed and their footing so precarious, he knew that he suddenly had an unexpected few seconds of freedom to get into the building. *Do it now*, he told himself, his mind racing, *before they realize.*

Webb hammered the baseball bat down on the clubhouse door. It immediately began to splinter and crack but it held tight. He swung the bat again, bringing it right over his head and crashing down on the door. The nails sunk into the wood and he had to yank them out as he prepared to strike for a third time. He swung the bat back, ready to heave it forward again, then pulled it back over his head with all the remaining strength he could summon up. This time it hit the door with a dull thud, and he saw that a chunk of flesh had been torn off a body behind him.

He glanced back and saw that the farthest advanced cadavers were moving forward again, attracted by his sudden strong movements and the noise he was making. A large group of them were edging closer. It was impossible to see exactly how many but that didn't matter. Many more were already following close behind. He shook the flesh off the end of the bat, heaved it back and swung it down again, this time with a loud grunt of effort and a satisfying crack as the top panel of the right-hand door gave way, leaving a large enough hole for him to be able to get his hand inside and force more of the wood away.

He could feel the first clawing fingers on his back now, then the deceptively soft impact of the first body crashing into him. Now working with a desperate, breathless speed he threw his bat down and pulled more of the wood away, enough for him to be able to shove his head and one arm through. It was virtually pitch-black inside the building and he could see nothing, but with his outstretched fingers he felt a wooden bar which had been carefully secured across the door—no doubt Martin's typically pedantic workmanship. He anxiously yanked it out of the brackets which held it in place, then dropped it down.

Another corpse grabbed Webb's shoulders, pulling him back. He allowed himself to be moved away for a fraction of a second, then shook himself free and ran back at the door. Despite the ground beneath his feet being greasy and covered with flesh and bone, he managed to build up enough velocity to hit the middle of the double-door with sufficient force to throw both sides of it open. Without stopping he ran into the darkness with arms outstretched, feeling his way through the shadowy building, not knowing where he was going.

Fighting with each other to get through the narrow gap, the first of hundreds of bodies followed Webb, the force of many more behind keeping them moving at a speed which almost matched his.

54

"You don't have a clue what you're talking about," Harte protested, shoving a handful of food into his mouth. "You've never seen so many of them as there were out there today."

Gordon shook his head and took a plate from Ginnie.

"And I don't want to know either," he said, sniffing at his food. "I saw more than enough, thank you. What's this?"

"Some kind of stew," Ginnie replied.

He poked at his food, stabbed his fork into a lump of something, then shoved it into his mouth and chewed it. Ginnie looked at his face expectantly. He nodded his appreciation and took another mouthful.

"Not bad," he said, trying to remember when he'd last eaten warm food.

"Remember that night back at the flats when you did the cooking, Gord?" Harte asked, laughing. "Fuck me, what was it again?"

"Some vegetarian rubbish," Lorna laughed.

"When was this?" Howard asked, struggling to see the others through the semidarkness. He sat just outside the main circle so that he could feed his dog without anyone complaining. All the others ever gave her were scraps, and after the way she'd fought today he thought she deserved more.

"We'd only been there a couple of weeks," Lorna continued. "Most of us went out looking for food, but Gordon pulls the old dodgy-hip routine and decided we'd all be better off if he stayed behind."

"I *have* got a dodgy hip," he protested.

"When it suits you," Caron mumbled.

"Anyway, he said he was going to cook a meal while we were all out, trying to make up for the fact that he was too scared to go out—"

"That's not true," he interrupted. "Honestly, Ginnie, it didn't happen like that. We were just—"

"So we left him cooking dinner while we're all outside risking our necks. Stupid bugger only went and fell asleep, then tried to convince us all that he hadn't. Burned the whole bloody lot! You should have smelled the stench! We had to chuck those pans out. I swear, you could smell it over the bodies, it was that bad!"

"And we made you eat it, remember?" Harte chipped in.

"Stokes loved it," Gordon answered back. "He wasn't bothered. Bit of carbon never hurt anyone, he used to say."

"Wasn't the food that finished him off, though, was it?" Jas said quietly. The mention of Stokes and his sudden demise brought the conversation to an abrupt halt.

"You're a bundle of laughs, you are." Harte sighed, annoyed that the mood had been spoiled unnecessarily. "Why did you have to say that?"

For an awkward moment no one spoke, choosing instead to concentrate on their food and their own thoughts. Harte was glad of the increasing darkness of the early evening. It made avoiding eye contact a simple matter. He was happy that they'd gone outside for the right reasons today, and they'd achieved far more than they'd ever expected, but he'd have been lying if he'd said he didn't regret what they'd done. They should have thought it through more carefully and involved the others from the start. Maybe Amir and Webb would still be alive if they'd planned things better. He didn't feel any sympathy for Martin, who sat groaning a short distance away, his head bandaged up. Maybe they should have bandaged up his mouth too, Harte reckoned. That bloody man was becoming a liability.

Until Jas had mentioned Stokes, the mood in the hotel had been becoming more positive and upbeat than any of them could have expected. Look at what we've achieved, Gordon had told them all a short while earlier: hundreds, possibly even thousands of bodies destroyed, and the hotel's defenses had unexpectedly been strengthened by Martin's inability to safely drive the bus.

"Anybody want another drink?" Hollis asked, suddenly feeling uncomfortable and looking for a distraction.

"Get me another can please, Hollis," Jas replied, his voice low as he thought about the helicopter and their missed opportunity today.

"And me," Harte added.

"Wine," Caron ordered.

"How much have you drunk today, Caron?" Lorna wondered.

"Have we got any wine left?"

"Think so, why?"

"Because if there's any left I haven't drunk enough."

Hollis got up and walked toward the bar, leaving the others laughing at the state the normally prim and proper Caron had allowed herself to get into. He'd only been gone a couple of seconds when the fragile silence in the rest of the hotel was interrupted by a loud crashing noise.

"What the hell was that?" Jas said suddenly, jumping up from his seat. "Was that you, Hollis?"

"Wasn't me," he shouted from the next room. "It was something out back."

He put the bottle he'd just picked up back down on the bar and ran through to the kitchen. The noise seemed to have emanated from the back of the building. It wasn't yet completely dark outside, but the interior of the hotel was filled with the typical shadow and gloom of a late winter afternoon, making it difficult to see details. He weaved around the equipment and supplies stacked up in the cluttered room, then stopped just short of the back door. There was something moving toward him. Something dragging itself along slowly. The smell of dead flesh filled the air. He picked up a carving knife from where it hung on the wall and raised it high, ready to slice the foul thing's fucking head right off.

"Don't . . ." it mumbled, breathing hard.

"Fuck me," he shouted with surprise. "Christ almighty, it's Webb! Quick, get some light in here."

Harte, Gordon, and Lorna were there in seconds, Harte carrying a battery-operated lamp which he switched on, revealing the bedraggled survivor in his full bloody glory. He was covered in the gray mire through which he'd crawled, with only the occasional flash of clear skin visible through the muck. He was struggling to breathe, his legs heavy with effort. He managed a single lurching step forward then fell back against an oven, knocking a pile of pots and metal trays over, filling the room with an echoing cacophony of noise. Hollis grabbed his slime-covered arm to steady him, then led him back into the restaurant.

"Is he okay?" Ginnie asked.

Howard's dog jumped up and began to sniff at Webb, who collapsed heavily onto the nearest chair. The dog cowered back and began to snarl. She let out a sudden bark and Howard immediately wrestled her away.

"It's just Webb," he said, trying to calm her down. "Just Webb . . ."

Webb looked at the faces gathered around him with wide, relieved eyes. He felt as if he'd had to run many times the actual distance he'd covered to get here. He never thought the time would come when he'd actually be pleased to see these people again. Even Lorna, Jas, and Hollis, whom he'd grown to hate with a vengeance, suddenly seemed like long-lost friends. Gordon passed him a bottle of water, which he drank from thirstily as the inevitable questioning began.

"What happened?" Jas asked. "We lost you."

"Amir took a wrong turn," he replied.

"You were supposed to drive around a field. For God's sake, how can you take a wrong turn in a bloody empty space?" Harte immediately interrupted. Lorna nudged him to be quiet.

"He got confused by the bodies," Webb explained. "Ended up on the golf course."

"So why didn't you turn back?"

"Couldn't. Too many of them."

"Where is Amir?"

He shook his head, and a brief moment of silence followed.

"How come you were gone for so long?" Jas asked.

"Car got stuck in a ditch," he mumbled. "Couldn't get Amir out. Think the crash killed him anyway. I did what you asked me to, though."

"You blew up the car?"

He nodded.

"Where?"

"On the golf course."

"With Amir in it?"

"He was already dead."

"And you made sure of that," Jas muttered under his breath. Hollis glared at him.

"Give him a break," he said angrily. "You're not helping."

"Webb," Howard asked, getting a little closer now that his dog had calmed down, "how exactly did you get back?"

Webb swigged more water and dropped the empty bottle on the floor.

"Ran," he answered, still struggling to think straight.

"We know that," Howard continued, his stomach suddenly twisting with nerves, "but which way did you run? Did you come back through the field and over the gate, or did you find another way through?"

Webb was shaking his head.

"No," he replied, "came back across the golf course."

"And how exactly did you get off the golf course and back into the grounds of the hotel?"

"Followed the music."

"So you managed to reach the clubhouse?"

"Came through it. Broke in and got out the back way."

Howard looked around. Had no one else realized what Webb was saying?

"What's wrong, Howard?" Hollis asked. Howard simply shook his head, unable to answer for a second or two.

"If he came through the clubhouse . . ." he began to say.

The penny dropped.

"Shit," Hollis said. He turned and ran out of the room and back through the kitchens. Lorna and Harte, who both now realized what was happening, followed close behind. Hollis was first to reach the back door. He flung it open and ran out onto the lawns behind the hotel complex.

Bodies. Hundreds, maybe even thousands of bodies were up ahead, steadily advancing through the gap in the fence that Martin had showed him days earlier. A huge, unstoppable wave of cold, dead flesh was now rolling relentlessly forward in their direction—enough decay to surround and swallow the entire hotel and everything in it and it was too late to stop it. There was no way they could hold back a crowd the size of which he'd seen out on the golf course yesterday morning.

"Oh, God," Lorna said with her hand over her mouth. "What the hell are we going to do?"

Hollis looked at her but couldn't answer. He couldn't think straight. It was impossible for any of them to appreciate the scale of what was suddenly unfolding around them.

"Fuck," Jas cursed as he rushed out into the open and pushed past the others. "We've got to get out of here."

"Where you going to go?" Hollis asked, still staring unblinking at the advancing dead.

"Anywhere," he answered, already sprinting back indoors.

"No point running," he shouted after him. "There's no way out."

"But we've got to do something," Lorna pleaded, grabbing hold of his arm and dragging him back inside. "Come on!"

Hollis pulled himself free and ran a short distance farther away from the building, trying to gauge the true size of the crowd which was surging closer by the second. He was distracted by a sudden engine roar and flash of light as Jas came powering around the side of the building on his motorbike, desperately looking for an escape route. Their options were terrifyingly limited. Bodies still tripped and stumbled through the gap in the hedge, making it impossible to even consider trying to get out that way, and the crash wreckage at the front of the building had rendered the road away from the hotel useless too. He accelerated forward, driving in a wide arc as close as he dared get to the farthest advanced cadavers. They seemed to increase their speed as he approached, moving toward him to try and cut him off. These bodies showed none of the reluctance and caution that some corpses had exhibited before now. Did they now understand the huge advantage they had over the living? he wondered. They were marching forward like an unstoppable invading army. For a second he rode parallel with them as they stormed relentlessly ahead. They were hugely outnumbered—thousands of corpses for every single survivor. Jas turned and rode back toward the hotel, his muddy wheels leaving a dirty brown mark across the letter P from Hollis and Martin's pathetic and now redundant cry for help.

"Block the door," Harte shouted as Hollis pushed his way back inside.

"What with?" someone's frightened voice shouted back from the shadows.

"Anything!" he screamed, and began to drag whatever he could find in front of the door. Hollis helped him, the two of them pulling on the top of a tall freezer unit and bringing it crashing down. Its doors fell open, sending loose metal shelves and racks flying, filling the building with more noise.

"Got to block every entrance off down here," Hollis said breathlessly, the clattering still ringing painfully in his ears.

"If we're not getting out of here," Harte asked, moving to one side so that Gordon and Ginnie could get past, "where are we going to go?"

"Need to stay by the supplies," Hollis answered quickly. "Try and fortify the restaurant perhaps? Maybe the Steelbrooke Suite?"

Harte disappeared into the shadows. Hollis followed, ushering Howard and Caron out of the way. He sprinted toward the Steelbrooke Suite, pausing only to glance into the restaurant. Webb was still sitting exactly where they'd left him, staring into space. Martin sat two tables away, slumped forward with his bandaged head in his hands.

"Come on," he yelled, "shift yourselves!"

Webb looked up but didn't move. Jas ran back from the front of the hotel and bustled into Hollis, distracting him.

"Leave them," he grunted, pushing his way toward the large conference room in the far corner of the building. "It's all their fault."

"You couldn't find a way out, then?" Hollis shouted after him. Jas disappeared into the darkness without responding.

Inside the Steelbrooke Suite, Lorna had already begun to pile tables and chairs against the doors and glass walls to strengthen them. Ginnie and Gordon were bringing in whatever food they could find and stacking it in the corner. Howard's dog rushed across the room at a ferocious speed, its pads and claws skidding on the parquet flooring, then she began to bark and howl furiously at the windows, pacing up and down beside the two glazed walls.

Hollis looked up just in time to see the first corpses slamming against the glass. They smashed against the tall windows, hammering at them with their fists, trying desperately to beat their way inside. In a matter of a few seconds what looked like hundreds of them had appeared across the full width of the back wall, spreading out in either direction, blocking out the little light which remained and dramatically reducing the already limited visibility in the room. Then, when the size of the crowd was enough to cover almost every square inch of glass, the bodies began to spill down the side of the building, moving slowly but with unstoppable intent and determination. Like a partially coagulated liquid they poured themselves around the outside of the hotel.

"We can't stay here," Gordon shouted.

"We can't get out of here!" Jas screamed, already on his way back to the other end of the building. "Get the front secured. Now!"

Everyone in the Steelbrooke Suite stopped what they were doing and ran through to the other end of the building. Some took the east corridor, others the west. Harte, who could outrun just about all of them, cut straight across the courtyard, throwing the glass doors open and barging through. He arrived in reception and found Jas struggling to push the wooden desk across the floor toward the door. He shoulder-charged the other end of the huge piece of furniture and it began to move, juddering awkwardly across the floor tiles.

"Get anything you can find to help block it up," Gordon ordered as he added his weight to the push behind the desk. Ginnie, Lorna, and Howard did as he said, disappearing into anterooms and store cupboards and bringing out everything and anything they could find to help seal the entrance. Another coordinated shove of the desk and it slammed up against the door, completely blocking it. The three men had just moved out of the way when Hollis dragged a tall-backed leather sofa up onto its end and pushed it over so that it dropped down against the desk at an angle, wedging it hard against the door frame.

"Shut that bloody dog up!" Ginnie screamed. Howard's dog was standing in the middle of reception, barking furiously at the glass. He reached down for her collar and tried to pull her away, but she stood her ground and refused to move, eyes fixed forward. He looked up and saw that the bodies had advanced all the way along the side of the hotel and had now begun to spread across the front. Through the gaps between upturned pieces of furniture he could see them moving continually, steadily surrounding the entire building. The steps leading up to the main entrance held them back temporarily until the weight of flesh still surging forward forced the leading cadavers to climb. Howard let go of the dog and helped barricade the doors with whatever he could lay his hands on. Rotting faces stared back at him through the glass and the bodies slammed their bony hands against the window continually. For a moment he thought he saw one of them grab the handle and try to pull the door open.

"Is that gonna hold them?" Harte asked, wiping sweat from his eyes.

"Going to have to, isn't it?" Lorna answered. Her voice echoed around the now almost pitch-black reception area. As well as shutting out the final shards of fading light, the haphazard blockade had changed the acoustics of the room, muffling the sounds outside and amplifying the noise indoors. "What now?"

Gordon and Hollis moved closer.

"Where will we be safest?" Gordon wondered.

"Right in the middle of the building?" Lorna suggested. "Either that or we should head up?"

"There's no way out if we go up," Harte said ominously.

"Don't think we have a lot of choice."

"We need to get out of sight," Hollis said. "A room big enough for all of us where they won't see us."

"We could try—" Harte began to say before being interrupted by a horrific scream from the other end of the hotel. It was Caron. He froze with terror, not wanting to know what she'd found. Around him others began to run toward the source of the sound. Even from a distance he could hear what was happening.

"They're inside," Caron cried, running down the west-wing corridor.

"How?" Hollis demanded.

"Swimming pool," Jas said, his voice full of desperation and disappointment. "Fucking things must have got in through the doors into the pool."

"Then block the bloody corridor off!" Gordon yelled, pushing past Caron and hurtling toward the pool and gym.

It was too late. By the time he'd got there the creatures were already swarming out into the open, steadily filling the marble-floored area in front of the restaurant, bar, and the Steelbrooke Suite. The dead moved with renewed speed, their progress helped by the pressure of others moving up through the narrow corridor behind them, forcing them forward. Within seconds their numbers were such that they burst through the doors into the courtyard and began to spill down the glass-fronted corridors on either side. In places the decorative glazing began to crack and give way under the pressure. The noise of the shattering glass seemed to excite the dead still further as they spread through the building.

"Up!" Jas shouted, loud enough for all of them to hear. "First floor, middle room. Trust me!"

With no other option, Lorna, Ginnie, and Howard began to climb the staircase at the reception end of the west-wing corridor. Caron and Gordon ran back down the hallway toward them, glancing back over their shoulders at the steadily advancing tide of corpses which washed after them. Hollis shoved them up the staircase, then turned to face Harte and Jas.

"What about Webb and Martin?" he asked, the nearest bodies now less than thirty meters away.

"Fuck them," Jas immediately replied. "We left them in the restaurant. With a bit of luck they'll have managed to block the door before they got in."

"All of this is Webb's fault," Harte seethed. "He doesn't deserve to survive."

"What about Driver?" Hollis demanded, the nearest bodies now close enough for them to be able to see the horrific detail in their dead faces. "We can't just leave him, can we?"

"He's probably dead already," Jas snapped. "Now come on, get upstairs."

Hollis didn't move, struggling with his conscience.

"Which room was he in?"

Harte was struggling too.

"East wing, top floor," he replied. "Can't remember which number . . ."

"Leave him," Jas said again, grabbing both men's arms and trying to drag them up.

"Oh, fuck it," Harte snapped, squirming free from Jas's grip and running down to reception, then back across and up the corridor on the other side.

"What the hell are you doing?" Hollis gasped as he disappeared

329

down. Jas shoved him again and they began to climb the stairs, stopping on the first landing where they could still just about see down to reception and over to the staircase on the other side of the building.

"Fucking idiot," Jas cursed. "Waste of fucking time."

Harte threw himself up the staircase at the end of the east wing, tripping on the final step in the dark and stumbling into the wall. He picked himself up and, ignoring the pain, ran along the top-floor corridor, opening every door he passed, still unable to remember where he'd left Driver and equally unsure as to why he'd bothered coming back for him. It was a stupid, spur-of-the-moment mistake but it was too late now. This was it. He'd found it. Room 39. He recognized a patch of torn wallpaper and a scratch just to the left of the door. He grabbed the handle, pulled it open and burst inside.

"Come on," he gasped, fighting for air. "We need to get out before . . ."

The room was empty. It was definitely the right one—there were trays of food and empty bottles of water and the bedding was dirty—but no Driver. Stunned, for a few dangerous moments Harte almost forgot the mayhem which was engulfing the rest of the hotel. He looked in the bathroom, under the bed, in the wardrobe . . . Driver wasn't there. Where the hell had he gone?

The sound of more glass shattering elsewhere brought Harte crashing back to reality. He raced back along the corridor and down the staircase again. Down below he could see the courtyard, rammed full of corpses, with still more trying to force their way in. They were at the bottom of the staircase too, and they were beginning to climb. With no other option he closed his eyes and accelerated, wincing with disgust as he crashed into the first cadavers. Shoulder down, he kept moving, battering his way through the surging crowd until he reached the reception area. A momentary respite and he was deep among the dead again, head down, this time racing toward the foot of the stairs leading up to the rooms on the west wing. Soaked with gore and gagging with the horrific, overpowering stench of decay, he began to force his way up, step by step. A hand grabbed his shoulder. Fired full of adrenaline, he clenched his fist and pulled it back to strike.

"Don't hit me, you fucking idiot," Jas cursed as he pulled him up by the scruff of his neck. "No good?"

"Not there," he wheezed breathlessly as they climbed to the first floor. Hollis and Lorna were standing on the landing waiting for them.

"What do you mean, not there?" Lorna demanded.

"He's cleared out," Harte answered. "Clever bastard's pulled a fast one on us. I bet there was never anything wrong with him."

"Clever bugger," Hollis muttered. "Had more brains than we gave him credit for. Just because someone's not talking all the time, doesn't mean they're not thinking."

He peered down the staircase. The bodies were climbing.

"What now?" Harte asked.

"Block it up," Jas replied. "Gordon and Howard are already doing the stairs at the other end. Just get what you can out of the bedrooms and throw it down. Those fuckers will never be able to get up here."

55

Webb had heard Harte moving around.

The sudden surge of bodies as they'd dragged themselves into the main part of the hotel from the swimming pool had snapped him out of his exhausted catharsis. With the rest of the survivors running around like headless chickens, devoid of any apparent aim or direction, he seized his chance to move. As the first corpses had appeared in the door of the restaurant he'd pushed past them, smashing them to the side before they'd even realized he was there. He left Martin behind, sobbing and wailing for help pathetically. When he looked back he'd disappeared, swallowed up by an unstoppable mass of decaying flesh.

Pursued by a surging stream of deadly corpses, Webb had fought his way to the nearest east-wing staircase. For a few anxious seconds he'd stopped at the top of the first flight and looked back down, watching the courtyard outside fill with an incalculable mass of rancid skin and bone, and then watching the bodies begin to drag themselves up after him. He knew they'd make it all the way upstairs eventually, it was inevitable. He breathlessly crawled up to the first floor and peered out of a small window overlooking the back of the hotel. The sun had disappeared, but just enough light remained for him to be able to see the massive scale of what was happening outside. Every inch of space around the hotel was filling with corpses, from the walls of the building right the way back to the boundary fence. And still they came! He craned his neck and saw that more of the tireless grotesques were continuing to force their way into the hotel grounds, ripping and tearing at others around them, desperate to keep moving.

Which room was it? Webb ran down the corridor, peeling off layers of sodden, stinking clothing as he moved. East wing, first floor . . . it had to be one of these. Something must have happened to stop Jas bringing the others up here, he thought as he yanked door after door open. Empty. Empty. Empty. He began to doubt himself. Was it definitely on this floor? Jas wouldn't have used the ground floor, would he?

Jesus Christ, they were already here! The corpses at the front of the crowd had already managed to drag themselves up onto the first floor. Had the sound of doors being pulled open and slammed shut made them move even faster? Struggling to contain his panic and soaked through with a desperate, nervous sweat, Webb watched as the first cadaver slowly hauled itself around and began to move down the corridor toward him, followed by an incalculable number of similarly decayed creatures. Had these things ever been human? In the disappearing light the lead creature looked like little more than a skeleton covered with the most meager layer of dripping flesh. It was naked save for a few scraps of cloth which hung around its neck and waist; every awkward, lethargic step it took forward seemed to cause it more damage. And yet it stared at him with cold, black eyes and moved toward him with unquestionable intent.

Room 18—empty.

Room 19—empty.

Webb looked up again and saw that the dead were coming along the corridor from both directions now. That meant that both staircases were blocked solid with bodies now. That meant there was no way out.

Room 20—empty.

Room 21—empty.

A sudden increase in the speed of the dead to his right distracted him. He turned and saw that the cadaver leading the pack had fallen. It immediately tried to get up again but was trampled and crushed by the feet of the many others following close behind.

Room 24. Found it.

With huge relief as he pulled the door open he saw a pile of boxes stacked at the far end of the room. He'd found Jas's secret store and, incredibly, he was the only one there. He waited out in the corridor for a few more seconds before shutting himself inside, knowing that it might be weeks before he emerged from this small and cramped hotel bedroom again. With the nearest bodies just a few meters away on either side, he took a deep breath and went in, immediately slamming, locking, and dead-bolting the door behind him. They were outside within seconds, hammering and scratching, baying for his blood. His heart racing, he dragged a heavy wardrobe in front of the door and pushed it over to wedge it shut. He knew that would be enough to stop the dead, or anyone else, from getting in.

Webb leaned back against the wall and began to weep with relief. *Thank God no one else can see me*, he thought as he wiped his face dry. He started to sob, but then put his hand over his mouth to stop the noise.

Can't let them hear me. Have to be completely silent. If I sit here and wait in silence, they'll start to disappear. Can't let them hear me.

Webb finally stood up straight and looked around the L-shaped hotel room. Where was the rest of the food? He walked farther in and saw that the initial pile of three boxes he'd seen was, in fact, the only pile. But Jas had stashed loads of stuff up here, hadn't he? So where was it? He'd seen him carrying several loads and when he'd crept inside between trips there had been much more than this . . .

He opened the top box—trying to be quiet, cringing at the noise of rustling cardboard—and looked inside. Food, drink, some clothing . . . he wished the dead out in the corridor would shut up so he could concentrate. All he could hear was their relentless banging on the door and the muffled sounds of fighting as even more of them filled the first floor and tried to force their way closer to him. There was maybe two weeks' worth of food here, perhaps a little more. What the hell was going on?

Confused and disoriented, Webb stepped back and tried to make sense of what he'd found. Was this the wrong room? Should he have looked in room 25? There was a piece of paper stuck to the front of the top box. He picked it up and carried it over to the window, struggling to make it out in the early evening gloom. A simple message was written in Jas's scrawled handwriting:

> *Webb, the stuff in the boxes is your share. I put the rest somewhere else.*

He sank to the floor under the window and covered his head with his hands. The damn banging outside was getting louder . . .

"Can't get anything else down there," Gordon announced breathlessly. Jas peered down the stairwell, which had been almost completely filled with furniture.

"Good," he said, satisfied that they were about as safe as they were going to be for now. "We'll keep checking, just to be sure they can't get through."

"Nothing's going to get through that lot," Lorna added. "It's the same at the other end. Don't know how we're ever going to get down."

335

"We'll worry about that later," Gordon replied. "I'm in no hurry to leave."

Jas turned around and walked back down the corridor. Harte and Hollis were coming the other way. They met in the middle and disappeared into the same room. Inside, Ginnie and Caron were busy shifting boxes of supplies, trying to work out exactly what they had and where they were going to put it all. Harte tugged Jas's sleeve and pulled him back.

"What's the matter?" he asked.

"Nothing," Harte answered quickly, his voice quiet. "Good idea, you clever bastard."

Jas shrugged. "No problem. I could see this coming, that was why I wanted to get away. Did it for myself, really."

Harte looked at him, unsure if he was telling the truth.

"Thanks, anyway," he mumbled.

Jas nodded and walked farther into the room, edging around the bed and stepping over boxes and bags of food and other supplies. He stood at the window and surveyed the devastation. He'd never seen so many bodies packed so tightly into a single space. *Maybe the helicopter will come back tomorrow*, he thought. *Maybe I'll try and find a way to get up onto the roof so they can see me. Then again, maybe I just won't bother . . . the harder I try, the more chance there is that everything will get screwed up again.*

He turned back around and looked at the other people he now found himself trapped with: Harte, Hollis, Lorna, Caron, Gordon, Ginnie, Howard, and his dog.

I can't afford to let anyone make any more mistakes. We've got nowhere left to run now.

Epilogue

ONE MONTH, THREE WEEKS,

SIX DAYS AND EIGHTEEN HOURS LATER

Sean walked back toward the hotel, his feet crunching through the late December frost. He felt uneasy. He had that same sickening feeling in the pit of his stomach that he used to get when he went back to work after a holiday. It had been a long time since he'd felt anything like this. Come to think of it, it had been a long time since he'd felt anything.

Why was he here? He kept asking himself the question over and over. It wasn't because he liked the people he'd left behind. Some of them were decent enough, but most he would never even have given the time of day to had he met them before all of this had happened. So was he doing it out of some misplaced sense of duty? Maybe he was. Truth was he just wanted some company. It had been more than seven weeks since he'd last spoken to anyone else and, much as he tried to deny it, he was lonely. *No one should be alone at Christmas,* he thought.

The streets were relatively clear now and he was able to move without fear of attack. Being able to risk using a car again had brought him some welcome freedom. The bodies no longer posed a threat now

337

that they had deteriorated to such an extent. Hard to think that the grotesque shadows of people which now littered the ground had ever caused such panic and fear. He looked at them today with pity, but also still with some contempt.

For the most part the dead were unable to move now. Very few could support their own weight and the majority had decayed to such a degree that they could do little more than lie helpless on the ground and watch him, moving only their heads and their dull, clouded eyes. Sean forced himself not to look back at them. Even after all this time it hurt to think that just about everyone he'd ever known and cared about was like this now.

Once on the run Sean had headed for a canal-side apartment belonging to his former boss which overlooked the center of Bromwell. After disposing of his dead ex-employer and her husband, he'd found himself with a relatively safe and secure vantage point eight floors above the devastation; from there he'd sat and watched the dead. In the absence of any other distractions they wearily dragged themselves along the otherwise empty streets, almost as if they'd been looking for help or simply a shelter of some kind. It disturbed him to think that these pitiful, abhorrent creatures might have retained some thought-processing capacity, perhaps even some level of memory or a degree of self-awareness. What if they'd understood what had happened to them? Might they have been lying there in the gutters knowing what they used to be, feeling the constant, gnawing pain of their gradual decay and waiting for the end to finally come?

Sean parked his car a short distance away from the junction that he, Martin, Howard, and Ginnie had blocked with trucks so many weeks ago. The same junction where he'd stood with Webb and practiced killing the dead. The same junction where he'd sat in a truck and waited for hours for Webb on the day he'd left the hotel, struggling with his conscience and his nerves, wondering whether he should go back to the others or take his chances on his own. He'd been so nervous and unsure back then, but his time on his own out in the open had changed him. He was ten times the man he'd been when he'd first arrived here all those months ago on his scooter in the middle of the night like a frightened school kid.

He climbed over the bonnet of the first truck. The vehicles blocking the roads were all still in place, he noticed. That was a good sign. He slid down to the other side, crossed the junction, then forced himself through the narrowest of gaps past the front end of the coach. He began to walk toward the hotel, wondering what kind of reception he'd get when they saw him. Would they be happy to see that he was still alive, or would they turn on him because he'd walked out on them? He hoped they'd understand. He paused for a moment and listened, hoping he'd be able to hear Martin's music. Nothing. That didn't mean anything, he decided. After all, there was no need to try and control the dead any longer. They weren't the problem they used to be.

Sean jogged around the corner and immediately found himself face-to-face with the wreck of the van and, behind it, the bus which lay tipped over on one side like a beached whale. His heart sank. What had happened? Had anyone been hurt? He climbed up the front of the bus and ran along its length. The hotel was visible in the distance, wrapped in a light mist. All around it the ground was covered in a deep, partially frozen, gray slurry—the remains of thousands of cadavers. The foul mire stretched all the way from the building to the road, but that didn't necessarily mean the people in the hotel hadn't survived. He wanted to shout out, but he couldn't bring himself to do it. Even after all this time he didn't feel comfortable making any noise out in the open like this.

He'd got used to dressing like a human being again. Sean lazed away his long, lonely days in the apartment wearing clothes he'd taken from the shops in Bromwell. When something got dirty, he threw it away. When he planned to spend any length of time out in the open, however, he reverted to the strong boots and over-trousers preferred by Webb, Hollis, and the others. He was thankful for the protection now as he jumped down onto the road and stepped into the partially frozen, once-human sludge. A paper mask over his mouth and nose did little to diffuse the horrendous smell, and his uncertainty increased as his feet sank into almost eighteen inches of liquid decay. He hated walking through this stuff. It was stupid, he knew, but he couldn't help thinking there might be something lurking deep under the surface which might somehow have survived and which might be about to grab him and drag him down. A hand attached to a perfectly preserved cadaver, perhaps, buried by chance deep under the fetid remains of hundreds more. There was a thin layer of ice on the surface of the slush where it had almost completely liquefied and dirty water had puddled. Apart from the crunch of the ice and the slip, suck and slide of his boots in the mire, the rest of the world was unnaturally silent and still. He focused on getting to the building up ahead.

"Anyone here?"

Sean's voice echoed uncomfortably loudly around the interior of the hotel. He'd reached the main entrance and had managed to force his way in past the desk, sofa, and other items of furniture which had been piled up against the door. His already low expectations sank further still when he walked through the silent building. The sludge in here was shallower than outside, but no less difficult to navigate and it was immediately clear that the corpses had had the run of the hotel. But had the others managed to get away before their shelter had been compromised?

The staircase at the reception end of the west wing was impassable and had clearly been blocked from above. With suddenly renewed optimism he ran the length of the corridor and found that the staircase at the far end of the wing had also been blocked in a similar way.

Could someone still be upstairs? Sean continued through the hotel, working his way through the narrow, slime-filled corridor which led to the swimming pool. The glass doors and some of the windows surrounding the pool had been smashed, no doubt by the pressure of the immense invading army of corpses which had obviously run riot here. The pool itself formed a bizarre and grotesque centerpiece, piled high with bodies which had stumbled into the noxious water and been unable to get back out.

Sean worked his way around the side of the building, looking up at the many bedroom windows.

"Hello!" he shouted. "Hello! Is anyone there?"

One first-floor window, he noticed, was open. He moved toward it as quickly as he could, wanting to run but not daring to speed up and risk losing his footing and falling into the germ-ridden tide of liquefied flesh around him. When he was almost directly underneath the window he risked shouting again.

"Can you hear me? Is anyone there?"

There was no response. He was about to continue farther around when he noticed a pile of semi-submerged mattresses on the ground. Whoever had survived the taking of the hotel by the dead, he decided, had managed to get away. He stared up at the window again and wondered who'd been trapped up there. Was it Webb, Gordon, Caron, or Martin Priest? Howard or Hollis? Lorna? Jas? Didn't matter now. They were probably long gone. He headed back inside.

On the way around to search through the kitchens and restaurants, Sean discovered that unlike the west, the east staircases were relatively clear; still soaked with the putrefied remains of hundreds of bodies, but passable. The entire east wing was ghostly silent save for the steady dripping of decayed flesh as it trickled down the interior of the building. He climbed up to the top floor, not expecting to find anything, but keen to check all the same. If anyone had been trapped

341

up here, his logic told him, then surely they'd have tried barricading the access points too? He opened a couple of doors but the rooms were empty, and then stopped when he remembered that Driver and his germs had been quarantined up here. He tripped lethargically back down the stairs to the floor below and shouted out again, listening to the way his voice echoed eerily across the empty first floor landing, wishing that someone would answer back.

Christ, he suddenly felt desperately lonely and low. He'd expected to find the others here, and the fact that they'd gone hit him hard. If he'd stayed he could have gone with them. He hadn't realized how much he'd craved company until it was clear that he was still on his own and it was going to stay that way. He continued back down to the ground floor.

Sean readied himself to leave. He called out a few more times, but he knew it was pointless. There was nothing to stay here for.

Room 24 East.

Emaciated, dehydrated, and sitting half-dressed, surrounded by his own waste, Webb leaned back against the wall under the window and covered his head with his hands. He wanted the voice outside to go away. Only silence was safe.

"Stop!" he screamed to himself, too afraid to say the words out loud. "Please stop! You'll bring the bodies back again . . ."

He curled himself into a ball and lay sobbing on the soiled carpet, waiting for the noise outside to disappear, terrified that the banging on the door was about to start again.

WARNING:
YOU WILL KILL TODAY

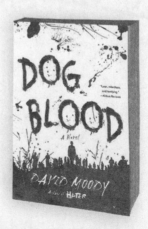

OWN THE ENTIRE CRITICALLY ACCLAIMED HATER SERIES

AVAILABLE WHEREVER BOOKS ARE SOLD

 St. Martin's Griffin   **THOMAS DUNNE BOOKS**

Outnumbered 1,000,000 to 1, a small band of the living face down the walking dead

Book 2

Book 4

Book 1

Book 3

"A marvelously bleak dystopian future where the world belongs to the dead."
—Jonathan Maberry, *New York Times* bestselling author of *Patient Zero*

St. Martin's Griffin   THOMAS DUNNE BOOKS